New Earth Chronicles

To the ones who almost gave up,

but didn't.

You were never alone.

Acknowledgments

This book would not exist without countless nights of defeat, uncertainty, heartache, redefining, and relentless belief in the power of storytelling.

I wrote this through the loss of love, struggle, and the haunting silence of nearly giving up. Every word is a testament to the storms I weathered, and the quiet strength it takes to keep going when nothing around you tells you to.

To my friends and family who encouraged me when I wanted to give up, you know who you are.

To the creatives, the dreamers, and those who've felt like outsiders: your voice matters.

And to every reader who picks up this book. Thank you for taking a chance on my world. It's just getting started.

— Joshua Aaron

Welcome to New Earth

Chapter I:
The Fall of Celeborn

This world… New Earth, was born of chaos. It was not a realm of comfort but of raw power, where even the strongest fell prey to the unrelenting tides of conquest. In the year 23,940 Orca, what we now call it on New Earth, the stars shone faintly over Celeborn's beleaguered castle, the kingdom's final hours had come. A cold wind swept through the ruined towers, whispering through cracks like the ghosts of the dead. The castle once stood as a symbol of hope, a sanctuary of shimmering white stone crowned by spires that reached for the heavens. But tonight, the air was thick with the harsh stench of smoke and blood, and the once-pristine walls bore the blackened scars of fire.

Bang! Bang! Bang! The heavy oak door shuddered beneath the soldier's fists, the echoes cutting through the cries of the dying below. Inside the dimly lit chamber, seven-year-old Marie clutched her younger sister, four-year-old Maya. Marie had inherited her father's golden hair and striking blue eyes, while Maya bore the deeper auburn tones and hazel gaze of their mother's Shikarian bloodline. The girls huddled beside the bed, casting shadows across their tear-streaked faces. Marie's chest heaved, each knock sent a tremor through her body. Maya whimpered, her tiny fingers gripping the hem of her sister's nightgown. "Mommy…" The whisper was soft, but its desperation struck like a weight. Marie swallowed, trying to steady her breath. Her trembling hands rose to cover Maya's ears. "Don't cry," she murmured, her voice too fragile to believe, "Mommy will come." Bang! Bang! Bang! Then, a voice. Low. Sinister. It slipped through the door like smoke.

"I know you're in there…"

The words slithered like a serpent, hissing in her ears, then coiling tight around her chest, squeezing the air from her lungs. It wasn't just any voice. Even at her young age, Marie recognized it. Everyone on New Earth did. It was the voice of the man who had brought war to their doorstep, the one whose very name made grown men tremble and children cry in their sleep.

Marie's grip on Maya tightened as her mind raced with all the terrifying stories she had overheard. Zion, the self-proclaimed ruler of New Earth, was said to wield power beyond comprehension. Some whispered he was part human, part otherworldly, a being forged from the chaos of the universe. Others claimed his tattoos, the dark markings that crawled across his skin, were cursed symbols granting him dominion over life and death. To Marie, he was simply the monster who had come to take everything she loved, her mother, her home, her future. And now he was here.

Another voice followed, light, mocking, and far too casual for the horror clawing at the door. "Come out, come out... wherever you are." A wicked chuckle echoed, and through the narrow slit in the door, a single eye appeared. It glinted with malice as its owner, a man named Haiti, one of Emperor Zion's trusted men. His wicked grin widened as he spotted the frightened girls.

At that moment, Queen Elena Celeborn burst into the room. Her long auburn hair flowed like a cascade of fire, a stark contrast to the dark urgency burning in her emerald eyes. She was a figure of both grace and power, her presence commanding even in the chaos that threatened to engulf her kingdom. She crossed the room in swift strides, the intricate embroidery of her royal gown catching the faint light of the moon. The fabric shimmered, its deep sapphire hue a tribute to the orb she carried, a gift from the Elders and the very heart of her reign.

Queen Elena was not just a ruler; she was chosen. Long ago, in the ancient sanctum of the Elders, she had stood before the great council. It was said that the Elders, keepers of New Earth's elemental power, could see the soul of anyone who dared seek their audience. They saw in Elena not only strength and wisdom but an unyielding compassion for her people. On that day, they bestowed upon her the sapphire orb, a relic as old as New Earth itself. It held the raw essence of the planet's elements: fire, water, air, and earth, a balance of creation and destruction. With the orb, Elena became the guardian of the realm, bound by duty to protect its harmony.

That's precisely why tonight could be the very nightmare we've been dreading. "Marie, Maya," she whispered as she knelt beside them, her voice trembling but firm. The sapphire necklace around her neck glimmered as if alive. She reached up, unfastened it, and placed it in Marie's small hands. "This is our legacy," Queen Elena said, her voice breaking. "You must protect it. Use it only when you are in grave danger." Marie looked up at her mother, confusion and fear etched across her face. "What's happening?" she asked, her voice quivering.

Queen Elena cupped her daughter's face, her touch warm despite the cold terror that gripped the room. "There's no time to explain. You must be brave, my loves." She rose, her eyes hardening. She took Marie by the hand, and Marie reached back for Maya, guiding her into the hall. The hallway stretched before them like a darkened void, the only light a solitary torch flickering on the far wall. Its weak glow danced across the cold stone, casting long, eerie shadows that seemed to move on their own. The air was damp, heavy with the faint metallic trace of blood.

Queen Elena gripped Marie's hand tightly, and Marie clung to Maya's just behind her. The girls moved in a silent line, footsteps light against the stone. Elena slowed her pace, glancing over her shoulder. Maya's small form trembled, barely keeping up. Elena's heart ached to scoop her up, to hold her, but she couldn't risk it. Not yet. "Stay close," she whispered, her voice so soft it was barely a breath.

Marie nodded, her wide eyes darting nervously around the corridor. Every sound, every creak of the ancient stone, every distant shout from the battle raging outside, made her heart leap into her throat. Her mother's fingers were firm, almost painfully so, but Marie didn't complain. That grip was her tether, her lifeline in this nightmare. Queen Elena moved with purpose, but her mind raced. She knew these halls, every twist, every turn, but tonight they felt foreign, as if the castle itself were conspiring against her. The walls, once symbols of strength, now seemed like traps closing in. *This is my fault,* she thought bitterly. *I should have foreseen this. I should have done more to prepare. To protect them.*

She glanced down at Marie, whose face was pale and determined despite the fear in her wide blue eyes, eyes that mirrored her strength, if not her color. Behind them, Maya clung tightly to

Marie's hand, her small frame trembling with each step, a soft whimper caught in her throat. Her daughters were too young to understand the full weight of what was happening, but Elena felt it like a crushing stone on her chest. She was their mother, their protector, and their queen. And tonight, she might fail at all three. As they reached the corner, Elena paused, holding up a hand to signal Marie to stop.

Carefully, Queen Elena leaned forward, peering around the edge. Her breath caught. A soldier stood at the end of the corridor, his back to them. The torchlight flickered across the polished armor of Zion's soldiers. The sigil of the empire gleamed on their chests, a mark of death. Marie's breath turned shallow. The room was too small. Too dark. She couldn't breathe. He held a spear, its sharp tip gleaming under the flickering torchlight. He shifted slightly, the polished leather of his boots scraping against the cold stone. Every movement was deliberate, controlled, like a predator waiting to strike. His eyes didn't blink, didn't wander. He was listening.

Elena pulled back quickly, pressing her daughters against the wall. Marie looked up at her mother, her voice trembling "What do we do?", she said. Elena crouched to their level, her green eyes sharp and focused. "Listen to me, Marie. No matter what happens, you protect Maya. Do you understand?"

Marie's lip quivered, but she nodded. "I promise." Elena straightened, her free hand rising, she whispered words in the ancient tongue of *Shikarian*, her voice carrying a melodic cadence that seemed to make the very air hum. Light began to spiral around her fingers, soft and blue, growing brighter with each passing second. Marie watched the light swirl with wide eyes, charmed almost, until her awe was shattered. "Mama!" Maya's scream tore through the silence. Elena whirled around, her heart plummeting.

One of the Emperor's soldiers had appeared from the shadows, his large, gloved hand wrapped around Maya's tiny arm. The child thrashed, her fists pounding against his armor, but it was like striking stone. "No!" Elena's voice rang out, her glowing hand erupting into brilliant blue flames. The soldier sneered, holding the struggling child like a trophy. "There's only one way out of this," he growled. His voice was low and rough, like gravel grinding beneath heavy boots. "Give us the M'ra Sphere."

Elena's eyes narrowed, her entire body trembling with fury. "By the order of the Elders, I shall give you no such thing." She raised her flaming blue hand, ready to strike… But before she could release the magic, a shadow moved behind her. It was fast, too fast. A strong hand clamped down on her wrist, twisting her arm behind her back. Pain shot up her arm as the flames sputtered and dimmed. Before she could react, another hand seized her throat, fingers pressing hard against her windpipe. She froze. The touch was familiar, the weight of it, the grip, the sickening closeness of breath at her ear. Her mind screamed what her body already knew. "Too slow," came the whisper.

Haiti.

His grin was sharp and cruel, his eyes gleaming with amusement. Ghastly tattoos snaked up his neck, dark and jagged, disappearing beneath his armor. With brutal precision, he gripped her throat tighter. The cold press of a blade touched her skin. "Move, and you're dead," Haiti hissed.

Marie stood breathless, her mother, the strongest person she knew, was trapped, powerless. Tears blurred her vision as she clung to the wall, paralyzed by fear. *Mommy…* Her throat tightened. She wanted to scream, to run, to do something, anything, but her legs wouldn't move. The room felt too loud. Too bright. Too scary.

Suddenly, slow, measured footsteps echoed through the corridor. Each one was soft, almost gentle, but the silence that followed made them deafening. A figure stepped from the shadows, tall and cloaked. No fanfare. No sound. Only presence. Elena's heart dropped. She recognized the silhouette. But not the man. Zion. The boy she once knew, the quiet, curious apprentice from another life… was gone. What stood before her now was a shell of stillness, a shadow wrapped in robes and ambition. His hood concealed most of his face, but she didn't need to see it. She felt it in his posture. In the way the air grew cold. In the terrible stillness of those pale, inhuman eyes slipped through the shadow. "Ah, Queen Elena," he said smoothly, his voice a deep, resonant purr. "Such defiance. Admirable, but ultimately futile."

From the shadows emerged another soldier, his heavy boots thudding against the cold stone floor. In his grasp, like a discarded puppet, was King Theodore, his blonde hair was tousled, damp with sweat, but still carried the effortless sweep of royal elegance. His chiseled jaw was tight with fury, and his blue eyes, so much like Marie's, burned with defiance even as the guards dragged him forward. The soldier dragged the unconscious king unceremoniously across the floor, the once-pristine gold and crimson robes of his station now tattered and smeared with blood and dirt. The crown that had once symbolized his authority lay dented and askew on his head, a pitiful remnant of the man who had stood proudly at the helm of New Earth.

Marie's breath caught in her throat. "Papa…" she whispered, her voice barely audible, but her trembling lips betrayed the depth of her fear. Theodore's face, pale and bruised, was barely recognizable. His strong jaw, once a mark of his unyielding resolve, was slack, and a deep gash marred his temple, the blood trickling down to stain his beard. The soldier came to a full stop in the center of the hallway, letting Theodore's body slump heavily against the floor. His head sagged against his chest, the crown barely clinging to his tangled hair. The father she once knew, strong, unwavering… was gone. "Ah, the king joins the party," Haiti sneered, his cruel smile widening.

Still gripping Queen Elena, he leaned forward just enough to nudge Theodore's side with the toe of his boot. "Didn't think you'd be conscious for the finale." Theodore groaned faintly. Marie's tiny hands clenched into fists as she fought the urge to cry out. Her father, the man who had once lifted her onto his shoulders to gaze at the stars, now lay broken before her. Queen Elena's composure faltered for the briefest of moments. Her emerald eyes flicked to Theodore, pain and fury warring within them. He had fought for them, for New Earth, until his last ounce of strength had been drained. "Elena," Zion's deep voice resonated as he stepped forward, his cloak billowing behind him. His gaze dropped to Theodore's motionless form, and he let out a low chuckle. "Your King looks… defeated."

Elena's jaw tightened, her free hand clenching into a trembling fist at her side. She wanted to scream, to lash out with every ounce of magic she had left, but she couldn't. Not with Haiti. Not with his grip tighter than a noose.

"Release him," she demanded, her voice cracking through Haiti's grip, despite the tears threatening to spill. Zion tilted his head, his inhuman eyes, gleaming with mockery. "Release him? Oh, my dear queen, you misunderstand. Your king belongs to me now, just as all of New Earth soon will be." The room seemed to grow colder as Zion bent down, gripping Theodore's chin and lifting his face. He studied the king as though he were inspecting a broken toy.

"He fought valiantly," Zion continued, his voice dripping with false admiration. "But even the strongest kings fall when faced with true power." Haiti let out a sharp laugh, and the other soldiers joined in, their voices echoing cruelly down the hall. Elena's heart ached as she watched Theodore's battered form, the man she had loved and ruled beside now reduced to a shadow of himself. But she couldn't show weakness. Not in front of Zion. "You'll pay for this," she said, her voice low and venomous. Zion paused, straightened, releasing Theodore's chin with a dismissive shove. "Oh, I'm counting on it," he said, a chilling smile curling across his lips. Elena glared at him, her chest heaving as she struggled against Haiti's grip. Zion's gaze dropped to her trembling hand, where faint traces of blue light still flickered. "The last of your magic," he mused. "A shame to see it wasted." His attention shifted to the object he pulled from his cloak. *The M'ra Sphere.* Its surface pulsed faintly, the pure white light within swirling like a captive storm. "When the sun rises," Zion continued, his tone almost conversational, "all will bow to their new King of New Earth."

"No!" Elena screamed, her voice shredded with desperation. Zion's lips curled into a cruel smile. He didn't raise his voice. He didn't need to. "Kill them both." Haiti moved without hesitation. The blade plunged deep into Queen Elena's back, and twisted. Her body jolted violently, then stilled, her breath caught in her throat like the calm before the storm. As if the world held its breath with her. Her emerald eyes locked with Marie's across the corridor, wide, wet, unblinking. Everything she knew. Everything she loved. Disappeared before her eyes. There was no more air left in her. Her pupil widened, catching one last glint of light before the color faded from them. The warmth left her gaze, but the gentleness remained. She collapsed from Haiti's grip. The sound of her body hitting the stone cracked through the silence like thunder. Blood spread fast, blooming across the floor in sharp contrast to the dull gray beneath her. The light in her hand, that stubborn, beautiful blue, flickered once… twice… then vanished. "Mommy!" Marie's scream pierced the air, filled with anguish that seemed to shake the very foundations of the castle. There would be no mercy. Not tonight.

Chapter II:
Dreams of the Past

Marie's eyes fluttered open, but the world around her wasn't the harsh reality of the campgrounds she had fallen asleep in. Instead, she found herself standing barefoot on a smooth, white surface that stretched infinitely in all directions. The air was thick and still, carrying a faint hum like a distant whisper. She looked down. The surface beneath her glimmered like polished ceramic, reflecting the vast expanse of a starless, emptiness above. Her breath echoed unnaturally loud as she stepped forward, the ripples of her movements disturbing the stillness. "Where… am I?" she whispered, her voice swallowed by the void. As if in answer, the hum grew louder, transforming into a faint melody that tugged at something deep within her.

It wasn't just a sound; it was a feeling, nostalgia, sorrow, and hope intertwined. From the distance, a figure emerged, walking toward her.

Marie's breath caught. She recognized that figure immediately. "Mother, is that you?"

Queen Elena stood before her, her auburn hair flowing as if caught in an invisible breeze. She wore a radiant gown of deep blue that shimmered like the sapphire orb, but her expression was solemn. Her emerald eyes held Marie's, unblinking, piercing through her like an arrow. Marie's knees buckled, and she fell to the ground. "Mother!" she cried, her voice trembling. "I… I thought you were…"

"Gone?" Elena's voice was soft but firm, cutting through the dreamlike haze. "I am." Marie's heart clenched, confused, tears pooling in her eyes. "How are you here? Is this real?" Elena tilted her head slightly, her gaze unyielding. "I came to give you a message, sweetheart." Marie opened her mouth to respond, but the words died in her throat. "You must listen to me," Elena continued, her voice echoing strangely. It was as if her words weren't entirely her own, as though they carried the weight of something beyond her. "You can never go back."

"What do you mean? Aren't you still here with me?" Marie whispered, confusion and fear prickling at the edges of her mind, going in and out of consciousness.

"What has transpired is beyond our control," Elena said, stepping closer. Her hand reached out, brushing against Marie's cheek, though the touch was fleeting, like the brush of a ghost. "The past cannot be changed, no matter how deeply you wish it to." Marie shook her head, tears spilling freely now. "I didn't ask for this. Any of this. Not even Maya. I just… I just want things to go back to the way they were." Elena's face softened, a flicker of sorrow breaking through her stern exterior. "That is not your path, my love. You carry more than you know. A destiny far greater than yourself." Marie stumbled to her feet, her fists clenched. "I don't want this destiny! I didn't choose it!"

Elena's expression hardened again, her voice ringing out like a command. "It chose you. The Elders chose this family as royalty. The prophecy is in the orb. Use it when necessary. You are the key, Marie." The white surface beneath them began to ripple violently, distorting the image of her mother. Marie staggered backward as shadows seeped into the dreamscape, curling around the edges like ink bleeding into water. "Marie…" a voice hissed, low and guttural, like the scrape of metal on stone.

Marie turned sharply, her breath catching as another figure emerged from the darkness. Haiti. But this was not the man she remembered. His form was a twisted manifestation of who he truly is, his features sharp and gaunt, his tattoos now writhing like living things against his translucent, cursed skin. His grin was wide, too wide, splitting his face with a wickedness that sent chills racing down Marie's spine. "You think you can run from this?" he sneered, his voice dripping with mockery.

"No, no, no! This can't be happening! Why are you here?" Marie spat, her voice shaking. "I am everywhere," he whispered, his figure moving closer, though his feet didn't seem to touch the ground. His words struck her like a blow, reverberating through the dreamscape. The rippling beneath her grew violent.

"You just want to be fooled!" he screamed. Haiti lunged at her, his twisted, ghostly form streaking through the air like a shadow torn from reality. His hollow, piercing eyes locked onto hers as he passed straight through her, his spectral

body phasing through her chest like a cold
whisper of death.

Chapter III:
A New World

The breeze was cooler here, carrying the faint scent of dry leaves and soil, like New Earth's autumn learning how to breathe again. The campgrounds were silent, save for the faint rustle of the wind weaving through the tattered tents. Nineteen-year-old Marie lay on the hard ground, her head resting on a thin pillow that did little to shield her from the cold. The sapphire necklace around her neck glinted faintly in the moonlight, its warmth contrasting against the chill in the air. Her eyes snapped open, but the world around her was the harsh reality of the campgrounds she had fallen asleep in. Her breath hitching as the remnants of a nightmare clawed at the edges of her mind. So many orcas had passed since the night at the castle, but the memory never faded. *Not in her dreams. Not in her bones.*

She sat up abruptly, her chest heaving, the dream, a vivid, terrifying echo of her past, still lingering. The camp was dark and still, her hands trembled as she touched the sapphire necklace at her chest. It felt warm, as though it had been pulsing with energy while she slept. Marie swallowed hard, her mother's voice echoing in her mind. *The past cannot be changed, no matter how deeply you wish it to.* And then, fainter, almost like a whisper carried on the wind: *You just want to be fooled.*

"Rough night?"

A voice out of nowhere. Marie turned sharply, her blue eyes narrowing as they met the gaze of a boy sitting nearby. He had been watching her, not in a threatening way, but with the quiet boldness of someone who didn't care if he got caught. His dark eyes twinkled with a strange mix of curiosity and mischief, and his awkward smile made him look younger than he probably was. *Why is he staring at me like that?* Marie thought, unsure whether to be annoyed or amused. "What?" she snapped aloud, tone clipped. The boy tilted his head, grin widening. "Playing hard to get, I see." Marie groaned and rolled her eyes, rubbing her temples.

"Who are you?"

He cleared his throat, sitting up straighter. "The name's Ronan," he said, his playful demeanor shifting to something more serious. Marie's gaze lingered on him for a moment, unimpressed. He was older than her, probably around twenty-five, with a sturdy build and an air of quiet confidence.

"Marie," she said finally, her voice soft but guarded. Ronan nodded, then leaned back, his gaze drifting to the horizon. "How'd you end up here?" She asked after a beat.

He sighed, the playful glint in his eyes dimming. "I'm a blacksmith or… I was. My father and I… we worked with what little tech we could salvage. We dreamed of something bigger… technology that could have advanced New Earth beyond anything Zion's goons could imagine. We could've changed the world." His voice faltered, and his gaze dropped to the ground. "But that dream died with my father. The Emperor…" He hesitated, and swallowed hard. "His soldiers made sure of that."

Marie caught the pause, the way his voice faltered, just slightly. He hadn't said Zion's name. As if speaking it aloud might summon… him. She studied Ronan, her annoyance melting into something softer. She knew the pain of loss too well. Ronan glanced around the camp, lowering his voice. "You want to know a secret?" He leaned closer to Marie.

"What is it?" Marie asked.

"Let's keep this a secret between you and me," he whispered. Marie's annoyance flared up again. "Well, spill it already."

"I'm leaving tonight." He leaned in more, his expression intense. "I can't live like this. Not anymore. The camps. The soldiers. Zion's reign, it's not living. It's just… surviving."

Marie's breath held as she met his gaze, steady, unflinching. She was more intrigued… Something about the way he said it made her pause. She looked at him differently.

"I'm escaping…," Ronan continued, his voice firm. "I have a plan. But I can't do it alone." He hesitated, then asked, "You want to be free?"

Darkness cloaked the camp as Marie and Ronan crept between the rows of tents. The sounds of snoring and the occasional crackle of dying embers were the only signs of life. Tension clung to the air as they moved silently between the tents. The faint light of the moon guided their steps as they crept toward the edge of the camp.

"Stay close," Ronan whispered, glancing over his shoulder.

Marie nodded, her heart pounding, her hand brushed against the sapphire necklace at her chest, its familiar warmth grounding her. They reached the camp's perimeter, where two guards stood at the gate. Ronan cursed under his breath. "There's no way past them without being seen," he muttered. But Marie had already stepped forward. "Wait, what are you doing?" Ronan hissed, his voice sharp with panic.

Marie didn't answer. Her focus was locked on the guards ahead. She sprinted toward them, sliding across the dirt just as they raised their weapons in alarm. Before they could react, she thrust her hands forward. A burst of sapphire hexes erupted from her palms, searing the air with intense heat. The hexes enveloped the guards in a swirling cloud of darkness, suffocating them in an instant. Their cries were brief before they crumpled to the ground, lifeless. Marie froze, her chest heaving as she stared at her trembling hands. Faint wisps of blue flame still flickered along her fingertips, casting ghostly light against the darkness. Her heart raced, the adrenaline giving way to something deeper.

Yes. She still had it. The sapphire necklace pulsed faintly, as though it recognized her. Its warmth was steady and grounding, but it wasn't the source. The magic didn't come from the necklace or the orb it guarded; it had always been inside her. Marie's breath hitched. *Mother's magic. It's mine now.* She felt the connection ripple through her, not to the object, but to the woman who had once worn it. Her mother's voice echoed, soft and distant, like a breeze through leaves: *"You'll know when it's time."*

Time for what? she wondered, her thoughts spinning. The answer felt just out of reach, but the raw power she had unleashed was proof that something had awakened, a legacy, a burden, and a destiny, all tied to her mother's bloodline. And yet, the orb's role lingered in her mind. Its presence pulsed faintly, as if reaching beyond her, an echo of something greater waiting to unfold. *What purpose?* she wondered. The question faded into silence.

Ronan stared, his mouth agape. "What the hell…" Before either of them could speak, a commotion erupted from the camp. More guards rushed toward them, weapons drawn. "Freeze!" One of the soldiers barked, leveling his weapon at

Marie. The sound of slow, cautious footsteps cut through the chaos. Emperor Zion emerged from the shadows, his long trench coat sweeping the ground as he moved, cloaked in darkness. His hood obscured most of his face, but the air seemed to thicken around him, heavy with authority and menace. Behind him, Haiti followed, his twisted grin glinting in the torchlight. "Well," he said, his voice unsympathetic. "Marie. You've caused quite the mess tonight, killing my men."

Marie didn't recognize the man, but something about the way the soldiers froze told her everything she needed to know. This was him. Her parents' murderer. Zion. She stepped forward, her eyes blazing as blue hexes ignited in her hands. "I'll do it again!" The guards immediately drew their weapons, aiming them at her and Ronan. Their movements were sharp, mechanical, trained to react without thought. Steel shined in the torchlight as multiple barrels locked onto them with lethal precision.

Ronan tensed beside her, and Marie could feel the shift in the air, the moment when fear and violence hung in perfect, deadly balance. "That's enough," Zion said calmly, waving a hand to signal the guards to lower their weapons. He chuckled softly, the sound cold and unsettling. "What is it to say that it won't happen again?"

"It won't," Ronan interjected, his voice steady despite the fear in his eyes.

Zion's gaze shifted to Ronan. "Ronan. I didn't expect for you to talk… considering I killed your father in an onslaught and at that time… there wasn't much to be said. What a coward. He couldn't even lift his head to look me in the eyes." He smirked, then turned his attention back to Marie. Despite the fear gripping him, Ronan lunged at Zion, "Why, you…" But the guards had already waved their weapons at Ronan, which put him at a halt.

"You have courage, little one. But courage is often the companion of fools," Zion said, his voice calm but cutting. He paused, his expression darkening. "Get rid of them and take the necklace." The soldiers surged forward, grabbing Marie and Ronan and yanking them apart.

"No!" Marie screamed, struggling against the soldier's grip.

Ronan thrashed, his voice raw. "Marie!" A soldier struck him hard, sending him sprawling to the ground. He curled inward, clutching his ribs, and for a moment, he didn't move. Marie's heart lurched. Memories of her father flooded her mind, the brutal strikes, the helplessness, the way he had looked. Ronan looked so small, so broken, just like the night Zion attacked.

Haiti stepped forward, delivering two more brutal blows that left Ronan gasping in the dirt. Marie's fury boiled over. *Is this what she meant?* Her mother's words echoed like a whisper in the back of her mind: *You'll know when it's time… Is this the time?* Marie didn't know. Maybe. Maybe not. "There's only one way to find out," she whispered.

Out of nowhere her lips moved on their own, forming words in the ancient *Shikarian tongue.* She didn't fully understand them. But something inside her did. The sapphire necklace floated from her chest, glowing fiercely, pulsing like it had been waiting. Her eyes, blue rimmed with burning sapphire, lit up the aura around her. The soldiers' grips faltered. Marie rose, effortless, suspended by something greater than herself. Her eyes bursting like the blue ocean at sea, speaking a native tongue, only her tribe could understand, rippling through the campgrounds like an earthquake. Her *Shikarian tongue* spoke. Higher. Faster. Like a quiet possession of a crooked doll.

"What is she doing?!" one of the soldiers shouted, his voice laced with panic. Zion's eyes widened as realization dawned. "No…"

The sapphire orb erupted with a blinding light, unleashing a massive shockwave that sent everyone sprawling to the ground. It shot upward, tearing through the night sky before disappearing into a wormhole. Zion's enraged roar echoed through the darkness, a sound of raw fury and despair.

***

In a world far from this one…

***

The echoes of chaos and destruction faded into the distance, giving way to the hush of a peaceful morning. Beyond the veil of worlds, Earth continued, untouched and unaware. Maple-lined streets curved through sleepy suburbs, where front lawns sparkled with dew and sprinklers hissed to life in perfect rhythm. Joggers passed by with earbuds tucked in, dogs tugged at leashes, and coffee brewed behind curtained windows. In

Westchester County, New York, the world felt steady. Familiar. Safe.

Birdsong cut through the morning haze, mingling with the soft hum of distant traffic. A yellow school bus rumbled around a corner, its brakes squealing as it came to a stop. The doors yawned open. Children poured out, their backpacks bouncing, their laughter rising in the air, blissfully unaware of what stirred just beyond their reach. But change was already on its way. By then, sunlight spilled through the thin curtains of Adam Greenfield's bedroom, casting golden streaks across the faded posters on his wall. The calm rhythms of suburban life carried on to his bedroom, the low hum of lawnmowers whispering through his window, the random bark of a dog. This was Earth. Ordinary. Untouched by the chaos brewing on New Earth… at least, for now.

He stirred, the serenity of afternoon mirrored in the rhythm of his breath. In his late twenties, he carried the kind of youthful charm that hadn't yet worn off, but the quiet sharpness in his gaze betrayed years of silent resilience. He sat up slowly, stretching his arms above his head as sunlight spilled through the window, casting gold across his face. He didn't need to be anywhere. Just simply him. Outside, the sky was a clean blue canvas, untroubled and open, a world that didn't yet know what was coming. The steady tick of the clock filled the room, its rhythm slow and deliberate. From downstairs came the faint gurgle of the coffee pot and the soft creak of a door. Katherine, maybe, back from one of her early errands. *Is that Katherine? I don't get to see her these days,* he thought. Adam's thoughts drifted, but not far. They never did these days.

He didn't know how, but something in his bones told him the days of quiet afternoons were numbered. The smell of cinnamon on slow mornings drifted in the afternoon through the air as Adam descended the staircase. The house was sleek yet warm, where polished floors met antique rugs, and the scent of fresh coffee clung to the air. It was the kind of place built by old money but held together by quiet habits, familiar creaks on the stairs, sunlight that always hit just right. Adam's bare feet met the cool polish of white marble with a practiced ease, but the comfort didn't settle like it used to.

In the kitchen, his sister, Katherine Greenfield sat at the table, absently scrolling through her phone as she ate. At twenty-five, she carried an air of effortless beauty, polished, but never forced. Her gold locket caught the sunlight streaming through the windows, a quiet fixture around her neck. She never took it off. Adam couldn't remember a time she'd been without it. There was a calm to her, a kind of practiced stillness, like someone who'd learned to keep her storms tucked behind a smile. Even now, with shadows hanging over the world, Katherine looked composed, graceful in a way that made people think she had it all figured out. But Adam knew better.

He moved to the refrigerator, retrieving a carton of milk and pouring it over a bowl of cereal. As the milk splashed over the flakes, Adam leaned against the counter, spoon in hand, watching his sister scroll through her phone. She was always scrolling lately. Always somewhere else. Never here. He took a bite, chewing slowly. What could he even ask? The silence between them wasn't uncomfortable, just… different. They were older now. Busier. Distant in ways that didn't have names yet. He cleared his throat, casual. "Any new boys you're talking to?"

Katherine didn't look up. "Don't start."

"What? I'm just asking."

"No one worth mentioning."

Adam smirked. "That bad, huh?"

Her thumbs abruptly paused above the screen. "Let's just say… some things aren't worth the energy." Her attention shifted back to the screen, where a message from Rose Blackburn, their childhood friend, lit up the display. A smile curved Katherine's lips as she began typing a response. "Are we going to the party tonight?" she asked, glancing briefly at Adam.

"Who's asking?" Adam smirked.

"Rose, duh," Katherine said with a teasing smirk, her tone light. She quickly typed a reply: *Yeah, we're still coming!* She set her phone down, her expression shifting to one of concern as she looked at Adam. "You're going to take it easy this time, right?"

Adam raised an eyebrow, his spoon halfway to his mouth. "What?"

"What?" Katherine echoed innocently.

"What do you mean by that?" Adam asked, setting his bowl down with a clink.

"Last time, you went a little crazy. You had too much to drink," Katherine teased, folding her arms across her chest.

Adam sighed, slightly annoyed. "I told you. I don't want to hear that story again." His eyes lingered on something familiar but triggering. *He wanted to run, but his legs stayed frozen. Like always. If he looked too long, he might start to feel again. He wasn't afraid of dying. He was afraid of failing, again.*

Katherine raised her hands in mock surrender. "Alright, alright," she said, though the teasing glint in her eyes remained.

Adam twirled his spoon in the bowl, the rhythmic motion lulling his thoughts into a darker place. The faint hum of a passing car outside pulled him back to a memory he tried to bury, the screech of tires, the sickening thud of impact, Eric's panicked voice echoing in his ears. The streets of Westchester County came rushing back to him, sharp, unforgiving. Shrouded in the dim glow of streetlights, their orange halos cast distorted shadows across the pavement. The screech of tires tore through the night, followed by a jarring thud that reverberated in his chest. Adam's hands gripped the steering wheel, his knuckles white as he sat frozen in the driver's seat. His breath came in shallow, uneven gasps as his wide eyes locked onto the body crumpled in the road ahead.

Eric Rowe sat in the passenger seat, his usual charm replaced by panic. "Come on! We have to go!" he shouted, his voice cracking. Adam didn't move. "Adam, we have to go!" Eric snapped, his voice rising with desperation. "The cops will be all over this, and I can't afford to go to jail. Let's go!" But Adam couldn't respond. His mind raced, replaying the moment over and over, the bone-jarring jolt, the shattering sound, the body falling to the ground like a lifeless ragdoll. His foot remained planted on the brake pedal, the car still idling, its headlights illuminating the aftermath of his mistake. The memory hit Adam like a punch to the gut as he sat at the kitchen table, staring into his bowl of cereal. He twirled his spoon absently, the milky loops swirling without purpose. "I never meant to hurt anyone," Adam muttered, his voice low, almost to himself. "If I could trade places with him, I'd do it in a heartbeat."

Katherine glanced up from her plate, her expression softening. "Adam, it was an accident." Adam shook his head, staring hard at the table. "Yeah, well an accident that I created," he said, his voice heavy with guilt.

"There's still plenty of time for change. You're already changing," Katherine said gently, her tone full of quiet encouragement. Adam didn't respond. *I know Katherine means well…it's not the same when you're the one sitting behind the wheel,* he thought. Brushing his hand against his jeans and moved toward the sink. He rinsed his bowl with quiet precision, the water running steady as he stared through the window above it. Outside, the wind stirred the trees, rustling leaves against the glass like whispers he couldn't quite make out. He dried his hands on the towel and paused, hand resting on the counter. Not everything could be fixed, but maybe some things could be faced. Behind him, Katherine watched in silence, her phone forgotten for a moment. The tension in the room eased slightly, but the weight of Adam's past lingered, an unspoken shadow that neither sibling could entirely shake.

***

Meanwhile, in the quiet streets of Westchester County, Rose Blackburn stepped out of her parents' house. At 27, she carried the calm confidence of someone who'd lived through just enough to know better, but still held on to hope. She wasn't the loudest in the room, but when she spoke, people listened. Always the thoughtful planner, the one who brought people together, Rose had a way of making even the smallest gathering feel like it mattered. Tonight's party was no exception. As she paused on the front steps, a soft breeze drifted through the trees, stirring the summer air. Porch lights flickered on across the neighborhood as if the world itself were holding its breath. Rose adjusted the strap of her bag, glancing up at the sky. Something felt different, not wrong, just… heavier. She didn't know it yet, but this would be the last night anything felt normal.

The thought clung to her like static. For the past week, she'd been waking up with her heart pounding, no nightmares, no visions, just a weight she couldn't shake. It made no sense. Life had finally found some kind of rhythm again. But tonight, as the sunset sang low and the wind shifted in unfamiliar patterns, the feeling returned. She blinked it away, grounding herself in the familiar: her shoes on the steps, the scent of cut grass, the glow of warm light from the hallway behind her. This was home. Safe. She wouldn't let a gut feeling rewrite the peace she'd fought to hold onto. Dialing her phone, she waited until the call connected. "Eric, are you on your way?" she asked, her voice full of warmth.

On the other end of the line, Eric Rowe cut through the early evening air, his long strides steady, almost too controlled. At 29, he still wore the build of a former athlete, broad shoulders, coiled strength, but the lightness was gone. Glory days under Friday night lights had long since faded into memory, replaced by something heavier. Quieter even… The city park sprawled out around him, golden light stretching through the trees, but Eric barely noticed. His hair, tousled by the wind, fell across his brow as he shifted his phone to his other hand. His fingers curled tightly around it, not out of nerves, but restraint. That was his way now. Always holding back. "Yeah, I'll be there in a few minutes. You sound excited."

Rose laughed. "Well, it's not every day I get you out of your cave. Try to have fun tonight. Promise?"

Eric smirked, but the expression didn't quite reach his eyes. He ran a hand through his hair, his fingers pausing at the nape of his neck, a reflex whenever things got too real. "No promises."

Rose rolled her eyes. "Urgh, you're so annoying," she said with a teasing smirk. "You're 29, Eric. When are you going to stop carrying this weight like it's your job?"

Eric chuckled, leaning against a park bench, letting his gaze drift to the evening sky. "Damn, Rosebud, you always this persistent?" His voice was light, but the humor didn't quite reach his eyes.

Rose huffed a laugh.

"Only when you give me a reason to be."

There was a pause, soft, but full.

Eric's voice dropped just a little, gentler now. "I'll see you tonight."

Rose blinked, caught off guard by the shift in his tone. "Yeah… see you." The moment she ended the call, her smile faltered. Staring at the phone, she hesitated, her thumb hovering over the screen as if debating whether to call him back. *Had she pushed too hard? Was she overthinking it?* They've been together for ages, but the nagging unease wouldn't go away, like trying to hold onto sand as it slipped through her fingers.

Eric had always been the type to carry the world on his shoulders, never asking for help, never showing cracks. She used to admire that about him, his quiet strength, the way he always seemed to have control even when everything around him was falling apart. But now… it just felt like distance. Like a wall built slowly between them, brick by brick. Her mind drifted to the early days, late-night drives with the windows down, his laughter filling the car, the way he'd grab her hand just because he wanted to feel her close. That version of Eric felt like a lifetime ago. Now, it was as if he were slipping from her grasp, and no matter how hard she tried, she couldn't hold onto him. She blinked, snapping back to the present as she stepped into the kitchen. The shift from memory to now was jarring, and the warm lights did nothing to calm the ache in her chest.

How could this be happening?

Does he still love me?

The questions hit like waves, subtle, constant, wearing her down. She rubbed her temple and stood still, listening to the quiet hum of the house around her. Of course he loves me… *right?* But doubt had already settled in, and the worst part? She wasn't sure if she was just

imagining it, or if she'd already lost him… and
was the last to realize it.

42

Chapter IV:
Elements of Hope

Adam pulled into Rose Blackburn's expansive home, its white columns bathed in moonlight. The deep growl of the Audi RS7's twin-turbo V8 rumbled to a halt. Sleek leather seats cradled the cabin, the scent of burnt rubber lingering, fresh traces of luxury from the last joyride. The glow of the headlights spilled across, illuminating the empty driveway. He gripped the Alcantara steering wheel, exhaling as he shut off the ignition... Something didn't sit right. Adam scanned the quiet street. No laughter. No thump of bass bleeding from the house. Not even another car in sight. Just the distant hum of crickets pulsing in the dark. His stomach coiled. Katherine shifted beside him, adjusting the emerald satin gown that hugged her figure. The porch light caught the shimmer of her gold locket, a gift from their father, something precious held space in it, Adam remembered. Katherine glanced around. Adam caught the subtle shift in her expression, tight, uneasy, as she turned to him.

"Why's it so quiet?"

His jaw tightened slightly as his gaze flicking toward the house. The windows were dark, revealing no movement inside. "Yeah… That's strange." He stepped out first, adjusting the cuffs of his slate-gray tuxedo, the subtle sheen of its silk lapels catching the dim light. Unlike his usual tailored black suits, this one had a certain lightness to it, as if it barely rested on his frame, the fine fabric whispering against his skin with every movement. The gunmetal embroidery on his cufflinks swirled like gusts of wind, intricate and smooth, a detail he'd never paid much attention to before. His muted navy tie, soft and understated, was neatly knotted, blending seamlessly with the pale mist-gray of his undershirt. He exhaled slowly as the night's eerie silence settled around them.

Katherine followed, her silver heels clicking against the gravel as she pulled her white faux fur stole tighter around her shoulders. A crisp breeze whispered through the night. She glanced at Adam, quick, assessing. "You look different tonight," she said, her voice edged with curiosity.

"What?" He glanced down at his suit. "It's not like we dress up for game night."

Katherine shivered. A cold breeze stirred through the trees, rattling the bare branches overhead. The scent of freshly cut grass and damp stone mixed with the faint trace of Adam's woodsy cologne as they approached the porch. He paused. Something about the wind felt… different. It didn't just move through the air; it carried something with it. A whisper. A presence. Adam rang the doorbell. A soft breath of wind brushed past his ear, faint, feminine. Almost like a voice. He blinked. *Did I just hear that?*

It didn't seem to faze Katherine. Maybe he imagined it. Still, a strange chill ran through him. Before the chime even finished, the door flung open. Rose Blackburn stood in the doorway, confident smile, the effortless charm of the girl next door. But Adam knew better. He'd known her long enough to spot the subtle cracks, the way her eyes didn't quite match the brightness of her grin. "Oh, my goodness!" she squealed, pulling both him and Katherine into a warm hug. But even in her arms, the way they lay around them, wasn't her. Not truly.

Her laugh rang out, light and familiar, but Adam caught the slight tremor in her breath. Was it nerves? Sadness? She was always good at this, masking pain with sparkle. Polished, magnetic, unshakable. And yet, as she pulled away, he swore he saw it, just for a second, that ache behind her eyes. Eric. He didn't need her to say it. He remembered the stories: the late-night drives, the windows down, her hand in his. The real Eric. The one who used to reach for her like it was instinct. That guy… left long ago.

"You made it!" she said brightly, stepping aside to let them in. The moment they stepped inside, the music hit like a tidal wave, contemporary beats reverberating through the walls. The house was alive: flashing lights, dancing bodies, the scent of perfume clashing with alcohol and something faintly floral. Adam leaned in close, lips near Katherine's ear. "Pretty loud in here, don't you think?!" he shouted over the music.

She nodded. "Yeah, no kidding!"

But then—

The world thinned. A pressure built behind his ears, subtle at first, like altitude shift. Then came a faint trickle, as if sound were slipping sideways. And beneath it, something else.

A whisper. Feminine. Not quite a word, just a breath of one. Not part of the music. Not part of the room. *Did I just hear that again?* He blinked, glancing at Katherine. Her lips moved, but her voice didn't reach him. Everything sounded off, dampened, warped, like a warble of static right before a speaker cuts out. *Get a grip. You're not losing it. You're fine.*

Then—

"Did you hear me?" Her voice snapped back into focus, loud and clear. She raised a brow, already over it. Eric appeared just in time, two drinks in hand, his grin sharp with mischief. "Drink up, bitches!"

Katherine chuckled. "Finally," she said, accepting hers, while Adam hesitated for half a beat before clinking his glass against hers. The ice shifted with a faint chime of crystal, cutting through the bass-heavy music as he took a sip, the burn of liquor smooth but sharp on his tongue, warmth trickling down his throat as he scanned the room. Then, Eric nudged his shoulder, voice low enough to be heard over the music. "Come with me for a sec."

Adam exhaled, setting his glass down. He had a feeling where this was going. He trailed after

Eric, dodging bodies and flashing lights, the bass still pounding like a second heartbeat. The deeper they moved, the heavier the air felt, thick with sweat, booze, and something else he couldn't name. Rose grabbed Katherine's hand and dragged her toward the living room, weaving through the crowd. "We haven't caught up in a bit!" Rose called over the music.

"Any new boys in your life?!"

Katherine leaned in, trying to hear. "What?! This music is too loud!" she shouted back. Then, almost to herself, Katherine muttered, "Why is everybody asking me that?"

Rose caught it… barely, but said nothing. Katherine straightened and called out, louder this time, "What?!"

Rose leaned in closer.

"I SAID, ARE THERE ANY NEW…"

Before Rose could finish and Katherine could ever answer, a partygoer stumbled into them, nearly spilling his drink. "RIGHT ON, DUDE!" the guy cheered, nodding at his friends.

Rose let out a groan and shoved him aside. "Okay, let's move before we get tackled." The words came out with ease, playful, effortless, the way they always did. It was so much easier to joke, to keep things light than to dwell on the rest, the quiet thoughts she tried to push down. She had been looking forward to this party, to losing herself in the noise, the movement, the energy. And yet, something about tonight felt… strange. Maybe it was just her. Maybe it was the unspoken tension with Eric, the way his voice had sounded on the phone earlier, distant, distracted, like his mind was somewhere else entirely. She shook off the thought, forcing a smirk as she looped her arm through Katherine's.

By the time Adam reached the kitchen, flickered in moonlight that shined through the glass windowed doors, the bass still pounded against the walls, neon lights strobing in hypnotic waves, but his mind was already bracing for what he knew was coming. *Why am I even going along with this?* The thought sat heavy in his chest, the weight of it growing with every step. He could feel it, thick in the air, pressing against his ribs. And yet, he didn't stop walking. Then he saw it, and it hit like a slap to the face. The counter was littered with bottles, half-empty glasses, and right in the center of it all… a rolled-up hundred-dollar bill beside a neat, white line of cocaine. Adam stopped cold. His chest tightened, not from surprise, but from confirmation. This was who Eric had become. The ache in his gut sharpened. The version of his best friend he remembered, the loyal one, the fearless one, felt further away than ever. Adam's stomach twisted. He rolled his eyes. *Of course. The same o' same o' Eric. Because why would it be any different? He's gotten worse.*

Eric leaned casually against the counter, plucking up a glass like it was just another night, another party, another accident. "So," he drawled, taking a sip. "Tell me something, Greenfield. How long has it been?" Adam didn't answer. He didn't need to. The sight alone was enough to stir memories he had spent years trying to bury. The nights spent chasing highs, losing himself in reckless abandon, convincing himself he was untouchable. The crash that always followed, the sickening weight of regret, lodged so deep it felt permanent. *What kind of question is that?* He thought he had left this part of his life behind.

And yet, here he was. Again.

Not again.

He clenched his fists, forcing himself to breathe. The temptation, the familiarity, it was all there, hovering just beneath the surface. Like an old ghost, whispering, waiting. Waiting for him to give in. Eric smirked, dipping his head as he ran a finger along the edge of the counter. "Relax, man. You look like you're about to be interrogated. It's just a little fun."

Adam's jaw tightened. "I told you… I don't do that anymore."

Eric exhaled a laugh, shaking his head like Adam had just said something ridiculous. "Come on. Don't be so dramatic. You were always the soft one between you and I." He leaned forward, lowering his voice, the familiar sweet-talking tone creeping in. "You used to love this. We both did. For old time sake just you and I again."

Adam clenched his fists. He hated this game with Eric, the way he twisted things, made it seem harmless, like it was just another night, another party, another accident, nothing to worry about. Like Adam was the one overreacting, the one being unreasonable for walking away. Because that's what Eric did. He laughed off consequences and morals as if he never had to answer to anyone, just himself. He shrugged off reality. He made destruction look like a good time.

Adam had fallen for it before. Too many times. And yet, here they were, as if the past hadn't happened, as if Eric hadn't watched him spiral, hadn't seen the aftermath, hadn't seen the dead body. As if Adam hadn't spent years crawling out of the hole he had buried himself in. His jaw tightened. *Not again.*

Eric picked up the bill, rolled it between his fingers, and arched a brow. "One hit. You and me. It doesn't seem so bad, right?"

Adam's pulse quickened. *Old times,* he thought. The old him wasn't someone he wanted to resurrect. The old him made bad choices. The old him almost ruined his life. Eric looked at Adam in that same arrogant manner "Oh, you're afraid of what will happen. Just like last time, eh? When you killed a man." Adam's eyes bolted. His fingers twitched at his side. His vision narrowed. He wasn't breathing, just staring, in anger. The only thing moving was the fury crawling down his spine. The room suddenly felt smaller, the air thick and suffocating, the music from the other room a distant memory like a distorted hum.

Why is he tormenting me?

Then—

Katherine's voice. "Hey, you guys…"

Adam spun around just in time to see her standing in the doorway, her expression shifting from lighthearted to horrified the moment her gaze landed on the counter. Silence crashed between them. Adam's stomach plummeted. "No! No! No! It's not what it looks like!" he shouted. But the look on Katherine's face, the hurt, the disappointment, hit harder than any punch he'd taken. It wasn't just anger. It was betrayal. Her eyes, dark and hollow, swallowed him whole. Like she had just lost faith in him. Her shoulders stiffened, every muscle coiled, as if she was willing herself not to feel anything at all. Adam had seen that look before, way too many times. And he hated that he was the reason for it. Before he could explain, before he could even try, she turned and walked out. *Fuck*, he thought.

Eric shaking his head as he turned back to the counter with the rolled-up bill. "She'll get over it," he muttered. His tone was casual, but Adam caught the slight edge in his voice, the way his fingers tightened around the rolled-up bill.

"I know you once did."

Adam swallowed hard, his hands balling into fists at his sides. *No. Not this time.* He clenched his jaw, as he forces himself to breathe. The weight of Eric's words dug into him like a dull blade, pressing against old wounds he refused to reopen. "That was a long time ago, Eric. You know I don't mess with this stuff anymore."

Eric exhaled, shaking his head. "It's all good, man." Without hesitation, he leaned over and snorted the line, rubbing his nose as if it were second nature. Adam turned away, jaw tight, pretending to focus on something… anything, else. He hated seeing this, hated the way Eric acted like none of it mattered. It was just a habit to him, a casual indulgence. He used to think like that too. Back when denial was easier. Back when he didn't care who got hurt. *Is he really doing this in front of me? After what just happened?* Trying to shake the discomfort from creeping in, and like always he mended the hearts of men, his friends, even his parents. Sometimes it was better for him to move passed it, to not rattle the cage. Adam cleared his throat. "So… anything new with you and Rose?"

Eric exhaled, rubbing the back of his neck. "Let's step outside." They pushed through the back door, greeted by a sharp gust of cold air and moonlight. Adam shivered, tucking his hands into his pockets. "Damn, it got cold quick."

Eric chuckled, his breath visible in the crisp air. "Yeah. Feels different tonight." He hesitated before speaking again. "I haven't told anybody else yet…"

Adam rolled his eyes. "And now you decide to tell me in the cold?"

Eric lowered his voice, barely above a whisper. "I want to marry her."

Adam's eyes widen. "Wow. Well, it's about time. You guys have been together for, what, a decade? I'm surprised she didn't find someone else by now."

Eric shushed him. "Keep it down. And if anyone knows about waiting forever, it's you."

Adam threw his head back, laughing. "Yeah, yeah, yeah. Sure. When the time is right." His smirk lingered for just a second too long before he shot Eric a teasing look. "At this rate, it'll probably be when we're all old and gray."

Eric narrowed his eyes at him.

Adam raised his hands. "Kidding. What happened to you? You can't take a joke anymore."

Eric exhaled, a half-smirk on his face "You mean... you can't take a joke?"

He glanced toward the sky. Adam followed his gaze, a strange stillness settling over the yard. The air still felt strange, like the world had momentarily paused.

Then, a breath of energy curled through the wind. Eric shook off a sudden shiver and motioned toward the door. "Let's head back inside. It's freezing." As they stepped back into the warmth of the house, the glass windowed doors swung shut behind them, cutting off the cold. But outside, the air lingered… unsettled. A stillness clung to the yard like breath held too long. Something had shifted. Something was watching. And it was no longer asleep.

Chapter V:
Veils of Deception

Deep beneath the soil in the backyard of Rose's house, something long forgotten trembled, its presence pressing against the earth like a heartbeat trapped beneath flesh. A whisper of power curled through the roots, ancient and restless, stirring the very foundation of the world above. The sapphire orb, once a sacred relic, once bound to a queen who ruled with wisdom and might, had been cast into the void, torn from its home, swallowed by the unknown. But even here, buried beneath a world that had long since forgotten its name, it was not dead. A fine crack splintered its once-perfect surface, glowing faintly like an ember refusing to die. Above, the air shifted. A quiet wind slithered through the grass, sending leaves spiraling upward as if drawn by an unseen force. Yet inside, the house remained alive with warmth and laughter, the pulse of music and conversation shielding its guests from the awakening force just beneath their feet. Then, the Earth's moon split in two. Not with sound, but with a silence so deep it screamed. The silver halves hovered apart, edges facing inward, like twin blades paused mid-strike. The air dropped a few degrees. Even the stars seemed to recoil. For a moment, the earth itself seemed to hold its breath, suspended in time.

And then—

Deep in the soil, a jagged crack snapped across the orb's surface. A soundless ripple pulsed outward, unseen yet felt, a force beyond comprehension, a power too vast to remain caged. The trees stiffened, their roots curling in protest as the soil split apart, and from the fractured heart of the sapphire orb, something began to stir. A murmur spiral through the air. A voice—ancient, shattered, barely a breath against the wind.

Save us…

Then, the earth trembled. Beneath them, the ground lurched as if it were breathing, exhaling a force long buried. The splintered sapphire orb pulsed, spilling ghostly tendrils of fog onto the dark soil. Vine-like tendrils erupted from the fractured gem, twisting violently, clawing their way through the earth. They slithered upward, wrapping around the wooden fence like starving fingers grasping for purchase. The air itself seemed to recoil. A static charge crackled through the atmosphere, unseen yet felt, like the moment before a storm, when the world holds its breath. The party carried on inside, music humming beneath the walls, unaware that outside, the very fabric of reality had begun to unravel.

Adam spotted Rose across the room, her crimson dress catching the light as she weaved past a group of laughing guests. She looked completely at ease, laughing at something someone had said. For a brief moment, her presence felt like a reminder of normalcy, something stable, untouched. Rose grinned, "Where have you guys been? You're missing all the fun!"

And then—

The party guests vanished.

Adam blinked. The air shifted. In an instant, the noise collapsed. The warm murmur of voices, the pulse of music, the laughter and clink of glasses. Gone. It was as if the house had swallowed its own breath and sealed itself shut. A hollow, unnatural hush crept in like fog, coiling around the room. He took a slow step forward, heart kicking against his ribs. Where moments ago, there had been motion and sound, now there was only a void. *What just happened?* Adam's eyes swept the room, desperate for movement. *Okay, now I'm losing it. This isn't real. This can't be real. Where are all the guest?* His grip on reality, already cracked by what he'd done in the dark, felt dangerously thin now, he was slipping, like a thread stretched to the breaking point.

The lights flickered. The scent of spiced drinks still hung faintly in the air, but everything else felt stripped. Emptied. The silence wasn't peaceful. It was wrong. Rose stood frozen mid-step, her smile suspended in place. Adam's throat tightened. A chill seeped into his spine, instinct screaming before his thoughts could catch up. Something wasn't right. Something was coming. He turned to the others, voice low and tense. "You guys… did you see that? Where did everyone go?" Adam caught Katherine's breath hitch in her throat as she stared at the now-empty space in front of her. The man she'd been talking to—vanished. Not a sound, not a trace. He'd been there, solid, grounded and now it was like he'd never existed. Like reality had simply erased him. Katherine jolted upright, her hands trembling. "What just happened?" Her voice cracked, thin and disbelieving.

He turned in time to catch the flicker of panic in Eric's face. His friend's eyes darted toward the kitchen, alert, searching. Adam followed his gaze. The women who had been laughing just a moment ago—disappeared. Their glasses still sat on the counter, untouched, ice barely melted. The air around the kitchen felt… off. Skintight. As if whatever had been there had vanished in seconds. The eerie stillness crawled under Adam's skin, a suffocating silence pressing against his ears. It was as if they had been erased from existence, their presence wiped clean from reality in the blink of an eye.

This can't be good, he thought.

Then, it hit.

A deep, growing tremor. Subtle at first. Then stronger. The floor shivered beneath

Adam's boots. The walls and the floorboards moaned. The house wasn't settling; it was a warning. The floorboards shuddered and creaked, the very foundation of the house seeming to writhe beneath their feet. Overhead, the chandelier swung wildly, glass pendants crashing against each other in a frantic, chaotic rhythm, like wind chimes caught in the grip of a storm. The golden light flickered, the bulbs dimming as if the house itself were gasping for air. Each jolt sent a fresh wave of unease through their bodies, the air around them thick with an unspoken dread.

Adam's eyes flicked to Rose just as she froze, staring at the walls. Her chest rose, stomach twisted, body stiffening like something had crawled up her spine. He saw her pulse flutter at her neck, fast, frightened. "What was that?" she whispered, voice barely above air. He glanced at Eric and caught the weight in his stance, the tightness in his chest, the way his breathing came in shallow, uneven pulls. His body looked braced, ready for something worse. Eric turned toward the windows just as the glass rattled in its frames, the tremor still rippling through the walls. But outside. Nothing. Not a gust of wind. Not even the sway of trees. The world beyond the glass remained eerily still, untouched by the chaos unraveling inside. Adam saw his friend's expression stiffen before he forced the words out, his voice low and strained.

"It felt like an earthquake."

But this was no earthquake.

The air hummed, a slow, low vibration, like the distant pulse of something massive stirring beneath them, rousing from an ancient slumber. A pressure built in the space around them, an invisible force pressing against their lungs, making the very air feel heavier. The temperature plummeted, the warmth of the house vanishing in an instant, replaced by an unnatural chill that slithered over their skin like unseen fingers. Adam's breath hitched. The energy around him buzzed, a whisper curling at the edges of his consciousness, like a storm waiting to break. *That's strange*, he thought. A strange static crackled through the room, raising the fine hairs on their arms, sending a whisper of something otherworldly rippling through the atmosphere.

Then, out of the dimness, ghostly white spheres materialized, their light rippling through the air like underwater moons, circling them in eerie stillness. The quiet that comes before an

abduction. Adam's legs felt like stone. He couldn't
move, couldn't think. Every part of him was
braced for impact, but nothing came. The earth
trembled beneath them some more, as if
something ancient and restless had finally been
freed. A guttural roar of wind howled through the
yard, a force so raw, so untamed, that the very
atmosphere seemed to shudder beneath its weight.
He clenched his fists, feeling the subtle vibration
in his fingertips, like static before a storm.
Something had changed. He glanced at the others.
The white lights flickered once, then disappeared.
And in that moment, Adam knew, something
inside them had shifted.

A deep sound emerged, like the earth itself
was growling, a rising tremor came again.
Fluorescent bulbs exploded in rapid succession,
sharp cracks echoing through the house as glass
rained down like shattered stars. The ceiling
groaned, wooden beams splintering as if an
unseen force was pressing outward, testing the
limits of reality. The walls pulsed, trembling as
something massive stirred beneath the surface,
clawing its way through. Then, the vines came.
Thick, gnarled tendrils punched through the
windows, snapping the frames like brittle twigs.

They slithered along the walls, curling around furniture like starving serpents, tightening, crushing. They wouldn't stop. They rummaged into the ceiling, creeping into every crevice, infesting the house like a living, breathing force of nature. It was like the world was turning inside out. The structure shuddered, a long, agonized creak rippling through its foundation.

The lamps hanging from the ceiling swayed violently before they were ripped from their chains, glass and metal shattering on impact. Bookshelves toppled, their contents spilling out like panicked voices lost in the chaos. Tables slid across the floor, pulled by unseen force, their legs screeching against the wooden planks. Then, the walls began to disintegrate, flaking away like in rapid curls, caught in a breeze. The wooden panels beneath it withered, twisting, curling inward as if time itself was unraveling inside the house. The air thickened, humming with an eerie, unnatural vibration. And in that moment… A roar of wind. The four suddenly turned just in time to see the wind howled, sudden and violent, as if the sky itself had cracked open. It tore through the space before them, slashing through reality like an invisible blade, creating a circular opening, an entrance, perhaps, to another world. A force beyond comprehension ripped into the house, sending debris spiraling like a hurricane trapped within the house walls, yet the four remained untouched, sucking chairs to the bottomless pit blackhole. The temperature plunged, frost crawling across the floorboards, through the four, creeping up the walls like frozen veins.

As the frost slithered higher, it reached the torn edges of the fractured wall, hesitated, then surged inward. A crackling burst of cold erupted through the opening as ice lunged forward, swallowing the frame whole. The wall convulsed, groaning under the pressure as crystalline spires jutted outward, weaving themselves into a jagged arch of shimmering frost-white, breathing out tendrils of vapor that curled through the air like living mist. The portal had formed, not built, but born, alive and thrumming like a heartbeat carved in ice. A doorway to somewhere else, but where? Another dimension? A place unseen, untouched, yet somehow calling to them. What had been sent away, cast down into their world for reasons unknown? And then, everything just stopped. The destruction ceased, as if the universe itself had taken a breath.

The air, once howling with chaos, fell into an unnatural silence. The house, no longer crumbling, seemed to hold its breath too, suspended between destruction and something else entirely. A cold calm settled over the space, not just from the ice, but from the eerie finality of what had just occurred. It felt as though the world had reset, but into something unfamiliar.

Frost coated the broken wood and cracked furniture, gleaming beside the eerie frost-white glow of the portal. Adam stepped forward slowly, boots crunching against the frost-laced floor. No words. No thoughts. Just breath, white and shallow in the cold air, as he stared at the impossible doorway still pulsing before them. His hand brushed the edge of a broken table. Everything else felt like a dream that hadn't ended. He turned to the others, voice dry.

"So… who wants to go first?"

They didn't answer. The others stood motionless, eyes locked onto the portal. Its glacial surface pulsed like a heartbeat, the icy wall humming with an energy that didn't belong in their world. The air crackled around it, sending shivers through their skin, not just from the cold, but from the sheer unnatural force radiating from the threshold. It wasn't just an entrance. It was alive. A boundary between worlds, waiting to be crossed. Their breaths came in shallow gasps, each exhale visible in the frozen air. The wind had stilled, yet an unshakable presence lingered, watching them, urging them forward. And beyond the veil of ice… something stirred.

The three turned to stare at him, disbelief flickering across their faces. Adam shrugged, hands lifting in mock innocence. "What? We don't exactly have a back door." He watched Katherine. She hadn't moved. Her arms hung stiff at her sides, fists clenched so tightly her knuckles had gone pale. Shoulders drawn, breath shallow, like her body couldn't quite process what had just happened. She wasn't panicking. Not exactly. There was something sharper behind her eyes. Fear, yes, but beneath it, logic. She was calculating. Breaking it down. The wreckage, the portal, the impossible shift in their world, all of it unfolding faster than reason could follow.

He knew that look. She was trying to find a way back. But there wasn't one. He felt it too, this creeping awareness that nothing was ever going to be the same. That what waited ahead was madness…

…yet somehow, still the only path left. She shook her head. "You say that like walking into some glowing ice wall is the rational option."

Adam arched a brow.

"I mean… do you see another door?"

Eric exhaled sharply, crossing his arms. "That doesn't mean we just step into some… something that literally tore a hole in our reality." His jaw clenched. "We don't even know what's on the other side."

Adam looked to Rose. She took a hesitant step forward, the glow of the portal flickering in her wide eyes. He noticed the way her breath caught, how her gaze lingered on the threshold like it meant something deeper, something personal. The shimmer of the ice danced across her face, reflecting a thousand memories he couldn't see. For a moment, she didn't speak. She just stared. Then… softly, like it had surprised even her, she said, "What if… it was meant for us?" The words hung in the air, weightless and heavy all at once. Adam felt something stir in his chest. Not fear. Not courage. Just… inevitability.

"There's only one way to find out," Rose added.

Adam didn't hesitate. He stepped forward and reached out, his fingers brushing the ice. *It's a bit chilly,* he thought. The cold bit into his skin, sharp and immediate, but beneath the frost, something else stirred. A pull. Not just an object, but a presence. An invitation. It tugged at him, like gravity, drawing him forward, calling him home to a place he had never been. *Let's hope Rose is right,* he thought. *She said, what if it was meant for us? She's always been the sharp one. This feeling… the cold… the ice… it's not repelling. It's guiding me. I couldn't possibly turn back now. Even if I wanted to.* Then, he stepped through. The cold surged around him like a living current, wrapping his body in a breathless silence. For a split second, the world behind him blurred, distant, dissolving into nothingness, as if it no longer wanted him back. It sucked him in.

Rose swallowed hard, her voice barely a whisper. "Do you think he's okay?"

Eric exhaled. "Someone has to go through to find out.

Across from them, Katherine's fists tightened at her sides. She didn't speak, just lifted her chin, eyes locked on the portal's glow. From where Rose stood, it looked like defiance.

Or maybe fear, buried so deep it wore armor. "I'll go," Katherine said.

Rose's heart jumped.

"Be careful," she murmured.

Katherine gave a small nod, nothing more, and stepped forward. The portal swallowed her like it had Adam. Rose blinked, a chill working its way up her spine. *Please let her be okay.* Then, only two remained. The cold nipped at her skin, but Rose barely felt it. She stood frozen. Her eyes flicked to the warped doorway of what used to be her home, the front hall where she once hugged her mom goodbye, the corner where her dad's boots always sat, muddy and waiting. All of it twisted now, coated in frost and shadow, like a memory that no longer belonged to her. A cracked photograph frame lay face down in the rubble. She didn't dare lift it. Her throat tightened. "Mom...? Dad...?" The words came out softer than breath, a question sent into a silence that had already answered. She hovered at the threshold; eyes locked on the portal's eerie glow. This was her home, her parents, her childhood, her memories, everything frozen behind her like it had already been erased. *"Don't forget your jacket, baby,"* the voice whispered, a phantom caught in the wind. Her body snapped to the direction of the voice like she seen a ghost. Her expression tensed. They never got an answer. Not to the yelling. Not to the pounding on the door. Not to the final scream before the world split apart. And now… there might never be one. The portal pulsed behind her, alive and waiting. She turned toward it, heart twisting. If she stepped through, there was no guarantee she'd come back. No promise she'd see them again. And yet… Something deeper called to her. Not the portal. Not the energy. But the feeling that maybe this was what she'd been meant to do all along. She took a shaky breath. *I'm not leaving them behind,* she thought. This is something they'd want me to find.

"You, okay?" Eric asked quietly.

Rose nodded. "Yeah."

Her body screaming to follow, but something held her back. The portal wasn't just an entrance to somewhere unknown, it was a threshold, a point of no return. Her fingers twitched at her sides, hesitant. Then she saw Eric. Beside her, he stood frozen, his jaw clenched so tight she could almost hear the grind of his teeth. His hands curled into fists, tension radiating off him like a live wire. He didn't speak, but she could see it in his eyes. He was calculating, weighing the risk, trying to make sense of something that made none. She could see it in the way Eric held himself, tense, unmoving. It wasn't fear exactly, but something quieter. A resistance. Like this final moment, standing at the edge, was the last piece of control. He wasn't ready to give up. She had never seen him hesitate like this before. He was the rational one. The steady one. But right now, he wasn't steady, he was stuck.

"Eric…" Her voice was softer now, coaxing him back from whatever thoughts were holding him still. She reached for his hand, her fingers brushing against his knuckles before slipping between them, lacing their hands together. His skin was cold, but his grip was strong. Solid. Grounding. They were in this together. She tried to push down the fear creeping up her throat. "Guess it's just us now." She felt Eric's fingers squeeze hers, steady and certain. Whatever fear lingered behind his silence, he masked it well. They stood side by side, facing the portal's glow, unspoken, but understood.

Whatever waited on the other side… they'd face it together.

And without another word, they stepped through. The ice pulsed, the portal shifting, almost like it was alive. And just before it sealed shut… something moved on the other side.

Chapter VI:
The Fire Within

Rose stepped through the ice wall, her breath hitching as a strange sensation washed over her. The moment her body fully crossed the threshold, the frigid light behind her dimmed, its glow flickering, then vanishing entirely. Darkness swallowed the tunnel. She turned sharply, her pulse hammering, her gaze locking onto the ice behind her. But there was no exit. No doorway. Only a wall of solid, frozen silence. *There's no going back now,* she thought, heart pounding. *Something about this place felt...* "Here, come on." Eric called gently. Rose blinked, adjusting to the pitch-black surroundings as her eyes gradually made out his silhouette. The tunnel stretched before them like the gaping throat of a beast, endless and hungry. They moved forward cautiously. The air was different here, heavier, unnatural. The further they walked, the colder it became, the temperature sinking past anything that should have been possible. Not just winter cold, but ancient cold, like something untouched, something that didn't belong to their world.

Their footsteps echoed, each step bouncing back at them like a whisper in the dark. Then, something skittered. Rose stiffened. A faint clicking sound scuttled along the walls. "What is this place?" Her voice came out hushed, breathless. She reached out, fingers grazing the frozen wall, and instantly tensed. It wasn't just ice. It was etched, carved, marked by something… by someone. The grooves were deep, measured, a story frozen in time beneath her fingertips. She inhaled sharply, dragging her fingers over the rough, jagged patterns. Warriors locked in battle. Swords raised, clashing, bloodless but brutal. And then, something else. Her breath hitched as her hands traced a colossal figure, towering over the rest. *These weren't just carvings. They meant something. They had to,* she thought. Something greater, something unknowable.

A shiver rolled down her spine, though not from the cold, as the open back of her crimson dress offered little protection. She swallowed hard, pulling her hand back, her fingers tingling from the touch. Whatever this place was, it had history.

And history never came without a price. Eric exhaled sharply, his breath visible even in the dark. "It's getting colder." His voice was right. The air had shifted again. It wasn't just cold anymore, it was pricking against their skin, creeping into their bones. Rose stiffened. Something changed. A pulse, a slither, moved along the tunnel walls. Her breath caught in her throat. The ice… was moving. Vein-like tendrils of frost curled inward, coiling and receding in slow, serpentine waves. They hugged the edges of the tunnel like roots crawling through soil, pulsing in rhythm. A little too smooth, too alive. She couldn't see them clearly in the dark, but she felt it. The whole tunnel… was breathing. *What is this place? What if they weren't meant to be here at all?*

Then—a glow.

A faint, blue light appeared ahead, pulsing softly, waiting. Eric's shoulders tensed, his gaze locking onto it. It wasn't just an exit. It was a threshold. And something was waiting on the other side… They pressed forward, drawn toward the glow. Rose stepped forward, her boots crunching against the ice as she and Eric emerged from the hollow tunnel, their breath sharp in the frozen air. A gust of wind cut through them, slicing like a blade, carrying a cold so deep it felt almost alive. Her fingers still tingled from the firestorm that had raged through her body minutes ago, but now… she just felt cold. Not just from the temperature, but from something in the air, in the stillness, in the way the world seemed to be waiting. Her crimson dress, sleek and elegant, had been perfect for the party, but here, it left her defenseless. The thin material clung to her legs, offering no shelter as the frost bit at her ankles. Her heels sank into the ice, making every step a struggle. Her eyes darted from Adam to the endless horizon of ice and snow. No buildings. No streets. No home. No New York. It was gone. As if Earth never existed.

The sky loomed overhead, an eerie shade of gray-blue, the clouds unmoving, heavy, as if pressing down on them. A lump formed in her throat. Maybe she had been in denial before. Maybe some part of her had thought they'd step through the portal and what? Find an answer? A way back? This shouldn't be real. But the ache in her lungs, the frost biting her skin, the sheer, oppressive silence all told her the same thing.

There was no way back.

She glanced at Eric, searching his face for something, logic, reassurance, anything, but he looked just as shaken. His breath was unsteady, his hands clenching and unclenching at his sides. For the first time, she realized just how fragile this moment was.

What if they weren't as strong as they thought?

The four stumbled onto the frozen terrain, their breath misting in the air as the biting cold cut through their skin like razors. It hit them all at once. This wasn't Earth. This wasn't the warm, crowded house party they had been standing on just moments ago. Adam shivered violently, gripping his arms. He was still in his dark fitted blazer and dress shirt, the once-crisp fabric now damp with melting frost. His dress shoes slipped against the ice, offering no traction, no warmth. He stood at the edge of the cliff, his breath frozen in his lungs. This couldn't be real. His mind scrambled to make sense of it, the jagged ice stretching for miles, the eerie silence where New York should have been, the absolute absence of home. It was like staring at a dream that had been shattered and pieced back together wrong.

He took a step forward, the ice cracking sharply beneath his boot. The sound echoed, too loud in the quiet. It sent a chill through his spine that had nothing to do with the cold. This wasn't just somewhere else. This was something else. He felt the weight of it pressing against his ribs, a slow, heavy certainty that wrapped around him like a noose. His hands curled into fists, knuckles whitening. He should have known something was off the second that portal swallowed them. And yet, standing here, staring out at the nothingness, the truth settled into his bones with a weight that refused to lift. In that moment, he thought, *They weren't going back.*

His stomach twisted. He had been the first to step through, the first to push forward, what if he had just led them into something they couldn't escape? He could hear the others behind him, their breathing uneven, their footsteps hesitant. They were looking to him now. And the worst part? He had no idea what to say. Adam's eyes flicked to Katherine. She clutched her sequined shawl tighter around her shoulders, her emerald cocktail dress offering little protection against the subzero temperatures. *The sheer sleeves might as well have been nonexistent,* he thought. Wind sliced through the fabric like knives against her exposed skin. She should have been panicking. She should have been screaming, crying, demanding an answer, but she wasn't.

Her gaze stayed fixed on the horizon, lips pressed tight, like she was calculating something, like she was trying to make sense of it all. Typical Katherine. Always analyzing. Always looking for answers. Trying to fit in a box, where there can be an explanation. Portals weren't real. Alternate dimensions weren't real.

And yet, here they were, he thought.

Beside her, Eric flexed his fingers to his sides, his button-down rolled to the elbows, and the slacks he had worn to look sharp at the party now looked stiff in the creeping chill we all felt. He rubbed his arms with irritation. His shoulders were drawn stiff, his jaw clenched, eyes scanning the endless ice like he could punch logic back into the situation. Adam didn't have to hear his thoughts to know the look, frustration simmering just beneath the surface. *Knowing Eric over the years, seeing him like this.. in the middle of nowhere. Not having everything at his requests. He hates it... I understand buddy,* he thought. Adam's jaw clenched, his eyes flickered, Rose slipped her hand into Eric's. *At least they have each other,* he thought.

He watched Eric's fingers twitch, then close around hers. The tension in his face didn't fade, but something softened, just enough. Adam looked away, heart sinking. Whatever strength they still had left, it was tied to each other now.

The four of them stood there, motionless, the weight of their reality finally pressing into them. There was no going back. No way home. No more pretending that this was something they could walk away from. This was real. And they had just crossed the threshold into a world they didn't understand. Snowflakes swirled in the air, the wind howling like a mourning cry through the icy expanse. Glaciers emerged in jagged formations, stretching endlessly beneath an oppressive sky. There was no sun, no stars, only an eerie, pale glow that hung over the land, casting long shadows across the frozen wasteland. Ice crunched beneath their feet, sharp as shattered glass, the cold biting through their clothes with merciless precision. It was vast. Empty. And utterly lifeless. Nothing but ice. Nothing but silence. Nothing but an endless void stretching into the unknown. Just endless, merciless cold. Rose's breath shook. "Oh my god."

Adam turned his gaze back to the horizon, his breath steady, but his pulse had quickened. He told himself it was nothing, just the wind curling through the glaciers, but deep down, he knew better. This place was too quiet. Too still. Something was out there. And it was waiting.

Rose took a shaky step forward. "Maybe we should try to go back."

Adam's voice was calm, but heavy. "I already tried that."

She turned to him, her stomach sinking. "What do you mean you tried?"

Adam's gaze didn't waver. "There's no way back in." *I assumed they knew,* he thought. The words landed like a stone in the pit of Rose's stomach. Silence settled between them, thick with an unspoken weight.

Eric exhaled sharply, dragging a hand through his hair. "That's not possible. Portals don't just... shut off." His voice verge on frustration, his breath visible in the frozen air.

Adam met his stare, unflinching. "Tell that to the giant ice wall that just sealed itself behind us." His voice was steady, but there was an edge to it, an unspoken frustration simmering beneath the surface. He gestured toward the towering wall of solid ice, its surface smooth and impenetrable, a frozen barrier that didn't just block their way back, it had erased it entirely. He clocked the tension building in Eric's face. His jaw clenched, shoulders tight, like he was bracing for impact. "No. No," Eric snapped, voice hard. "We're not just trapped here. There has to be another way back." His breath came out in sharp, uneven puffs, curling into the frozen air. Adam could see it; Eric was barely holding it together. The way his fists flexed, the edge in his tone. That ripple of unease? It was there, just under the surface. And if he was starting to crack, that meant the reality was sinking in for all of them.

Nearby, Katherine dropped onto a frozen slab near the cliff's edge, arms wrapped tightly around herself. Her emerald dress shimmered faintly in the pale light, but the glamour was gone, replaced by quiet dread. Adam caught her staring out into the wasteland beyond, her face unreadable, but her body stiff, like the silence itself had pinned her down. Her gaze flicked toward the distant ice vines winding around a glacier, their movements unsettling, slow, deliberate. Alive. Just not natural. She looked like she wanted to speak, but her voice barely carried.

Adam heard it anyway. He watched Rose cross her arms, rubbing at her shoulders like she was holding herself together. Her voice cracked when she finally snapped "So what? We just accept that we're stuck? That we're not going home?" It wasn't just anger. There was fear there too. He could hear it, the fear buried under the words. Adam inhaled slowly, his fingers curling into fists. "Freaking out isn't going to help."

Rose snapped her gaze to him, eyes blazing. "Oh, I'm so sorry if my reaction isn't as chill as yours. My life just got ripped away from me, and you want me to calm down?"

Adam's jaw tightened, snapped his gaze at her. "I never said that. You know exactly what I said." For a second, he almost said something sharper, the kind of truth that leaves scars, but the words stayed trapped behind his teeth.

Eric sighed, stepping between them, his hands raised. "Okay! Let's not do this. We need to think." His voice was firm, but his eyes flicked toward Rose. "There's no point in arguing." Rose shook her head, turning away from them, her hands still clenched.

Katherine finally stood, arms still wrapped around herself. "What do we do now?"

Adam's lips parted, then hesitated. The weight of their eyes was crushing. Katherine waiting. Eric watching. Rose still fuming. For the first time, he didn't have an answer. They were looking to him now. Like he was supposed to know what to do. Like something inside him should just… click. But all he felt was the cold. The vastness. The fear. A gust of wind howled past them, carrying with it something strange, a whisper, distant, barely audible.

Rose stiffened. "Did you hear that?"

Eric tensed beside her.

Katherine swallowed hard.

"I thought it was just the wind."

Adam turned his gaze back to the horizon, his breath steady, but his pulse had quickened. *What was this place? And more importantly, who else was here?* Something else was out there.

And it was waiting.

Chapter VII:

Fugitives of Fate

Elsewhere, where hours slipped like minutes and hunger crept in unnoticed, beyond the thinning's frost, another change was taking shape, slowly, quietly, like breath exhaled beneath the winter moon. Ice blanketed the earth in a hush, muffling the world with shimmering stillness. The landscape stretched like a forgotten dream: silver trees sheathed in rime, their brittle limbs sagging beneath frozen dew. Frost latticed every branch and stone, turning even death into something beautiful. A windless silence hung over the land, broken only by the crunch of boots on crusted snow and the distant crackle of settling ice. Adam's breath plumed before him in rhythm, each exhale ghosting into the air. The cold sank deep, numbing thought and motion, but he pressed forward. There was something sacred about the hush, something eerie, too.

As if the land was watching. As if it knew. He glanced back at Katherine, who lagged a few steps behind. Her arms wrapped tight around herself, shoulders drawn inward. Lips pale. Breath quick. She didn't speak; she didn't need to. He saw it in her eyes: the ache, the weariness, the bitter resolve. Stopping wasn't just dangerous; it was a death sentence. The world shimmered with quiet menace, its beauty almost cruel, less a landscape than a mirage carved from ice and silence. Fractured light danced across the trail, casting ghostly reflections. Ice-crusted thorns jutted from the ground like warning signs. A frozen cathedral, reverent, watchful, cold. A winter wonderland sculpted by forgotten gods, delicate and deadly in equal measure. But even that was shifting. Somewhere ahead, beyond the veil of white and hush, something warmer stirred.

The terrain groaned with each step, as if protesting their presence. Ice splintered beneath their boots in hairline fractures that spiderwebbed and vanished just as quickly. The once-solid crust had begun to crack, not just in sound, but in feel. Adam felt it: a tremble beneath his soles, like the earth was warning them. He met Katherine's gaze. No words, but the same thought moved through them: something was coming. And it wouldn't wait for them to be ready. "Keep up with us," he said, his tone edged with quiet urgency, though he softened it just enough to avoid making it sound like an order. They were all struggling in their own way, but stopping wasn't an option, not here, not when the terrain was shifting beneath their feet.

Katherine gave a small nod, arms tightening around herself as she forced her legs to keep pace. Her breath came in uneven puffs, visible against the cold, and her steps had grown slower, heavier. Adam watched her chest rise in short, shallow bursts, too quick. It wasn't just the cold. Something else was digging into her. Fear, maybe. Fatigue. He couldn't tell. But whatever it was, it was eating at her. And still, she pushed on.

Adam slowed his pace, breath curling out in ghostly wisps as something dark snared the corner of his vision. He turned his head and saw it, thin, deliberate, rising like a scar against the sky. A trail of smoke. It cut through the pale clouds with unnatural precision, too smooth, too vertical, like a blade slicing heaven in half. It wasn't the wild scatter of a brushfire, nor the dying plume of some long-fought battle. This was… intentional. A beacon. Or a warning.

His gut twisted. They weren't alone. He stared for a moment too long, his mind spiraling with possibilities. *A settlement? Survivors? An ambush?* There was something unnatural about the stillness beneath that smoke, how the wind didn't scatter it, how it rose in silence. As if the land itself was holding its breath. And maybe he was, too. He didn't speak. Not yet. The air around them was already thick from the argument, the kind of silence that isn't peaceful, just full of unsaid things. He felt it pressing against his skin, coiling around his chest. The blame lingered in every sideways glance, in the fact that no one walked at his side anymore. It wasn't fair. But it wasn't new. *When it goes wrong, it's always me.*

He gritted his teeth and shifted his weight, the memory of Rose's words, sharp and exact, still echoing in his mind. He didn't blame her. Not really. She was scared. They all were. But that didn't stop the bitterness from curling in his gut. Or the loneliness. Or the dread. He glanced back. Katherine was hugging herself, eyes down. Eric's jaw was tight. Rose, she was watching the same smoke now, her expression unreadable. But Adam wasn't fooled. The tension clung to all of them.

The smoke continued to rise, unbothered, undeterred. Like it knew they'd seen it. Like it was waiting. It wasn't just the smoke in the sky, it was the smoke between them, the unspoken tension, the mistrust. His heart thudded harder in his chest. Who else was out here? And were they already watching? *Should he say something? Would they even listen?* "There's smoke in the mountains. We should head over there… It's the only sign of life we've seen." Rose's voice was firm, but Adam caught the thread of uncertainty beneath it.

He followed her gaze to the distant peaks, jagged and veiled in mist, untouched by time. They wouldn't reach them tonight, not even close. But something about them felt inevitable. Everything would be different. The air around him thrummed with tension, like the earth itself was waiting, for them, or for whatever came next. Eric followed Rose's gaze, his jaw tightening. Adam noticed how his fingers flexed at his sides, restless, like he was already bracing for whatever lay ahead. The smoke meant people. And people meant answers. But it also meant danger. Adam had seen Eric make hard calls before, always calm, always certain. But this time, something was off. "That's our best bet," Eric said. Adam heard the strain in it. He wasn't sure who Eric was trying to convince them, or himself.

Adam hesitated for a moment, his eyes lingering at the dark fume rising beyond the treetops, twisting against the soft glow of the sun-dappled canopy. There was something about it that unsettled him, a whisper of instinct clawing at the back of his mind. It reminded him too much of the night everything changed. Every step forward felt like stepping deeper into something they weren't meant to find. But before he could voice it… "Come on," Eric said, his voice clipped and low. "We have a long way ahead of us."

Adam watched his breath curl into the frozen air, vanishing into the vast nothingness ahead. Tension clung to his posture, tight shoulders, clenched jaw. He didn't say it, but Adam could feel it in the silence: hesitation wouldn't save them. He inhaled sharply, forcing down the unease twisting in his chest, gripping onto resolve like a lifeline. Every instinct screamed that whatever lay ahead wasn't meant to be found, but turning back wasn't an option.

The dark fume in the distance pulsed against the sky, a silent omen, daring them to come closer. Whatever was waiting beyond those trees, those mountains, there was only one way to find out. The frost beneath his boots no longer crunched as loudly, just softer, wetter somehow, like the world was changing beneath them.

He followed the others as they pressed forward, their steps growing steadier as the unforgiving ice gave way to softer earth. The once-frozen terrain slowly dissipated into patches of damp soil, revealing towering trees ahead, their thick canopies filtering warm, golden light through the branches. The shift in the environment was stark, where there had once been nothing but frost and lifeless terrain, now there was the scent of damp moss, the distant murmur of unseen creatures. Katherine slowed, her breath uneven as she leaned against a fallen tree trunk. Her fingers dragged along the rough bark, steady, almost deliberate. Adam watched her, catching the way her hand lingered, like she needed to remind herself the world was still real.

He stepped toward her, his voice low with concern. "Are you all right?" She gave a shaky nod, but Adam wasn't convinced. The exhaustion in her eyes said more than words ever could. His jaw tightened. He had to be the steady one, the one to keep them moving forward. But how much longer could he keep pretending he wasn't just as lost as the rest of them? She was cold, exhausted, barely holding herself together, but so was he. He just couldn't afford to show it. He exhaled sharply, forcing the thought aside. "Let's take a break." His voice came out even, controlled, because someone had to be. Rose stopped and cursed under her breath. "These heels aren't making it another step." She kicked them off without ceremony, then grabbed the hem of her crimson gown and tore it just above the knee with a sharp tug. "This isn't home anymore." Katherine followed suit, ripping the slit in her emerald dress higher with a hiss of frustration before slipping off her own shoes and stretching her bare toes against the mossy ground.

Eric shrugged off his blazer with a grunt and rolled up his sleeves, letting the cold air hit his skin, revealing forearms streaked with dirt and strain. Adam stripped off his blazer and tie, letting them fall beside a broken log. He knelt to untie his dress shoes, slipping them off with a wince. The dirt felt foreign beneath his feet, soft, damp, and strangely alive. One by one, the remnants of the party — the fabric, the polish, the pretense, fell away. They weren't guests anymore. They were survivors. Adam watched Eric scan the area, his fingers twitching like he was ready to throw a punch at the air itself. Tension hung off him like steam. He rubbed a hand down his face, slow, like trying to wipe the day off. "Yeah, let's take a break," he said, voice low. Then, almost to himself, he muttered, "Feels like the tail end of a bad trip."

Adam smirked, a hint of a laugh in his tone. "I mean, you did just snort up half a roll before we got sucked into this nightmare."

Eric let out a sharp laugh, shaking his head. "Shit, maybe I am hallucinating." He gestured vaguely at the shifting terrain. "Would explain the whole winter-wonderland-to-mystical-forest thing."

Rose rolled her eyes, unimpressed. "Well, unless your drug-fueled delusions come with a five-star hotel, we still have to figure out where the hell we are."

Eric and Adam exchanged a look, shaking their heads. They already knew how she was. No point in arguing. As they settled onto a moss-covered log, Adam caught Katherine glancing toward the forest that stretched beyond them, rigid posture, alert eyes, something pulling at her like instinct. The tension was still there. But it felt different now. Softer. Like, for the first time since the smoke, they could breathe. Adam caught the shift in her expression. "Where are you going?"

"There's no food," she replied, already stepping away. "I'm going to find some."

Adam frowned, glancing at the towering trees and the vast unknown stretching before them. "You don't even know this place, and you're going into the forest?"

Katherine met his gaze, unwavering. "I'm hungry. Aren't you?"

Adam hesitated. *Of course I'm hungry. Just not sure I'm willing to die for it.* He watched Katherine step toward the trees like she hadn't just said the most reckless thing imaginable. He sighed. "Yeah, I am." His eyes flickered to Rose, watched her eyes track Katherine's retreat. She crossed her arms, a smirk tugging at her lips. "You'd think she'd be a little more grounded."

Eric huffed a quiet laugh, shaking his head. "She's stubborn, that's for sure."

Rose stepped up beside them, her arms folded tight as she stared toward the lake. She looked distant, like her thoughts were still somewhere back in the trees. A quiet hung between them until she finally asked, "So, what do you guys think this place is?"

Eric huffed, arms crossed over his chest. "Your home turned inside out."

Rose shot him a glare, but Adam smirked at the sarcasm. "Whatever it is," she said, her voice barely above the wind rustling through the trees. "I just... I hope our parents are safe."

Adam watched her as she spoke. Something in her voice cracked, softer than usual, more vulnerable. He didn't know what memory crossed her mind, but the way she looked out over the lake... it reminded him of his own. His mom's laugh. The steady tone of his dad's voice on stormy nights. For a moment, he held onto those sounds, uncertain if he'd ever hear them again.

Eric's expression faltered, just for a moment, a crack in the carefully composed mask he always wore. Adam caught it, subtle but there. Eric exhaled slowly, shoulders easing, though the tension didn't fully leave him. Adam noticed something else, too, his voice. It was softer than before, not like when they'd trekked through the glacier. It was calmer now. Or maybe just tired. Like he was trying to believe it himself. "It's going to be okay." The words hovered in the air between them, fragile, uncertain, because none of them really knew if it was true. He pulled Rose close, his arm settling around her. She didn't pull away. Adam watched as she leaned into him, just for a moment, her eyes closing with something like relief. The quiet between them felt heavier now, not peaceful, like they all knew better than to believe it would last. But safety was fleeting.

Elsewhere, separated from the group, Katherine moved cautiously along the dirt path, her boots sinking slightly into the damp earth. The forest around her felt untouched, its towering trees standing like sentinels of an age long forgotten. The air was thick with the scent of damp moss and rich earth, the distant rustling of unseen creatures hinting that she was not entirely alone. As she passed brittle, lifeless plants, something unnatural happened, the moment she moved beyond them, they stirred, their shriveled branches stretching, leaves unfurling into lush, vibrant greens. Trees that had seemed dead just moments before now stood tall and strong, their roots twisting into the ground as if awakened from a deep slumber.

She halted, her breath catching. Slowly, she turned, staring at the transformed path behind her. The plants had grown, because of her. A shiver rolled through her, not from fear, but from the weight of realization settling deep in her bones. It wasn't just the eerie stillness around her or the unnatural way the air felt heavy, it was the understanding that something had shifted, something irreversible. The world she thought she knew was unraveling before her eyes, revealing truths she wasn't sure she was ready to face. And yet, despite the chill creeping up her spine, she couldn't turn back now.

Ahead, the earth stirred, reshaping itself with quiet intention, forming a narrow path that led her deeper into the heart of the forest. The once-untamed ground seemed to welcome her, guiding her steps toward a thicket of wild blueberries nestled between the towering trees. The bushes were heavy with fruit, their deep blue hues standing out in striking contrast against the vibrant greens, as if nature itself had painted the scene just for her. A soft breeze rustled the leaves, carrying the sweet scent of ripe berries through the air, as though the forest was offering her a gift, a sign that, for now, she was exactly where she was meant to be. Swallowing hard, Katherine hesitated before reaching out, her fingers grazing the plump berries as if testing whether they were truly real. The weight of the moment pressed against her, this wasn't just hunger, it was survival. Something unnatural had guided her here, something she didn't understand, but the gnawing emptiness in her stomach outweighed her fear. She plucked a handful, feeling the cool, firm texture against her palm, the scent of crushed fruit lingering in the air.

She had no idea what was happening to her, no explanation for the way the forest seemed to respond to her presence, bending, shifting, listening. But right now, none of that mattered. The others were tired, hungry, and worn thin from the weight of the unknown pressing down on them. They needed food, and for whatever reason, the forest had provided. For now, she wouldn't question it. The sky had dimmed to a dusky violet by the time Katherine emerged from the trees. She stepped toward the others, her hands cupped carefully, filled with small, ripe blueberries.

Katherine extended her hands, offering the small handful of blueberries she had gathered. "It's not much, but it'll have to do for now." Her voice was steady, but Adam caught something else beneath it, maybe fatigue, maybe guilt. An apology without the words. He took a few and gave a quiet nod, forcing a small smile.

Rose grabbed one and popped it into her mouth without hesitation. No comment, no sarcasm. Just a bite and a blank stare. Adam watched her chew and felt the weight settle in his gut, not hunger, but the realization that this was it. A few berries, enough to keep the edge off for maybe an hour. If that. They weren't starving, not yet, but the thought lingered like a splinter: *what if this was the best they'd get?* His stomach gave a dull twist. He ignored it. Right now, survival didn't care about satisfaction. You took what you could get. Eric, however, eyed the berries like they were an insult. Adam caught the subtle curl of his lip, the flicker of skepticism that crossed his face before he spoke. "That's it? We're really out here playing survivor over some damn berries?" He gestured vaguely at the forest, like he expected a buffet to materialize from the trees.

Adam rolled his eyes. *Here we go again.*

Katherine shot him a look, her patience wearing thin. "Unless you know how to magically conjure up a Michelin chef, this is what we've got." Her tone was sharp, edged with exhaustion.

Adam recognized it immediately; it wasn't just about food. It was everything. The long hours, the constant uncertainty, the weight of the unknown pressing in from all sides. Eric exhaled sharply, rubbing his temples before muttering, "Man, I would kill for a burger right now. Or a damn protein bar."

Adam glanced over at him. That voice, half-joking, half-serious, was typical Eric. The kind of hunger he complained about sounded more like a mild inconvenience than a real problem. Like he'd never actually gone without. Rose smirked, tossing another berry into her mouth with a flick of her wrist. "Careful what you wish for," she mused, chewing slowly. "Something out here might take you up on that offer." Her voice was light, teasing, but beneath it, something unspoken lingered. Eric rolled his eyes but didn't argue. He plucked a few berries from Katherine's hand, muttering under his breath, "I don't know... maybe something that had a pulse."

The words hit like a whipcrack. Adam's breath caught, just for a second. The moment was small, barely a flicker, but it slammed into him with the force of a collapsing ceiling. A pulse. His chest tightened, his body stiffening as his mind betrayed him, dragging him backward. A memory surged forward, violent and unbidden, headlights slicing through darkness, the wet crunch of metal, a body sprawled across pavement. The air had been thick with the scent of burning rubber, his knuckles bone-white as they gripped the wheel. The moment stretched, endless, as his heartbeat thundered in his ears, refusing to let him forget.

His fingers twitched, as if they could still feel the ghost of that night, the suffocating grip of shock, the sick realization that nothing would ever be the same. He swallowed hard, forcing the lump in his throat down. *Did Eric even hear himself? Did he even care? Or was this just another thing he could toss aside, bury, pretend it never happened?* The weight of it sat between them, thick as the roots beneath their feet. Adam exhaled sharply, pushing the past away. *Not now.* He forced his voice to stay even, casual, though his jaw had tightened. "Yeah? And what exactly do you plan on hunting?" He turned to Eric, flashing a dry look, the tension laced beneath his words. "You gonna wrestle a deer?"

Eric scoffed, rolling his shoulders as if shaking off the weight of the moment. "I'd have better luck than starving out here."

Rose let out a quiet snort. "Right. Because if there's one thing we can count on, it's your survival instincts." Eric shot her a glare, but it held no real heat. The weight of exhaustion had dulled the edges of their bickering, leaving only the hollow ache of uncertainty in its place.

As the night settled over the forest, the air turned crisp, carrying the scent of damp earth and lingering smoke from their dwindling fire. Shadows stretched between the towering trees, their jagged edges swaying with the shifting light. The four huddled near the fire, their bodies heavy with exhaustion, silence settling in where words no longer had a purpose. Katherine curled into herself, tugging her sequined shawl closer, though it did little to block out the cold. She was exhausted, her limbs heavy, but the freezing air clung to her skin like a second layer, making sleep impossible.

Adam lay on his back, staring at the canopy above, his blazer pulled tight over his chest. Sleep tugged at him, but his mind refused to quiet, the weight of the unknown pressing deep into his bones. The cold nipped at his exposed skin, a cruel reminder of how unprepared they were. Slowly, his body surrendered, exhaustion dragging him under. Beside him, Rose had already drifted into a restless sleep, though her arms remained locked around herself in a feeble attempt to hold onto warmth. Her dress was too thin, the silky fabric now a cruel joke against the brutal reality of their situation.

Eric sat on a fallen log, fingers flexing against his slacks. The fire had kept them from freezing outright, but the embers were dwindling, and the warmth was fading fast. Even with the blazer, the cold clung to him, his usual confidence stripped down to something quieter. Somewhere in the distance, an owl hooted, a low, mournful sound swallowed by the vastness of the unknown. Eric exhaled, rubbing a hand over his face before grabbing the makeshift bucket they had salvaged earlier. With a quiet grunt, he stood and made his way to the fire, tilting the bucket just enough to let water slosh against the embers. The flames hissed in protest before fizzling out, plunging their surroundings into a thick, ink-black darkness.

Then—*a snap*.

Eric's head jerked up. His breath hitched as he scanned the treeline, the hairs on the back of his neck rising. Something had caught his attention. A flicker of movement… barely there, but enough to make him go still. Whatever it was, it had rattled him. The forest swallowed sound, the crackling fire now a ghost of memory in the vast, suffocating quiet. No wind. No distant night creatures stirring in the underbrush. Only silence, unnatural, absolute. But something was there.

Beyond the reach of what little moonlight pierced the canopy, the shadows thickened, shifting, bending in ways they shouldn't. Between the tangled roots and gnarled branches, something crouched. Watching. Its presence coiled in the air, unseen but suffocating, pressing against the edges of the night. The darkness stretched, heavy and endless, as if it, too, was waiting. It pressed against the treeline like a held breath, thick and unmoving. Shadows clung to the branches, shifting ever so slightly, as if something moved just beneath them. Whatever was out there, it wasn't just hiding. It was watching. Then, a step. Another. A loose branch, brittle with age, cracked beneath their foot, then *snap*.

Eric's eyes narrowed toward the sound. His shoulders stiffened, posture tight, as he gripped the bucket with both hands, knuckles white against the metal. Not as a weapon, but as if the weight of it anchored him. He stood still, head tilted, listening. Waiting. But there was no one. No movement. No breath. Just the waiting hush of the trees. The silence stretched too long. Too still.

After a moment, Eric let out a slow breath and shook his head. Whatever he thought he'd heard… it was gone. His movements slowed, weariness creeping into his limbs as he turned back to the fire pit. He set the bucket down and ran a hand through his hair, muttering something under his breath, too low to catch, but sharp enough to carry frustration. Unseen, the flicker of shadow melted into the dark, slipping deeper into the trees. They had to be careful, had to stay hidden. The four of them weren't ready to see yet.

Not like this. But the shadow had seen them. Had felt their presence like a whisper in the dark, so close, yet still worlds apart. A few minutes later, they found a hollowed-out tree, the opening just large enough to slip inside. It wasn't much, cold, cramped, but it would do for now. They curled into themself, pulling their cloak tighter around their body, and let exhaustion take under. The forest held its breath. And the night carried on, unbothered by the ghosts that wandered beneath its watchful sky.

Chapter VIII:

Whispers of the Elements

The first stirrings of morning crept over the horizon, casting long, golden shafts of light through the towering trees. What had once been an eerie, frost-laced woodland had transformed overnight. The snow had vanished without a trace, replaced by dense greenery and thick underbrush, as if the forest itself had exhaled and become something new. Moisture clung to every surface, turning bark slick and moss luminous beneath the dawn. The scent of damp earth was rich and full-bodied, tinged with something older… something ancient. It wrapped around them like a veil… grounding but not comforting. The world felt different now. The very air buzzed with a quiet hum, charged with something unseen.

Above, the canopy stretched high and tangled, filtering light into kaleidoscopic rays that danced across the forest floor. Leaves rustled in a breeze that hadn't been there moments ago. A breeze that spoke, soft and knowing, like the forest had been waiting.

Adam stirred, eyes blinking against the filtered morning light. As he shifted upright, his gaze landed on Katherine just a few feet away. Katherine's eyes fluttered open. Something was different. She pushed herself up with a sharp inhale, the ground beneath her no longer cold and barren but lush with greenery. Vines curling around roots, delicate wildflowers bursting in vibrant clusters, stretching toward the early light. The entire area had transformed overnight, as if nature itself had awakened. Her heartbeat quickened. This wasn't normal.

"Katherine?" Rose stirred beside her, blinking against the light. Her voice was still thick with sleep, but the tension in her tone was undeniable.

Adam watched her stand abruptly, her eyes darting across the transformed landscape. "Where did all these come from?" she murmured, almost to herself. There was a sharpness to her posture, a flicker of awe, and maybe unease in her voice. Then, louder "You guys!"

Eric jolted awake at her voice, his body sluggish from exhaustion as he pushed himself upright. Adam blinked rapidly, already seated, the remnants of a dream still fading into the recesses of his mind. But the moment his vision cleared, his breath grasped. The barren forest floor they had collapsed onto the night before was unrecognizable the lush greenery stretched around them, vines curling along the tree trunks, and wildflowers blooming in clusters where there had once been only dirt and decay. Eric exhaled sharply beside him, running a hand through his disheveled hair, his expression shifting from groggy confusion to wary disbelief.

Towering trees surrounded them, their trunks twisted with thick vines that had not been there before. Vibrant petals, delicate and otherworldly, unfurled lazily beneath the rising sun. The ground was soft beneath their hands, damp with morning dew but alive, buzzing with an energy none of them could explain. The forest had changed. "Whoa," Adam breathed, his gaze sweeping over the transformed landscape.

Katherine turned to him, her brows furrowed in thought. "This wasn't here last night… it's like something made it grow.

Before anyone could respond, Adam saw Rose jolt, her breath hitched, sharp and ragged, like someone had poured molten steel down her throat. Her body tensed as if something inside her snapped. Heat shimmered off her skin in waves, visible even from where he stood. She looked sick… no, possessed. Something was twisting through her, writhing and clawing to break free.

"Guys…" Her voice cracked. Adam's stomach dropped. He watched her stumble back, legs buckling beneath her as she collapsed against a tree stump. Her fingers dug into the bark, nails dragging down like she didn't even realize it. Her whole body shook. Then, her pulse roared. A strange light pulsed beneath her skin. And in the next second, the fire erupted. A scream ripped from Rose's throat, raw and deafening, just before the flames burst from her body. Adam flinched, instinctively shielding his eyes as a blinding inferno engulfed her, swallowing her whole in light and fire. The force of the eruption hit like a blast wave. Trees bent. Leaves curled and turned to cinders mid-air. The very ground cracked beneath the heat, grass wilting into ash.

Adam staggered back, his heart slamming against his ribs. The fire whipped around her like it was alive, snaking up her limbs, coiling along her spine, writhing into the sky like it had been trapped inside her for years and had finally broken loose. Through the blaze, he could barely make out her form, just a silhouette burning bright in the chaos. "Rose!" he shouted, the sound ripped from his throat. She didn't respond. Maybe she didn't even hear him. She was just burning.

He stared as Rose's body lifted off the ground, suspended by the fire itself. The flames curled through her like threads of power, crackling along her limbs, wrapping her in heat that didn't consume, but carried. There was no scream now. Just a trembling breath, her chest rising and falling like she was at war with her own body. "I…" she gasped, her hands clawing at her chest, fingers trembling. "I can't stop it." Even the fire didn't want to stop.

Eric threw an arm up against the heat. "Somebody do something!"

Adam's heart thundered. *Do what exactly?* Instinct drove him forward, even as everything in his brain screamed to stay back. The same pull he'd felt at the portal, the same whisper in the wind. It was here again, louder than ever. He reached out, his hand trembling, fingers stretching toward her. The moment his skin brushed the edge of the heat, the wind answered. A violent gust slammed into him, knocking him backwards. He stumbled; breath ripped from his lungs.

Katherine flinched beside him, her breaths coming sharp and uneven. Adam caught the flicker in her eyes as they darted between him and Rose. "She's… she's not burning," Katherine said.

Not a question. A realization. And a terrifying one. Adam's heart pounded. The flames around Rose shifted. Not wildly, but with intention. They moved like they knew her. Like they were listening to her heartbeat.

Eric stepped forward, fists clenched tight. "Rose, you need to control it!" His voice was steady, but Adam heard it. The fear, threaded beneath the urgency.

Rose tried. Adam could see it. But the fire pulsed again, feeding off her panic, exploding outward, knocking them all back. Eric cursed as he hit the ground. But when he pushed himself up, his hands squelched against the dirt, not with sweat, but with something else. Water. He froze. His palms were wet. More than wet. His fingers trembled as he lifted his hands, watching in disbelief as droplets dripped along his skin, forming out of nowhere, rolling down his wrists like condensation on glass. "What the hell…" he breathed.

Adam barely registered Eric's shock. He could hear something else… whispers. The wind was speaking again. But this time, it wasn't just a murmur. It was calling his name. His head snapped to the side as the breeze shifted, curling around him like a phantom touch. Leaves lifted from the ground, spiraling toward him, drawn by something unseen. The murmur deepened. Distant voices moved with the wind, threading through the air like ghostly breath. A sudden chill swept over his skin, brushing through him.

He turned sharply, breath catching as the air stirred again, this time with form. Wind spun tighter before him, weaving itself into the shape of a hand. It reached for him, its unseen fingers curling, brushing his cheek in a fleeting caress. The touch was neither warm nor cold, but powerful. Charged with something ancient, then, it vanished. Out of nowhere the wind folded inward and slammed into Adam's chest, knocking him backwards. His breath hitched as he stumbled into the ground. His pulse surged. An invisible force snapped into place like something lost had returned. The air thrummed around him, alive with energy. It wasn't just the wind. It was a presence. A presence that had chosen him. For a second, Adam knew it.

He turned his head just in time to see Eric crouch beside Rose, his expression tight with concern. Eric reached for her hand, his voice low but urgent. "We gotta get you out of here." Rose shook her head, trying to steady her breath. But Adam could see it, she was slipping through Eric's grip. More than droplets dripped along his skin, a hose of water puddled around them, funneling from his hands. Then Adam caught it something still burned inside her. A sickly heat shimmered in the air around her, thick and unrelenting. She gasped, her shoulders twitching like she was holding something back. "I… I'm burning up," she whispered.

Eric didn't hesitate. "Come on, we can't stay here." He reached for her again, pulling her upright. Tighter this time. Their hands met and the air cracked. A sudden ripple of heat pulsed from her chest. Not like before. This was smaller. Tighter. But no less wild. Adam felt it before he saw it. A pressure shift. A warning.

Then—

Rose let out a strangled gasp. Her back arched as golden light flickered beneath her skin. The fire surged again, not as a wave, but a strike. A violent whip of flame burst from her arm, snapping through the clearing like a lightning lash. Eric stumbled back, shielding his face. The fire didn't consume her this time, but it fought to. It lashed outward in jagged bursts, desperate, chaotic, as if testing her grip. Rose clenched her fists, teeth bared, eyes fiery red. "No," she hissed. "Not again…" And then, as suddenly as it came, the fire recoiled. Collapsing inward. A final spark hissed into the air and vanished. She dropped to her knees, panting hard, eyes wide, smoke curling from her fingertips. The blaze was gone. But Adam could still feel it. Its power hummed beneath her flesh, coiled like a waiting beast. Silence stretched between them thick and electric. alive.

The clearing felt suspended, like the world itself was holding its breath. Smoke curled upward in lazy spirals, dancing in the dim light. No one moved. No one spoke. The air was too hot, too still. The ground beneath them was part scorched, or muddy. The scent of ash and slush clinging to the back of Adam's throat. He looked at Rose, knees planted, shoulders rising and falling with each ragged breath and for a moment, she didn't seem like Rose at all. She looked like something reborn. Then a branch cracked in the distance. Adam's eyes snapped up. He finally spoke, his voice quiet, but firm. "Guys… I don't think we're alone."

Rose stiffened. Eric's shoulders squared, his hand drifting toward his side. From behind, a shadow emerged from the hollow at the base of the scorched tree, their movements slow. Measured. Unseen. Like someone who'd just been inches from being roasted alive.

Muscles tensed. Breaths hitched. For a moment, the weight of fatigue was swept away, replaced by something raw. The sharp prickle of danger settling into their bones. The morning light bled through the trees, casting shifting shadows across their faces. Whatever Adam had felt it was enough. Enough to cut through the fog and set every nerve on edge. He didn't move at first. His pulse still raced, and the whisper of the wind hadn't left him, it lingered in the back of his mind like an unfinished sentence. Katherine's voice cut through the haze. "Who else would be out here?"

Eric scoffed softly. "You say that like we even know where here is." His fingers flexed at his sides, that same nervous tick he always had. He glanced around the trees, shoulders tense, like he expected something, or someone, to come charging out at any second. "What exactly did you hear?"

Maybe I am hearing things, Adam thought. His jaw tightened. How the hell was he supposed to explain the snap, or the wind without sounding crazy? He wasn't sure what he heard. He swallowed, heart hammering. "The wind," he said. "It… spoke." Silence dropped like a weight.

Eric blinked. "The what?"

Adam exhaled, jaw clenching. Saying it out loud made it sound even worse. But he had felt it. He hadn't imagined that voice, that presence winding around him like it knew him. "It wasn't just wind," he said. "It was voices. Like… someone was trying to say something to me."

Eric stared for a beat, then dragged a hand down his face. "Great. First, mystery garden. Then Rose goes full inferno. And now you're hearing voices in the wind."

Katherine didn't respond right away. Her gaze lingered on Adam, eyes narrowing just slightly as they flicked to his hand, then back to his face. She didn't say anything, didn't laugh or roll her eyes. Just stared like she was working something out in silence. "What did it say?" she asked quietly.

Adam hesitated. "I don't know. But it felt like a warning." A breeze stirred the leaves above, gentle but deliberate. Adam's gaze lifted. He couldn't shake the feeling that something unseen was still listening.

Eric let out a rough breath and raked his damp fingers through his hair. "So, what now? You think we have powers or something?"

Adam didn't answer. He looked down at his hand, the one the wind had touched. He flexed his fingers. Something stirred beneath his skin. Something new. Something lightweight. "At this point, are you really surprised?" he said quietly. He wasn't even sure who he was talking to.

Rose shifted beside Eric, her breath still ragged. She looked at her hands, watched how heat shimmered across her skin. "Or maybe… this was always meant to happen."

Adam turned toward the distant mountains, where a faint curl of smoke rose against the sky. His gaze sharpened.

Katherine stepped forward beside him. "We have to get to where that smoke is." No one argued. Because deep down, they all felt it. Something had changed. And this… was only the beginning.

A dense, towering forest stretched for miles, its trees gnarled and ancient, their thick roots clawing through the earth like skeletal fingers. Vines hung low like nooses, draped in eerie silence. Mist curled through the underbrush, veiling the path ahead. The deeper they moved, the more the air felt wrong. It was too still, too heavy, like the forest itself was watching. Their steps slowed. The terrain grew uneven, each root threatening to trip them, each shadow stretching too far. A distant snap echoed somewhere to their right. No one spoke of it.

Adam inhaled sharply as the wind brushed his skin. But this wasn't random it moved with strange intent, circling his back, nudging him forward like a breath with purpose. He paused, tilting his head, listening. There it was again, a whisper, or maybe just the memory of one. Not a voice, exactly… but it felt like something unseen was trying to speak. The gust passed through him again, and for a fleeting second, it felt familiar.

Guiding. Watching. He clenched his fists and scanned the trees. Nothing. Only the eerie, suffocating stillness.

Up ahead, Rose's arms wrapped tightly around herself. Adam watched her fingers twitch at her sides, the movement slight but not missed. She looked down, and he caught the moment her gaze locked onto her own hands. Something flickered there, a shimmer of embers curling along her fingertips before vanishing. She shook her hands out, quick and subtle, as if trying to dismiss it. Adam's chest tightened. He remembered the fire, how it had erupted from her, how it had nearly swallowed everything.

Eric rubbed his hands over his face with a frustrated groan. "Are we even going the right way?" he muttered, not loud but not exactly under his breath either. He scanned the trees like a man searching for answers in a maze with no exit.

Adam turned his head slightly, catching the way Eric slowed when he noticed Rose's reaction, how her shoulders tensed, how she looked down again at her hands like they weren't her own. Eric's tone softened. "Are you okay?"

Rose gave a small nod, her voice barely audible. "Yeah… just cold."

Adam didn't believe her. But he said nothing. Katherine halted up ahead. Adam's gaze followed her just as the dirt beneath her boots rippled outward, thin, like a breath beneath the surface. She gasped and stumbled back.

"What was that?" Katherine muttered.

Adam watches, eyes narrowing.

"You felt that too?"

Katherine hesitates, then slowly nods.

"I think… I think I did that."

A beat passes. No one moves. Then, a whisper rustles through the trees. Not the wind. Something else. A shadow flickers between the trunks. Too fast to track. Then, a low, deep, and unnatural sound vibrates through the still air. It's not the wind. Not an animal. It almost sounds like… breathing. Beside Adam, Rose stiffens. Her arms fold tightly across her chest, and Adam catches the edge in her voice when she whispers, "Do you feel that? Like… like someone's watching us?" *Okay. She felt it too. At least I am not the only one going crazy,* he thought. And from the look Eric shot her, so had he. The presence was real. Lurking, unseen, but there.

The deeper they walk, the more the forest contorts into something unnatural. The trees, once majestic, now lean at warped angles, their bark warped and split like skin stretched too thin. The ground shifts beneath their feet, forcing every step into a silent test of balance. A damp, heavy stillness chokes the air, broken only by the low creak of limbs swaying without wind. And beneath that… something else. A hum, faint and droning, rides the silence like a predator biding its time. The deeper they go, the more the air thickens, not just with fog, but with a foul, metallic tang, like blood in water. The forest no longer feels like a place. It feels like a presence waiting to be seen.

Then, up ahead, the darkness shifts to what once looked like thick black smoke begins to dissolve, unraveling like an illusion. A massive black stone chamber emerges, towering and ominous. The instant Adam lays eyes on it, the smoke vanishes completely, like a mirage breaking. Rose suddenly grabs his arm, yanking him back. "STOP!" Her voice cuts through the silence abruptly. They all freeze. Adam turns toward her, heart thudding. Her grip is iron-tight. Her chest rises and falls too fast, her wide eyes fixed on the chamber. *She looks like she's seen a ghost.*

"We've been walking this whole time," she says. "That wasn't there before."

Eric squints at the structure. "What are you talking about? It's right there."

Adam says nothing, but the wind stirs again, stronger this time. It presses against his shoulders like a warning. He narrows his eyes. The air around the chamber feels wicked. Thick and dreadful. Its dark stone is veiled in time, etched with forgotten symbols. They've arrived. But something dead is waiting.

Chapter IX:
The Sacrifice

The black smoke that had once billowed from the chamber's roof began to thin, unraveling like mist at dawn. It didn't drift… it simply vanished. Gone in an instant. The air grew unnaturally still. Not just quiet. Adam's breath hitched, and for a second, he wasn't sure if the others noticed. No wind. No sound. Just the soft crunch of their boots and even that felt like too much noise. He blinked up at the structure now clearly visible ahead. The chamber loomed tall, monolithic, and sinful. Its black stone surface was slick, as if it had just rained, but the air was bone dry. Symbols etched and faded, wrapped around its form like ancient scars. No birds. No insects. Not even the hum of energy from within. It sat in the forest like it didn't belong there. Like it had been waiting. Adam swallowed. *We've been walking for hours. That thing wasn't there before.* He clenched his jaw. *Right? I haven't had real food. I'm starting not to believe my own thoughts.* His eyes narrowed. Maybe Rose wasn't exaggerating this time. She could be dramatic as hell, but she wasn't stupid. *Still… how does an entire building just appear out of nowhere?* Something about it rubbed him the wrong way. Not just the sudden appearance, but how his body felt near it. Tense. Like standing too close to a speaker playing a song you couldn't hear. He took a slow step forward.

"Wait…" Katherine's voice cut through the silence like a pin drop in a tomb.

Adam turned. She was staring at the chamber, brow furrowed, lips parted slightly. "That smoke…" she pointed. "It's gone. Completely."

Adam followed her gaze. *She was right.* The haze that had once cloaked the structure like a veil had vanished, as if it had never existed. But they'd all seen it. Hadn't they? His eyes scanned the space between the trees, hoping for answers. Nothing. No wind. No movement. Not even the sound of birdsong. "We're being played," he muttered.

Rose took a hesitant step forward, her gaze locking onto the massive stone doors. Symbols. Faint, intricate carvings stood out against the aged surface, their meaning just out of reach. She brushed her fingers over them, wiping away centuries of dust. "Ancient symbols. What could they mean?" she whispered.

Something tugged at Adam's memory. Not his, exactly, but Rose's reaction lit a spark, like she was remembering something he didn't yet understand. She squinted at the carvings, tracing the engravings with her fingers. Then it clicked for her. "These… these symbols represent the four elements." She turned to them, more certain now. "Earth, Water, Air, and Fire." The words sounded heavier than they should have… like they weren't just words, but a warning. Or a prophecy. She glanced toward the looming chamber. "These symbols… they're telling us something. We need to get inside."

Adam wasn't convinced. His arms tensed at the idea of walking through yet another ancient door. The last time he did that, they ended up here. Changed. Lost in this forbidden world, branded by something they didn't understand. The memory crawled up his spine like ice. Another portal. Another unknown. He folded his arms. "How do you know these elements are for us?"

Rose inhaled, and the frustration in her eyes said *Seriously?* "Just earlier, I was burning up, boiling hot. Adam, you heard voices in the wind. Katherine made an entire garden bloom. And Eric… you produced water from your hands. Tell me that's normal. Tell me this is all some giant coincidence." She scanned their faces, arms folded now, daring any of them to offer a better theory. "Because if you can explain it, I'd love to hear it."

Adam hesitated… then smirked. "Well… we were just at a party, and we did take a lot of shots earlier. And Eric…" he tilted his head with a look, teasing, "you were kind of doing that… uh… cokey-coke thing back there."

Eric exhaled, deadpan. "If we do this… there's no going back."

Adam's smirk faded. He looked up at the black stone doors again. They stood like gravestones. "Do we even have a choice?"

Katherine stepped forward, calm and steady. "Let's see if this works."

The four of them approached the chamber doors. Above each, the engraved elemental symbol glowed faintly, like it had been waiting for them all along. Below the symbols: circular openings. Just large enough for a hand.

Eric stood before the Water symbol. Rose claimed Fire. Katherine moved to Earth. And well Adam found himself in front of Air. A thick, breathless silence fell between them. The stone underfoot grew colder. Adam's hand hovered. *Is this the moment everything changes? Or are we part of a sick game?* One by one… They plunged their hands inside.

A sudden, searing hiss ripped through the stillness. Then a sharp pain. Sudden. Inescapable. A metallic snap. A burning slice deep into their skin. Too fast to stop it. Too late to pull away. Blood smudged the stone, trickling into the ancient carvings like an offering. They all yanked their hands back violently, gasping.

"Ah!" Rose's cry rang out first.

Adam flinched as a sharp sting exploded through his own palm. He yanked his hand back, hissing through clenched teeth. "What the hell."

Across from him, Katherine gasped, staggering a step. Eric cursed under his breath, flexing his fingers. Adam's eyes darted to the others, each of them recoiling, cradling their hands. Blood shimmered in the dim light, pooling in their palms like some kind of sick ritual. The stone didn't just recognize them. It marked them.

A low, mechanical groan rumbled from deep within the chamber, the sound ancient, grinding, like something long-forgotten stirring awake. The walls shuddered violently, dust and loose debris trickling from above as if the entire structure had been waiting for this moment.

The carved symbols pulsed with an eerie glow, their faint light flickering, absorbing, drinking in the fresh sacrifice. The very air felt thicker, charged with something unseen, something watching. Something had been awakened. Something shifted behind the doors. A deep clunking noise echoed, gears grinding into motion. The air vibrated, the doors swung open. Darkness. A long, pitch-black corridor stretched before them, swallowing their presence in its void-like depths. The faint, wavering glow of torches lined the walls, their firelight casting restless shadows that danced like ghosts against the stone. Along the surface, strange carvings of ancient warriors loomed, figures frozen in time, their once-powerful forms now eroded and faceless, stripped of identity by centuries of decay.

The deeper they looked, the more unsettling the images became, as if watching, whispering secrets lost to the ages. Adam's skin prickled. Not from cold, but from something deeper, some primal warning crawling up his spine. His breath caught as he stepped forward, eyes scanning the faceless figures on the wall. The others followed. Behind them, the stone doors groaned and slammed shut with a thunderous boom. Dust shook loose from the ceiling. They turned, startled. But it was too late. The chamber had sealed. Adam's eyes met Katherine's, and for a flicker of a moment, he saw his sister enveloped in fear. *Another door. Another portal. The last time we walked through a portal, we ended up here.* Every detail felt intentional. Like they weren't just entering a ruin… but a tomb. A suffocating stillness hung in the air, thick with the weight of something forgotten… or something lurking.

Eric ran his fingers along the engravings, his voice low. "What is this place?"

Katherine frowned.

"I can't see a damn thing."

Adam stepped deeper into the chamber, boots crunching against the dust-caked stone. The air was heavy, stale with age and something else, something harsh. Beneath the scent of ancient rock lingered a faint metallic tang, cold and biting, like rusted iron… or dried blood. It struck the back of his throat like a warning. His chest tightened as he scanned the room, a part of him instinctively bracing… though for what, he didn't know.

From somewhere deep in the chamber, a single droplet of water echoed as it fell. A sharp, deliberate, like the tick of a countdown. The torches along the curved walls flickered erratically, casting long, warping shadows that danced across the carved stone. Etchings shimmered beneath the flame; runes etched in a language he didn't recognize. Yet felt wrong to look at for too long. Shadows crawled across the ceiling like they had lives of their own, distorting into shapes his mind refused to name. Cold air whispered through unseen cracks, carrying with it a low hum, too low to be natural. Not wind. Not breath. Something else. Something watching.

He caught sight of Rose ahead of him, her eyes narrowed, expression unreadable. She moved slowly, gaze locked on a cluster of low, rigid slabs, four of them, positioned in a wide arc at the heart of the chamber, each one angled toward a dark circular drain embedded in the floor. Adam frowned. The arrangement felt wrong. Too precise. Too ritualistic.

His gaze drifted across the chamber. Along the right-hand wall, a row of alcoves was carved into the stone, shallow hollows barely lit by the flickering torchlight between them. Some held rusted shackles. Others bore stains too dark to name. A few were empty… but not clean. Dust disturbed, as if something had once lain there. As if others had come before them and failed. Smudges streaked across the stone. *Oh my god,* he thought.. His unease deepened as the torchlight behind him flickered, casting shadows that seemed to shuffle across the walls, silent witnesses that vanished when he turned.

Rose stepped closer, her fingers brushing along the timeworn surface of one slab. Adam watched her pause, stiffen. She traced the grooves embedded in the stone, the dark stains barely visible beneath the dust. Whatever she saw, it rattled her. She didn't flinch outwardly, but he could see it in her posture, the way her breath gathered, and her shoulders drew in ever so slightly. She turned to them slowly, and when she finally spoke, her voice came out low and strange, like it wasn't meant to be heard. "It's a sacrificial chamber."

The words hit harder than if she'd screamed them. A single droplet of water fell from the ceiling and struck the floor. The sound echoed. No one moved. Adam's stomach knotted. Her tone wasn't dramatic, wasn't performative. It was reverent. Like speaking it aloud gave it power. *Rose isn't being dramatic this time. Something bad is in here with us. We have to get out now.* The atmosphere seemed to darken, the chamber's secrets pressing in around them, waiting to be acknowledged. Shadows clung to the walls, refusing to move, as if watching. The air thickened, almost like suffocating, but more deliberate, carrying the weight of something old… something waiting to be awakened. It hadn't felt like they had stepped into a room. It felt like they had been swallowed.

The moment the words left her lips, a guttural growl ruptured from the deepest shadow, low, wet, and crawling with rot. It sounded like a corpse trying to speak, vocal cords long decayed but still desperate to be heard. The stone groaned in response, as if the walls themselves remembered pain. And in that moment, the chamber didn't just feel haunted, it felt hungry. The torches flickered violently.

Katherine froze. "What was that?"

Adam's grip tightened around the torch.

Say something. Anything.

"I don't know."

A massive, hulking shadow shifted at the far end of the chamber, its outline barely distinguishable from the darkness itself. For a breathless moment, it seemed to stretch and coil, like a beast waking from centuries of slumber. The air thickened, and an instinctive dread settled over them, as if they had just been noticed. A voice followed. A low and guttural, laced with a growl that vibrated in their bones. Ancient, but twisted, like something once human, now warped into a dark mockery of speech. The words slithered through the chamber, heavy and venomous, carrying a malevolent promise that chilled the air around them. "Orcas ago, I took the M'ra Sphere. I thought I could command it… bend it to my will." Still submerged in darkness, the figure drifted slowly through the shadows, gliding from the far corner toward the center of the room, unseen but felt.

Its presence twisting through the air like smoke. Chains scraped faintly along the stone, echoing like a death knell as the shadow shifted. "I tried to possess it myself."

None of them could truly see it. Only feel the weight of something wrong. The voice grew heavier, thick with something inhuman.

"In doing so, I deceived it."

Rose took a slow step back.

Something about this… screamed death.

"It whispers promises… until you are no longer yourself. You think you can control it. But the Serpent's Call twists around your soul and once it has you… it never lets go." He exhaled, a rasping, bitter breath. "It cursed me. Bound me to the underworld. All for thinking I was worthy." The figure moved closer. Now, in the dim light, the flames trembled, dimming, as though suffocated by something unseen. A towering figure began to materialize from the shadows, not walking, but gliding. His form flickering between substance and smoke. A heavy, tattered cloak billowed around him without wind, frayed edges dissolving into wisps of shadow. Beneath the hood, there was nothing human, just a trace of shape, like smoke behind a veil. The air turned cold, thick with the scent of sulfur and decay, as though the underworld itself exhaled through him.

Haiti.

And then he spoke, a voice fractured and layered, echoing with the whispers of countless souls bound to his curse. "What you seek is not what you want. What you desire is unattainable. I can promise you… I'll make it better."

Eric stiffened.

"What are you trying to say?"

Haiti stepped forward, his presence suffocating, they all saw… an abomination. A hollowed-out reaper, a figure scraped clean of anything human. They froze in the weight of fear. Terror struck them. "To give you wonders of your lifetime." His voice darkened. "It embraces a special power among those who are destined. To take this offer, you must lose what your heart desires... A heart for a heart."

Adam's blood ran cold, frightened, he's never seen something so grim. The phrase didn't stick, it felt ancient. Like they'd just been bound to something they didn't understand. His jaw tightened. "And what if we don't want to take this offer?"

Haiti's lips curled into a slow, wicked grin. "It's not a choice."

A ghastly specter of what once was: rotted flesh stretched over glimpses of jagged bone, constantly shifting and reforming, as though his body could no longer decide what it wanted to be. Hollow sockets burned with a faint, sickly glow, pulsating like dying embers trapped in eternal darkness. From the ends of his long, skeletal fingers, black ichor dripped and evaporated into nothing. The last remnants of a body he could never reclaim. His presence radiated malice. Katherine stumbled back behind Adam in fear. He instinctively stepped in front of her, shielding her from Haiti's horrifying presence. "What you sow is what you will reap," Haiti murmured.

It stepped forward to the drainage groove, or rather, glided, his form wraith-like, barely seeming to touch the ground. The tattered hem of his cloak drifted behind him like mist clinging to bone. Fingers like ivory talons emerged from the folds of fabric, clutching a handful of fine white powder. The four exchanged glances: fear mirrored in every eye. Adam's grip tightened around the torch, his breath shallow.

"What is it doing?" Katherine whispered.

Haiti's hollow sockets gleamed. He knew they were watching. In one smooth, deliberate motion, he scattered it across the stone floor. The air trembled, particles swirling into unnatural spirals, suspended midair as if time itself paused.

Adam said nothing. He didn't move. None of them did. They were too scared to run. Too afraid to breathe. The first time they've seen anything like this. Something in the room had shifted… and whatever it was, it wanted blood. Black goo erupted from the dust.

The inky substance slithered across the stone like a living shadow, twisting and contorting until it unfolded into a hovering form; a black spirit, its shape both formless and terrifyingly defined. It loomed above them, its hollow gaze like voids that pierced straight through flesh and bone. Wisps of darkness trailed from its edges, curling and dissipating with a faint hiss, as if whispering secrets no living soul was meant to hear. The atmosphere grew suffocating, pressing against their chests, and for a moment, even the flicker of Rose's fire dimmed.

It lunged. A blur of darkness surged downward, like a coiled serpent striking from above. The chamber trembled as the force descended, suffocating and swift. But before it could reach them—

"You will not touch them!"

Marie's voice cracked through the chamber like a bolt of thunder as she leapt into the fray, cloak billowing behind her. She brought her staff down with crushing force, the impact reverberating through the stone floor. A shockwave exploded outward, the black entity shrieking as it split apart mid-air, recoiling into the shadows as if scorched by divine fire.

Haiti roared, his shape flickering and distorting like torn shadow fighting against flame. His fury twisted the very air around him. With a guttural snarl, he thrust out a hand, tendrils of black magic unfurling like smoke, laced with whispers and venom, racing toward Marie in a violent surge. But she stood firm, her staff already in motion. The runes etched along its length pulsed with ancient light as she twirled it once, catching the curse midair and absorbing its energy until it dissipated harmlessly into the stone around her. She looked older now, no longer the young woman who had stepped through the palace halls all those orcas ago. The lines of time touched her gently, but unmistakably. Somewhere in her late thirties, maybe even forty. A woman shaped by years the others had not lived. Her features were refined, her presence commanding. Not a girl at all. A woman. A guardian. And something else entirely. "GO! IT'S YOUR ONLY CHANCE!" she ordered.

The four didn't hesitate. They bolted toward the back of the chamber, boots skidding against the cold stone. Heartbeats thundered in their ears as they dove behind towering walls of carved rock, seeking whatever cover they could find. From their hiding place, they could only watch as Haiti and Marie collided with the fury of ancient forces unleashed. Marie thrust her hands forward, unleashing a massive wave of blue flames that roared across the chamber. Haiti whipped his cloak upward in a desperate attempt to shield himself, but the flames broke through, slamming him into the far wall with bone-cracking force. The stone fractured on impact, deep splinters spiderwebbing outward as the entire chamber shuddered violently. Dust and debris rained down, the echoes of power lingering in the air.

From behind the stone wall, Adam saw Katherine edge out slowly, her gaze locked on Marie. There was something silent exchanged between them, a flicker of recognition maybe, or something heavier. Then Marie nodded. It was subtle, but Katherine straightened, like the nod had told her exactly what she needed to hear.

Without hesitation, Marie strode forward, gripping her staff tightly. At the bottom of its sleek design, a hidden mechanism shifted. A blade flared out, sharp and gleaming in the dim torchlight. Each step she took echoed through the chamber. As she approached, she saw it, Haiti was still breathing. Marie didn't hesitate. She plunged the blade straight into his chest.

Haiti's eyes snapped open wide, shocked, and almost human in that final moment. His form convulsed violently, the decayed shroud of his existence trembling as the curse began to unravel. The flickering shadows and rotted wisps of flesh peeled away in slow, twisting layers. For a fleeting instant, his shape softened into that of a frail, hunched old monk, skin paper-thin, eyes sunken with remorse. But even that form could not hold.

His body dissolved into translucent wisps of light, lifting like ashes on a dying breeze. What remained was a spirit, pale, weightless, and free. Its hollow gaze met Marie's, not with fury or regret… but with acceptance. For the first time in centuries. The spirit died with a secret and drifted upward, fading into the air like scattered embers. Yet the chamber did not fall silent. The air still pulsed with something lingering… as if he was not truly gone. Some curses, she knew, never left. They simply waited. Marie exhaled slowly, the tension in her shoulders finally releasing. She yanked the staff back, but there was no blood. Only a faint residue of shadow clinging to the tip, like smoke refusing to die. Only then did she speak. "It's all right to come out now." Her voice was soft but steady. A promise that the danger had passed. She turned, her gaze finding them: Adam, Rose, Katherine, and Eric, frozen behind the stone, eyes wide, breath caught, like children caught in a nightmare. Silence hung thick in the chamber.

And then, Eric broke the silence.

"Who the fuck are you?"

Chapter X:
The Guardian in the Shadows

The forest lay still, cloaked in shadows beneath a sky painted with endless stars. The crackle of firewood snapped through the quiet night as Marie knelt beside the unlit pit. From her satchel, she drew a small pouch, loosening the drawstring with care. A fine, silvery powder shimmered in the moonlight as she sprinkled it over the dry wood. She whispered something ancient, words none of them could understand, and waved her hand slowly over the pile. The fire roared to life, its flames swirling with unnatural colors: blues, golds, and deep purples flickering in hypnotic patterns. Marie looked up, her expression serene but commanding. "I am Princess Marie Celeborn."

Rose stared, her voice barely above a whisper. "How... how did you do that?"

Marie's gaze stayed on the dancing flames. "I studied magic with my mother," she said softly.

"She taught me to bend small things, to turn water into branches, earth into tools, light into warmth." She paused, the firelight flickering across her face. "My father taught me duty."

Katherine leaned forward, brow furrowed. "Then... what are you, really?"

Marie held her stare, unimpressed.

What kind of question is that? Of all the things she'd faced, curses, traitors, death itself. But it was this question that made her want to laugh. "I'm human," she said, voice cool as the firelight dancing in her eyes.

Adam shook his head. "Then how do you explain that blue flame back there?"

Marie's lips curved into a faint smile. "Magic. It's been in my family for generations. Woven into our blood long before any of us understood it."

Eric's voice broke through, tense.

"Where are we? What is this place?"

Marie lifted her palm over the fire. The flames shifted, swirling into shapes. First, a molten sphere of light, then slowly forming into two celestial bodies: one, a swirling blue and green planet, New Earth, and the other, its pale, cratered moon.

The four leaned in, breathless. The fire deepened, transforming into a vision that surrounded them. The crackle faded, replaced by a hum of cosmic silence. Above them, galaxies spun, stars pulsed with ancient light, and planets drifted through an endless sea. Slowly, a swirling globe began to form, a luminous world of blue and green, orbiting its pale moon, spiraling closer, until they felt as though they could reach out and touch New Earth itself. "New Earth," Marie began, her voice low and reverent. "A new age… a different time." She paused, letting the fire's glow dance across her features. "It's been told for generations, for every year spent on Earth, twelve orcas pass here. We exist as an alternate universe to yours, living parallel… yet separate."

Above them, the universe unfolded, galaxies turning in vast celestial rhythms, stars flickering like whispers of forgotten stories. One globe spiraled closer, vibrant and alive, wrapped in swirling clouds of blue and green, its pale moon faithfully circling beside it. New Earth. A world reborn. A different age. A story only just beginning.

The edges of the night dissolved, and the vision took hold. The vision pulled them in. They stood, or rather, felt themselves suspended high above vast emerald plains, crowned by a towering mountain that pierced the clouds. At its peak, a grand temple ascended from the stone, its ancient pillars weathered by centuries, yet still defiant and magnificent. Within its heart, four hooded figures gathered in a perfect circle, their hands raised skyward, elemental power humming around them: Air, Fire, Water, Earth.

In the beginning, Marie's voice continued, *New Earth was founded by the Four Elders. They wielded the purest elemental forces each tied to an element that shaped New Earth's breath: the sky, the flame, the river, and the root. For a time, this world thrived in perfect harmony.* The vision darkened. A shadow cracked across the skies. From a jagged crater, alien creatures burst forth: monstrous, winged beings brandishing cruel weapons. The Elders braced, their powers intertwining as they fought against the onslaught. *But outsiders came. Malakan invaders. They sought to claim what was never theirs.*

Images flashed:

— Soldiers torn apart in the mud.

— Beasts cried as they were struck down.

— Warhorses collapsing, their blood pooling beneath shattered hooves.

The vision slowed. The Elders stood together, forming a perfect circle atop the temple ruins. Their hands lifted, power spiraling between them, light gathering, brighter than the sun. *In desperation, the Elders unleashed their combined power. They wiped out the invaders, but at a great cost.*

A brilliant burst of pure energy erupted, sweeping across New Earth in a radiant wave, obliterating the invaders and leaving silence in its wake. The light faded, revealing a shattered temple, stone cracked, and rubble strewn across sacred ground. The Elders fell to their knees, breath ragged, their strength spent. Slowly, they helped one another rise, their faces worn with exhaustion. Below them, the fields stretched silent, littered with the lifeless bodies of the Malakan invaders. The price of their protection.

The vision shifted again. The light around them rippled, melting into golden hues of dawn. Broken lands slowly healed; fields once charred by war bloomed green and alive. Villages emerged from ash and rubble, small fires of hope burning once more beneath vast, open skies. Peace felt fragile… but for a time, it held.

Centuries passed. New Earth rebuilt itself, dividing into tribes, striving for balance.

The five watched as villagers rebuilt shattered homes, their hands rough and weathered from long days of labor. Children chased each other between freshly thatched huts, their laughter echoing beneath skies that once rained fire. Women gathered at the wells, sharing food and stories, hopeful smiles masking the weight of memories. But beneath the beauty, shadows lingered; whispers of past horrors that refused to fully fade.

In a quiet, candlelit chamber, one Elder lay weak and trembling, each breath thin and ragged; a whisper pulled from the edge of life itself. His skin, pale and fragile, trembled with every shallow rise of his chest. Yet in his gaze, there lingered the faint glimmer of purpose, refusing to be extinguished. His brothers knelt beside him, their hands gripping his as though they could hold him here by sheer will. Eyes glistened with unspoken grief, centuries of loyalty and brotherhood passing between them in silence. They whispered ancient prayers and final words, knowing their time and New Earth's peace was slipping away with each fading breath, sacred moments from centuries past.

The day they swore to protect this world. The storms they calmed together. The light they carried when shadows threatened to consume.

Their voices cracked under the weight of history and impending loss. His weakening hand squeezed theirs, frail, but steady as if to say: *I am still with you… for this last task.* Tears welled in their eyes, not for the farewell they knew would come soon, but for the responsibility they now carried: to ensure that his final gift to New Earth would not be in vain. Outside, the winds howled against the ancient stone walls, as though the world itself braced for what must come.

In their final years, they knew peace could not last. Corruption was inevitable. And they... were fading. The vision brightened, shifting to the temple's summit once more. The Four Elders stood together, their robes billowing in the rising wind. Their faces were solemn, yet resolute. *They knew the time had come.*

Their hands glided toward the heavens, power drawn not from stone or artifact, but from the depths of their very souls. Light poured from their palms. Not magic. Not element. Something deeper. Essence. It shimmered, soft and golden, tinged with the translucent glow of spirit. The

light converged above them, swirling into a
radiant mass. It twisted and folded in on itself,
condensing into a perfect sphere. It pulsed once…
then again… like the heartbeat of something
newly born. In the center of their circle, the
sphere hovered in a silent, powerful eternal way.
In what we know it as:

The M'ra Sphere.

Not forged by hand. Not summoned by
spell. Created from unity. Sealed in sacrifice. A
final gift to the world they swore to protect. A
steady, radiant heartbeat as if the very soul of New
Earth thrummed within its core, alive and
watching. It glowed not just with power, but with
hope, a fragile promise that light would always rise
from darkness. Yet beneath that brilliance lingered
a silent warning, looping, and waiting. The power
unchecked can twist, corrupt, and devour. The
sphere pulsed with all that was good… and all that
could be lost.

They created The M'ra Sphere. In unity, it brings
life. In greed, it brings ruin. The Sphere doesn't grant
power; it magnifies what's already in your soul. The land

always listens to The M'ra Sphere. In balance, it breathes. In chaos... your darkness crawls back out.

It was creation and sacrifice thru manifest, the culmination of lifetimes spent guarding balance. A beacon of hope, forged not without pain, but with purpose. It shimmered as a promise to future generations... and a silent reminder that all power comes at a price. In its light was legacy; in its shadow, the cost they would bear forever.

It was meant to bind this world together. To preserve balance. To keep evil at bay.

But even as the M'ra sphere pulsed with radiant energy, darkness began to seep in. The light dimmed, swirls of shadow coiling around the orb. White lightning flickered inside it, but its purity faltered. *And should that power fall into the wrong hands...* Marie's voice turned grim, *...New Earth will face its end. The M'ra sphere pulsed, not only with life but with something deeper, something ancient. It absorbed the very essence of its creators,* Marie's voice continued softly through the vision, *their sacred abilities passed into its core. Host Augmentation, the power to magnify the strengths or weaknesses of whoever dares to wield it. And the Serpent's Call... a whisper in the darkness, deceiving, seducing, twisting desire into ruin.*

Before their eyes, *The M'ra Sphere* dimmed. Its brilliant white glow suffocated beneath swirling black clouds. White lightning crackled violently within, flashing like serpents trapped beneath glass, desperate to strike.

After their long hibernation, the Elders sought noble hands to protect the M'ra Sphere, Marie's voice carried on. *My tribe, the Shikarians, were chosen. My mother and father, Elena and Theodore Celeborn, led our people with honor. We fought for righteousness… won and lost countless battles.*

The sphere pulsed one last time… then dimmed. The vision shifted, carrying them forward through time.

After centuries of peace, the Elders could sense the weight of their fading strength. The balance they fought so hard to protect… would not hold forever.

The vision freezing moments in time:

— Hordes of Shikarians locked in fierce combat on bloodied fields.

— Elena and Theodore, in battle, blades fought beneath storm-lit skies. Victory hard-won.

And then… they gave birth to me. And my younger sister, Maya.

The vision softened: two newborns cradled gently in their parents' arms, their tiny breaths steady and pure. Elena and Theodore stood tall, crowned not by birthright, but by the will of the people, chosen to guide, to protect, and to preserve balance until destiny called forth the worthy. Their eyes glistened with hope and purpose, knowing the weight of New Earth's future now rested in their hands… fragile, yet filled with boundless promise. *The tribal council chose them… they were crowned King and Queen of New Earth.* The crackle of embers faded, swallowed by a silence so complete it felt sacred. Even the night seemed to hold its breath, the weight of ancient truths pressing gently against the world. In that hush, time itself stilled as though all creation waited, listening.

And together, Marie's voice whispered with reverence, *we became whole again. United under the oath to protect New Earth from those who would see it fall.* The vision shifted once more. A cold winter night blanketed the palace in stillness, frost glistening along stone archways and glass windows like threads of silver lace. Within the grand hall, King Theodore and Queen Elena sat upon their thrones, their posture regal, their eyes solemn, yet touched with humility. The air was heavy with reverence; every gathered soul bore witness to this sacred moment, hearts swelling with hope and trust. The weight of New Earth's future now rested in their hands, fragile, yet filled with boundless promise.

The great doors creaked open, and silence fell once more. The gathered crowd gasped softly as four hooded figures entered the hall, the Elders themselves, ancient and frail, their presence commanding and otherworldly. Their footsteps echoed on polished stone as they approached the dais, each step measured, as though time itself slowed to honor them. One Elder spoke, his voice like wind over distant mountains. "We come bearing gifts." Without another word, they thrust their hands forward, ancient power crackling at their fingertips. From the void between them, light twisted and coiled, drawn as though from the breath of the cosmos itself. Slowly, it gathered into a brilliant orb: *The M'ra Sphere*, radiant and alive, its glow pure and untamed. It pulsed with a steady rhythm, each beat echoing through the hall like the heart of New Earth itself.

The great hall became a cathedral of silence. Even the torches seemed to dim, as though bowing to the power before them. King Theodore and Queen Elena ascended from their thrones, every step slow, reverent. Their robes trailed behind them like flowing banners of silk, catching the glow of the braziers. Each movement was careful, as though honoring the moment with their very breath. The air seemed too still around them, all eyes watching as they descended the dais to stand before the ancient beings.

The sphere's glow painted their faces in hues of silver and white, a soft light shimmering across their features like moonlight on water. Their breaths came shallow and measured, though beneath their regal composure, hearts pounded with awe and uncertainty. The weight of the moment pressed against their chests, each heartbeat echoing the sphere's steady pulse. In that sacred silence, destiny felt tangible, shimmering between them and the ancient power before them. Before them pulsed ancient power… not merely magic, but the breath of destiny itself. A promise written in the stars… now entrusted to their mortal hands.

Queen Elena's fingers trembled as she reached forward, the weight of generations pressing on her shoulders. King Theodore placed a steady hand over hers, grounding her and himself, as they accepted the sphere's radiant glow. In that moment, the world seemed to exhale… and New Earth's fate shifted, forever marked by their courage to hold what could never truly be possessed.

"It looks to the darkest of hearts," the Elder intoned solemnly. "You must not let evil touch it, or it will be the end as we know it." The Elders lifted their hands, frail yet unwavering. From their palms, light began to stir valiantly, not conjured, but drawn from deep within, as if they pulled threads of their very spirit into being. Colors bloomed: a brilliant white for Air, fierce crimson red for Fire, deep sapphire for Water, and rich emerald for Earth. The energies swirled, dancing between them in graceful arcs, weaving together like strands of destiny.

"We give you the gift of the gods," the Elder continued, his voice reverent. "We bless your family with magic, to protect the crystals and the M'ra Sphere. But know this you cannot possess the crystals yourselves. Only they will know who is worthy. They must only be used to call upon them… when the time comes."

Slowly, the lights entwined, coalescing into a single radiant crystal: a sapphire orb necklace shot through with veins of color, pulsing like a living heart. It floated gently down, resting in Queen Elena's outstretched hands, warm and weightless… yet heavier than any crown. In that moment, the legacy of the Elders became more than history, it became trust, sacrifice, and hope, cradled in mortal hands. Tears glistened in her eyes as she looked upon it. The weight of trust, sacrifice, and legacy all captured in a single, luminous stone. *That day,* Marie's voice echoed softly through the vision, *they understood the importance of the M'ra Sphere.*

The illusion shimmered softly, shifting into a memory long buried beneath time. Above the clouds, metallic vessels hovered like silent predators, sleek, otherworldly crafts that drifted just beyond New Earth's atmosphere. Then, without warning, they deployed their payload, pods streaking like comets through the sky, descending toward the unsuspecting world below. *They came from a world called Lyra… a planet fading into ruin.* Marie's voice drifted like wind through the memory. *They offered peace in exchange for a place of solace. But it was not peace they sought. They had heard whispers of New Earth… an infinite world with resources, untouched and teeming with life.* Her voice softened, heavy with memory. *They arrived for the food we harvested with our hands. The waters that healed. The roots that cured disease. They came for what their dying world could no longer give.*

The scene shifted. New Earth bloomed before them, not the ravaged realm they knew, but a memory, untouched and whole. Sunlight spilled across rolling hills, gilding the grass in hues of gold and emerald. The air was impenetrable with the scent of soil, sweet grain, and something floral, almost ethereal. Villagers moved in rhythm, their hands working the land with quiet reverence… plucking ripe fruit from bending trees, gathering tall stalks of corn, their laughter rising like songbirds in the breeze.

Children chased one another between rows of wheat, their giggles weaving through the rustle of leaves. Somewhere, a distant bell chimed, not as warning, but as celebration, marking the end of a bountiful season. Everything breathed. Everything lived. New Earth gave without demand. Its soil brimmed with healing roots, its rivers ran pure, untouched by corruption. Crops grew tall without poison, and the air carried not the weight of industry, but the hush of harmony. It was a planet unlike the dying worlds beyond the stars, a place where life thrived in rhythm with the land itself. To the Lyrans, it was more than a haven. It was the last great resource the galaxy could not manufacture. A world worth saving. A world worth deceiving. The Lyrans, cloaked in the faces of villagers, moved among them. Smiling. Sharing. Pulling corn from stalks and handing it to neighbors with warm eyes and patient nods. They blended in like whispers. Anticipating. *But their emperor… he knew why they had come, Marie* murmured, as if the memory itself still lingered in the air. Then another shift.

He was younger then, not the feared figure spoken of in rebel whispers, but a boy on the edge of manhood. Hunger lined his face, and his frame was lean beneath dust-stained garments, the kind worn by those forgotten by fortune. His eyes, sharp and restless, darted between vendors and guards, calculating risk with every breath. He moved swiftly through the market outside the castle, drawn by the scent of fresh bread wafting from a nearby stall. Without hesitation, his fingers curled around a warm loaf, as if survival itself depended on it. The guard yanked his arm with a snap, jerking him off balance. Zion stumbled, his knees nearly buckling as his palms scraped the dirt. The bread lay crushed behind him, forgotten.

Gasps broke like glass through the crowd. Vendors turned away. Mothers shielded their children. No one stepped forward. They didn't want to believe. New Earthians wanted peace and harmony.

Moments later, he was dragged through the marketplace like a criminal, past stalls he once walked by in silence. His boots scraped stone. A pillar slammed into his shoulder, he bit the inside of his cheek, refusing to cry out, even though pain is all he could think about. Pride, brittle as it was, held his spine upright. Children stopped mid-laughter. A otherworldly creature growled, then whimpered. An old woman crossed herself, whispering a name not meant to be spoken ever. *He did not rise alone,* Marie's voice softened. *Even then, the wind carried whispers… whispers of something watching him. Guiding him.*

Zion kept his gaze low, but in his chest, fury kindled like kindling to a spark. Not rage for being caught… but for being seen as less than. By the time they reached the castle gates, his body had stilled. But inside, where no one could reach, he burned. And the fire was only just beginning. In the next instant, Zion was hauled through the palace gates. Within the throne room, he was thrown to the floor. The cold stone met his trembling knees as he looked up, eyes sunken with hunger, filled with fear and humility.

"Please," he whispered. "Forgive me… for I was only hungry. Let me serve you. Let me prove my worth."

King Theodore and Queen Elena exchanged a glance, uncertain at first, yet moved by the desperation before them. Then, a soft nod from the King. "A thief by circumstance, not by heart," the King declared. "We will not turn away a boy in need."

A flicker of compassion from the Queen. She stepped forward, her golden robe trailing behind her. "What is your name?"

The boy's voice cracked as he spoke. "Zion."

"Then rise, Zion. You shall serve within the palace and earn your keep with dignity." Queen Elena said with quiet authority, the weight of mercy behind her words.

Marie's voice echoed softly through the illusion, her tone hushed as if remembering a wound: *He was pleading, begging the King and Queen to let him go. In exchange for his sins, he convinced them to offer his life to be their servant. But he knew what was on*

New Earth… The M'ra Sphere. The core of this world. They intended to invade, to kill, and to destroy anything that stood in their way. And they did exactly what they said they were going to do.

The image stilled for a breath: Zion, kneeling in the throne room, head bowed in false humility, as though the darkness within him had not yet awakened. But he was no orphan. No desperate boy. He was the birth of an Emperor. And his deception was only just beginning. The illusion trembled, as if resisting the memory that followed. Shadows stretched across the light, bleeding into every corner like ink in water. A low hiss curled beneath the surface, soft, beckoning. The vision shifted once more, pulling them into a truth whispered only in nightmares.

Zion stepped into the vault's heart, where silence clung like mist. There, encased in crystal and shadow, pulsed *The M'ra Sphere.* All radiant and rage. The light it emitted was not warm, but cold and sentient, alive with intent. As he drew closer, the glow intensified, casting a pale shimmer across the walls… until it reached him. Reflections of cold, white light glimmered in Zion's eyes, twin shards of a power he didn't yet understand. His breath hitched. He couldn't look away. *The M'ra*

Sphere called to him, not with words, but with hunger. A low hiss slithered through the chamber, too soft to be real, too insistent to ignore.

Somewhere beyond the vault's edges… something appeared. Not a sound, not a shape, but a presence. Watching. Waiting. The one they do not speak of: *The One Who Cannot Be Named.* The shadows felt thicker here, as if they were listening. Zion's spine tensed, though no one was there. Yet deep within the hush, a whisper curled like a serpent: silent, patient, ageless. Something ancient stirred behind his expression, curiosity twisted into longing. The whisper of power had found a listener.

Marie's voice returned, barely audible, carried like a memory through the illusion: *He believed that if he could lay his hands on it, it would grant him ultimate power… a new reality where he would reign as king.* The illusion darkened. The walls of the grand chamber formed in shifting light, their golden inlays catching flashes of unseen lightning. Time had passed: Zion was no longer a boy, but a man cloaked in power and veiled fury. Marie's voice returned, low, and steady, as if dragging each word from a wound. *It consumed everything about him. Orcas later, he returned, not as a servant, but as a sovereign, pleading with the King and Queen to hand over the M'ra Sphere. He confessed… said the Elders had sent him to reclaim it. That it was never theirs to hold.*

Zion stood before King Theodore, who remained poised at the far end of the grand chamber, the golden banners of New Earth draped behind him. The Emperor's voice rang through the vast hall, sharp with frustration, echoing off the stone like a threat unanswered. *"That's because you're not listening!"* Zion snarled. *"The Elders sent me to take it back before it's too late!"*

The King's eyes narrowed. "The M'ra Sphere belongs to the kingdom," he said, voice low but resolute. "You were never its keeper. That truth was written long before you arrived." King Theodore straightened. "You were never sent," he said firmly, threading through each syllable. "The Elders entrusted The M'ra Sphere to this kingdom orcas ago. It was their final act of faith in us. And you… you've twisted that into ambition."

Zion's fists clenched. "You're wrong," he hissed. "You don't understand what's coming. They chose me! I am the rightful one!"

Queen Elena stepped into the chamber from the high archway, her silhouette framed by the golden light above the grand steps. She paused there, as if the air itself held its breath. Zion turned toward her, his face wild with urgency. For a heartbeat, something in him softened, hope, perhaps, or a flicker of the boy he once was. But whatever remained faltered the moment her gaze met his. Her spine stayed straight, her expression unreadable, but behind her eyes, something broke. There was no warmth in her stare now. Only realization. A truth that had waited too long to speak. "You were a boy once," she said, her voice soft yet firm, "who asked to serve. What stands before us now is not that boy." A beat of silence passed.

Then King Theodore's voice cut through the chamber like a blade. "Guards!"

Marie's voice slipped into the memory, heavy with sorrow. *Little did the Emperor know… the Elders had passed the M'ra Sphere to the kingdom many orcas ago. They saw through the illusion of power and chose balance over dominance.* Footsteps thundered down the hall. Two guards burst into the chamber, gripping Zion's arms as he resisted, eyes blazing with betrayal. "You are not to remain in this kingdom," King Theodore declared. "By order of the Shikarians… you are charged with treason."

A distant rumble shook the vision. Marie's voice lowered into a whisper. *Then the storm hit.* Lightning split the sky like a curse, merciless, all rage, and glory, casting Zion's face in a flash of fury and shadow. The thunder that followed was not from the heavens, but from within him, a roar of something ancient and unleashed. In that moment, the storm was not above them. It was him… wrathful, deranged, and no longer human. The illusion around them wavered, edges fraying like burned cloth, and the vision began to unravel. Marie saw what she could never forget.

Her mother's back was turned. Her father slumped to the side, frozen, eyes wide with disbelief. A shape moved behind Queen Elena, silent and sudden. Haiti. A blade pierced through her body with merciless precision. A gasp escaped her lips. A shudder. Blood trailed down her gown like falling petals. "Mommy!" Her knees buckled.

A scream echoed across the chamber, but it wasn't the Queen's. It was Marie's. Then silence fell, cruel and absolute. The Queen collapsed, her face striking the stone floor. And the light in the chamber died with her. And Zion, no longer the boy who asked to serve, had become something else entirely. Something… wicked. Twisted by sorcery. Crowned by delusion.

Our new Emperor Zion.

Chapter XI:
Ashes and Answers

The wind stirred again, sharper now, a bit colder. Brushing through the tall trees with an eerie hiss. Adam barely moved. The fire crackled behind him, but his eyes stayed on the sky, on the way the branches above groaned and thrashed like something unseen was crawling through them. The gusts pressed in from all sides. Leaves whispered. Not just sound, but sensation, like the forest itself had seen what they saw. And it was afraid. He felt Katherine shift nearby. Maybe she looked up first. Maybe she felt it too. But Adam couldn't take his eyes off the trembling canopy.

Then Marie's voice cut through the silence, soft but absolute. "The Elders are long gone… but their power still remains," she said. "The Sapphire Orb chose you."

No one spoke. Adam stood frozen, the words echoing in his skull like a bad dream. *The elders are long gone… but their power still remains. The sapphire orb chose you.* He blinked, heart hammering in his chest. *Does she actually believe that? A group of barely functioning adults were meant to save a world they just found out existed. Is this lady serious? Does she hear herself?* He dared a glance at the others. Katherine's arms were crossed, but her knuckles were pale. Eric's jaw was tight, unreadable. Rose didn't even blink, like she was trying to process the impossible one frame at a time. The air felt heavier now. Not like before, when it was just the fog or the trees closing in, but heavier inside him. Like something ancient had cracked open, and now it was watching them. He swallowed, unsure if the weight in his chest was fear… or something worse. Obligation.

Marie leaned forward, eyes gleaming in the firelight. "New Earth is dying. Zion's perversion is twisted by the M'ra Sphere, corrupting our harvest, our land, our people. We're going to need all your help to get it back and restore balance to New Earth."

Adam's heart pounded. He clenched his fists and stepped forward, his voice trembling, not from weakness, but from disbelief. "We are not fit to fight his army," he said, trying to steady his breath. "Let alone what's in this forest. What makes you think we can help you?"

Marie didn't hesitate. "You were called by prophecy, she said. "Chosen through blood… through time. The Sapphire Orb carried the Elders' final hope. And it led me to you. When I cast the orbs, it searched for the worthy ones. It gifted you with New Earth's founding elements. Deep within ancient blood. You're the only ones powerful enough to stop him. You were meant to save us!"

Adam lashed out. "Prophecies don't save people. People do."

"Prophecies guide. But people choose. That's what makes you different, Adam. You still have a choice." Marie said calmly.

Adam didn't know what startled him more, her words or the fire in her voice. She wasn't just someone carrying a legacy. She was someone who had lost everything. And maybe… she wasn't so different from them after all.

Eric narrowed his eyes. "How can we trust you?"

Marie inhaled sharply, her jaw tightening. "My parents were once King and Queen. Emperor Zion, who is all war and rage, murdered them and took the throne. All he wants is power. To destroy everything that stands in his way. To not fight back would dishonor my parent's name." She looked at each of them, her voice low.

"Trust me, I want him dead."

Silence hung in the air. Adam crossed his arms; eyes fixed on the fire. Then he flicked his gaze to Marie. "You mentioned the M'ra Sphere. Why does everyone want it?"

Across from him, Marie stared into the fire, its glow flickering across her face. Her eyes weren't just reflecting light; they were holding something else. Something old as time. Something broken. She finally spoke, but not like before. Her voice had changed, a bit quieter now, steadier. Like she was speaking to more than just them.

"The M'ra Sphere… it doesn't just grant power. It reveals what already lies within. That's what no one tells you. In the right hands, it brings balance. In the wrong ones…" She hesitated. "It consumes. It destroys. It whispers. And when the day comes… It waits to test us all."

A little later… The fire crackled in the distance, casting faint, shifting shadows through the brush. Its glow pulsed gently across the forest floor, painting the trees in flickers of gold and coal. Marie lay on her side, facing away from the others, her body still, her breath steady beneath the dim wash of moonlight. From a distance, she looked peaceful… yet something in the air suggested that peace had come at a cost. Katherine stood a few feet away, watching Marie with narrowed eyes. Silent. Guarded. Then she turned and walked back toward the group huddled near the other side of the fire. "She's asleep," she whispered.

Eric leaned in. "Do you believe what she said?"

Adam watched Marie. Rose had her arms crossed, gaze fixed on the fire like it held answers. "It all makes sense," she said finally, voice low. "What happened back in that chamber. Why she wants to kill…" She hesitated. "…Zion."

He sat near the edge of the group, hands clasped tight in front of him, staring into the fire as if it might burn the confusion out of him. His chest felt heavy, not just from the vision, but from the silent truth none of them wanted to say out loud. That maybe… just maybe… they were part of something too big. His mind flashed back to the chamber: Zion stepping forward, eyes like voids; Queen Elena gasping as the blade struck;

the sound of Marie's scream echoing like it belonged to someone else. He remembered the helplessness. The stillness. The cold in his limbs that made him feel like a ghost in his own body. A chill slid down his spine. He blinked hard and looked away, as if the fire itself had turned on him. Then he rubbed his temples, trying to shake it all loose, the memory, the pressure, the impossible weight of what they were being asked to become. "How can we trust her?" he asked finally, his voice low, guarded. "How do we know she's not one of them?"

The fire crackled between them, casting slow-moving shadows across Rose's face. She didn't answer right away. Adam noticed the way her eyes lingered on Marie, like she was calculating answers for her. Then they flicked toward him. She held his gaze, just for a moment, like she could see the storm behind it. Then she spoke, voice soft but steady. "She saved us, Adam," Rose said. "I don't think she's lying."

Katherine shifted beside her and nodded. "I'm with Rose on this one, you guys."

Adam turned to Eric. Eric turned to Adam. They didn't say a word, just exchanged a look. The kind that said, *Of course, the girls are sticking together.*

Eric snapped, "We don't know this lady. She could be leading us straight into a trap."

Katherine raised an eyebrow.

"She did save our asses, though."

Adam squinted into the woods, jaw tight. "Okay… but did she? Or are we just pawns in someone else's game?"

Rose folded her arms, eyes flicking to Eric. "She's the only one who knows what the hell is going on. I trust her… a little."

"'A little gets you killed out here." Eric scoffed.

Adam rubbed the back of his neck and glared between them. *Great. We're about to die and these two are bickering like it's group therapy.*

Katherine shifted beside them. "So does talking like a paranoid dad, Eric."

Eric folded his arms. "Good. Then maybe someone around here should be the paranoid dad."

Katherine rolls her eyes. "Oh boy."

Adam blinked. *You were literally high on something two days ago, but sure Dad of the Year.* He didn't say it out loud, but the glare he sent Eric probably got the point across.

Eric huffed. "If there's any slight change in her plans," he said, looking between them, "we turn back around. Got it?"

The fire crackled on, low and steady, but none of them felt its warmth anymore. They didn't speak again. Not as the flames burned lower… not as the wind stirred the edge of the trees. Across the clearing, Marie still slept motionless, breath slow, as if untouched by the weight of the night. Her face was serene, almost fragile in the firelight, but there was a tension beneath it, a quiet strain just beneath the surface. Her body rested, but her spirit was moving, drawn elsewhere, following a thread no one else could see. Deep beneath the calm… her mind was already reaching…

Lightning slashed across the night sky, illuminating the tall arched windows of a distant stone tower. For a brief moment, the entire room was bathed in silver, shadows stretching across the stone walls like reaching hands. Rain whispered against the glass in a steady rhythm, soft but persistent, as if trying to speak through the silence. But inside, all was still untouched by the storm, yet somehow holding its breath. Ronan slept soundly beneath heavy blankets, his chest rising and falling with the calm breath of deep slumber. The room around him was dark and richly adorned, faded tapestries, gold-rimmed bookshelves, and flickering candlelight that glowed against carved oak walls. A kingdom long forgotten still clung to this place. And he, its last heir, had almost learned to forget it too.

"Ronan."

The voice was soft, feminine, distant. Barely louder than a breath. But it pulled him from the edges of sleep, familiar in a way that made his heartbeat change. He stirred, shifting beneath the covers.

"Ronan, where are you?"

"Ronan!"

Lightning cracked again, louder this time, closer, like the sky itself had ripped open. The sound rolled through the chamber like distant thunder chasing something unseen. For a breathless instant, the room exploded in a burst of white, every shadow cast into stark relief. Ronan's eyes shot open, heart pounding as if something had called him from beyond the storm. "Marie," he whispered. Ronan's breath slowed. The room had returned to stillness, but the echo of Marie's voice lingered, soft, pleading, and distant, like wind brushing through the cracks of memory. He sat in silence, listening to the rhythm of rain tapping the windows, the flicker of candlelight dancing against the stone walls.

Far away, somewhere beyond the storm, she was already moving. A pale gray sky hung low above the forest, thick with clouds that hadn't yet broken but promised rain. Through the tree, Marie led the others in a quiet line, careful with each step. Adam kept his distance, watching her move ahead. She walked like she'd been here before. Like this place had been waiting for her. The path sloped downward, slick with moss and damp earth, where murky water trickled between bulging rocks, like veins beneath wounded skin. A low fog clung to the ground, coiling around their boots, swallowing sound, and blurring the edges of the trail. The air was thick, not just with moisture, but with something else. A presence. Almost reverent, like the forest itself was holding its breath. Gnarled roots jutted from the sides, forcing them to balance with every step, while the scent of wet bark and unseen decay filled the air. Above, branches tangled like skeletal fingers, casting fractured light across the path as if the forest itself were watching.

Then the air shifted. It felt wrong. It was still. Too Still. Branches that once whispered above them now stood motionless, like even the wind had abandoned this path. Adam stepped lightly, but every crunch beneath his boots echoed too loud. The trees were darker here. Sickly, somehow. He glanced at the others. No one said a word. Maybe they felt it too. The heaviness. The pull. Something beneath the surface of this forest was shifting. Not natural. Not safe. And somehow… it knew they were coming. Marie's staff rested in her grip, its smooth blackwood shaft tapping softly against the earth, steady, like a heartbeat guiding them forward. The satchel at her side bounced gently with each step, its contents secure but faintly shifting beneath the layers. Adam watched her for a moment longer. She moved like the silence didn't bother her. Like she belonged in it.

Above them, the branches swayed and murmured, as if the forest itself were listening to their passage. Katherine's voice broke the silence. "Where are we going?"

"To Ronan's," Marie replied, eyes scanning the path ahead.

Adam glanced at her. "Who's Ronan?"

Marie glanced back briefly. "An old friend."

They walked in silence for a moment longer, the crunch of shifting rock beneath their boots the only sound. Adam kept his eyes low, watching the mist curl around his ankles like a living thing. Each footfall echoed faintly, swallowed almost as quickly as it came. It felt like the forest was holding its breath. Even the wind had gone still, like the trees themselves were listening.

"What is this place called?" Katherine asked.

Marie turned slightly, as though she hadn't heard at first. "New Earth."

Katherine blinked. "New Earth?"

Marie came to a stop. She turned to face them fully, her staff planted firmly in the ground. "Yes," she said quietly. "New Earth."

They stared at her, eyes lingering with a mix of disbelief and uncertainty. The weight of her words hung in the air, thick and unanswered. Then slowly, one by one, the group began to move again, hesitant at first, as if their bodies remembered how to walk before their minds caught up. The silence between them spoke louder than words ever could. Then Katherine asked the question that had been building in all of them, sitting just beneath the surface like a pressure waiting to break. Her voice was soft, almost afraid of the answer. "What happened to our Earth?" The words seemed to hang in the air, fragile and impossible, like a memory they hadn't dared to grieve until now.

Marie didn't stop walking. Her eyes stayed on the path ahead, her voice barely more than a breath. "That place… it's not where we left it."

Adam blinked. "Wait, what does that mean?"

Marie only shook her head. "Some doors… aren't meant to reopen."

Adam stared after her, heart pounding like it wanted out of his chest. The others passed him without a word, Katherine, Rose, Eric, each one wrapped in their own thoughts. But Adam's lingered. The weight of it all clung to him like damp air… not just because something was lost, but because part of him still lived in what used to be. The man he killed wasn't a secret. Eric had seen it. Katherine had known. Rose was the only one left in the dark. But the shame? That never left. It crept into moments like this, the still ones, the quiet ones, when there was nothing left to distract him. The guilt. The doubt. The question he couldn't shake: *Is this who I am?* And whatever Marie meant about Earth, about doors that shouldn't reopen something in the way she'd said it… the quiet finality in her voice, the weight in her eyes, it struck deeper than he expected. It wasn't just sadness. It was resignation. All he knew was this didn't feel like fate. It felt like a sentence. Like he'd been dropped into someone else's war, someone else's prophecy and now, they were expected to save New Earth, even if they didn't understand it.

Marie didn't slow down. She lifted her staff and pointed ahead. "Ronan's castle is just beyond the ridge," she called. "We don't have time to stop. Keep moving."

They reached the edge of a towering cliff, where the forest gave way to a vast, breathtaking gorge carved deep into the earth. Below, a veil of mist coiled through the chasm like a living thing, obscuring the bottom in a ghostly haze. Across the gorge, in the far distance, stood Ronan's castle, ancient, stoic, and gleaming faintly through the mist. Its spires rose like broken crowns against the sky, the clouds clinging to its stone as if trying to veil whatever still remained within.

Eric stepped forward and exhaled, awestruck. "Wow."

The others came to stand beside him. From this distance, the castle looked like something out of a forgotten legend. Its stone towers pierced the sky like broken teeth, jagged and proud against the mist. Clouds curled around its highest spires, veiling parts of it like a secret half-remembered. The wind carried a distant howl, as if the land itself remembered what had once been lost there… or what still lingered within.

Without a word, they began their descent down a narrow passageway that carved its way into the rocks below. The path sloped sharply, slick with moss and scattered with loose stone, forcing each step to be slow and deliberate. Gnarled roots curled like claws across the trail, and towering rock formations flanked them on either side, not closing in, but rising high, casting long shadows as they wound deeper into the gorge. A thin mist clung to the air, cool and metallic against their skin, carrying the scent of damp earth, lichen, and something older like forgotten bones buried deep in the stone. Marie took the lead, her staff tapping rhythmically against the ground as she moved with certainty, though her eyes remained fixed ahead, as if the path held more than just stone.

"What kind of place is this?" Rose asked quietly, scanning the terrain.

Marie's voice came without turning. "Some say it's cursed. Others say it brings blessings."

Adam squinted toward the towering shapes beyond the mist. "What do you say?"

Marie paused mid-step. Adam noticed her grip tighten on the staff, knuckles white, body suddenly still. She didn't look back, but there was something rigid in the way she stood, like the air had changed around her. He followed her gaze, not quite to the castle itself, which was now obscured by mist and rock, but to the vague silhouette through the haze. It was like watching her stare down a ghost. Grief flickered across her expression, but only for a heartbeat, before she buried it beneath that same quiet resolve. The silence stretched.

"Let's not forget we have a job to do," she said, her voice low, steady… but edged with something unspoken. Something sacred.

They pressed forward without question. Eventually, the group stumbled upon a small clearing nestled between two towering boulders, their jagged edges framing the space like ancient guardians. The wind died down here, muffled by the natural stone walls and the curling branches overhead that cast shifting shadows across the forest floor. The faint sound of running water whispered in the distance, weaving beneath the hush like a hidden stream. Somewhere deeper in the woods, an animal called out in a low, rasping cry. Grateful for the brief shelter, they slowed to a halt, chests rising and falling in quiet exhaustion. For a moment, no one spoke, they simply listened to the stillness, catching their breath and grounding themselves in the eerie calm.

"This is too much," Katherine muttered, wiping sweat from her brow. "We've been walking for hours without a break."

Marie nodded. "We'll stop here. See if you can find water. And we'll need something to eat."

They each scattered to the edges of the clearing, some slumping against rocks, others leaning into tree trunks or stretching out along fallen logs, their bodies aching from the long descent. The air hung thicker here, like the forest was holding its breath, and even the wind seemed hesitant to stir. The quiet felt unnatural, not peaceful, more like a pause before something unseen revealed itself. Eyes, real or imagined, pressed in from the shadows between trees… because in this place, something always watched.

Eric nudged Rose gently. "Rose… are you hungry?"

"A little," she said. Her gaze shifted toward the shadows between the trees, quick, almost cautious. Adam caught the flicker in her eyes and tensed, suddenly aware of how quiet the forest had become.

"Shh," Marie whispered sharply. Adam watched her freeze, grip tightening on the staff, body tense like a drawn bow. Rose, Katherine, and Eric turned to her in sync, pulled by the sudden shift in her stance. Marie's eyes didn't move. Whatever she saw beyond the trees, it had her locked in place.

Adam lingered a few steps back, pulse quickening, unsure what he was supposed to be seeing. He followed her gaze to the treeline.

Through a narrow clearing and across a shallow stream, a massive grizzly bear prowled the riverbank. Wet fur clung to its hulking frame as it swiped at fish with clumsy, crushing force, completely unaware it was being watched.

Marie stepped forward, calm and composed. She whispered the Shikarian words under her breath "Vash tal'kai en'derrah." The syllables curled like smoke in the air. The bow shimmered faintly in her grip; a raw ancient and very much alive arrowhead pulsed with a sapphire light. Then, with unshaken focus, she loosed the arrow straight between the bear's eyes. The arrow pierced the bear's skull with brutal precision, burying deep between its eyes in a flash of sapphire light. The beast collapsed mid-charge, its massive body crashing into the earth with a deafening thud that echoed through the gorge. Blood pooled quickly beneath its head, dark and steaming against the cold soil. Marie didn't flinch, she lowered her bow, eyes fixed and unreadable, then strode forward with silent authority to claim the kill. Behind her, no one spoke.

Adam leaned against the base of a gnarled tree, turning a snapped branch between his fingers. The bark flaked beneath his thumb. His eyes flicked between the others, Eric and Rose gathering firewood, Katherine checking the bear. Then something shifted in the air. A whisper. Soft. Not wind. It slithered through the trees like breath through bone, threading between the branches, curling around Adam's ears. "Come," the voice hissed. "Alone. Don't bring the others." Adam froze. The voice hadn't come from the clearing. It was in his ear. Inside him. He looked up. For a moment, he didn't know why, but his feet we're already turning, already moving, the snapped branch falling from his fingers. Like something was waiting for him. There, nestled between thick roots and overgrown thorns, was the entrance to a cave. Narrow, low, and pitch black. A wooden den carved into the earth. The shadows around it didn't move. They waited. Still. For someone to enter.

I can't stop.

He knew that much. But it didn't feel wrong. It felt like letting go, like slipping into something warm and familiar. "Or suffer the consequences," the voice whispered again.

Adam stepped forward slowly. Something in the air shifted around him, heavy like the sun pressing its heat onto you, like walking through a dream he couldn't wake from. His boots pressed into the damp earth with a muffled crunch, but he barely heard it over the thrum rising in his chest. Each step pulled him further from the others… and closer to something he didn't understand, but couldn't ignore. The others were too distracted to notice, still dealing with the bear, still talking in hushed tones.

He took another step. The wind shifted. It wasn't just the cave pulling him forward, it was something older than language, older than reason. A gravity that sank past skin and bone and into the place where guilt lived. Into that space no one could see, the one he hadn't dared look at in weeks. The man he killed. The blood he couldn't wash off, no matter how many rivers he crossed. It wasn't just the murder. It was what came after: the silence, the distance, the way people looked at him and didn't ask. The way he started to believe maybe he was the monster. But now… something else was watching. Calling. And for the first time since that night, Adam didn't feel shame. He felt seen. And that terrified him more than anything.

He stepped into the cave, the cool air wrapping around him like a second skin, damp, and laced with something that didn't belong. The scent of stone and rot filled his lungs, piercing and metallic, as if the earth itself had bled. Somewhere deep within, water dripped in slow, careful intervals, echoing like a warning in the dark. At the far end of the den, nestled in a jagged alcove, something glowed… pulsing faintly, like it was breathing… Could it be?

A light. Faint, pulsing, but alive.

Then he saw it—

Suspended in midair, a perfect sphere hovered above a tall, narrow wooden stand as if gravity had forgotten it. The light radiating from it wasn't steady, it flickered, shimmered, like breath caught between heartbeats. Every inch of its surface shifted in silent motion, as if *The M'ra Sphere* itself was made of memory… or something older. Adam couldn't look away. It called to something in him, not with sound, but with presence. His feet moved before he could stop them. The M'ra Sphere did not resist. It welcomed him. It began to pull.

He didn't understand how or why, only that his body answered a call his mind didn't have words for. It was like being drawn into a current beneath the surface of thought. Older than language. Older than time itself. Then came the sound. A slithering hiss. Soft. Subtle. Like breath slipping through cracked stone. At first, Adam barely noticed it, just noise, just air. But it persisted. Louder. Curling through his mind like smoke through a keyhole. It slid into thoughts he hadn't dared to think. *You're not broken.* The hiss grew forcefully, coated, wrapped around like a blanket, warm, but suffocating, like a chorus of serpents whispering promises just beneath an earshot. It didn't need words. It was a command written in instinct.

It feels good. The power.

His fingers twitched. His breath shallowed. He knew he should pull away. But the sphere did not resist, nor did his hands reach for it. It welcomed him. And somewhere deep down... he wanted to be welcomed. The sound soared to a crescendo, rising, coiling, sinking into the space where guilt lived. The man he killed. The silence afterward. The distance he created. The weight no one saw. *This can't be possible,* he thought. It didn't demand penance. It offered something else. Something easier. A way out. Adam's pulse slowed. The reflection of the pure white *M'ra Sphere* shimmered in his eyes as he stepped closer. The Sphere glowed brighter now, with the intensified hiss clawing at his ear, hissing, pulsing in time with something ancient in his bones. And for a moment, under that sound, under that spell, he believed, this could fix him. *It wasn't my fault! I'm not a murderer!*

And then, a voice.

"Adam?"

The voice wasn't just a sound; it was a rupture. Sharp. Almost dreamlike, but very much real. It sliced through the cocoon of hissing and heat, shattering the trance like glass underfoot. The sound stopped. The pull broke. Light drained from his eyes as *The M'ra Sphere*'s reflection vanished from them. He staggered back a step, breath catching in his throat. Eric's voice had pulled Adam from the translucent void and for a moment, it felt like waking up underwater. The world returned in fragments: sound without shape, light without meaning. His chest stiffened, lungs slow to remember how to breathe. It was like surfacing from a dream you didn't know you were having… only to realize something had followed you out. "Adam, what are you doing in here?" Eric stood at the mouth of the cave, his silhouette sharp against the glow.

Adam turned, disoriented. He opened his mouth, but the words barely came.

Was it all an illusion this whole time?

How long was Eric standing there?

Did he... what if he heard me?

Come on, think of something quick.

He has to know. That I...

"I... I saw..." His gaze drifted back toward the alcove, but the Sphere was gone. The light had vanished. The hum had faded. Nothing there. Only darkness. *Am I going crazy?*

Eric stepped closer, slow and careful as if Adam might break. "Hey," he said, quieter now. "You all right?" Adam didn't answer. He couldn't. The words were still tangled somewhere between fear and shame. Eric's brows pulled tight, but he didn't push. "Come on," he said gently. "Let's not get separated out here." He turned, giving Adam the choice to follow.

Still dazed, Adam nodded. He didn't fight it. Didn't argue. But as he followed Eric out of the cave, something inside him stayed behind. Something that had been seen. Something that had been marked. And whatever it was... it wasn't done with him. It wanted to kill him.

Chapter XII:
The Last Safe Place

Marie felt it before she saw it, something fractured beneath the soil. The deeper they went into New Earth, the more the world around them twisted out of harmony. Roots cracked underfoot like old bones, dry and gnarled, refusing to carry life. Streams ran through the land like veins, but the water moved wrong. It was too thick, too slow, like it carried secrets it couldn't let go. In places, it swirled murky and dark, as if grief had sunk into the soil and risen back up through the current. It didn't shimmer. It didn't sing. It just watched. Even the wind had changed. Where it once whispered through the leaves like a friend, now it stood still, listening. Watching you. Marie tightened her grip on her staff. Nothing in this part of the forest felt sacred anymore.

It was like the earth had been silenced. The Elders used to say that New Earth breathed in cycles, balance and chaos, creation and decay, but now the decay had grown teeth. And it wasn't just the terrain. The trees leaned like dying sentinels. The birds had stopped calling. Shadows lingered longer than they should have, and even the fog carried weight, pressing against her skin like a warning. And somewhere behind it all... the wind waited. Not whispering. Just watching.

Marie stood still, her breath low and measured, eyes scanning the treeline. The air here wasn't right; it hadn't been for many orcas. Not since the Sphere was stolen. The trees were quieter now, too quiet, their roots twisted in unnatural ways, as if the land itself was resisting something it couldn't fight. She could feel it in the ground beneath her boots: an imbalance, subtle but growing. The M'ra Sphere was alive. Somewhere out there, it pulsed and New Earth pulsed with it. *It's already begun,* she thought, gripping her staff tighter.

And they don't even know it yet.

She crouched low behind the brush, staff braced at her side, eyes locked on the treeline. Her senses strained beyond what sight could offer: listening, sensing. The earth here didn't just hold silence. It held memory. Ruin. Roots torn and twisted, pulsing with energy that didn't belong.

The moss no longer whispered life, it clung to decay. Something was feeding on the land itself. The deeper they ventured, the more the balance of New Earth unraveled. She narrowed her eyes. It was subtle, but she could feel it: the pull of the Sphere, distant, heavy, in different. Like a sun growing colder. Whatever this place used to be, it wasn't anymore. She glanced over her shoulder, catching the others still stepping out of the den.

Eric and Adam emerged together, the cool air brushing their faces like a veil newly lifted. The sharp scent of moss and damp earth hit them like a bulldozer through drywall, loud in the nose, all grit and memory. Just ahead, the others crouched low in uneasy silence, pressed behind bulging rocks and tangled brush, barely breathing. Their eyes were locked on something unseen in the distance, as if the forest itself had paused to listen.

"Stay low," she whispered, more to herself than anyone else. She had seen this kind of stillness once before. Just before the fall of her family's sovereignty. Before Zion took the throne. She knew what came after this kind of silence. Blood.

Eric's brow furrowed. "Why is everyone so quiet?"

Marie didn't speak. Just simply lifted a hand, eyes scanning the forest. "Shhh."

The forest held its breath with them, eerily still, too still. Even the wind had quieted, as if the trees themselves were ready and waiting. Then, through the heavy silence, came a sound, a sharp and clean snap. A twig cracked somewhere in the distance, unmistakable and close enough to shatter the illusion of safety. Rose stiffened, her voice barely above a whisper. "What was that?"

A monstrous sound echoed through the forest, a sickening blend of gurgle and shriek that sent a jolt through Marie's spine. It wasn't human. It wasn't animal. It was one of Zion's. A Prylyn creature lunged from the trees, its form nothing but a shifting mass of slick, black ooze. Empty sockets glowed faintly where eyes should be, and its mouth split open in a snarl of glistening, razor-sharp teeth. It landed behind her. Marie spun, just as the creature's arm slammed into her chest, launching her across the clearing. Her body struck a tree with brutal force, bark splintering on impact.

The creature leapt again, landing in front of her with grotesque grace. Marie exhaled sharply. Blue energy sparked around her wrists, forming sharp, knife-like gauntlets on both hands. She surged forward and, in one clean strike, cleaved the creature down the middle. Its screech tore through the trees as it dissolved into black vapor. "Go!" she shouted.

More Prylyn creatures erupted from the shadows, their arms morphing into long, metallic rods. They fired blasts through the trees, energy bolts slicing through the air toward Eric, Adam, Rose, and Katherine. "Come on!" Eric barked, grabbing Rose's hand. The group ran. Behind them, Marie fought like a tempest. One creature grabbed her arm. She twisted, slammed her forehead into its face. It reeled backward, stunned.

The forest exploded into intense motion as Eric, Adam, Rose, and Katherine sprinted through the trees, arrows slicing past like angry whispers. The air pulsated with danger, each step a chance they were willing to take. Then, a sharp cry rang out, Katherine stumbled as an arrow struck the back of her thigh, her body twisting mid-run before collapsing to the ground. Adam skidded to a halt, heart lurching, and doubled back without hesitation. Adam turned instantly, rushing to her side. "Katherine!" He slipped her arm around his shoulders, lifting her up as she limped beside him.

Eric and Rose dove behind a thick tree trunk. A Prylyn took aim. Eric spotted him a second too early. "No!" He yanked Rose down. An arrow thudded into the bark inches above her head. Nearby, Adam found cover behind another tree, gently lowering Katherine to the ground. "You, okay?" he asked.

Katherine winced, gritting her teeth. "Yeah… just help me not bleed out."

Back in the clearing, Marie staggered as a Prylyn slammed into her again, this time with the hardened rod that replaced its hand. She caught herself, breath sharp but unbroken. Her hand flew to her back, drawing her staff in a smooth arc. The blade-tip leveled at the creature's throat, gleaming blue in the fractured light. They circled each other, predator and guardian, both waiting for the first move. Another snarl echoed in the distance. Marie turned just enough to see Katherine clutching her leg, blood soaking through the thin fabric of her gown. The Prylyn's arm morphed into a rod of blackened steel, its jagged point aimed precisely at her chest.

Marie didn't hesitate. She lunged forward, driving her staff through the creature's side in one swift, brutal motion. As it collapsed, she spun on her heel and bolted toward Katherine, the forest blurring around her as instinct took over. She dropped beside her, pulling a strip of cloth from her belt. One of the enchanted wraps she'd always had on hand. Quick, practiced hands tied the cloth tight around Katherine's thigh. A faint shimmer passed through it as the healing threads activated.

Katherine hissed in pain. "You're not even gonna count to three?"

Marie gave a faint grin. "Didn't have time for one."

Behind them, the brush split again. Louder this time. A blur tore through the canopy in a fast, deliberate, thunder motion. Hooves struck the forest floor like war drums slowed in time—*doom… doom… doom…* Leaves spiraled upward in a chaotic dance as the rider burst into the clearing, cloak unfurling behind him like a banner of battle forgotten. He was tall, broad-shouldered, and cloaked in midnight leathers, the mark of New Earth's forgotten bloodline etched along his bracers. A blade gleamed at his side, kissed by the last breath of sunlight. He didn't shout. He didn't hesitate. He leapt from the saddle in a single, fluid motion, sword drawn before his boots met the soil.

The Prylyn lunged. Ronan Valemont standing tall and fearless, met it mid-charge, steel sinking deep in a single, silent stroke, in a precise moment. The creature didn't stand chance, it fell twitching to the moss, already forgotten sunken in the soil. He stood over it without a word. The wind curled around him like it remembered his name: Mighty protector of New Earth. Returned from myth. Marie stepped back, retracting her staff. Her chest heaved with exhaustion.

Ronan turned to her, eyes sharp with concern. "You alright?"

Marie smirked faintly. "Never better."

He hasn't changed… still that same old handsome guy… Still has the chiseled cheekbones… Just older. Wiser. But still carrying the weight of what they took from him all those orcas ago.

The others approached. Adam still supported Katherine as they joined Marie and Ronan. Katherine stared up at him, blinking through the pain. Her gaze lingered on his frame, tall, broad-shouldered, cloaked in midnight leathers. Something unreadable passed through her eyes, too fleeting to name. "Are you… Ronan?" she asked.

He nodded slowly, a smirk tugging at his lips. "There's so much I need to teach you."

Chapter XIII:

And Then... Nothing

Before she opened her eyes... something felt wrong with the warmth. Katherine stirred, blinking into golden light. Soft wind whispered through the curtains, carrying the scent of pine and something sweet... cookies, maybe? The sweet smell was almost too close to natural. Sunlight dappled across her face, she lifted a hand to shield her eyes. Her hair felt freshly brushed, her body wrapped in soft clothes she didn't remember putting on. Everything was warm. Familiar. Yet also quiet. Too quiet. Like she lived in a dream. She sat up slowly. No noise. Just calm. Her bedroom looked exactly as she remembered it, photos on the wall, her favorite scarf draped over the desk chair, the old green quilt folded neatly at the edge of the bed. Everything looked right. Too right. Like it had been waiting.

She rose, every detail pressing against her memory like it was trying to convince her it belonged. But something tugged at the back of her mind, an ache she couldn't name, a wrongness she couldn't place. The silence in the room felt full. Charged. She swung her legs over the bed and stood, bare feet meeting cool wood. Then… voices. Too particular. And her gasp remembered a familiar horror. Could it be? Are they alive? One voice being Adam. Another one… Dad? Her heart deepened with excitement.

She opened her door and padded softly down the hallway, the wooden floor cool beneath her steps. At Adam's room, she paused, exhaled, something in her chest tugging, only to find it empty. A quiet ache settled in her ribs, but the voices down the hall kept echoing, like a thread pulling her through fog. She followed them, each step slower than the last, as if her body already knew what her mind hadn't caught up to yet. The living room glowed with warm light and decorations. Streamers. Confetti. Balloons. Party favors. A cake sitting on the side table, with candles lit.

"Is this thing working?" her father's voice called.

"It's on, Dad. You don't see the red light?" Adam replied, a younger version of him off-camera.

"Oh, that's what that is?" James said.

"Oh my gosh, you're getting old," Adam teased.

"Alright, alright. Go get the presents. She'll be here any minute."

"I know, that's what I've been telling you." Adam let out a breath and gave a dry smile, the kind that came with an invisible eye-roll. His tone was flat, like he'd said it a dozen times before and now he was just humoring the slow ones.

"What?" James said, blinking like he'd just rejoined the conversation from another universe.

Adam gave the camera one last look, half smirk, half eyeroll as if already over the moment. Katherine turned the corner and slowed, heart thudding in her chest. The living room burst into a blur of streamers, confetti, and familiar faces.

"SURPRISE! Happy Birthday!" her mom, dad, and Adam all shouted in perfect unison. Their voices echoed off the walls, wrapping around her like a warm breeze caught in a dream.

She stopped cold. Katherine's breath caught in her throat "Mom?" Her voice cracked. "Dad? Oh my God..." she whispered.

Suzanne's smile beamed at her like sunlight through glass, a soft, glowing, impossibly perfect smile. There they were. All of them. Adam. Her mom. Her dad. Alive and well. Suzanne stepped forward, arms outstretched, holding a neatly wrapped box.

"This is for you," she said, her voice sugar-sweet and just a second too delayed. Katherine stepped into the hug. The embrace was warm... but her mother's hands were ice-cold, fingers pressing too stiffly against her back. Her dress scratched like burlap against Katherine's cheek, wrong and somehow.... Off. As they pulled apart, Suzanne's smile faltered, just for a blink, and something about it looked fractured. A sliver of her teeth flickered in the light, too white, too still. Too perfect.

For a heartbeat, Katherine swore she saw a ripple run across her mother's face, like a dropped pebble on glass. The gift box was small but felt heavier than it looked. A dense kind of weight, like it was full of stones. It landed with a dull knock in her hands when she adjusted her grip, and the faint scent of burnt metal and blown-out candles floated up with it.

"Smile for the camera!"

Adam chirped again.

But this time, his voice seemed to overlap itself, one version slightly faster than the other, like two recordings playing in tandem. The room dimmed for half a second, lights pulsing. The chandelier above flickered like a glitching frame in a film reel. Then, everything returned to normal. Or… something close to it.

Katherine blinked, her smile faltering. Her heart pounded, not from joy this time, but a crawling unease that slithered up her spine. They turned to her, smiling as if nothing had changed, as if years and planets and pain hadn't passed between them. Their laughter was effortless, their joy unshaken, like a memory stuck on loop. They watched her open presents, applauding, nodding, laughing along, as if the act itself was sacred. Katherine mirrored them, talked and laughed and played along, but her heartbeat never settled. Something inside her buzzed, like a wrong note humming beneath the melody, off-key, but no one else seemed to hear it.

"Smile for the camera!"

Adam's voice rang out again.

Katherine's heart dropped just for a second. Her head tilted slightly, looking to Adam, as if something about the words didn't sit right. His expression was the same as the joyous and affectionate Adam he was known to be, but then it clicked. A flicker of unease crossed her face, barely visible, but there. But that wasn't Adam talking, it was the same as before. The same tone. The same rhythm. The same words. Overlapping itself once more, like a recording skipping in real time. She blinked. For just a second, their faces shifted: her mother's jaw too wide, her father's smile too still, Adam's eyes flickering with a static that didn't belong. Then it was gone. Perfect smiles again. Perfect moment. But something had broken behind them. And this time, she felt it.

"What's the matter, honey?" her mother asked gently.

Katherine's eyes widened.

"How is this possible? You're… here."

Suzanne smiled, serene and soft.

"We've always been here, Kate."

And then, just for a breath… her smile vanished.

No transition. Just gone. A sudden frown. Flat, and hollow. No remorse. Then she grinned again. Her eyes wide. Her lips slowly curly up her face. Tightening. Like the air around her face had skipped a frame.

James tilted his head, a crease forming between his brows. "What's going on, sweetheart?"

Katherine turned to Adam, her voice dropping. "Follow me to the kitchen."

Adam raised an eyebrow. "Why?"

"Are you going to the party tonight?" she said quietly, as if recalling something from before.

Adam smirked. "Who's asking?"

Her expression tensed. She blinked rapidly, lips parting in confusion, like the words had surprised her as if it happened days ago. But recalled from a memory.

"You're twenty-five. Why do you need to sneak out?" Adam asked calmly.

"Let me have my moment," Katherine said with a faint smile. "I'm still daddy's little girl." Katherine paused in confusion. The words felt strange in her mouth. Like metallic in her tongue. Like they didn't belong to her... Why would she say that?

Adam tilted his head. Something shifted behind his eyes, like a thought cracked through. "Where is Marie taking us?" he asked.

Katherine terrified. "What?"

But Adam said nothing. He just smiled… Just smiled. The kind of smile that didn't reach his eyes. His face held an unreadable expression. Like a mannequin trying to remember how to move. Like a fractured thought. He blinked. Once. Slowly. Then his eyes followed Katherine's. Unblinking now. Wide as a hawk before the strike. Too precise. Too focused. As if he wasn't watching her, but mimicking where she looked. Like he was trying to remember how to be human. "Where is Marie taking us?" he asked, voice low. "Katherine, do you trust Ronan?"

Her breath immovable. Struck with fear. "What? What is going on?" she whispered, stunned. She didn't move. The air had shifted… thick now, laced with static. Something was wrong. Something had fractured. "How did this happen?" she asked softly. "How did we come back?"

He blinked at her. "Come back from where?"

"New Earth," she said, breath trembling. "It was real."

Adam's face didn't change. His tone stayed calm... almost too calm. Like the words weren't his, just ones he'd been taught to say. "I have no idea what you're talking about."

She turned to the living room, no one was there, and then slowly, back to the kitchen where Adam stood. Her mother was already there, in an instant, in her daughter's face, reaching out. Katherine swallows gently, fear steadying her movements.

"Honey," Suzanne said gently, her voice calm... too calm. "What you see here... isn't real."

Then, that same voice echoed behind Katherine. "Honey, what you see here... isn't real." She turns to the mimicking voice. Terrified. The air dropped like a weight. Light flickered once... then again. Katherine stepped back. The warmth drained from the walls like blood from a body. "No," she whispered. "How is this possible?"

Adam looked at her. Not with guilt... but with pity. Then his eyes glitched, wide, unblinking, like something behind them had cracked. His eyes met hers, wide and hollow. "It's happening again," he said. "And you still don't remember." He grabbed his own hair and yanked his head back, baring his throat to the sky. Katherine's breath froze. The knife rose. Fast.

"No!" Katherine screamed.

In an instant Adam cut his throat open. But nothing happened. No blood. No pain. Just silence. And then… he disintegrates. His body unraveling into ash and shadow, scattered on a wind that came from nowhere. Her father vanished next, his form folding in on itself like crumbling paper. Then her mother… gone without sound, her hand still outstretched mid-reach before it disintegrated. The kitchen cracked. Not splintered. Cracked. Like glass under pressure. Katherine narrowed her gaze to the walls. The walls trembled and began to shrink around her, groaning inward until every window spidered with cracks. Glass splintered toward her like threads of lights, slicing across her skin. Even the air seemed to collapse, trembling as if the house were exhaling its final breath. And then, came the sound. A deep, roaring groan. Not a scream. Not thunder. Something worse. It was the sound of the world ending. The house shattered into pieces. Katherine falling into the dark unknown. And then… Nothing.

Not dark. Not quiet. Just… absence. Katherine floated in it. Pitch black. No floor. No sky. No air. No breath. She opened her mouth and screamed. A raw, aching sound. The kind of scream that tore from her chest like a broken promise. But there was no echo. No one to hear it. Not even herself. Everything was just... gone.

Chapter XIV:
The Breaking Point

Katherine jolted awake, her palms were shaking, and her gasp trapped in a half-remembered dream, trying to hold herself together. Rain lashed against the carriage window, sharp and merciless, a harsh contrast to the silence of the void she'd just escaped. Her chest lifted and fell, but she didn't speak. She didn't move. For a moment, she wasn't sure where, or when, she was. The world was cold again… too cold. A faint whisper echoed through her mind. *It's happening again.* She blinked rapidly. But there was no voice now. No falling. Just rain. Outside, through the streaked glass, she caught the blurred shapes of Marie and Ronan, hunched beneath soaked cloaks, guiding the horses through the storm. The wheels creaked. The carriage groaned. Her fingers trembled against the seat.

Across from her, Rose slept with her head against Eric's shoulder. Adam leaned near the far corner, breathing steady, eyes closed, his face half-shadowed in the dim light. They were here. All of them. But this wasn't New York. This was New Earth. And nothing felt the same. Rain continued to hammer the sides of the carriage as Katherine blinked, trying to steady her breath. She shifted slightly, pressing her back against the seat. She exhaled slow, careful. The dream hadn't followed her. Not entirely.

Rose stirred, rubbing her eyes. "You said something in your sleep," she murmured. "I couldn't tell what it was." She blinked away the haze of sleep, her mind still tethered to whatever strange images had floated behind her eyelids. But Katherine's expression pulled her fully awake, the way her eyes darted, how her fingers trembled faintly against the leather seat. Katherine's hand drifted toward her locket, fingers brushing its golden edge like a reflex. She didn't look at it. She never did. Something was off. Even if she couldn't name it yet, she felt it settle between them like a weight.

Katherine froze. "I…" she started, but her voice trailed off. Whatever words she'd spoken in the void had vanished with it. "I don't remember."

Rose didn't press. She simply offered a quiet nod, and for a moment, the space between them felt warmer, softer. Like understanding, without explanation. A thunderclap cracked through the sky, shaking the world outside. The carriage shook slightly as the wheels shifted over cobblestone. Outside, the storm was ruthless. The rockaway carriage rolled into a wide, stony driveway that curled toward a towering palace, its dark silhouette slicing through the rain.

Ronan snapped the reins. "Whoa, whoa, horsey," he said as the animals slowed to a halt.

Marie turned in her seat, glancing back at the group. "We're here. Let's get inside before we drown out here."

Eric sat up slightly, turning toward Adam. "Remember our plan," he whispered.

Adam nodded, jaw tight. The rain outside beat harder against the wood as he pushed the door open. A blast of cold struck his face. And then he saw it: the palace towered in front of him, bigger than he'd imagined. A bit older. Colder. The kind of place that didn't speak. It simply stood. Towering. Timeless. A monument to something bigger than them all. He exhaled, the breath catching in his throat. "Whoa…"

One by one, Katherine, Rose, Eric, Marie, and Ronan stepped down from the carriage into the downpour. Rain soaked their cloaks within seconds, the wind whipping around them as thunder rolled somewhere in the distance. Ronan moved past Adam with a grin that held too much pride to be casual, like the storm belonged to him. His boots splashed through shallow puddles as he led the way, unbothered by the cold, as if he'd waited years to bring someone back here.

"You like it?" Ronan said, grinning. "Can you believe Zion never stepped foot here? Maybe he thought it was beneath him. Or maybe… he knew better."

Adam, drenched, turned slowly. His breath held for a second longer. "It's… massive." Behind him, the others stared with the same expression, equal parts awe and disbelief. Beyond the rain-slicked steps, the castle's rear stretched into a towering stone wall. Carved directly into the cliffside, it wasn't just architecture; it was domination and reverence combined. A sprawling courtyard opened before them, its cobbled floor rimmed with mist, and in the distance, arched stone fences framed an elevated garden, lush, half-wild, and heavy with New Earth's kept secrets.

From high above, a series of waterfalls spilled down from the rock wall, cascading like silver ribbons through carved spouts and moss-covered channels. The water didn't just fall, it danced, refracted through the courtyard torchlight like a living veil. Vines curled around twisted iron fences. Ferns rustled at the base of crumbling statues. Ivy gripped every surface, claiming it like time itself had grown possessive. A lone tree bloomed in the far corner, twisted, silver-leaved, its roots reaching into stone. The storm only made it more surreal, like nature itself was offering a strange kind of welcome. One forged in beauty, decay, and forgotten bloodlines. For a moment, the group paused, soaked and speechless, as if they'd stepped into a place that didn't belong to them. Marie didn't wait. She hurried toward the front doors. "Come on," she called back. "We've got work to do."

As they reached the entrance, Ronan's butler swung open the massive double doors without a word. Warm golden light spilled out into the rain, casting halos over wet cloaks and muddy boots, like some forgotten cathedral welcoming ghosts. The heat from inside met the storm like opposing forces, fogging the doorway in a thin veil of steam. For a brief moment, it felt less like crossing a threshold and more like stepping into something legendary.

Inside, the group stepped into a grand marble hall lined with sconces and ancient tapestries, each one etched with a story long before their time. The walls soared upward into vaulted ceilings, their arches kissed with gold filigree and soft candlelight. Their footsteps echoed across the polished floor, every drip of rain from their cloaks swallowed by the grandeur. Adam's eyes scanned the structure. It didn't feel like a fortress built by war; it felt crafted with purpose.

Marie's voice broke the silence. "Ronan's father built this place from scratch," she said softly. "Every stone laid by hand. He believed the land could be protected without destroying it." Adam in thought, absorbing the weight of that heritage. *Maybe… she is telling us the truth after all.*

Ronan turned toward them. "You're going to need all the training you can get," he said. "You've got an hour. My butler will show you to your rooms." He walked off as he spoke, already shouting down the hallway: "There's fresh clothing upstairs!"

Eric stepped closer to Rose, who tilted her head. "Do you trust them now?" she asked.

Eric didn't answer. Not yet… The butler appeared, quiet and efficient, as if summoned by the air itself. His footsteps made no sound against the marble, and his posture was so precise it felt practiced. Without a word, he gave a small bow and motioned for them to follow. The gesture was simple, but something about it carried weight, like they were guests in a place that remembered everything.

No one followed her. Not yet. And Rose was glad. She needed a minute. A room. A breath of her own. Rose paused at the threshold as the door opened. The butler gave a polite nod, silent as ever, then stepped aside. She entered without a word, and the door clicked shut behind her. The room was beautiful… technically. Ornate. Elizabethan. Heavy with tapestries and carved wooden trim. It looked like a portrait more than a place to sleep. She stood there, unmoving, eyes scanning the lavish details. It wasn't hers. It wasn't home. Just another performance set in a world that never asked if she wanted to audition. She stood at the vanity, motionless, brushing her damp hair with one hand, the other resting on the wooden edge. The mirror reflected a face she barely recognized, tired eyes, lips set in a line too firm for someone her age. But it wasn't her expression that held her gaze. It was the mark.

Nestled at the side of her neck, just above the collarbone, near the slope where her jaw curved… It pulsed faintly beneath the skin. A symbol, sharp and curved like flame trapped in glass. Not a bruise. Not ink. Something marked. It hadn't been there before… but somehow, she knew it had always been waiting. The glow was barely visible, like the dying light of coals, subtle, but undeniable. It didn't flash. It breathed. Her hand rose slowly to touch it, fingers hovering as if afraid to make contact. The warmth surprised her. Not burning. Not painful. Just… present. A quiet confirmation of something she hadn't asked for. Her throat closed in.

Why? she thought. *Don't cry. Not now.* It wasn't fear, not exactly, just the sinking sensation that whatever this was… this heaviness… it wouldn't let her go. It was burning an inferno inside her chest. She exhaled slowly, the weight of it all pressing behind her ribs, as she turned toward the wardrobe. Gowns hung neatly in a row, corseted, layered, medieval as hell. She stared for a moment, just stared, her jaw twitching. This was the kind of place that expected women to smile politely and burn quietly. Not her.

She closed the wardrobe doors with quiet finality, the sound barely more than a click. Then she leaned her head against the wardrobe door for a moment, eyes closed, exhaling through her nose. Earth was starting to feel like a fever dream, dim, warm, and gone. She missed the hum of the city at night. The simplicity of a hot shower. The smell of her favorite blanket, still laced with laundry detergent and memories. And Eric… she missed him in ways she didn't want to name. Back there, he had been quiet comfort. Here, he was something else, braver, bolder, maybe even a little broken. And she didn't know how to reach him now. Not without cracking open parts of herself she'd worked so hard to seal shut.

She blinked fast. Once. Twice. But she refused to let it take her. Her jaw locked. Her eyes stung. No tears. Not here. Not in this place. Not yet. She turned from the closet and sat on the edge of the bed, elbows on her knees, staring at the flickering sconces across the room like they owed her answers. But they offered nothing. Just fire. Just flicker. Just emptiness. She took a breath, deep and shaky, and whispered to no one:

"I have to do this."

A tear slid down her cheek before she wiped it away, like it had never been there at all.

Somewhere else in the palace… The hallway was quiet. Too quiet. Adam moved slowly, every step muffled by the soft grain of the stone beneath him. Something drew him forward… not a sound, not a voice, but a feeling. A tug. He passed a door, barely ajar. Paused. A subtle draft kissed his cheek as he pushed it open. Inside was shadow and silence. The study breathed age, bookshelves stretched floor to ceiling, loaded with worn tomes and curling scrolls. The air carried the scent of dust, ash, and old ink.

On a small table by the door, a single candle flickered beside a stack of unopened letters, the flame swaying like it had been waiting. He stepped further inside, footsteps soft against the stone floor. At the far wall, a heavy desk sat cloaked in dusk, its edges worn smooth from years of use. A single book lay at its center, leather-bound, thick-spined, the kind of object that felt more placed than forgotten. The title glinted faintly in silver: *Chronicles.* Adam reached for it without thinking. The leather was cold beneath his fingertips, worn at the edges. The cover creaked open in his hands. Inside the flap, a line of handwriting curled across the page, deliberate, dark ink that had weathered time:

Property of Ronan V.
To finish what my father began.

He turned a page carefully, handwritten pages, diagrams, pressed sketches of ancient tech. Notes in Ronan's handwriting:

I was too young. I didn't understand the cost of silence. They left me alive, but survival isn't the same as being saved.

Some pages were newer, others stained with age. As Adam turned the next page, he noticed the handwriting had changed, less refined, more angular. Older ink. A different voice entirely. A symbol: four elemental shapes

surrounding a central void. Beneath it, hastily
scrawled in faded ink:

*We are close. If we succeed, this could change the
face of New Earth. The conduits beneath the palace show
promise. The way they pulse with stored energy. But it must
remain hidden. If Zion finds out, he will destroy everything.
He cannot know. He must not know.*

A smudge trailed off at the edge of the
parchment, like the writer had left in a rush. Adam
swallowed. He flipped again. The handwriting
returned to Ronan's. Slanted. Tight. Heavy.

He knew.

You knew, didn't you, Father?
That he would come for us.
I still remember the sound. The fire.
The pain when you left this world.

If we had just one more day,
maybe we could have…

The ink trailed off. And then, at the bottom of the page, softer:

Always, beloved father.
Always.

Adam's fingers lingered on the page. The words pressed into his chest like a wound that hadn't closed. He slowly turned one more page:

They will be the protectors until the time has come…

And there it was again, beneath the prophecy, another name written in darker ink, as if recently added:

The One Who Cannot Be Named

He stared at it a bit longer. Something about that name sparked curiosity. Interest. Then, without meaning to, he whispered: "The One Who Cannot Be Named."

The candle near the doorway flickered, then died in a snap, like something unseen had snuffed it out. The silence thickened, pressing in from all sides, wrapping the room in a sudden, eerie stillness. Adam's back straightened, goosebumps crawled up his spine, every instinct on edge. A shadow swept across the hallway beyond the open door.

Then—

"What are you doing in here?"

Marie's voice. Steady. Unshaken.

He turned quickly, snapping the book shut like it had burned him. She stood in the doorway, one hand still on the frame, her silhouette sharp against the flicker of candlelight. Her expression gave nothing away, no judgment, no surprise, just that unnerving stillness she wore so well. For a moment, neither spoke, the air between them sat heavy with whatever truth Adam hadn't meant to find. "I… I didn't mean to intrude."

She didn't answer right away. Just stared at him, the flicker of light catching in her eyes like it might reveal something buried. It wasn't anger. It wasn't approval. It was the kind of silence that made you feel like you'd asked the wrong question, even if you hadn't spoken at all.

"Come," she said at last. "We have training to do." Adam cast one last glance at the study; at the secrets he wasn't meant to find.

They followed Ronan through the corridor, the walls alive with a soft, golden light that bathed every carving and banner in a warm glow, their footsteps echoing softly against the polished stone. High above, the ceiling arched like the ribs of an ancient beast, laced with metallic veins that shimmered faintly when they passed beneath. The air here felt different, cleaner somehow, the castle itself had been holding its breath until now, and Adam slowed for half a step, feeling it wash over him. There was history here, written in stone and silence, and some part of him, the part he rarely let speak, wondered if he belonged to it somehow.

Ahead, the hall opened into a vast, dome-like chamber. Katherine slowed to a halt as they crossed the threshold, her mouth parting in visible awe. Around them, the chamber stretched wide; walls gleaming with a faint metallic sheen, ceilings veined with hidden conduits that caught the light like trapped lightning. She turned slightly, her gaze sweeping over the intricate architecture as if trying to make sense of it all. Adam saw the wonder in her eyes and knew she was feeling it too: this place wasn't just old, it was alive. "Whoa. This place is huge…" she breathed.

At the center of the chamber, four circular platforms stood side by side, each one glowing softly with a pale silver light that pooled across the polished floor. Wires and conduits ran beneath the glassy surface like veins, pulsing faintly as if the room itself was breathing. Above them, suspended in a glass-walled booth built into the far wall, Ronan and Marie moved behind a sprawling control panel, their figures briefly illuminated by the cool blue glow of the screens. From up there, they seemed almost detached, watchful, but steady like captains steering a ship none of them knew how to sail yet.

He pressed a button on the console, his fingers moving with a confidence born of long-forgotten drills. Somewhere above, unseen mechanisms stirred to life, humming faintly through the stone walls. A low vibration passed through the chamber, subtle but unmistakable, like the castle itself was holding its breath. Then his voice broke the stillness, clear and commanding as it echoed through hidden speakers overhead. "Each of you will have your stations. Step up. The platform will read your DNA."

Adam, Katherine, Eric, and Rose exchanged quick glances, a silent mixture of nerves and unspoken excitement passing between them. Adam hesitated for half a second before stepping forward, the glow of the platform painting soft halos around their feet. His boots thudded against the surface, slick, cold, and unfamiliar, and he swallowed the tight knot forming in his throat. Whatever this was, it was too late to turn back now.

As they took their places, a calm female voice filled the chamber, crisp and unwavering. It echoed softly off the polished walls, neither mechanical nor warm, just clear, efficient, and inhuman. Adam's gaze flicked briefly toward the glass booth above, where Ronan and Marie watched in silence. The moment stretched, taut and expectant, like the breath before a race begins.

"Welcome, Eric Rowe, Adam and Katherine Greenfield, and Rose Blackburn. Training will begin momentarily," the Aegis Unit announced.

On the glass monitors above, the Aegis Unit logged their vitals in real-time: pulse steady, temperature normal, respiration controlled. Beside each readout, a new metric flickered to life, faint but unmistakable. Buried deep within their physiology, the elemental signatures registered at last, fragile sparks of something ancient waiting to awaken. Ronan studied the screens, his expression unreadable. His voice came again.

"Let's begin."

There was a beat of silence.

"Eric Rowe, begin," the Aegis Unit announced.

From the corner of his eye, Adam caught Eric rubbing his hands together, a little too sharp. He was trying to act casual, but the tension bled through every small movement, visible in the tight set of his shoulders. Adam exhaled quietly, the knot in his stomach tightening. If Eric was nervous, he was doing a terrible job hiding it and that didn't exactly make Adam feel any better.

A few steps away, Katherine thrust her arms out, her jaw clenched in concentration. She tried to summon gauntlets of rock around her fists, but the stones barely stirred, crumbling apart before they could take shape. A flicker of frustration crossed her face, quick and sharply aimed. Rose extended her hand; fingers curled like she was cradling an invisible flame. For a heartbeat, nothing happened. No spark. No heat. Just empty space and her lips pressed into a stubborn line, like she could will it into existence if she just tried hard enough.

Adam swallowed and turned inward, cupping his palms a few inches apart. *Come on,* he thought, *you've faced worse than this. Don't freeze now. They're counting on you.* He focused on the air between them, urging it to pull together into a sphere. For a moment, he thought he felt something, a soft vibration, a quiver in the air, but it collapsed in on itself before it could fully form, vanishing as if it had never been there at all. The frustration between them crackled like static, invisible but palpable, heavy enough to weigh down the room. It coiled through the air, threading between them, a shared failure none of them wanted to name. Adam felt it seep into his chest, tightening around his ribs like an unseen hand. No one spoke, but the silence was thick with the sting of almost.

Ronan's voice cut through the tension like a blade. "Stop."

Marie stepped forward, her fingers tapping the secondary control panel. Her voice echoed across the chamber, gentle but clear, resonating off the metallic walls. "Your abilities are tied to your emotions. Your heart. Think of when we summoned you, when we called you to New Earth. Your past was forgotten. Your new life began here. Not knowing who, or what you are, led you to this moment."

Adam stiffened, heat prickling under his skin. Not knowing who you are. Not knowing what you are. The words struck deeper than he wanted to admit, scraping across the hollow places he'd tried to ignore. He wasn't just some blank slate dropped into this world. He had a life once. A real one. And now they wanted him to pretend none of it mattered. Heat soared in his chest. His hands curled into fists before he forced them to relax, the anger burning low and steady. Fine. If that's what it took to unlock whatever they were looking for he'd find a way.

For a beat, the words hung heavy in the air, sharper than anything else she could have said. Ronan turned his head slightly toward Marie, studying her with a brief, unreadable look, a silent confirmation that he understood, and agreed. No more coddling. No more hesitation. They had to find their strength now, or not at all. A sharp hiss broke the heavy silence as a small hatch opened near Eric's platform. From it, a narrow pedestal ascended smoothly into view, bearing a simple stone vase balanced at its top. The vase looked almost ceremonial, its surface rough and unadorned, like something unearthed from a forgotten altar. Adam's gaze flicked to it instinctively, the pressure shrinking in his chest, whatever came next, it wasn't meant to be easy.

Eric squared his shoulders and closed his eyes, inhaling sharply. When he exhaled, a swirling ribbon of water poured from his palms, fast, almost violent, snapping around his wrist like a noose. The coil pulled tighter than he intended, yanking his arm downward with a strength that wasn't entirely his. Eric jerked against it, muscles straining, the cold bite of the water bleeding into his skin. A raw, broken grunt escaped him, half pain, half fury, as he fought to keep from collapsing under the force. For a moment, it felt like the current was using him rather than the other way around. His breath caught, panic flashing in his chest, before sheer will wrestled the magic into submission. Gradually, the water slackened, sliding into a smoother curl as he forced it back under control.

Eric's eyes snapped open, and with a growl low in his throat, he hurled the water toward the vase. The stream lashed out like a whip, slamming into the stone with brutal force. A crack split the air, sharp and final, as the vase exploded into shards across the platform. Eric staggered a step back, chest heaving, the raw sting of effort burning through his muscles. For a breathless second, he just stood there, hands shaking, heart hammering, staring at the destruction he had made.

"Excellent," the Aegis Unit announced.

The word rang hollow against the heavy silence. Adam gave a half-smirk, tilting his head. "I thought you weren't into this superhero bullshit old man," he said, voice low but teasing. Eric didn't answer. Just rolled his shoulders back and stared at the shattered vase like it had personally offended him.

Ronan nodded.

"Next up, Katherine Greenfield."

Katherine gave Adam a look; a sharp, almost desperate beneath her calm exterior. He caught her eye and answered with a steady nod, masking the knot forming in his chest. Jaw tight, Katherine stepped forward and planted her feet wide apart, every movement stiff with barely restrained tension. For a heartbeat, Adam thought she might crack under the pressure, but then she set her shoulders, stubborn as ever, daring whatever came next to break her. The room shuddered beneath their feet, low at first, then stronger, enough that Adam instinctively braced against the platform's edge. Out of the corner of his eye, he saw Eric shift, widening his stance like he was ready to catch something. Rose clutched the side rail of her platform. Even Marie, high above in the booth, leaned forward with a hand braced against the console.

Loose stones skittered across the polished floor, drawn toward Katherine like filings to a magnet. Her eyes had gone stark white, the glow spilling into the charged air around her. "Guys?" she gasped, her voice cracking under the weight of it all. Her outstretched arms stiffened, fingers curling upward as if cradling an invisible sphere, but it wasn't smooth or shining.

It was coarse, jagged, born from the debris clawing its way across all corners of the floor toward her. Muscles locked against a pressure no one else could see, the chamber groaning faintly under the gathering force. From every corner of the chamber, dirt, stones, and broken fragments launched toward her, coiling and spiraling like a storm gathering around its center, around her. Whatever this was, it wasn't Katherine commanding the Earth. It was the Earth reaching for Katherine. The dirt-molded sphere trembled violently in her grasp. It was too large, too raw to fully control, and with a sharp crack, Katherine's steady collapsed, and it hit the floor. The debris exploded outward across the polished surface, scattering into a wide, messy ring. She staggered back, clutching her chest, her whole frame trembling from the strain.

Adam's pulse hammered in his ears, the raw charge of the power still clinging to the air like smoke after a fire. For a moment, no one moved.

No one spoke. Even Ronan, from the glass booth above, leaned forward slightly, studying her with a mix of interest and concern. Then the Aegis Unit's voice cut through the heavy silence, calm, crisp, and almost jarringly polite:

"Superb."

"Please step forward, Adam Greenfield."

Adam wiped his palms on his pants. His heart was hammering against his ribs, but he forced himself forward, stepping onto the platform. Marie triggered a new hatch. A fragile glass orb lifted into view, small, delicate, almost taunting in its simplicity. He flexed his fingers once, twice, trying to ground himself. He could feel the currents of air rushing through the vaulted space, cool and restless. He pulled at them, slowly at first, shaping the currents between his palms. A shimmering bubble of compressed air began to form, quivering, spinning faster and faster until the ball itself blurred from sight. The pressure mounted, tugging at the edges of his control. The air around him thickened, then whipped into a swirling gale. His boots scraped against the platform as he struggled to hold steady.

He didn't realize at first—

—but his body was rising.

An inch.

Another.

The invisible forces he pulled at were lifting him, buoying him upward, as if the very air had decided to carry him. *I'm floating. I'm really floating.* Then a jolt of fear stabbed through him like a blade through his heart. His mind racing through thoughts: *The man's face. A pool of blood. Pieces of glass. Limbs contorted. The corpse. Death.* Eric's voice, distant and ragged: *"Adam, MOVE!"* Adam's breath hitched, his pulse slamming into overdrive.

NOT HERE! NOT NOW!

The air bubble trembled. Cracks spiderwebbed through the current. Then the invisible force collapsed in on itself. Adam crashed back down onto the platform, landing hard on his side, pain jolting through his ribs and shoulder. The impact blasted a shockwave across the floor, rattling the platforms and scattering loose debris like dead leaves. From the corner of his eye, Adam caught a glimpse of Ronan and Marie behind the glass—

Ronan's face unreadable. Marie's mouth pressed too tight. No words. No sympathy. Just the heavy, crushing weight of their silence. For a second, everything was still, just Adam's labored breathing, the sharp ring of failure in his ears. He pushed himself up onto his elbows, heart pounding, not just from the fall, but from the glimpse of what he couldn't outrun. Above, in the glass booth, Ronan leaned forward slightly, exchanging a brief, unreadable glance with Marie. The Aegis Unit's voice broke through the tense silence, calm and clinical: "Excellent."

Adam tensed as Rose stepped forward, her movements stiff, almost reluctant. She climbed onto the platform and took a long, trembling breath, then another. From the booth above, Marie's voice crackled through the intercom:

"Just remember it's all about control."

Rose squeezed her eyes shut.

Control. Got it.

She inhaled deeply, willing her body to still, but the heat started anyway. It slithered along her spine, coiling under her ribs like a living thing desperate to be freed. *Oh no, not again.*

She clenched her teeth, trying to suppress it, but the fire didn't listen. With a violent snap, the heat exploded outward. Flames erupted from her skin in a deafening roar, swallowing her in a wall of blinding gold. The blast knocked her off balance, driving her to one knee. The fire raged higher and more violent, tearing at the air around her. Adam flinched backward instinctively, feeling the heat slam into him like a solid punch. Beside him, Katherine stumbled against the platform rail. Eric took a desperate half-step forward, hand reaching out. "Shouldn't we help her?!" He shouted toward Ronan.

"No! Wait,"

Ronan barked back through the intercom.

Marie's voice cut sharply through the crackling flames: "Can she reach five thousand Kelvin?"

Eric swore under his breath, panic raw in his voice. "Are you insane?! She needs help!"

Without warning, Marie slammed her hand on a red button, another hatch slid open near Rose's platform, three stone targets rising into view, perched on slender pedestals. Inside the inferno, Rose, fully fledged in flames, staggered upright. Her hands shaking, her eyes burning molten red. *I have to do this. Try to control it.*

Through the blaze in her eyes, she saw Eric's hand reaching, pleading, but she shook her head minutely, gritting her teeth against the fire threatening to devour her from the inside out. The flames fought her even now, writhing against her grip, but she forced them to heel. Calm around her body. A fireball coalesced in her palm, unstable, quivering, but real. Sucking in a deep breath, Rose aimed at the first target and fired. The pedestal exploded in a blast of stone and flame. She twisted, wobbling, her knees nearly buckling, but she clenched through the tremors, summoned another fireball from her palm and fired. The second pedestal shattered with a satisfying crack. The third, her vision blurred at the edges.

The world leaning in around her. But she would not fall. She hurled the last fireball and the final target disintegrated in a brilliant shower of sparks. The fire clung to her stubbornly, flames crackling along her skin, but strand by stubborn strand, she dragged it inward, forcing it back under her will. *Easy now. Attagirl.* When the flames finally died, Rose was left panting, swaying, her body smoke-streaked, trembling, but upright. The Aegis Unit's voice broke the stunned silence: "Superb."

Eric bolted toward her, catching her just as her knees gave way. "You, okay?" he asked, voice low with fear.

Rose nodded, leaning heavily into him for a breath before forcing herself upright, still trembling, but standing. "Yeah, I'm okay," she softly muttered. Not strong yet but getting there.

From the platform, Adam watched her stagger, watched Eric catch her, watched her push herself upright like it cost her everything. The fire was gone. The targets were gone. But the way Rose stood there, still fighting, still trying to hold herself together somehow hit harder than the explosion itself. Adam's heart stiffened, eyes boiling with grief this time. The words he didn't say burned hotter than the flames ever had. He finally thought it and without knowing how much it terrified him, he knew very much, it was true.

This world wasn't just going to test them.

It was going to tear them apart.

Chapter XV:
What If We Die Here?

The silence that followed the trials wasn't peace, it was the silence of aftermath, of wounds that hadn't stopped bleeding. The training chamber gleamed like nothing had happened, but Adam still smelled the scorched air, still felt the phantom bruises crawling beneath his skin. Their bodies had survived. Their spirits hadn't. And somewhere deep inside, Adam knew: This world wasn't just testing them. It was preparing to break them. Up in the booth, Ronan allowed a faint, satisfied nod. Marie didn't smile, but her posture eased slightly. Ronan leaned over the intercom again, his voice cool and precise: "Now, let's take it to the next round."

The training floor rumbled again, deeper this time. Like something ancient waking beneath their feet. Metal gears groaned beneath the surface, and the ground began to shift. Massive stone tiles split open, then rotated downward like inverted puzzle pieces. In their place emerged a full-scale combat arena, vaulted, spacious, and menacing. Along the walls, tall glass panels slid open to reveal racks of weapons: swords gleaming with deadly precision, crossbows strung taut, spiked axes, curved daggers, and relics that looked like they belonged in a war museum, not a training vault. Ronan's voice carried again, low and firm. "Choose your weapon."

Below the observation deck, the group hesitated only briefly. Then, with a hydraulic hiss, the booth doors opened. Marie descended the eastern steps, her presence as sharp as ever, joining Katherine and Eric at the far end of the arena. Ronan moved in the opposite direction, his boots echoing across the stone as he approached Adam and Rose. No longer voices behind glass, their mentors were now close enough to study their posture, their breath, their fear. The test wasn't over. It had just become personal.

Adam's gaze flicked across the room, noting the subtle shift in energy. Marie moved to stand beside Katherine and Eric near the opposite end of the arena. Her presence was cool and commanding, very watchful in a way that felt almost maternal. Meanwhile, Ronan remained near Adam and Rose, eyes sharp with a silent intensity. There was no mistaking the intent now. They were being tested… purposefully.

Rose moved first, stepping toward the weapon vaults with unshaken focus. Her fingers curled around a pair of Kali sticks, lightweight, deadly, and fast. Adam followed, scanning the arsenal before settling on a katana with a long, blackened blade and a grip wrapped in worn leather. It wasn't the flashiest weapon, but it felt balanced. Like something that had survived the same war he had. On the opposite end of the chamber, Eric unsheathed a broadsword with a clean whistle of steel. Katherine retrieved a reinforced combat staff, testing its weight with a quick spin.

The four of them converged near the center of the arena, two against two, blades and breath steady beneath the weight of unspoken tension. Brothers faced brothers. Sisters faced sisters. Whatever bond they shared outside this moment dissolved beneath the hum of steel and the crackle of expectation. There were no alliances now. Only instincts, muscle memory, and the hunger to prove they belonged here. Adam squared off with Eric, both gripping their weapons like extensions of their will. Rose matched eyes with Katherine, neither blinking, neither backing down. Adam lifted his blade, grin flickering with a wink. "Do they make good weapons… or toys?"

Ronan, standing just behind him, replied in a quiet voice, measured, but with an edge. "That depends on how seriously you take your opponent."

Across the way, Marie crossed her arms and addressed her own two. "Don't think. Feel. The moment you hesitate, you lose."

The air thickened with anticipation, stretched taut like the moment before a storm breaks. Eric's knuckles flexed around his grip, the muscles in his jaw locking with focused aggression. Katherine's stance lowered, precise and poised, her eyes scanning for the slightest weakness. Rose didn't blink, didn't even breathe, her entire frame coiled like a flame about to ignite. Adam's grip tightened, and his breath slowed into something controlled, sharpened, ready. And then…

Eric moved.

Ronan said coolly.

"Remember, your enemy is your friend."

Ronan let the words settle. "They're not here to kill you. They're here to teach you how not to get killed."

Eric didn't respond with words. He just rolled his eyes and lunged. The clash of steel rang through the chamber, sharp and sudden. Adam caught the first blow with the flat of his blade, but Eric twisted fast, striking him across the cheek. Pain flashed white, and Adam dropped to one knee. Across the arena, Katherine charged hard. Rose was ready, she pivoted low, spinning into a sharp roundhouse aimed at Katherine's knees. But Katherine jumped, just in time, and as she landed, she whipped her body into a counterstrike, her boot slamming into Rose's chest. The impact cracked through the room.

Rose flew backward, hitting the mat with a breathless thud. From the sideline, Marie didn't flinch. But as Katherine straightened, pride flickering behind her eyes. Marie spoke cold and clear: "Don't gloat. Help her up," she said. "One day she'll be the one pulling you off the ground."

Katherine hesitated… then stepped forward and extended a hand. As she pulled Rose to her feet, something about her posture shifted, just slightly. A renewed strength in her shoulders.

A flicker of uncertainty in her eyes. "Are you alright?" Katherine asked, almost too quickly.

Rose nodded, her breath still catching. "Never better," she said, but there was something in her voice, something deeper. Not wounded. Not angry. She sounded… unbreakable. Adam watched them closely, the flicker between them stirring something uncertain in his chest. But then, he felt it. That weight again. A stare. Ronan stood across the room, arms folded near the opposite wall, silent as ever. Yet Adam could feel his eyes on him. Heavy. Measuring. Like a blade pressed against the back of his thoughts.

Adam turned, and that's when it hit. A surge of water exploded from Eric's outstretched palm, fast and forceful. Adam didn't think. His hands shot up in reflex. The air around him shivered. Bent. Then snapped outward. Wind burst from his palms in a tight spiral, crashing against the water like a living shield. The spray ricocheted off the barrier and rained down across the chamber, soaking everyone in its path. Silence. Then a burst of laughter filled the room.

Eric stepped back, blinking water from his lashes. "Okay," he said, chuckling. "That was new."

Adam exhaled slowly, shaking the wind from his fingers like a spark he'd almost let catch fire. "Guess I'm finally listening to you."

"You better," Eric muttered, smirking. "If we're gonna survive out there."

Adam smirked back. "You mean save the world," he said, "in style." They all stood in silence for a beat, dripping, breathless, changed. The steam rising from their skin clung to the air like ghosts of who they'd been before the trial. No one spoke. There was nothing left to prove, only the quiet understanding that something inside them had shifted, and there was no going back.

Adam's blade hung at his side. Water dripped from his sleeves as he flexed his fingers again. The katana felt lighter now, or maybe he was stronger. Something in his chest stirred, then flickered to his fingers, not power exactly, but purpose. A rhythm. Something activated. Across the room, Rose sat up, rolled her shoulders, and gave Katherine a knowing glance. Not wounded, more awakened. Whatever was changing inside them… had already begun. Girlfriends who just knew each other without saying a word. They didn't have to speak. Marie's eyes flicked toward

Ronan. He gave a slight nod. The trial was over. But the war was coming.

Soft slumbers fell quietly over the fortress, whispering through the night, the air still damp from the earlier trial. Somewhere in the distance, the wind brushed against stone and the garden. Adam moved through the dim corridors, footsteps soft on the cold floor, until he reached her door. He knocked once. A moment passed, then the door creaked open. Katherine didn't say anything at first. She just turned and walked back toward her bed, sitting down like the weight of the day had finally caught up to her. "What's up?" she asked over her shoulder, her voice low, almost hollow. Adam stepped inside, closing the door behind him. He could tell something was on Katherine's mind. He joined her on the edge of her bed, shoulders brushing each other with a playful tap. "How are you feeling?" he asked.

Katherine didn't answer. She stared ahead, blinking slow, like her thoughts were somewhere far off. Adam nudged her gently again. "Come on," he said. "There's something bothering you. I can tell."

She tried to smile, but it twisted halfway through, melting into a frown she tried hard to forget. "I miss Mom and Dad."

Adam's heart fluttered for a moment. The thought of his parents felt like a distant memory. It hadn't hit him yet. "I know. Me too."

She hesitated, then glanced away, her voice barely above a whisper. "It was weird… I had a nightmare earlier. In the carriage."

Adam looked at her.

"What kind of nightmare?"

"You were in it," she said after a beat. "But you were acting strange."

He blinked. "Strange how?"

Katherine shook her head.

"Never mind." A pause. "Do you ever think we're gonna see them again?"

"I hope so," he said quietly.

There was another pause. Longer this time. No words needed to be said. Even the wind outside seemed to still, like the whole world was waiting for someone to speak. Then her voice broke through the silence, barely above a whisper.

"What happens if we die here?"

Adam didn't speak right away. His gaze drifted to the wall across the room, then past it, to some invisible point in the future he couldn't see. *Katherine has a point. What if we die out here?* For a moment, it felt like everything stopped. The question swallowed him whole. He saw flashes of cold, unlit corridors. The sound of screams swallowed by smoke. Himself, alone, bleeding, calling for help that never came. It frightened him. And even worse, he wasn't sure they'd survive this. But he smiled anyway, for her. Because sometimes pretending was the only thing holding the fear back. "We won't," he said. "Let's make sure that doesn't happen, okay?"

She blinked looking to Adam.

"You promise?"

"Yes," he said looking down at her.

She didn't reply, but when he wrapped his arms around her, she leaned into it. Her forehead rested lightly against his chest, and for a moment, neither of them had to carry the weight alone. The silence returned, but this time, it felt like something safe. Just quiet enough to hold them both steady, like the world had paused to give them a moment of peace.

The quiet stretched between them and outside, the wind stirred again, soft and steady, brushing against the windows like a whisper. It moved through the room in faint drafts, not cold, but just enough to remind them they weren't alone. Katherine's voice broke through the stillness. "Do you honestly think we're ever going to see Mom and Dad again?"

Adam exhaled, slower this time. "I sure hope so," he said, and this time the smile reached his eyes. "If they saw us today… they'd be really proud."

Steam curled thick through the bathroom, clinging to the mirrors and tiles like mist after a storm. Eric stood beneath the stream, naked, the water pouring hard over his head, craving down the defined lines of his body. His hands rested against the wall, head bowed, eyes closed. Just soaking in the abyss. Letting the boiling hot water press against his skin. He wasn't thinking at least, not in full sentences. Just fragments. Feelings. Images. Everything they'd been through was catching up to him, pounding into his skin harder than the water ever could. He finally reached for the knob, turned it slowly until the shower hissed into silence. The room exhaled with him.

Eric grabbed a towel from the counter, wrapped it around his waist, and stepped out of the glass enclosure. He moved in silence, wiping condensation from the mirror with the side of his hand. The chill in the air hit instantly, a sharp contrast to the heat he'd just left behind, but he barely noticed. He was still inside his head. His reflection stared back, hollow-eyed, damp hair clinging to his forehead, a war still echoing behind his gaze. Then he saw it. Just beneath the curve of his jaw, above the collarbone… something new. A mark, faint but distinct, swirled like water caught in motion. It shimmered slightly, as if it had been waiting beneath the surface of his skin all along. Not carved. Not tattooed. Just… there. His fingers brushed over it. It was warm, barely, but pulsing, like a second heartbeat. He didn't flinch. Didn't speak. Just stared at it for a long moment, the silence wrapping tighter around him. Whatever this was, it wasn't going away.

The hallway was dim, lit only by the low flicker of ancient sconces that lined the stone walls. The castle had gone quiet, its echoes softened by nightfall. In his room, he let the towel fall from his hips and tossed it onto the nearby chair, dragging another smaller towel across his shoulders and neck to wipe away the lingering steam. He froze mid-step. Someone was standing in the doorway. He turned and saw her. His beautiful girlfriend who he'd love so deeply.

Rose didn't speak. She didn't need to. The light from the corridor behind her kissed the edges of her figure, but her focus was on him. On the man in front of her, his silhouette outlined by steam, skin still damp, muscles firm with restraint. There was a moment, brief but full, where she couldn't look away. She'd known him for years. Through war. Through distance. Through silence. But standing there like this… it felt different. Like something between them had already begun.

He took a step toward her.

"Hey," Eric said, barely above a breath.

"Hi," she replied, just as softly.

She stepped forward. So did he. Neither rushed. But neither hesitated. They met in the center of the room, chest to chest, breath to breath. Eric's hand found her arm, his touch slow and in awe as his fingers slid along her skin. Their eyes locked, and the space between them disappeared. "I can control it now," Rose whispered.

Eric's thumb paused in its motion. "I don't want to hurt you."

"You won't."

She wasn't sure if she was lying. But standing this close, feeling his warmth, his body, his breath, she didn't want to retreat. His presence steadied her and set her on fire in the same breath. This was the boy she trusted. The man she wanted. And even if it was dangerous, she needed to feel him choose her. Just this one time…

Their lips met before either of them could think twice. It wasn't soft, it was hunger finally uncaged. Their kiss was molten, threaded with all the things they hadn't said and the danger they both carried. Eric guided her toward the bed, hands never leaving her body. She fell back onto the bed, and he followed, his weight settling above hers like a shield. The heat built fast, too fast. Rose wraps her legs around Eric, her hands slid up his back, gripping tighter. She could feel it building inside her, the heat, the pressure, something that wasn't entirely hers anymore. But she didn't stop. Not yet. She wanted to believe she could hold it. Eric's mouth traced her collarbone before finding her neck, his breath danced, leaving heat wherever it touched. He wasn't rushing. He was savoring every moment. The passion that lingered between them all these weeks finally cracked open and still, they wanted more.

As she held him close, Rose opened her eyes. And they were red. Not flushed. Not passion-warmed. Flaming red. Eric's hand had just caressed her thigh when it hit him. A surge of heat, not warmth, but inferno and pain, traveled from her mouth into his. It burned through him precisely, piercing his organs, like consuming fire. His body seized. His lips parted, about to speak, but then he froze. Red flushed across his face. His chest convulsed. His muscles tensed. The heat hit him like a shockwave, searing from her mouth into his, his chest, his bones. He gasped, once, hard, then reeled back, stumbling off the bed and hitting the floor with a thud. "I'm… I'm sorry!" Rose gasped, eyes wide, hands trembling.

He sat upright, chest rising and falling in uneven bursts as he clutched at his ribs. He didn't speak. He's not sure if Rose scorched his vocal cords or not. The burn had already begun to fade, but the memory of it clung to his skin. It wasn't just pain; it was something deeper and intimate. Like he'd been struck by lightning and kissed by fire in the same breath, and his body hadn't decided which to recover from first. The spark or the kiss of death. He closed his eyes, inhaled sharply… and exhaled.

"It's okay," he said.

And somehow, he meant it.

A beat passed.

Then something shifted.

The pain in his chest dulled, then suddenly disappeared altogether. The raw sting in his throat faded into warmth. He looked down at his hands, half expecting to see blisters… but there were none. His skin was smooth. Whole. Unmarked. He blinked once, then again. He couldn't believe his eyes. The ache had vanished as if the fire had never touched him. Whatever was inside of him now, it wasn't just power. It was transformation.

Something greater.

Something thriving.

Looking for attention.

And it was no longer asking permission.

Chapter XVI:
The Reaping

The air was colder than it had any right to be. Adam stood near the edge of the war table, fingers drumming lightly against the polished stone surface. He wasn't thinking about battle formations or strategy, or at least, not yet. His mind was still with Katherine. With her voice in the dark. *"What if we die here?"* The words had stuck to him like residue. Not fear. Just… weight. The kind of weight you didn't speak aloud because it already lived in your bones. The wind howled against the castle walls, carrying with it the ghost of something coming. Inside, the others began to arrive. Eric walked in first, quiet as ever. His expression unreadable, but Adam saw it, the subtle stiffness in his shoulders, eyes zoomed to the floor. Whatever had happened between him and Rose, it had left a mark.

Marie came next. She took her place on the opposite side of the table, her eyes sweeping across the room like a general inspecting soldiers, calculating and cold. But Adam noticed the way her fingers tapped twice against her hip before she settled. She was anxious. Even she knew what they were about to do wasn't just risky, it was reckless. Rose entered a few beats later. She didn't look at Eric. She didn't look at anyone. Her jaw was tight, her eyes sharper than usual. But her hands trembled, just once, before she clasped them behind her back. Then came Katherine, she walked in like she had something to prove. She met Adam's eyes across the table and didn't look away. *Oh, she's definitely thinking about it. He could see it in her eyes. The same thought that kept him up at nights: What if we die here?*

Ronan was already there, leaning against the far wall, arms folded across his chest. His expression was also unreadable, but his eyes, something about his eyes… missed nothing. He watched them gather in silence, like pieces on a board he'd arranged once before, in a war he still carried in his bones. The weight of that history sat heavy in the room, though no one dared speak of it. "Everyone's here," he said, pushing off the wall. "Good."

He stepped toward the war table and unfurled a faded map across its surface. Time had worn the parchment thin, the ink smeared in places like old blood. But the red markings remained, sharp, deliberate, and glaring like warnings carved by war itself.

Marie's voice cut through the stillness. "This is not a test. This is real life."

Adam swallowed hard, the weight of it capturing in his heart. *Life. They forget what life once was.* So, this was it, the line between training and war, between wondering and knowing. No more questions. No more delays. Just the reaping… and whatever waited for them on the other side.

Ronan's fingers brushed one of the red markings, then he turned and flipped a dial on the embedded console. A soft hum filled the room. The surface beneath the map vibrated, and the old parchment dissolved into light. The table flickered to life. A holographic map shimmered upward, New Earth, outlined in bright emerald, its regions pulsing in shifting hues. The same red marks now hovered like scars above the terrain.

Adam squinted at the display, arms folded tightly across his chest. He wasn't sure what he was supposed to see, just shifting colors, lines, and blinking zones that meant more to Ronan than to him. But something in the room had changed. The others stood straighter now, their bodies pulled firm with attention, eyes locked forward.

Ronan swept his hand through the projection, flipping through digital layers like the pages of a memory. With a sharp motion, he zoomed in on a familiar structure; fractured and ruined. *The Sacrificial Chamber.* Adam's gut tightened. "Wait..." he said. "You want us to go back there?"

Marie didn't flinch. "Our best chance is returning to trace any residual energy that could lead us to Zion," she said. "The M'ra Sphere's pulse is stronger now... If we're going to act, it has to be now."

Adam's lips parted, a protest already forming, uncertainty pressing against his ribs. *How come they don't know where Zion is. They don't know if we can trust them.* He didn't like the sound of this plan, didn't like how close it brought them to the place that had nearly killed them. But before he could speak, Ronan cut in. "Leading us to him brings us closer to The M'ra Sphere," he said. Like it was simple. Like it was obvious.

Eric scoffed, stepping forward. "Hold on. Aren't we storming your old place? You forget where you live? Better yet, where he lives."

Katherine let out a sharp breath, smirking, holding a laugh in. Marie turned, sharply, eyes leveled. "That castle?" she repeated, voice cutting like ice. "That was never mine. Zion built that twisted monument from blood and ruin. My home. My castle. My legacy still stands. Sealed since his reign began." She took a step closer. "What he's done to this planet is inexcusable."

Eric started to speak again.

"And before you continue, for orcas, we tried searching for Zion's new fortress, but it is buried deep beyond somewhere in the forbidden storms. A land we hadn't stepped foot on. That's why you are here. So, you ought to keep your mouth shut," she said flatly. "About things you don't understand."

Ronan smirked, clearly amused by the tension, but said nothing. Adam glanced between them, catching the faint twitch in Eric's jaw.

Good, Adam thought. *At least someone shut him up.* But something in Marie's voice caught at

Adam. Not just confidence. Certainty. She spoke like she knew the Sphere was close. *But how?* He hadn't felt anything. But maybe she had. Maybe she was always tied to this place in a way none of them understood. Still, the idea sat heavy in his chest. If the M'ra Sphere's pulse really was growing stronger… did that mean it was destabilizing? Being twisted? And if it was reacting to Zion, was it calling out? Or crying for help?

Around the room, Adam saw it. The shift that happened when fear didn't speak but settled into the body. Rose stiffened slightly, her jaw clenched in defiance rather than doubt. Katherine's arms crossed tight over her chest as she threw a glance sideways at Marie, searching for something unspoken. Eric didn't move at all, but the corner of his mouth twitched, barely, and in that stillness, Adam felt it: they were all bracing for something they couldn't name.

Concern hung in the air like fog, thick, quiet, and clinging to every breath. No one said anything, but their silence spoke louder than panic ever could. It was the kind of stillness that came before something broke. The kind that told Adam they all felt it… even if no one dared name it.

"You should all be alert at all times," Ronan added, his voice colder now. "We've done readings. There's still a presence in that place. Something spirit-like. It calls itself Haiti."

Eric scoffed under his breath.

"Yeah, we met him."

Katherine rolled her eyes. "This should be fun," she muttered, too low for Ronan to catch, but Adam heard it. He didn't blame her. He lingered for a moment longer; eyes locked on the glowing image of the broken chamber. The last time they were there, something inside him had cracked. This time... something else was waiting to break. He turned and followed the others out.

Marie didn't wait for questions. She moved quickly down a narrow corridor, her cloak sweeping behind her like a shadow with purpose. The others followed in silence, the weight of what they'd just agreed to pressing down on every step. The hallway widened at the end, opening into a cold chamber Adam hadn't seen before: circular, with tall obsidian pillars surrounding a smooth platform etched in faint runes. The space was quiet, part armory, part altar. Just a quiet reverence, as if this place remembered power.

Ronan stepped forward, silent, and gestured to the obsidian table in the center where four garments lay folded with care. These weren't medieval tunics or flashy suits. They were something else entirely, crafted for purpose, not presentation. Adam stood still as the others moved around him. His set was matte black, form-fitting but breathable, with a flexible structure that responded to motion and temperature. The threads were interwoven with air-reactive fibers that seemed to hum faintly in the silence, shifting just enough to make him feel the space around him. Nothing extravagant. No symbols. Just function, light and fast, like the element inside him.

Adam's fingers hovered just above the fabric. It was cold with a warm ease. A subtle breeze. It felt… alive. Like it had been waiting for him. He drew in a breath and laid his palm flat across the material. A hum vibrated under his skin, barely there, but real. The threads reacted to his touch, shifting subtly with the air around him, like wind recognizing its own. His suit didn't just fit, it knew him.

This wasn't just protection. It wasn't even power. It was a reflection. Of the boy who stepped into this world broken… and the man walking out transformed. He wasn't ready. But the world wasn't waiting. Adam gracefully pulled the suit on without a fight.

Beside him, Rose slipped into her gear: sleek, streamlined, and forged with flame-resistant weave. A faint shimmer pulsed beneath the surface only when she moved, as if the suit knew what she carried. It absorbed the heat rather than reflected it. Katherine's suit was more robust, stitched in deep brown-black, with reinforced joints and plated seams designed for impact. The material bent with her, absorbing tension without giving. Silent strength it mirrored.

And Eric, calm, unspoken, secured his own gear: fluid layers of tactical fabric treated to resist water. It gleamed softly in the light, edges beveled like wave crests. Perfect for stealth. For speed. Adam's hands lay on his chest for a beat longer. The uniform clung at first, then settled, syncing with the rhythm of his breath. A hum beneath his ribs. Not magic. Not power. Just readiness. Marie watched from the edge, silent as ever. She had enchanted them, woven the suits with both elemental significance and functionality. No capes. No apexes. Just tools for what lay ahead. Adam exhaled. *So, this is what it feels like to be one of them.* The pressure in the air was changing again. This was it. The last calm before the storm. *They're not even sure how to use this power.*

The air here felt… different. Denser. Like the walls were watching. Marie stepped onto the platform and turned to face them. "Stand close," she said.

Adam hesitated, just for a second, caught between instinct and uncertainty. But something in Marie's voice pulled at him, not with authority, but with quiet certainty. It wasn't a command. It was something that made it feel like stepping forward wasn't obedience… it was trust. Katherine stepped beside him. Eric and Rose flanked the edges. None of them spoke. How could they? When they're going back to a place that once tried to kill them.

Marie raised one hand to the air, her other resting against her chest. Her fingers moved, not quite a gesture, not quite a spell, but something in between. Her lips parted in a whisper. No English. No tongue Adam recognized. It was *Shikarian*— ancient and musical, shaped more by breath than sound. And yet, he felt it. In the back of his skull. In the center of his chest. The air shimmered with ancient magic. A spiral of sapphire light curled around Marie's hand, starting at her fingertips, then lashing out to theirs. It wound inward like a tightening vortex. It wasn't a beam. It was a grip. A force wrapping through their bones, sight, and breath. And just as Adam exhaled…

They vanished.

In a split second, they had arrived unraveling from the vortex. Adam stumbled, the sudden shift from castle to wilderness knocking the breath out of him. It was his first time. His stomach turned, hard, like scrambled eggs. Not from fear, but from the way his insides felt… untethered. Like someone had taken a scoop of ice cream and dumped it in water inside him during the warp. Dissolving away. It hadn't quite come back together yet. *I feel like my stomach is going to fall out.* His boots sank into soft moss, and he blinked against the pale light filtering through the warped canopy above. The air tasted wrong, damp, metallic, almost sour. Up ahead, the Sacrificial Chamber loomed: half-crumbled and choked in vines, as if the forest itself had tried to forget it ever existed. But something was different.

The land, once vibrant and strange, now looked wounded. Veins of black ooze spiderwebbed across the roots and stones, leaking from the chamber and the forest floor like a disease clinging to the sick. Some puddles of it remained. It clung to trees, soaked into the soil, coiling like a parasite around the Sacrificial Chamber. Adam stared at it, throat dry. *Was this The M'ra Sphere's doing?* The rot… the decay… *Was this what Marie meant when she said New Earth was dying?* For the first time, he didn't just believe her. He felt it, like the world itself was crying out beneath their feet.

It hadn't always been this way. Adam remembered the first time he saw New Earth, icy cold, but lush terrains under golden sun, wildflowers dancing in the wind, skies so clear they looked painted. Even the air had felt alive then, pulsing with quiet magic. Now, that same wind carried the stench of rot. Corrosion. The trees were quiet. Hollow. The sunlight, dimmed. The plants didn't speak. It was like someone had drained the color from the world and left only shadows behind.

Beside him, Marie straightened her spine, her boots sinking slightly into the corrupted soil. The faint glow in her hand flickered, brighter for a moment, then dimmer, as if even her magic sensed the sickness in the ground. Her eyes swept the ground like a commander surveying a battlefield, but something in her posture had shifted, more rigid, more alert. The land wasn't just altered. It was warning them. And Marie, more than anyone, seemed to understand what that meant.

Adam stepped forward, the silence wrapping around him like a warning. Behind him, Eric's jaw was tight, his eyes sweeping the forest as if searching for something just out of reach. Rose crossed her arms, rubbing one shoulder, her gaze flicking toward the trees, not curious, but cautious. Even Katherine, usually unshaken, hesitated before stepping ahead, her fingers grazing the hilt of her dagger like she needed the feel of it. None of them spoke. And neither did the forest. Even the wind seemed to hold its breath, as if the land itself was waiting for something to go wrong.

"I'll look over here," Rose said, her eyes drawn to the treeline.

Marie didn't argue. She simply gave a short nod. Adam watched Rose drift toward the trees, her movements slow and deliberate, like she was listening to something the rest of them couldn't hear. Leaves rustled faintly above her, though no wind stirred, just the breath of something ancient watching them from the shadows. Adam's pulse quickened. It wasn't fear exactly, but a tension that pressed against his skin, that crawled into his lungs. The forest didn't feel empty. It felt anxious. Like the land itself was holding its breath for someone or something...

Eric, Katherine, and Adam approached the ruins, their steps slowing as the weight of the place pressed down on them. The stones were cold beneath their boots, damp with age and memory, as if they'd once soaked up blood and never quite dried. Cracks split across the ground like veins, fractured lines that seemed to pulse with something ancient, something watching. Marie stepped toward a patch of disturbed earth, and froze, her breath catching in her throat before she crouched, drawn to something the rest of them hadn't seen yet.

A pile of white powder lay there, too clean, too deliberate to be natural. Its shape was strange, almost sculpted, like something had formed it with intention. Marie crouched slowly, her breath catching as the wind shifted. And then the outline sharpened, cheekbones, a brow, a grin carved from ash. A face. Half-buried in the dirt. Sculpted from powder. Grinning. Marie fixated on the image. Her stomach turned. It wasn't just a face. It was his. She knew it the way a nightmare isn't over, just waiting, purely waiting for the right particular moment to…

"Haiti," she whispered.

The name hit the air like a curse. And the silence twisted tighter. Back in the forest, the moss damp beneath his boots. The three of them moved slowly, Adam's eyes scanning the ground near the edge of the ruined chamber. Broken stones littered the area, splintered, cold, and lifeless. There was no sign of the Sphere. Just wind curling through the trees, and a silence so deep it pressed against Adam's eardrums, as if the forest itself was holding back a secret. Then something shifted.

Air rippled in front of Eric; subtle at first, like a heatwave bending the horizon. Then it deepened, distorting the space around him as if reality itself had been tugged loose. A pressure built in the air, low and humming, just before the ghost began to take shape. A faint, like steam rising from a cold surface. Haiti. A sudden chill slipped through the trees. The air swollen, distorted like heat bending over pavement. Adam straightened just as the air in front of Eric shimmered, like a shape began to form. Faint. Ghostlike. It floated in the air before Eric, its edges flickering like a mirage. Then it leaned in, so close he could feel the cold curl of breath against his ear. "Give up now," it whispered, low and wet, "or suffer the consequences."

Eric jerked back, the gasped in his throat, echoed faintly. The voice had been low, almost warm, but laced with something foul, like rot hidden behind silk. Before he could react, the figure dissolved, vanishing into the trees with a laugh that resonated too long, too deep. It clung to the branches like smoke. Rose stepped from the woods, brushing bark from her fingers casual, but something in her posture looked guarded. The forest clung to her skin, as if it hadn't wanted to let her go. She stopped a few paces from the others, but didn't speak right away. "Any luck?" she asked.

Eric shook his head. "No."

Suddenly, the air cracked, sharp and violent, like the snap of a bone. Moments later, Adam dropped from a tree branch above, landing in a crouch with barely a sound. Dust swirled around him as he rose, eyes scanning, breath steady, but his pulse was racing. Something was wrong. He could feel it.

"Nothing up there," he said.

This is too weird. The silence. Something's off.

Katherine froze ahead of him, her posture suddenly rigid. The air shifted, thick, electric, like the sky before a lightning strike. Adam's pulse kicked. Something moved behind the trees. Then it came, grotesque, twisted shapes bursting from the brush. Dozens of Prylyn creatures, skin stretched thin over bone, eyes glowing like molten ore. "You guys!" Katherine shouted. "We have company!" The group turned, falling into instinct.

Marie shouted, "Everybody to your post!"

The five of them locked into formation, backs pressed together, eyes scanning the twisted landscape. Around them, shadows shifted, grotesque forms circling just beyond the trees, limbs twitching with unnatural intent. The forest itself felt like it was breathing with the creatures, closing in with every heartbeat. No one spoke. There was nothing to say, only the silence before the storm. Adam's chest tightened. "Come on," he said, scanning the creatures. *What are we doing?* he thought. *They're going to kill us.*

Marie's voice rang out. "Now!"

Adam surged forward, the wind rising with him, not to vanish, not to flee, but to strike. The air answered like a curved spring, snapping beneath his feet and flinging him straight toward the nearest creature. He barely registered the speed, just the rush, the blur, the target. Then came the impact: not his, but the creature's. Its arm morphed mid-motion into a jagged rod and swung hard, hammering Adam across the ribs and launching him backward like a rag doll through air. He flew, crashing backward into the stones of the chamber, he hit the ground hard. Dust swirled. *What the hell just happened?* he thought.

The creature roared, a guttural shriek that cracked through the air like splitting bone. It stood in the mouth of the chamber, blocking Adam's path, its right-hand twisting into a jagged blade. Adam's lungs burned, his limbs still sluggish from the earlier blow, until something surged inside him. The wind didn't just rise; it flooded his veins. Strength coursed through his arms like a dam breaking, veins dilating.

Adam's gaze locked onto the beast. "Shall we?" he whispered. He didn't wait for the answer. The air detonated around him. He rocketed forward, his fist colliding with the creature's jaw in a blur, one moment left, the next right, his movements bending space like a whipcrack. Before it could react, Adam flipped midair and launched both feet into its chest, hurling the beast out of the chamber in a thunderous crash.

Outside, Katherine stumbled back as a horde of Prylyn creature charged her. She lifted her hands in instinct, ready to shield herself and the earth answered. Rocks ripped from the ground like teeth from a jaw, circling her like armor. Her eyes widened. "I'm doing this," she breathed. She hurled them forward in a single, violent thrust, smashing the creatures in a crushing wave. Rose pivoted with a snarl, flames bursting from both palms. Fire spiraled out in twin lashes, scorching the incoming wave. Her pupils gleamed, heat burning hotter with each breath until her eyes blazed crimson-red. One Prylyn leapt, but Rose swept her hand and ignited it midair, the creature reduced to a fire-wreathed shriek.

Eric didn't speak. He didn't flinch. Two creatures stalked toward him, eyes burning, movements jagged. He braced himself, fists clenched, but there was no weapon in his hands. Only breath. Only instinct. The first lunged from the right, Eric ducked and drove an elbow hard into its side. But before he could recover, the second slammed a fist into his gut from the side. He staggered, then the first returned, smashing him in the face from the right. His head whipped left, just in time for the second to strike again from the opposite side. Left. Right. Left. Blow after blow landed like a rhythm meant to break him. But through the ringing in his skull, something stirred. Cold. Calm. Deep.

He staggered back, breath ragged, blood at the edge of his mouth. His muscles ached. His vision blurred. The creatures snarled, closing in. He didn't think. He just lifted one hand. And it happened. A surge of cold grew through his veins, violent, untamed, like the ocean had been hiding all along. Then a torrent of water burst from him, slamming into the creatures with enough force to lift them off their feet, hurling them skyward like broken leaves. He exhaled, barely steady. Then his knees buckled, and he collapsed to the ground, soaked and shaking, the rush of power leaving his limbs hollow.

Marie exhaled slowly, the battlefield still crackling in her blood. Across the clearing, a Prylyn creature writhed against a splintered tree stump, its body mangled, but not dead. It hissed through black bloodied teeth, one arm twitching, the other dragging uselessly at its side. Its eyes gleamed, not with strength, but spite. Marie's gaze turned to ice. She didn't move fast. She didn't need to. She stepped forward in one deliberate stride, lifted her hand. The air snapped. Invisible force looped around the creature's throat like a tightening noose. It shrieked.

Not a battle cry. Not a curse. A scream. A raw high-pitched animalistic scream. The kind you didn't hear on battlefields, because no one lived long enough to make it. Its claws scratched deep grooves into the dirt, legs kicking out, spine arching. The whine in its throat was ragged now, screaming for air. Its eyes bulged, veins straining. It tried to speak… beg maybe, but Marie only tilted her head slightly.

And then—*snap.*

The sound cracked through the trees like a gunshot, sharp and absolute. The creature's body seized violently, limbs twitching with the last sparks of life. Then it crumpled, spine folding against the stump like broken scaffolding. Black ooze pooled beneath it, slow and thick, as if even the forest wasn't ready to absorb the violence.

Damn, Adam thought. *She's not the same teacher who led us through the woods.* There was no patience left in her now. No grace. Just precision and war. Some things you just don't talk about.

Rose had veered off slightly, standing just beyond the others in a pocket of trees, half-shrouded by twisted trunks and overgrowth. Not far, but far enough. Close enough to hear them. Too far to be seen. She turned just in time to see a Prylyn creature retreating through the brush, limbs twitching in panic. Her hands ignited without hesitation, a fireball coiling in her palm like a living thing, heat crackling up her arms. She hurled it forward with precision. The flame struck the creature mid-sprint, and in an instant, it was ablaze, screaming, thrashing, then collapsing into a smoldering heap of what it used to be, as the forest swallowed its dying shrieks. Very peculiar.

Something tapped her shoulder. Twice. Not a breeze. Not Eric. Something else. It was cold. Premeditated. It curled against her skin like frost with fingers. Aching for her. She turned, slowly, feared pour into her as if her body already knew. And there he was. Haiti. Floating inches from her, death stared her in the face. Half-shadow, half-specter, his face a mask of

something older than death. She didn't have time
to scream. Didn't have time to run. She froze and
knew there was no going back.

Haiti jolted into her like a possessed
demon, no struggle, no sound, just a rush of
blackness that folded her from the inside out. Her
spine arched like it was being pulled by invisible
strings. Arms stretched to the sky. Mouth wide
open. Too wide. Frozen in time. Her jaw
unhinged in a silent gasp. She couldn't move, but
she could see everything. Her eyes flared with a
sick, yellow trace that wasn't hers. Then her body
snapped abruptly. Bones cracking. Not once. Not
twice, but three times. A violent jerk, forward.
Rearranging her bones. Then another vicious yank
sideways. A brutal pull, making her head slant
with her mouth wide open. Rose stood motionless
like a puppet. Arms tied to the sky. The tips of her
toes touch the ground like a dancer caught mid-
performance. She whined a painful shriek like a
puppy longing for their owner, but no one could
hear.

Then—*snap.*

She collapsed like glass shattering on the
floor. Face pale. Head turned to the side. Eyes
wide. Jaw unhinged. Limbs twisted. Just lifeless.

Marie turned back. "Is everyone all right?"

"Yeah," Katherine called, scanning the edges of the clearing.

Eric didn't answer. He looked around and froze. "Wait," he said. "Where's Rose?"

Adam and Katherine turned toward him, instincts flaring like a warning bell. The air had shifted, but heavier, like it was pressing inward from all sides. Adam felt it slide beneath his skin, a prickling tension that told him something had gone terribly wrong. *Where are you? Why did the air feel like it was mourning something they hadn't lost yet?*

Then, beyond the trees, just past the veil of shadow. They saw it. A ghostly carriage glided between the trees, drawn by pale, eyeless horses whose hooves never touched the earth. The wheels turned slowly in midair, creaking with a soundless rhythm that made the forest seem to hush in reverence or fear. It wasn't real.

It wasn't alive.

Inside the carriage, barely tethered to the world, was Rose. Her body shimmered like mist sculpted into form, translucent and pale, bound in crisscrossed chains that draped over her shoulders like an X. Heavier links wrapped around her waist and ankles, pinning her to the carriage floor in quiet domination. Her eyes were wide… too wide. Glassy with panic, rimmed with a shimmer of ghostly light. Her mouth moved in a desperate cry, lips trembling, jaw slack, but no sound came. Just that unbearable silence. A single tear slid down her cheek, vanishing before it ever reached her chin, like even her grief had been erased by whatever took her.

"ROSE!" Eric bolted forward.

"ROSE!" Adam echoed, racing beside him.

They tore through the trees, branches clawing at their skin, the forest itself resisting their chase. The ghostly carriage floated faster ahead, wind spiraling around it, trees bowing in its path like servants to some unseen doom. Adam and Eric, both lunging forward arms outstretched, breaths ragged. Rose reached back, mouth stretched in a silent scream that refused to close, her eyes locked with theirs in frozen desperation. Her translucent fingers trembled as they reached toward Eric, but before they could touch, the chains crisscrossed over her shoulders yanked her backward, dragging her down with a violent jerk. Her body contorted unevenly, flinching against the pull, as if the agony had snapped her spine in two directions. Eric pushed harder, gasping, "Come on, baby" he breathed. "Come on." but the distance stretched. Stretched even further. Eric's hands, his fingers, almost touched hers, the tip, just the tip, but in a single blink, she was gone.

The carriage. The horses. Her hand. All of it dissolved into mist before his eyes, like a dream shattered by waking, too fragile to hold. One second, she was there, reaching, trembling, pleading. The next, nothing but smoke and silence. No sound. No trace. Just a gaping absence where Rose had been.

Simply gone.

Chapter XVII:
What Remains

He used to laugh like that. The memory hit before the sound did, Eric's laughter echoing across cracked pavement, two boys chasing each other through the sunlit ruins of some Old Earth playground. Sneakers scuffed. Elbows bruised. Eric had shoved him off the rusted slide once, then pulled him back up with that crooked grin, always daring, always louder than the moment. Back then, everything had felt simple. Unbreakable. Adam blinked. The echo was gone. The only thing chasing them now was silence.

Adam stood at the foot of the hut on the castle grounds, the canvas curtain shifting in the wind. The sounds inside were impossible to ignore, wood cracking, something metal crashing to the floor, Eric's voice breaking through it all like thunder without form. He didn't cry out names. He didn't scream words. Just noise. Grief didn't always come in language. Sometimes it came in waves, and Eric was drowning inside them. Adam's hand hovered at the entrance, unsure. *I'm not sure what to say here. Eric was always the bigger brother to me.* Part of him wanted to go in. Part of him didn't think he had the right.

Then, a cup smashed against the wall. A chair overturned. The wind kicked again, pushing the curtain aside for Adam to see him. The silence hit Eric first, it was too loud, too empty. A mess of furs and supplies cluttered the cot in the corner, the place where Rose would've been by his side. The place he couldn't look at. Not yet. He moved slow, like each step was a fight. His hands found the edge of the dresser and in one sharp motion, he swept everything from it. Bottles, scrolls, maps, they crashed to the floor, shattering or rolling away. He didn't care. Eric stood in the middle of the wreckage, eyes hollow. Blood stained his knuckles. His fists trembled at his sides. Something had broken, maybe the dresser. Maybe Eric himself. Then, finally, the tears came. He collapsed into his hands, his body shaking. No words. No breath. Just the guttural ache of someone breaking, too exhausted to scream.

"I'm tired of pretending I don't feel anything. She was taken," he whispered.

"And I couldn't save her."

Adam stepped inside. "Eric," he said, softly, barely more than a breath. The name felt foreign here, like it didn't belong in this wreckage, like saying it out loud might shatter what little remained. He wanted to help, to say something that mattered, but everything felt small in the face of Eric's grief. "Why didn't we go now? Why didn't we go save her?" Eric asked, voice cracked.

Adam exhaled.

"If we had, they would've ambushed us."

The air was thick with dust, grief, and the sharp scent of blood. Everything sacred had been torn apart, and now only silence answered back. Eric turned, his face blotched and raw, tears streaking down his cheeks like wounds that couldn't close. His eyes were red, swollen, barely able to see through the ache. His chest heaved, not from breath, but from everything he'd been holding back, like the weight of the world had finally cracked open inside him. For a moment, he looked like a man torn in two, grief spilling from every seam.

"It's not over," Adam added.

"You don't know that," Eric snapped. "Just go away. Leave."

Adam didn't move. And for a moment, just a breath, he wasn't in the hut. He was twelve again, feet kicking up dust on a cracked basketball court, laughing as Eric tripped over his own shoes and faceplanted with a dramatic "oof." They'd spent that whole summer together, racing bikes, making up games, chasing curfews like enemies. Eric had always been louder. Bolder. The one who threw punches first and thought second. But even then, Adam had been the anchor. The one who pulled him out of trouble, or dove in with him when trouble got too deep.

Now, staring at him through a haze of tears and broken walls, Adam realized something awful: somewhere along the way, they'd stopped saving each other. He didn't speak, didn't step closer. He just stood there, anchored by something he couldn't name. Guilt, maybe. Or the fear that one wrong word might push Eric further over the edge. Eric stormed up to him, eyes wild, fists trembling at his sides like they were holding back a storm. "Don't you see?!" Eric shouted, voice cracking under the weight of it. "We lost everything, our homes, our families… and now

Rose! She was the last thing I had left! The only thing that made this worth surviving. And you're standing there like it doesn't even matter!" His breath hitched, chest heaving as if saying her name took something from him he couldn't get back.

"It's not like that," Adam said quickly. "We can get her back! We're going to get her back. I promise." He wasn't sure if he believed it. Maybe he was trying to convince himself more than anyone else. The words came too fast, too firm, like armor he'd thrown on in desperation. But someone had to say it. Someone had to believe, even if it felt like hope was hanging on by a thread. If he let the doubt show, Eric would fall apart. And if Eric fell apart... maybe they all would.

Eric stepped up further, shoving past, but Adam didn't move. He shifted with him, blocking his path. If Eric veered left, Adam mirrored him. Right, the same. He wasn't being aggressive, just steady, like a wall built out of desperation and belief. His eyes searched Eric's, trying to find the part of his friend that hadn't shattered.

"Eric."

Adam's voice softened. "Just promise me you won't lose yourself in this." He hesitated, swallowing back the rest. "I know the feeling all too well. You just have to get to the other side of it now."

Eric's face twisted. "All these false promises," he spat. "Get out of my face."

"Listen," Adam pressed, "if you just give Ronan and Marie some time, they'll—"

Eric's fist cracked across Adam's face, a raw, desperate blow. The sound echoed in the hut like a gunshot, sharp and absolute, bouncing off the walls like a warning. Adam's head snapped to the side from the impact, as he stumbled back, hitting the ground hard, palms catching the dirt behind him. The taste of blood spread warm and metallic across his tongue. His jaw throbbed, but the sting wasn't what hurt the most. It was the look in Eric's eyes, the betrayal, the loss, the fury.

"Why would I believe a murderer," Eric grudgingly said.

The words hit harder than the punch. Not because they were wrong, but because they weren't. For a second, the silence held, until Adam remembered: Eric had blood on his hands from that night, too.

FLASH—

Adam's palms immobile. Eric's voice, sharp through the chaos: *"We have to go!"* Headlights stuttering across the windshield. Sirens swelling behind them. Adam sat frozen behind the wheel, shaking, silent, unable to move. Then, Eric at the driver's door, yanking it open. *"Get in the passenger seat!"* Adam didn't argue. He slid out, hands still stained in regret, dazed. Eric took the wheel. Not a word between them. Just silence and the unspoken agreement they'd never talk about it again. The memory faded, but the weight of it remained.

Maybe they weren't brothers anymore. For a second, the world held still, no wind, no breath, just the sting blooming across his jaw and the silence that followed, louder than the hit itself. Adam stood up, wiped his lip, then said, quietly but sharp, "You don't get to blame everyone else," he said quietly, "just because she chose something you didn't want." Eric didn't answer. He just stared, jaw clenched, eyes hollow, then stormed out, the flap of the curtain snapping closed behind him. Adam stood alone in the wreckage, lip bleeding, heart heavier than he'd ever admit. The silence left behind wasn't peaceful. It was personal. And somehow, it hurt more than the punch.

The throne room was silent, but not empty. Ancient carvings lined the obsidian walls, etched symbols worn by time, yet still pulsing with meaning. Flickering torchlight cast long shadows across the black marble floor, bending with each movement like the room itself was watching. Chains clinked in the distance, and from behind iron bars lining the walls, caged Prylyn creatures hissed low, their eyes darkened with unnatural light. The chamber felt alive, as if the walls themselves had learned to hold their breath in the presence of something unholy.

Rose knelt at the center, shackles binding her wrists to the stone floor, her hair clinging to her face in damp, sweat-soaked strands. The air pressed in, cold, metallic, and old, like the walls themselves remembered violence. She could hear her heartbeat in her ears, but her expression stayed still. Whatever waited in the shadows, she wouldn't give it the satisfaction.

Then—

She heard it. A soft shuffle. Not loud. Not rushed. Measured. Intentional. Like footsteps carved from shadow itself, drawing closer with every breath. Her muscles tensed, but she kept her head down. Whoever, or whatever, was coming… she'd face it on her terms. From the far end of the room, heavy footsteps echoed off the stone. Not fast. Not showy. Just… precise. Like someone who believed the world would bow, simply because he entered it.

Emperor Zion.

He emerged from the gloom behind the throne, not conjured, not summoned, but revealed. A man, tall and composed, cloaked in black. His steps were deliberate, unhurried, like a predator savoring the moment before a kill. The temperature shifted, like the room itself bowed in fear. Rose stood her ground, but every instinct screamed. She raised her chin, met his eyes. And froze.

Not because of him… but because of what moved behind his eyes. A flicker. An immoral, inhuman. Something else stared back at her, through him, something older than his rage.

They call it The One Who Cannot Be Named… watching through him. Waiting.

Smiling at her. Just smiling.

Chains clinked as Rose adjusted her weight, kneeling in the center of the throne room, wrists bound to the cold stone floor. The air pressed in, dense, ancient, and watching. She refused to show discomfort, even as her eyes flicked upward to meet his. Whatever this was, whoever he was, she wasn't going to cower.

"I know who you are." His voice was calm and measured, like a verdict already written. He remained standing, gaze fixed on her, unmoving, unnerving. "That kind of fire? It doesn't belong in their world."

Rose glared at him, the fire beneath her skin still burning despite the cold bite of iron around her wrists. She wouldn't flinch, not in front of him. But before she could summon a response, a ripple of cold passed through her, like a shadow brushing the edges of her spine. It wasn't fear exactly... but something far more primal, like the room itself had leaned in to listen. "Wouldn't you like to know," Rose replied, her tone cold, defiant.

Zion's smile was thin, unbothered. "Little one, your anger is misplaced. I'm not your enemy. I'm here to bring order to the chaos."

"By killing innocents?" Rose cut in, her voice laced with heat even as she tried to hold it in. The fire inside her surged.

"By restoring balance," he said, voice low. "Through discipline, this planet can finally become what it was always meant to be. Abundant. With the right resources," he added.

Something twisted churned in her gut. *Resources.* That word always meant bodies, land, blood when people like him said it. The fire beneath her skin pulsed again, begging to rise.

"You're insane," Rose spat. "You think by destroying the planet's core you'll save it?"

Zion's gaze didn't waver.

"New Earth is dying."

"It's all because of you your planet is dying. Not us." Rose seethed, fury blazing through like wildfire.

His jaw flexed, the calm in his face faltering, for the first time, she saw anger, not pride, in his eyes. "The power of The M'ra Sphere can transcend us. Transcend the universe. I'm the only one willing to do what must be done."

She stared at him, trying to make sense of the calm in his voice. *Does he even hear himself? This wasn't strategy. It was delusion. A man so far gone, he thought genocide could pass for vision.*

"Then there's you," he continued. "I'll need a right-hand man when the dust clears. Someone with vision. Strength. Fire."

"Why me?" Rose asked.

"Why not the others?"

"You're too smart for your own good," Zion said. "You possess one of the most volatile elements of all. Fire consumes, yes, but it also purifies. It belongs beside me." He stepped forward, shadows trailing behind his cloak like ash in water. "I wouldn't offer," he said quietly, "if I didn't think the feelings were mutual."

Rose's eyes sharpened. Her voice didn't rise, but it cut. "I would never join you." She lifted her chin; gaze fixed on him without flinching. "Not in this life. Not in the next." Her voice dipped to a near-whisper, low and sharp:

"I'd burn first."

And in that moment, she felt it clearly, her flame wasn't just rage. It was resistance. Determination. A force that would never bend to the likes of him, no matter what tricks or illusions he conjured.

Zion's expression darkened; disappointment slid across his face like a blade. "You're right," he said, his voice like smoke on glass. "I don't need you." He turned toward the chamber's center. The chains around Rose clinked as she shifted, watching him with a glare that could've burned steel. He raised his hand, not to cast a spell, but to gesture… gently, reverently. "This world is already listening."

The black goo at the center of the chamber pulsed once. Then again. As if stirred by recognition. A low hiss slithered through the stone like a breath held too long. The ground quivered. Cracks spidered out from the puddle of darkness. Something moved beneath the surface, slow, cautious, sinful. Then the shapes began to rise. Not born. Not summoned. But formed.

The shapes climbed from the sludge in silence, twisted bodies forged from rot and ash, bone and smoke. Four of them. Towering. Mounted. Cloaked in shadows that rippled like dying firelight, kneeling, heads bowed. Their skin wasn't smooth, nor scarred, but marked. Strange sigils and lines pulsed faintly beneath the surface,

as if etched into their very bones and risen
through the flesh. Not ink. Not art. Something
older. Meant to separate them from anything
human.

Rose didn't breathe. She couldn't. She
stared at them kneeling before Zion, beasts pulled
straight from nightmare. Asterius. Vienna.
Barricade. Jarvis. The names rang like curses she'd
never heard, but somehow… understood. Her
stomach twisted. This wasn't power. This was
desecration. *What the fuck is going on?* She thought.

She wanted to scream. Or run. Or maybe
both. Instead, she clenched her jaw and kept her
mouth shut. Zion didn't need to see her fear at all.
*Marie would know what to do in this moment. Katherine
would be ready. Eric would charge in without thinking.
Adam… well, Adam was Adam. He'd do his best to save
all of us. But she was alone. Chained. And scared out of
her mind.*

"Rise, my children," Zion said.

They stood up in unison, towering and
still, like statues carved from war itself. Shadows
clung to their forms as if reluctant to let go. One
of the Horsemen turned its head to Rose, slow,
deliberate, inhuman. A sound like bone grinding
against stone whispered through the chamber. Its

eyes hadn't even opened, but somehow, Rose felt them. Watching. Selecting. As if he already knew which one would burn first.

Then—

Asterius flicked his eyes fully open, gaze upon Rose, like both of them were stuck in a nightmare. Rose didn't flinch; she didn't need to. The fire inside her was already boiling beneath. "When I get out of here," Rose snarled, "I'll kill you myself."

"My child," Zion replied, already turning back toward his throne, "there's so much more you still need to learn."

The afternoon sun filtered through the arched windows in fractured streaks. Eric sat in the dim light of his chamber, shoulders low, arms resting on his knees. Dust hovered in the stillness, catching the light like fragments of thought. He hadn't moved in some time. Hadn't slept much, either, not since Rose. His eyes dropped to the floor.

Then—

Central Park.

He and Rose sat on a bench in the middle of the city, laughter rising like music above the noise. She leaned into him, ice cream in hand, light dancing in her smile. She set her paper ice cream cup on the bench and reached for his face, thumb brushing his cheek, her gaze locking with his. "I love you," she said.

Eric smiled. "I love you too."

Then came the knock. Not part of the memory, too sharp, too thick. It echoed once, then again, louder. Her smile stayed frozen in place, but her head tilted, past Eric's eye line, too slow, too precise. Eyes locked on a shape the dream hadn't invited in.

Knock. Knock.

The sound grew louder. Muffled. Real.

The knock came again.

Eric scuffled in his bed, waking up to a nightmare, that he couldn't run from. His eyes fluttered open, a sharp breath dragging him back to the present. The bench was gone. So was the warmth. So was Rose. She wasn't next to him as he hoped. In his room was stone walls, Elizabethan, dappled light through his windows, silence, yet cold.

Knock. Knock.

Louder this time.

He blinked, disoriented, then dragged a hand down his face as if trying to wipe the dream away. A lingering chill clung to his skin. Another knock echoed faintly through the door. He turned toward it, slower this time, like he already knew something was waiting. It creaked open. Katherine stood in the hall, her braid slung over one shoulder, a shadow behind her eyes.

Katherine hesitated.

"Ronan has something to tell us."

Eric didn't answer. But something in her voice, or maybe in the stillness that followed, tightened in his chest. A weight. A warning. As if whatever waited behind that door was already moving toward them.

Chapter XVIII:
Into the Lair

The war room pulsed with quiet energy, glowing panels, flickering holograms, and the low hum of voices preparing for war. But Adam stood still, unmoving in the chaos. He lingered near the edge of the table, silent. The space was wide and circular, carved from dark stone with ancient glyphs along the walls, though now, the old world was eclipsed by maps and movement. A large holographic display floated above the center of the table, casting pale light across the room. The map flickered in shades of red and blue, slowly rotating; Zion's Lair now highlighted in crimson.

Adam's eyes stayed fixed on it. He didn't move, didn't shift. The others around him, Katherine, Eric, Marie, spoke in clipped voices, their urgency sharpening with every new detail. But Adam felt the stillness inside him widen. Rose's capture wasn't just a loss, it was personal. It echoed in him like a wound that hadn't closed.

He shifted his stance. Eric still hadn't spoken since Rose was taken. Katherine was quieter too. And Marie… Marie kept looking over her shoulder, like the past was following her in real time. Then the holograms shifted: Zion's lair rising in red.

Ronan approached the center console and turned a dial. The map pulsed, expanding into a more detailed view. "Marie found traces of her," he said, eyes flicking toward the flickering red outline. "Residual energy left behind, from Haiti."

The others went still. "She's being held in the dungeon beneath Zion's lair."

Adam's jaw tensed. "Are you sure?"

Ronan nodded. "Yes. And in some ways," He hesitated. "I'm glad it was Zion. This gives us a chance to fully map his territory."

Adam didn't respond right away. Something about the way Ronan said it, it didn't sit right. *Glad it was Zion? As if that made it better. As if Rose being in danger was somehow a strategic advantage.* He watched Ronan closely, his stomach coiling with unease. Was that how leaders spoke? Or was that how people lost themselves in war? For a brief second, Adam wondered if Ronan even saw them as people anymore… or just pieces on a map fighting for their hierarchy. They didn't ask for this. No one did.

With a sweep of Ronan's hand, the topography shifted. The image twisted and reformed, layers peeling back to reveal the underground system beneath the lair. Ronan paused, fingers hovering as he zoomed in on a dark pocket of tunnels. "There. There she is." he said. "It may be difficult to take down," Ronan revealed.

Katherine stepped forward, arms folded. "Why would it be difficult?"

Ronan didn't look at her at first. "Because it's surrounded by fire."

The word hit Adam harder than it should have. *Fire. We're up against fire now? What is this world?* It wasn't something you can extinguish; it was part of all of them. Rose. Alive. In danger. And somewhere out there, twisted beyond recognition. Ronan's jaw tensed. "It's forbidden territory," he said. "The land beyond the storms… Zion turned it into a furnace. Nothing grows there now."

Adam stared at the glowing outline on the map, now reduced to nothing but cinders and silence. The idea of Rose trapped in that wasteland churned something dark in him. Not just anger. He wouldn't let that be her ending. Not there. Not like that. His gaze narrowed. "Then how do we get inside?"

Ronan answered without flinching. "You, Katherine, and Marie will fly above, take out any guards along the ridge. Eric and I will cover the ground."

A heavy silence settled between them. Marie stepped forward, her voice calm but commanding. "Saving Rose isn't our only objective," she said, her eyes sweeping over each of them. "The M'ra Sphere might be nearby. It has a way of pulling at your thoughts, distracting you when it matters most. Don't let it. If any of you gets a chance to take it. Do it."

Adam exhaled through his nose, still staring at the red shape pulsing at the center of the table. Zion's Lair. A fortress of stone and fire. And somewhere in its heart, Rose was waiting. He didn't say a word. But inside, the storm was building. The hangar buzzed with quiet movement, some of Ronan's soldiers checking weapons in the background, generators humming softly, shadows stretching long beneath the dim overhead lights. Adam stepped into the space, his boots echoing on the stone floor. Ahead, Eric stood alone, zipping up the front of his battle suit from waist to collar. No words, just tight movements. Mechanical. Controlled. He adjusted the collar, then stared forward, distant.

Adam approached slowly.

"Hey bud," he said, voice low.

"You ready?"

Eric didn't answer. He stared at Adam, just for a second, then turned his back and started to walk away. Adam reached out, hand catching Eric's arm. "This is it. We're gonna get her," firmer now. Eric froze for a beat. Then he pulled his arm back, calm, but cold. "Don't worry," he muttered, without turning around. He walked off into the shadows, leaving Adam standing there with silence thick between them.

Adam didn't move. He stood frozen, hand hanging low to his side. The air around him felt heavier, like their friendship had just broken, and no one else noticed. He wanted to believe Eric didn't mean it, that it was just the stress, Rose, and the weight of what they were all about to face. But that voice, that look... it cut deeper than it should have. And now, with the mission ahead of them, there was no time to fix it. No time to say more. Just silence. And whatever came next.

The breeze at nighttime was warm up here, carrying the faint scent of blood and bone, like the land beyond the storms were learning how to bury the innocent in the ash again. Moonlight cut through the fog like a blade, pale and ghostly, washing Zion's lair in a haunting glow. The mist curled across New Earth's airspace, slow and deliberate, as if the sky itself were holding its breath. No wind. No sound. Just the cold pulse of waiting: New Earth bracing for the coming fracture. Above the lair, the sky cracked. A jagged platform of rock split through the fog, riding the wind like a battering ram. Katherine stood at the front, her eyes glowing white, hair whipping violently as the air curved around her. Behind her, Eric and Ronan balanced on other slabs of stone, flying fast, the three of them slicing toward the lair like a blade unsheathed.

Below, two Prylyn creatures hunched at the portcullis, limbs bent at unnatural angles, their movements twitchy and reptilian. Though they had no true eyes, the hollow sockets in their skull-like faces tracked the air above, sensing shifts in pressure, catching tremors most beings would miss. One tilted its head, let out a low hiss, tongue flicking like a sensor, nostrils flaring as if sniffing out heat or fear. The other stiffened, claws twitching against the stone, head snapping sideways in a motion too fast to be human.

The shapes grew larger.

Not birds—

Legends.

Katherine leveled her stance, extended one hand, the platform of rock lifted up with her intact, shards of stone, sharp and fast as arrows— blasted forward. The first Prylyn didn't even scream. The second burst apart, his body erupting into black goo, splashing like oil across the entrance. Ronan and Eric dropped from the air, off the platform rocks, in near-perfect sync, their silhouettes slicing through the fog as boots met stone with practiced ease. Dust curled up in spirals beneath them, trailing the heat of movement.

Katherine followed a breath later, her boots striking with a weighty, bone-deep thud. No words. Just war in motion. Heavy as ever. No one said a word. The sky above the lair split with motion. From the ground, Ronan barely glanced up, but what he saw was unforgettable. Two figures, silhouetted in silver-blue moonlight, cut across the clouds like avenging spirits.

High above, Marie and Adam, side by side, soaring through the air with a precision no human should possess. The moon crowned them, casting ghost light on the weapons in their hands. Adam, his eyes radiated white, hovered in the air, heart thudding like war drums in his chest. His fingers tightened around the hilt of his blade. The cold wind wasn't just wind; it was the pressure of what came next. He glanced sideways at Marie. They were already legends, or so the world had whispered. But legends didn't feel fear like this… did they? Marie turned her head just slightly, nodding once to Adam. Adam exhaled, sharp and quiet. *I guess we're doing this.* Without a word, they dove.

Adam angled his descent like a falcon mid-hunt. His sword locked to his side, he twisted midair, aiming directly for the Prylyn creature posted atop the tower. The Prylyn never stood a chance, Adam struck first, blade spearing through the thing's chest as black goo burst into the wind. Marie descended, landed a second later, silent as shadow, deadly as flame. Her descent barely stirred the dust before she surged forward, eyes locked, motion like a blade drawn from silk.

Her dagger flashed once in the moonlight, slicing across the Prylyn's throat in a single, fluid arc. The creature convulsed, black sludge pouring from the wound in thick, bubbling streams, like tar spilling from a cracked pipeline. It clutched at nothing. Collapsed in pieces. No sound. No soul. Just the echo of Marie's breath as she stood over it, already turning for the next.

Adam turned toward the other Prylyn creature, moved as one. Precise and deadly. The creature he'd struck had burst apart mid-air, no blood, just a spray of thick, black sludge that hissed as it hit the ground. Adam's stomach turned. That wasn't armor. That wasn't human. Whatever these things were… they hadn't started this way. There were more. There had to be. The two they'd taken down were just sentries, distraction, maybe. If he flew over the gates now, he'd light a signal flare for the entire lair. No. He couldn't. Stealth was the only way this worked.

He caught Marie's eye. She gave a single nod, already stepping past the corpse at her feet. Time to move. Adam stepped to the edge of the tower, his breath tight in his chest. Below, through the thinning fog, he spotted them, Ronan, Eric, and Katherine, gathered at the base of the lair, already in position.

Adam flew beside the others, his arm wrapped around Marie's waist as they cut through the fog together, silent and focused. Their boots struck the stone in unison, the impact sharp, final, like a seal closing behind them. But as his soles met the ground, something in him pulled back. The lair pulsed with wrongness, its stone too smooth, too cold, like it had been melted and reformed by something unholy. Fog coiled at their feet, but it wasn't just mist, it clung like breath from a sleeping beast, rising from cracks that hummed with a faint, sickly glow.

Adam didn't need to look at Marie to feel the tension in her body. This wasn't just a fortress. It was a warning. A tomb pretending to be a palace. For a second, the five of them stood still. No words. There didn't need to be. Just the cold press of anticipation, like the air before a storm, heavy and waiting. Ronan stepped forward, scanning the shadows along the outer wall. "There's a side corridor near the east tower," he said, voice hushed. "It should lead to the council chamber. If Zion has records… they'll be there."

Adam nodded once. His eyes flicked upward toward the tower he and Marie had just cleared. No movement. They slipped into the lair without another word, shadows swallowed by stone. The lair was quiet. Too quiet. *I don't like this feeling. Something about it just… makes my skin crawl,* he thought.

They moved through shadowed corridors, boots soft against ancient stone. No alarms. No guards. Just the cold breath of a fortress holding its secrets too tightly. Every step echoed like a warning. Then came the chamber, heavy door, rusted handle. Marie stepped forward, palm glowing faintly as she whispered something in a tongue older than the walls around them. Faint blue light shimmered across her palm as the magic surged into the lock. With a soft click, there, the mechanism released. The door creaked open, revealing a wide chamber beyond. The council room opened like a wound.

No one was inside. They slipped in quickly and quietly, the heavy door clicking shut behind them like a held breath. Shadows stretched long across the stone floor, cast by the flickering torchlight embedded in the walls. At the center of the room stood a large oval table, its surface buried beneath scattered papers, brittle maps, and rusted ledgers layered with dust. Marie moved toward a stack at the far end, her steps slow, deliberate. Her fingers hovered just above the parchment before she began to sort through it, each page whispering under her touch, her hands trembling with the weight of what she hoped, and feared, to find. She paused. This wasn't an ordinary paused. Like she seen a ghost. Her heart fluttered with the loss of air in her lungs.

Could it be? How?

The others moved around her, quiet and careful, but their presence dulled to background noise. Her world narrowed to the scattered papers beneath her hands, the feel of parchment edges, the brittle crackle of old ink, the quiet whisper of memory clawing its way back. There it was. A document. Her sister's name written at the top:

Maya Celeborn.

The parchment was aged, edges curled with time, but the name was clear. Unique. Those eyes. That jawline. Her lips. That nose. Older now, but still the same. Her fingers trembled. Across the header, thick red letters screamed what her voice couldn't:

SOLD.

Marie stared at the word, just stared, her stomach turning inside out on itself. It wasn't just a transaction. It was a sentence. Orcas ago. A life stolen. Labeled. Filed away like inventory. As if Maya's life did not matter to anyone. Marie folded the paper with slow precision and slipped it into her coat, sealing it close to her chest. Her jaw locked. She didn't speak. She couldn't. There wasn't time for grief. She hadn't felt the weight in her heart this heavy… not since… her parents. Her King and Queen. Now wasn't the time for mourning a loss. Only fury. That never stopped her before.

Across the room, Adam glanced at her, just for a second. He didn't ask. He didn't need to. But the weight in his eyes said it all. She turned away before it could land. The grief. Before it could soften her determination. A silence lingered, then the rustle of more parchment paper broke it. Nearby, Eric combed through another stack erratically. His voice dropped to a whisper. "Where are you, Rose?"

Katherine leaned over the far side of the table, the dim light throwing slashes of shadow across the map and her face. Her gaze swept the parchment paper with calm precision, studying the layered ink and charcoal that outlined Zion's lair. Then she stopped, finger pressing firmly into a square marked near the lower quadrant, its corners darkened like a bruise. "There," she said quietly. "The dungeon."

Adam's stomach clenched at the word. *It seemed like we just got here, and our friend was sent to some demonic dungeon. She must be scared. I know Eric is.* The image of Rose chained in the dark flickered behind his eyes. He stepped in closer, gaze locking on the mark Katherine had pointed to. It wasn't just a location. It was a deadline.

Ronan stepped closer, his eyes narrowing as he followed her finger. "Excellent." He scanned the rest of the map. "For The M'ra Sphere... it would make sense to keep it at a higher vantage point, more secure, easier to defend."

He turned toward the window, and paused. A glint caught his eye. Through the fog, the tip of a tower awakened in the distance, gleaming faintly under the moonlight.

"There," he said, pointing.

"In the tower."

He pivoted to face them.

"Adam, go with Marie and locate Rose. Katherine, you're with me. We'll retrieve the M'ra Sphere from the northern tower."

A beat passed.

"And Eric, you can…"

He stopped. The room fell quiet, tension drawing tight like a wire. Even the soft shuffle of movement halted as the others looked up, sensing the shift. Ronan's gaze remained fixed, something had caught his attention. The air felt heavier, as if the moment itself demanded silence.

Adam turned. "Eric?" *Why would you leave? You're gonna get yourself killed... He was always the hothead. He never listens. Not to me. Not to anyone.*

The space behind them was empty. Adam exhaled. He already knew. There was nothing he could do. The moment Ronan hesitated; he'd felt it in his gut. Eric was gone. Not out of defiance, but out of desperation. For him, this wasn't strategy or duty. It was love. Raw, reckless, and aching. Rose wasn't just missing; it was the girl he only ever loved, and she was slipping away by the minute. And Eric… he couldn't bear to lose her again. No, not again. Adam stared into the dark corridor, the silence pressing heavier now. He understood. All too well. Because if it were someone he loved? He'd already be running too. Marie's eyes widened as the realization sank in.

"He's gone."

The hallway was empty… eerily so. No guards. No flicker of movement. Just the steady echo of Eric's boots against the stone, swallowed quickly by the walls. His shoulders were set, his pace deliberate, but something about the silence around him felt wrong, like the lair was watching, breathing every footstep he took. Ahead, the corridor curved toward darkness, leading him deeper toward the dungeon.

Then—

Creak.

Eric stopped mid-step. The sound coiled through the hallway, sharp and sudden against the silence. He turned his head slightly, muscles tensing, brows creased as he strained to listen. Another creak. Closer this time.

He turned around slowly, his eyes scanning the corridor behind him. But nothing… just the stretch of stone and shadow, untouched. The silence pressed in, thick and unmoving, as if the lair itself were holding its breath. No footsteps. No flicker. Just stillness… too still in fact. Too quiet… The air had changed. It no longer felt still, it pressed in closer, heavier, like the hallway itself had started breathing. The temperature dipped, subtle but sudden, threading cold along the back of his neck. Something unseen was watching him. Eric didn't know better.

Just beyond the flicker of torchlight, the faintest distortion shimmered in the hall, barely perceptible. A woman-shaped ripple in the air, limbs too still, too invisible, too precise. The space around her pulsed faintly, like heat off decaying flesh. Yet invisible. Light bent as an illusion across her form, as if the world refused to look directly at her. Something ancient decrepit watched through that invisibility… and it wanted blood.

Vienna.

She materialized a few feet behind him, her form snapping into focus like a secret exhaling in the dark. Her skin was so pale it seemed to catch the light wrong, half-there, half-vanished. Strange markings laced her arms like inked cracks in porcelain, pulsing faintly beneath the surface. She didn't move. Didn't speak. Just stood there, still as a statue, head tilted slightly, her silence was more violent than a scream. Something about her calm, the way she breathed like a predator with infinite time, made the air itself recoil.

Then, without a sound, she turned, slow and smooth, like slipping into water, and faded from sight. No shimmer, no flash. Just invisible, like light bending around her until she was gone. Somewhere in the dark, she was already warning the others, ghosting through the lair like a whisper through the air, a whisper… the hunt had begun.

The corridor narrowed, stone pressing in on both sides as Eric moved deeper into the dungeon's throat. Each step echoed softer now, absorbed by the damp silence. Then, just ahead, a low grinding sound broke the hush. Metal scraping stone. Like the keys spoke to him. Rose lifted her head. She'd heard it too. Footsteps. A silhouette behind the bars. Her heart lurched:

Eric. She exhaled. For a moment, she didn't trust her own eyes. The dark had warped her thoughts for days, twisting hope into hallucination, faces into shadows, memories into lies. But this wasn't a trick. That voice… those eyes. The way he moved. The way he marched to her like…

A tremor ran through her chest, not from fear, but relief so sharp it felt like pain. He'd come when the world she knew had crumbled. Against all odds, against every wall Zion had built, he found her in the dark. And for the first time in days, she remembered who she was. "Eric!" she cried out, as she pushed to her feet.

"I'm getting you out of here," he said, already searching the walls for the key.

Her eyes flicked to the side.

"Eric, the wall."

But he didn't stop. His hands found the rusted keyring, fingers moving fast despite the weight of urgency pressing down on him. The cell door swung open with a groan, and she surged forward, barely able to speak his name. Her limbs moved before her mind caught up. The rusted chains at her wrists scraped as she stood, her whole-body trembling, not from fear, but from something deeper. A trust she hadn't dared touch

in years. Eric grabbed a second key, fumbled
briefly, then slid it into the cuffs. Click. They
snapped open. The metal clattered to the floor like
broken shackles.

Then he pulled her close, not out of
impulse, but out of instinct, like his arms had been
waiting for this exact moment since he first met
her. She sank into the warmth of his chest, hard
muscle beneath soft fabric, rising and falling with
breath he didn't realize he'd been holding. He
smelled of firewood and mahogany, just like
home. His arms wrapped around her with the
desperation of a man who'd tasted life without her
and refused to ever feel that emptiness again. Her
fingers clutched the back of his elemental garb,
anchoring herself to the only constant she had
left. In that moment, there was no war. No pain.
Just them. The wave of two heartbeats crashing
into the silence together. Fire and water.

"I won't lose you again," he whispered.

"You won't have to," she whispered back.

Their lips met in a crash of cool waves and
passion, slow at first, then a rush of desire. Rose
clung to him like he was the only solid thing in a
world crumbling beneath her, fingers curling
tighter around his neck and the back of his head.

The kiss was a promise, a plea, a memory of every moment they had lost and everything they still hoped to have. He gripped her waist, pulling her closer, like the world was ending and she was the only thing left worth saving. Time blurred around them, just the fierce, trembling need to feel alive in each other's arms. Their lips had stopped in motion; heads pressed against each other. The silence in the world says it all. They opened their eyes and looked at each other. "I want to be with you every step of the way." He said. "I'm not gonna let anything happen to you."

The weight of his words hung in the sky, she loved him as much he loved her and his words, his protection, his love was enough in a twisted world they found themselves in. Eric didn't wait for the moment to settle, his fingers laced with hers, firm and certain, as if letting go for even a second might undo everything they'd just reclaimed. He wouldn't take a chance with that. He moved first, swiftly, focused, guiding her with the instinct of someone who'd already imagined losing her again. Rose followed without hesitation, their joined hands the only anchor in a world about to ignite. "Come on," he said. "We have to get out of here."

They escaped the dungeon as two runaway fugitives, heart to heart, two shadows slipping back into the dark, hearts still racing from the kiss that had nearly broken them. Their footsteps echoed softly, swallowed quickly by the silence of the lair. Stone walls closed around them like a throat holding breath. And somewhere, just beyond the edge of sight, something watched in silence, waiting patiently.

The hall stretched in eerie silence, as if the stone itself were holding its breath. Each footfall landed soft but thoughtful, their boots skimming over the ancient floor like whispers in a tomb. Shadows pooled along the edges, curling inward like teeth waiting to bite. Adam and Marie moved quickly but carefully, every step a silent vow not to be seen, not to be heard. Ahead, a Prylyn stood guard, twitching, vaguely humanoid, its skull-like face locked in blank watchfulness.

Marie pulled Adam back with a sharp glance, her breath held tight in her chest. She edged toward the corner, lifting her palm slowly, fingers spread steadily. A soft remembrance of once was… her Mother, Queen Elena, guarded her and Maya, as a little child, just now she guarded Adam. It felt too real. Too surreal in the moment. As if her mother was there with her. But that all faded away when a soft glow coiled in her hand, pale blue and pulsing like a heartbeat, threads of light swirling between her fingers like mist woven from willpower. The energy built in silence, now a lethal whisper in motion. She released it, the blast streaking down the corridor like a phantom arrow, fast and merciless.

The blast struck silent, no flash, no warning, just a sharp, invisible force. The creature spasmed violently, limbs seizing in jagged pulses as if trying to resist death itself. A guttural hiss tore from its throat, thin and wet, before it collapsed sideways with a sickening thud. Black goo spilled from its mouth in thick streams, bubbling like tar, pooling beneath its skull-like face as the last tremor left its body, defiantly.

"Come on," Marie whispered.

They stepped past the body, boots silent on the stone. The stench of scorched air and something fouler clung to the corridor, lingering like breath held too long. Adam didn't look down, but he felt it, the weight of what they'd just done pressing against the silence. Behind them, the creature's body twitched once, then went still.

Adam kept his eyes forward, but the image of the Prylyn seizing on the ground replayed in the back of his mind. Not with fear, but with calculation. These things weren't alive in the way he understood life. They didn't bleed. They didn't cry out. And yet… the silence they left behind felt heavier than a scream. His hands curled into fists at his sides, muscles tense. Whatever waited deeper in this place, he could feel it watching.

Then—

A voice.

Low. Smooth. Threaded with something foreign. It didn't come from in front of them. Or behind. It moved through the walls:

I see you've brought help. Curious… I wondered which one of you would find the courage to crawl this far.

Adam stopped cold. *This is it.* His arm twitched, instinct reaching for a weapon he didn't have. But this wasn't a fight of swords, it was something strange and a bit deeper. The voice coiled through the stone, wrapping around his spine like a chill. Whatever was speaking… it already knew they were here.

Did you think I wouldn't notice? That I'd just let you take what's mine?

Mark my words, your friends will never see the light of day again.

A long silence. Then—

BOOM.

A blinding flash of light flooded the corridor, searing the darkness with a burst so bright it left afterimages in its wake. An instant later, sirens erupted, an ancient, metallic wail that rattled the stone and set the air vibrating. The sound wasn't just loud; it was angry, a mechanical shriek that echoed down every hall like the lair itself had come alive. Lights above flickered violently, bathing the walls in red pulses, casting everything in a feverish, warlike glow. The ground thrummed beneath their feet. The fortress wasn't warning them. It was hunting them and this time the lair had awakened.

Chapter XIX:
Ambushed

Sirens screamed, flushing through the halls. A metallic wail tore through the lair, sharp, violent, remorseless. It wasn't just an alarm. It was a shriek of something ancient waking up. Blood-red glyphs ignited along the walls, burning through the gloom like eyes snapping open in the dark. Shadows convulsed across the stone, twisting in jagged shapes that moved wrong, like they weren't cast by anything living. The stone itself seemed to shudder, as if the lair was coming alive. At the top of the corridor, in a different hall, Ronan and Katherine skidded to a halt. "We've been ambushed!" Ronan growled, his voice cutting through the chaos like a blade.

Katherine's eyes flashed.

"We have to find the others!"

There was no hesitation. No time to process. Ronan's boots were already pounding against the stone, his form a blur of forward motion driven by instinct more than thought. Katherine followed close behind, her breath cutting sharp through the rising noise, fists clenched tight at her sides. The corridor twisted ahead like a throat ready to swallow them whole, but neither slowed. Whatever waited in the dark, they would face it head-on.

Elsewhere in the lair, the Prylyn creatures stirred. They hadn't slept so much as gone dormant, hunched, twisted forms convoluted into the darkness like malformed statues, waiting for breath. Their limbs twitched first, silent, insect-like movements scraping against stone. In narrow cabins and shadowed cradles, the air thickened with their reawakening, the scent of sulfur rising as if the lair itself exhaled something ancient and wrong. But the sound of the alarm jolted them awake like a flame to dry leaves. One by one, they snapped to life, bodies jerking upright, limbs twitching as if remembering muscle and movement all at once. Their wicked skull-like faces turned in unison toward the corridor. Then they charged. At high speed. Hungry for pain. And the unshakable instinct to kill. A dozen. Then a dozen more.

Flooding from side corridors and chamber cracks, they stormed toward the center of the lair with insect-like precision, clicking, screeching, limbs scraping stone as they charged. Outside, in the main corridor, the final echo of the siren was swallowed by the grinding roll of steel. The portcullis gates stood sealed, silent, unmoving, as if the lair itself had anticipated the invasion and snapped shut in defense. There was no escape.

While the battle erupted below, Adam and Marie charged into the upper hall. They darted around the corner, boots pounding against the stone floor. A view of the main corridor stretched below them, enclosed by rusted beams and slotted windows. Adam skidded to a stop at the window, and halted. Down below, the lair had erupted into chaos. *Where are you Eric and Rose?* He could see Ronan and Katherine locked in battle, Prylyn creatures swarming like insects in every direction. Blades clashed. Grunts and screams echoed off the stone. Ronan's sword cut a clean arc through two attackers, while Katherine drove her fist into another's throat. But they were outnumbered. Badly. The pounding.

Adam's pulse slammed in his ears. *They're not going to hold.* For a second, he just stood there, helpless and furious. *Why didn't we come sooner?* Katherine was fighting with everything she had, but her stance was slipping. Ronan was fast, too fast for most of the creatures, but even he looked winded. Adam clenched his fists. He didn't care what plan they'd made to retrieve The M'ra Sphere, none of it mattered if Katherine died before it began.

He glanced up, and spotted the rusted roof hatch bolted to the upper frame of the lair. Without a word, he raised his hand. He concentrated. Harder this time. Inch by inch. Air spiraled around his wrist like a serpent and then launched upward with a sharp burst. The old lock shattered with a metallic *crack*. A hidden ladder groaned and unraveled, crashing down with a metallic rattle. "Adam!" Marie called out. "What are you doing!?"

"We have to help them!" He shouted.

He was already climbing. Two rungs at a time, he hauled himself up the ladder toward the top of the castle. The hatch resisted at first, then gave way with a creaking screech as he forced it open. Wind slammed into his face. The air up here felt different, colder, thinner, thrilling around the molten fire that surrounds Zion's Lair. As he climbed over the hatch to the rooftop, he heard it, the whispers again. The wind was speaking to him. Something about it… made the voice indistinguishable. Not like last time, not like the forest. This time it called for him to jump.

Marie hesitated at the bottom. Adam looked down at her, and the look in his eyes told her she wouldn't be able to stop him from doing the unthinkable. Muttering a curse under her breath, she grabbed the ladder and climbed up. At the rooftop, Adam stepped to the edge of the tower, eyes locked on the battlefield below. From here, the carnage stretched in every direction, Prylyn creatures and warriors pouring in through the main corridor like a wave. Alongside the screeching creatures were men, or what used to be men, bearing Zion's insignia and eyes hollowed out with black rot.

Katherine was already mid-combat, rocky gauntlets encased her hands, jagged and pulsing with raw Earth energy. Each punch echoed like stone on steel, locked in a brutal exchange with a monstrous figure that oozed black sludge from its mouth: Jarvis, the pale, disjointed figure with black sludge dripping from the corners of his mouth like a hungry werewolf, feasting for blood.

His limbs moved out of rhythm, like a puppet cut from its strings then dragged back into motion. His movements were inhuman, disjointed, jerking and twitching as if something inside him was fighting to get out. She struck first, a rocky gauntlet slamming into his chest, but Jarvis barely flinched. They traded blows back and forth, Katherine dodging low, countering fast, her fists coiling rock, reforming, wrapped in Earth's fury.

Dust flared with every strike, but still, Jarvis kept coming for more. Nearby, Ronan was blade flashing through three of Zion's men in a wide, devastating sweep. Blood sprayed the floor. He turned, parried another strike, then drove his sword clean through a Prylyn's abdomen. Adam's eyes narrowed. Something moved behind Katherine, two Prylyn creatures crawling through the shadows, slipping toward her blind side while she fought Jarvis. His chest tightened. *No.* Without hesitation, with the voice he heard, the wind, he stepped onto the ledge and jumped.

"Adam!" Marie shouted behind him.

The wind obeyed his call. It surged around him mid-air, guiding his descent as his body flew toward the nearest creature. He landed hard, legs wrapped around the neck base, onto the Prylyn's should top. The thing screeched, but Adam didn't give it a chance. With a flick of his hands, the air condensed like a lasso around its throat. Adam held his hands steady for a beat longer. Then with a slight turn of his hands, the air surged—

Snap.

The creature crumpled. Adam flew upwards and flipped in the air, valiantly like an eagle soaring through the sky before landing. Marie landed beside him, the wind catching the edge of her cloak as she hovered down gracefully. Her eyes swept the chaos, already pulsing with focus. A door burst open to their left. Eric and Rose charged in through the side, eyes focused. Marie gave Rose a quick glance.

"Welcome back," she said.

"Things are about to get ugly."

Before Rose could answer, Marie charged forward, her staff humming with power. She unleashed a blast of energy that surged like a shockwave, slamming into three Prylyn and sending them hurtling backward. A stillness fell across the corridor, sharp and sudden. The Prylyn stiffened mid-charge, their claws twitching inches from impact. Limbs locked. Mouths stretched open in snarls that never finished. Even the wind around Adam stilled, like the air itself refused to move. *I have a bad feeling about this.* Then a voice cut through the silence, loud and piercing:

"ENOUGH!"

The sound reverberated through the stone like a god striking the earth. Echoing. Everyone froze. Adam's head snapped up. *That's him. Zion. The one Marie has talked about. We are going to finally meet him.* A figure emerged from the shadows beyond the corridor, cloaked in black, his steps slow and deliberate. He didn't walk like a man. He glided like a verdict. Adam had never seen him before, but the air told him everything. Stone cold. Condemning. Corrupted. There was something unnatural in the way the space bent around him, as if the lair itself retreated in his presence.

Emperor Zion. He was tall, composed, yet steeped in malevolence, his very stance radiated a monstrous presence. A fine cloak dipped in black tar, draped from his shoulders, its hem dragging like smoke. His eyes were obsidian shards, reptilian like. Beneath his outer robe, glimmers of scale peeked through his skin, faint and iridescent, like a lizard cloaked in armor. His gaze found Marie. "Queen Marie," he said, as if the title tasted bitter. "Still pretending to lead… even when The M'ra Sphere won't answer you."

Marie's fists clenched, gripping the staff glowing at her side.

Zion stepped forward, slow and precise. "You never give up. Always clawing your way back in. Just like your mother and father… fighting the good fight."

Her breath deepened like a caged animal waiting to be set free. Adam saw it, the flicker in her eyes, the way she stood still like she almost cut someone's throat out. All pure rage. Marie slammed the staff to the ground like a warning.

"You murdered them!" Marie spat. Her voice cracked, not with weakness, but with fury restrained. "You murdered our King and Queen!

Adam stared at her, stunned by the force behind her words. It wasn't grief, it was fury sharpened over orcas of silence. Fury given breath for the first time. Zion tilted his head slightly, amused. "Ah," he breathed, almost gently.

"So, you remember."

Adam's hand hovered near his side, air stirring again. He didn't know the story, but he didn't need to. He saw it in Marie's eyes. This wasn't strategy. This was blood born from ache. Zion's fingernails began to extend, elongating like obsidian claws from his fingertips, until the edges gleamed beneath the lair's low torches. He didn't lash out, not yet. He simply tilted his head. "I'd be happy to do it again," he said calmly.

Marie didn't flinch.

"You will pay for what you did."

Zion's smile was small, full of contempt. "I'm not concerned about you."

She took a step forward, staff now pulsing with raw light, gripping it tighter. "It's not me you should be afraid of."

Zion's smile faded. The wind shifted again. He took a single step forward, his voice cold and deliberate. "This was never a rescue mission… it was always a trap…You will perish just like your parents did."

Adam barely noticed the silence that followed. He was too busy watching Ronan. He hadn't spoken, not once since Zion had stepped forward, but now his hand flexed around his blade, knuckles pale. Too pale. Ronan's eyes locked on Zion with a fury that didn't burn…it festered. Adam gasped. He knows what happened. He knows Zion didn't just take Marie's parents. He took Ronan's father, too.

Then—*snap.*

With a flick of Zion's hand, the battlefield snapped back into motion. The Prylyn screamed. Blades clashed. Shouts rang out. And from the northern wall—

BOOM.

The sound struck through the lair, like thunder meeting lightning, Barricade tore through the wall like a battering ram carved from nightmares. He wasn't armored. He was mutated. Towering, hulking, and bristled with thick black hair throughout. His jaw jutted forward unnaturally, tusk-like teeth protruding from lips that barely moved, smoke hissing from his flared nostrils with every breath. His shoulders cracked with each step, his bones thickened by something far from human.

He charged, his heavy limbs pounding against stone as he barreled straight for Rose. She turned sharply, eyes blazing. Fire surged from her hands, a jet of heat roaring through the corridor. But it barely slowed him. With one massive swing, Barricade knocked Eric aside like a ragdoll. Then he lunged, grabbing Rose by the wrists mid-blast and hurling her through the air. Her body spiraled, flames trailing like comets behind her until she slammed against the far wall. She collapsed to the ground. For a breath, there was only smoke and the crackle of burning debris.

Rose stirred. Her body pulsed. Glowed. Then she… Ignited! She flamed on, fire coursing over her entire body, her uniform untouched beneath the blaze. Heat shimmered around her like a living aura as she lifted into the air, spiraling upward, her limbs unfurling like a firestorm breaking free. Her eyes locked on Barricade. Then she launched, a streak of fury, slamming into his chest with a thunderous crack that sent him flying. He crashed into the wall behind him, fracturing beneath the impact, and went still.

Across the castle, Eric pushed himself out of a pile of broken brick, dust clinging to his uniform. Zion's men rushed him from both sides.

He raised his hand, water pulsing at his fingertips, and summoned gauntlets of rippling current around his fists. Snapped. Gauntlets locked place. He struck the first soldier with a powerful jab, crack, and then spun to knock the second into a wall. A third charged. Eric pivoted, disarmed him, and kicked the enemy's sword into the air.

"Catch!" The blade curved in the air.

Adam turned just in time to catch the blade, its weight jarring, the steel heavier than he remembered, like it had absorbed the blood it spilled. The impact stung through his wrist, but he gripped tighter, muscles straining. The corrupted soldiers closed in, too many. He couldn't hesitate. Not now. Not with everyone watching. Not with Zion still breathing. His breath hitched.

The pressure wasn't just in the air, it was inside him, coiled and rising. He lifted the sword. *Move, Adam!* And he did. Steel clashed with claws, air swirling beneath his boots as he dodged a strike and drove the blade into the next attacker. But something shifted. Energy. Something coming from above. Adam blinked, and the world didn't move with him. His limbs tensed like a magnetic pull, stiffer then a brick. He couldn't move.

Something… someone was locking him in place. Not with force, but with a telekinetic illusion. The air shifted. The silence thickened.

Adam felt it like gravity had changed. A sharp gust rippled through the air, he turned toward the sound, just as Asterius slipped through it, stepping out of nothing like he'd been waiting on the other side. Asterius moved with liquid grace, swift, almost too perfect, like a vision conjured instead of being born. His blade came first, fast, and precise. Adam blocked it with a grunt, steel ringing against steel. Asterius leaned in close, their faces nearly brushing, his breath was cool. Intentional. "You're even prettier up close." Asterius winked.

Adam's pulse jumped, but he didn't let it slow him. His instincts kicked in, every muscle coiled with precision. He twisted away, jaw clenched, and thrust his palm forward, releasing a tunnel of air so sharp it cut through the chaos like a blade. It hit square in the chest, sending Asterius flying, the force of the blast ripping him off his feet. He slammed into the stone wall with a deep, bone-snapping thud that echoed through the corridor. Cracks spiderwebbed behind his body on impact, dust raining down from the ceiling.

For a moment, Asterius didn't move, just slumped there, smoke curling around him. Adam barely had time to breathe before he sensed another shift. Through the raid, Eric had just unleashed a massive tunnel of water, sweeping through a cluster of Zion's men like a wave of war. Bodies slammed to the ground, soaked and staggering. But the air around him shimmered, warped, like heat off pavement. Too hot to touch. And then blinked out of existence altogether. An invisible force struck, sudden and brutal. Vienna materialized mid-stride, her hand snapping around Eric's throat from the front, locking him in place. Her other hand clamped down on his wrist, twisting the sword toward his own chest. Eric struggled, but her grip was hard to break lose. He steadily raised his free hand, palm open. Vienna caught the movement a second too late. He was aiming for her face. She cursed and launched a brutal kick to his groin.

Eric huffed, the impact folding him in half as they both went flying. They crash-landed into the northern tower, glass and stone exploding outward on impact. Eric hit the floor first, the wind knocked clean from his lungs as dust rained from the ceiling. Pain lit up his ribs, but he forced himself to roll onto his side, coughing through the grit in his throat. Slowly, his eyes swept the crumbled hallway. There was no sign of Vienna.

Drip.

Somewhere in the distance, water dripped against stone, slow, steady and hollow. The silence felt unnatural, like the air itself was holding its breath. His eyes locked on the opening, the one they'd smashed on impact. Something was coming. The breeze from the opening, he could feel it. He could feel her presence. He just didn't know from where. He raised his hand and just fired. A tunnel of water blasted through the opening. It hit something. Vienna's form shimmered, lost balance, and dropped out of the tower with a scream. Eric exhaled, and wiped his face with the back of his hand. This fight wasn't over. Not even close.

Not far from the Northern tower, Marie drove her staff into the gut of Zion's men. He fell, unconscious. She turned, saw a massive, jagged hole punched through the side of the Northern tower. Without a word, she took off, flying through the shattered corridor, smoke rising in her wake. The cold was deeper here, not just in the air, but in the bones of the place, like the lair itself had been drained of life long ago. Light barely touched the corridor's edges, flickering and fading as if even flame refused to stay. The wind had vanished. Stillness clung to the corridor, like the hallway itself was holding its breath.

Eric walked slowly, sword dragging at his side, each step louder than it should be. The walls narrowed. Cracks spidered beneath his boots. Something unseen pressed in from all sides. And then he saw it. He turned. A black chamber door stood at the far end. Monolithic. Ominous. It hadn't just been shut. It had been waiting. Still. Nothing stirred around it, not even dust. Sound itself seemed to hesitate before reaching it.

The corridor stretched endlessly ahead, narrowing, each step echoing deeper into a space that felt more tomb than a hallway. Eric moved toward the door, breath tight, blade in hand. Behind him, footsteps. "Eric," Marie said, she stepped beside him without a word, her breath slow, her shoulders squared. He turned, relief flickering in his eyes, just for a moment. Silence poured between them, swallowed by the weight of what loomed ahead: A hiss, a slow sound like a slithering snake remained at the door. Their gaze locked on the black door, but her mind was already past it. "This is it," she said.

Eric glanced at the frame. "Are you sure?"

Marie didn't flinch. But deep down, she felt it, every inch of it. That door didn't just hide the Sphere. It hid the ghosts of everything she'd lost, her parents, her kingdom, her freedom. It had taken so much from her already. And now she had to walk straight into its jaws. The moment she waited for, orcas ago. She squared her shoulders, stared ahead, and lied, only a little. "Positive."

He stepped forward, gripped the locked handle. "There must be some other way."

Marie exhaled slowly. "It won't be easy."

She raised both hands. Blue light coiled around her fingers, soft at first, then growing into luminous threads of sapphire energy that spiraled across her hands. The metal groaned. A sound like ancient bones grinding against stone filled the corridor as the blue glow snaked outward, gripping the door's edges with invisible hands. And then, with force and focus, she bent the frame inward until the black door cracked open like a rib cage.

The door groaned open into a cavernous chamber swallowed in shadow. Marie stepped in first, her boots echoing against cold stone. The vaulted ceilings stretched high above, ribs of old architecture fading into darkness. But there, hovering in the center was the source of it all.

The M'ra Sphere.

It hovered silently atop its stand, white light pulsing like a heartbeat. No chains. No guard. No barrier between it and them. Just raw, radiant power, suspended like an exposed nerve in the dark. And then he heard it. A hiss. Not a mechanical sound. Not breath. Something ancient. Primal. It slithered into the room like a curse unraveled, curling around the walls, wrapping around his spine, his eyes, his mind.

It drowned out everything, the hum of silence, the drip of condensation, even his own breath. Eric slowed. His shoulders relaxed. His sword lowered. She saw the glow reflected in his eyes, white and very much alive, casting him in a halo that didn't belong. The slithering hiss grew. Louder this time. His steps grew slower. Shallow.

Hypnotic. Eric was suddenly in a trance, no words, no force could stop him.

"No," she breathed.

But he didn't hear. He kept walking. Stalking towards The M'ra Sphere. Somehow it made his mind forget the pain he was drowning in. His Home. His family. And even Rose, although he got her back who's to say one of the four won't be next and for a moment, this stillness Eric is in, he wouldn't be able to help them. Tiny goosebumps trickled up his spine throughout his body. His eyes, wider beyond comprehension, were learning, and absorbing the very essence of the Sphere. The hiss looped in louder this time.

Marie straightened, every instinct in her body retreating. She knew this magic. Not because she studied it. Because The M'ra Sphere didn't need permission. It whispered to those who looked for answers. It found cracks and filled them with seduction. This time it was Eric, and it was trying to consume him. She didn't think. She moved. Marie yanked a velvet cloth from her satchel and hurled it forward, over the Sphere in one clean motion. The hiss shattered violently like whispers from a ghost of the past.

Gone. Like it had never been there. For a heartbeat, the silence was heavier than sound itself. Marie's chest rose, shallow, as if even the air feared to move. Eric stumbled backward, gasped, blinking hard. He couldn't remember what he was doing a second ago. Everything was a blur. He looked at Maire, like waking from a dream he couldn't name. Marie didn't wait.

She strode forward, grabbed the Sphere, still humming beneath the fabric, and slid it into her velvet crossbody bag. The weight of it hit her like a stone in water, but she didn't falter. Not now. Not again. She didn't breathe until the hiss was gone. Even then, her chest stayed tight. The Sphere may have been covered, but its hunger wasn't silenced. Not truly. And she couldn't shake the feeling… That it had already taken something from Eric. Marie tightened the strap of the bag across her shoulder. Her voice was steady.

"Let's go."

Marie moved fast, unaware that far above them, eyes were already watching. Eyes that felt the M'ra Sphere's absence like a knife to the chest. Zion stood at the highest balcony of the lair, unmoving, a lone shadow above the chaos below. Fire licked the courtyard. Screams echoed through the smoke. And yet he did not blink. Then, his body stilled. A sharp pain bloomed beneath his ribs. His hand gripped the fabric over his heart. *The M'ra Sphere.* Something flickered behind his eyes, not fear. Something about him shifted. A thread, invisible but vital, felt severed. Power… slipping. Without a word, Zion turned, his cloak sweeping behind him as he disappeared into the darkness.

Rose blazed across the lair, fully engulfed in fire, her body a streak of living flame. Every step scorched the ground beneath her, her presence a burning rebuke to the chaos around her. She fought with relentless precision, hurling blasts of flame in tight arcs and vicious bursts. Streams of fire erupted from her hands as soldiers closed in, only to be swallowed by the inferno, their screams lost beneath the roar of her fury.

Above her, Adam soared into view, his white eyes as snow, locked onto the chaos below. He halted midair, boots hovering just above the ground. The wind answered, first a whisper, then a shriek. It coiled around him, wrapped in a cocoon in furious spirals as he raised his arms, drawing the current tighter and tighter. Then, with a sharp motion, he released it, unleashing a roaring hurricane that blasted through the advancing line of soldiers and Prylyn creatures, tearing them from their feet like leaves in a storm.

Something flickered below. Zion was gone. Adam's chest tightened. Not from exhaustion. From knowing. *He's going for the Sphere.* "He's headed for the Sphere!" Adam shouted, voice cutting through the storm.

"Not if I get there first!" Rose yelled, her flames snapping around her, zipped to the inside of the lair, vanishing into the shadow corridors. Katherine, witnessing the charge, raised her arm without a word. Adam swooped down, caught her hand mid-leap, and carried her through the air. They landed at the base of the staircase leading into the lair. Inside the dim corridor, Katherine moved quickly. With a sharp motion of her hand, the earth obeyed, stone walls groaned and particles from the ground, coiling, sealing the entrance behind them.

Adam continued forward, his steps fast but cautious, the echo of each footfall swallowed by the stone walls around him. The hallway split ahead into two narrow corridors, both dimly lit and eerily quiet. He paused at the intersection, scanning both directions, left and right, his breath shallow, his body stiff. Then, without a word, he turned left. Katherine followed close behind, silent but ready. The scream echoed down the corridor, sharp and distant: Rose. *Rose. She must be down this way. Wait, why can't I…* He thought.

Adam stiffened. Not from fear, something else. It crawled beneath his skin like static, invisible but undeniable. A prickling sensation climbed up his spine, colder than instinct, deeper than nerves. Something was wrong, and every cell in his body knew it, long before his mind could understand why. Katherine turned to him, alert. "What's wrong?"

He tried to speak. Tried to move. But his throat tightened, and his legs rooted to the floor as if the hallway itself had clenched around him. His breath shortened. His instincts had locked him in place, like his body was screaming a warning his thoughts hadn't caught up to yet.

Then—

A low rumble began, subtle at first, like pressure shifting inside the walls. It wasn't mechanical. It wasn't natural. Adam's eyes flicked upward just as Katherine's head snapped toward the ceiling, both of them tracking the sound as it slithered through the stone like something hunting just beneath the surface. "Go!" he said sharply.

The rumble stopped. The hallway flashed, just once. A shadow passed through the light, there, then gone, like a glitch in reality. And suddenly, he was there. No warning. No sound. Just motion and force. Adam barely had time to blink before the man was on him, slamming him into the wall. His back hit stone with a crack, and a forearm pressed hard into his chest, pinning him like prey. The corridor seemed to still around them, as if the space itself recognized the threat. His breath vanished. Pain cracked across his back. The man leaned in, calm, composed, elegant even, in the worst way.

He turned his head toward Katherine. "No hard feelings," he said, smirking. That's when she froze, recognition flashing across her face. Adam didn't know who he was. But the moment their eyes locked, he understood one thing, he wasn't leaving this hallway the same.

Asterius.

He tilted his head, studying Adam for just a second longer than necessary. "You're different," he said, soft, almost curious. And then, he winked. Before Katherine could react, his hands clamped around Adam. A twist of light. A ripple in the air. And suddenly they vanished.

No ground. No sound. Only the feeling of falling without motion. Darkness cradled him like a void, cold, weightless, infinite. Adam blinked. Once. Twice. Still nothing. Then, light. A pulse of sickly green flickered around him, revealing smooth stone beneath his feet. The air pressed against his skin like wet glass. Asterius stood at the far end of the room, eyes glowing a venomous yellow. Like a still doll waiting for the kill.

Adam's heart thrashed in his chest. He stumbled back instinctively, the silence choking him more than any scream ever could. "Where am I?!" he shouted, voice echoing too long, like the space itself didn't know how to hold it. "KATE! ERIC! ROSE!" Asterius said nothing. Didn't move. Just stared. Adam turned, desperate, and found a stone statue beside him... Rose? No... the shape was wrong. He reached out and waved his hand through it. It dissolved into dust. His throat tightened. "What is this place?"

Asterius's voice slid through the silence like a whisper behind glass. "It's just a figment of your imagination." Then, he disintegrated. No sound. No warning. Just gone. The room rippled. Stone became smoke. The floor became sky. And Adam was alone again. But something had changed. It was pitch black again. The silence wasn't just absence now, it pulsed. Like breath. Like memory. Shapes flickered in the dark haze. First one, then many. Stone markers rising from the mist, like a burial. Gravestones. Adam staggered forward, drawn toward them like a moth to a flame. Names carved in cracked marble glinted in the half-light, blood seeping out:

ROSE BLACKBURN

ERIC ROWE

KATHERINE GREENFIELD

"No…" His voice came out broken. His hands trembled as he reached for one. Cold stone. Solid. Real. Then a fourth marker emerged, slower than the others. Taller. Centered. He didn't want to look. But he did.

ADAM GREENFIELD

His knees nearly gave out. It wasn't just fear. It was a knowing, deep and terrifying. Some part of him had already accepted this. Some part of him… believed it. His breath caught in his throat. He turned to run and slammed into a wall.

No… not a wall. A hallway. Flickering green lights stretched out endlessly before him, just like the one he'd been in before. The air was thick with static, the scent of smoke and dust curling through the corridor. His heart beating fast. Limbs shaking. Eyes wide. Holding on like it was his final breath. A picture hung crooked on the wall, framed in black, its image warped.

But he knew it. It was the hallway. The one he'd just escaped from. The one where Katherine had stood beside him. Adam stepped toward it, breath unsteady. He reached out and the moment his fingers touched the frame the ground collapsed beneath him. A roar of wind. Glassed cracked under pressure. A spiral of black.

He was falling—

no bottom,

no end,

just the pull of gravity

and silence that screamed.

The light vanished. The air turned icy. Then, impact. Adam slammed onto solid ground, a pitch-black floor that stretched in every direction. No walls. No ceiling. Just endless, suffocating dark.

"Hello?!" he called out, voice trembling.

"Eric?! Katherine?! Rose?!"

…No answer.

"Can anyone hear me?!"

The silence pressed in harder, a presence all its own. Then his voice came back to him but perverse. Malevolent. "Eric?! Katherine?! Rose?!" the echo repeated. "Eric?! Katherine?! Rose?!" A deep thrum emerged in the distance. A sound like a war drum—

Doom.

Doom. Doom. Doom. Doom.

Then another voice—

his voice—

but it didn't sound like him anymore.

"Who are you talking to?"

Adam's breath hitched. He turned in a slow circle, scanning the dark. "This isn't real," he whispered. "This isn't real." But it felt real. Too real. The air bit at his skin. The dark watched him. Then somewhere deep down, he wasn't sure he wanted to know the truth. And then it came, a growl. Low. Ancient. Not from the shadows, but from inside his chest. As if something had noticed him… and was hungry. A pair of long, black taloned claws extended, dripped in black smoke, reached for his shoulder in the dark, barely a touch, eager to snatch him away. Then the voice answered again: "You can't run from it forever."

Images flashed—

brief, sharp,

like polaroid snapshots slamming into his mind.

Snap. Snap.

Blood.

Fire.

His own face, smeared in blood.

And behind it all—

The man he killed.

The truth.

The guilt.

The weight.

Then—

In the distance, faint and flickering: a green glow. A hallway. Framed like a painting suspended in the void. The same hallway. The same warped image. Adam ran toward it, legs shaking, pulled like a moth to a flame again. His hand reached for the picture again. This time, he didn't hesitate, he wanted to leave this nightmare.

WHOOSH.

A slam of air. A flash of blinding light. The pressure hit him all at once, like being yanked through space and spit back out. The void vanished, replaced by stone beneath his boots and the sour bite of torchlight in his eyes. He stood in the hallway. But it wasn't the same. The stone beneath his feet felt colder, slick with dampness that clung to the air like sweat. The walls were darker now, distorted, like they'd absorbed the fear left behind. Faint green light shimmered along the surface, bending and twitching like reflections from some unseen pool, as if the corridor itself was breathing.

Then—

Rose's scream echoed, twisting and warping down the corridor in fractured layers. The sound shimmered unnaturally, glittering through the air like broken glass caught in a beam of green light. It didn't just bounce off the walls, it slithered, threaded into the stone itself. Adam spun toward it, heart pounding, his instincts overriding the fear. Footsteps echoed behind him, sharp, fast, familiar. Adam blinked, the hallway still swimming in and out of focus. His limbs felt heavy, like he'd been underwater. He swayed, bracing himself against the wall. His head throbbed. His mouth was dry.

What the hell just happened…?

Katherine's voice cut through the haze. "Adam!"

He turned, dazed. Eric and Katherine were rushing toward him, faces tense, eyes scanning him like he might vanish again. "We've been looking for you everywhere," Katherine said, gripping his arm.

Adam's voice came out hoarse. "Where…
where were you?" But the real question sat heavier
in his chest. *Where was I?* He pulled himself
upright, trying to make sense of the world again.
"I think…" he started, breath shaking. "I think
Zion has Rose."

Before anyone could say another word
Rose's scream ripped down the hallway, shrill and
brutal, like it was being dragged through a
thousand mouths at once. Like an echo. Then a
shadow. A flicker of movement at the far end of
the corridor. A figure emerged, ghost-like at first,
but solid in the next breath: Zion. One arm
wrapped tight around Rose's neck, dragging her
with him. Katherine gasped. Eric doesn't answer,
his body tenses, his jaw clenches. And then… he
runs. "Rose!" Eric shouted.

"Wait! Eric!" Adam shouted, but he was
already gone.

Zion disappeared around the corner,
taking Rose with him. His voice echoed behind
them like a curse: *If you want the girl… come and get
her.*

They reached the corner and stopped, nothing. Zion and Rose were gone. Just sudden emptiness. At the turn of the corner, the end of the hall stood a black door, cracked open, pitch-black inside. Nothing, but unease, untold secrets, even the stench of death crept out from the opening. Eric stared at it, his breath shallow. "This is where he took her," he said quietly, almost to himself.

Adam stepped forward. "It's a trap. If we go down there, we die with her." Eric's hands clenched at his sides. He hesitated, just for a second. Then he looked at them both, something sharp behind his eyes. "I'm not leaving her again," he said. And before either of them could stop him. He ran faster than a bolt of lightning.

"Eric!" Katherine yelled.

"Eric! No!" Adam's voice cracked.

He reached the door, it was heavier than he anticipated, he persisted, shoved it shut behind him, locking them out. Katherine and Adam ran to the door seal; it was too late. It's locked. No sound from the other side. "Damn it," Adam muttered, slamming his palm against the door. They looked around, there was no other way in. Not this time. "Fuck." It wasn't just a door. It was a line, and Eric had crossed it alone. "Come on," Adam said, turning to escape. "We can't stay here." Together, they ran, back toward the lair grounds, the shadows closing in behind them.

Eric leaned his head against the black door, chest heaving, breath ragged. It stayed there for a moment longer. The weight of it all pressed into his spine, into his ribs, into his heart. He didn't know what lay before him. He took a deep breath and only knew Rose was the one worth saving. He did it for her. He exhaled and turned. And the world had changed. The hallway was gone. The lair had vanished. No one else was here.

In its place, was sand, wind, and the sun. And at the far edge, a cliff that dropped into nothing. The sky stretched out like fire on glass. He scanned the area, to his mind, it was something like falling cliffs. All deserted.

At the far edge, Zion. Holding Rose by the throat, dangling her over the abyss like a sacrifice. Her body hung limp, her feet just inches off the cliff's edge. She wasn't moving, her eyes rolled back like a hollow possession, no pupils, all Eric saw was white. He gasped. Her hands twitched. Her breath came in shallow bursts, quick, desperate, almost failing. Zion's fingers tightened her neck. Her legs kicked once, then stiffened, her boots scraping against air. She was losing oxygen.

"Take another step," Zion growled, "and you'll see how far she'll go." Eric halted. His eyes locked onto Rose's, wide and terrified.

"Please, don't do it," he said, voice cracking.

Zion smirked, cold and monstrous. His fingers unclenched with casual cruelty. He let go. Rose fell, limbs flailing, swallowed by the void beneath.

"ROSE!" Eric yelled. He lunged forward with a strangled cry, but there was nothing to catch, she was already gone. He crumbled inward to his knees, whimpering like he had lost his whole world, that whole world was Rose.

Behind him, the wind shifted, sharp, unnatural, like something unseen had passed through the space. Zion. He didn't leave right away. He lingered long enough to watch Eric break, eyes gleaming with cruel satisfaction. "It will all make sense soon, my child", he said. Then he vanished in a blur of darkness and light, gone, like he'd never been there at all. Not even a shadow remained.

The weight of what Eric had seen driving the air from his lungs. His hands trembled uncontrollably, fists clenching against the cold sand beneath him. His chest caved inward, breath caught between a sob and a scream. Even after the silence...

Rose plummeting endlessly. *Is this what death feels like?* She thought. Her eyes flickered opened, she gasped at the fall, her body ignited mid-fall, flames twisting around her like a Phoenix reborn. She soared, soared upward, her death sentence transforming into strength, into power. She felt the air leave her lungs. Not from fear, because there was nothing left to hold on to. And she remembered. *I am the fire.* Light poured from her like a solar flare, and the air bent around her in reverence. She surged higher, faster, until the edge of the cliff came into view again. A blinding glow bloomed over the cliffside. Fire and gold it illuminated and there he was, Eric, her lover, her soulmate. She saw his broken heart. His soul. She would never hurt him.

She gently hovered just above him, flames humming around her in soft spirals. She extended her hand. On his knees, Eric looked up, eyes wide, like he'd seen a ghost, breath stunned. In awe at most. How could this be? She floated above him, flame still flickering, eyes calm. Eric calmly reached for her, shaking. Her flame didn't burn him, it cradled him. Warm and alive. He slowly pulled her close. Her boots touched the ground as the flames receded. As soon as the fire went away, he strapped her in a hug so tight there was no room for her to let go. He couldn't possibly let her, not after what he just faced.

"I have you now," he whispered, like a vow. Above them, the air stilled, the sun curling around them like a prayer half-answered. Rose held on to Eric, a little unsteady, but the fire behind her eyes hadn't gone out. It transformed. She was no longer that girl we thought we knew. Something in her changed. Now the raid was over, but she sensed something.

And then she remembered:

He came for blood today.

Tomorrow, he'll carve out our hearts.

Chapter XX:
The Aftermath

The infirmary inside Ronan's palace wasn't much, just stone walls, low lantern light, and worn medical cots scattered like remnants of an older war. The air smelled of burnt herbs, old ash, and something faintly metallic. Bandages crinkled. Soft murmurs drifted between healers and soldiers, barely louder than the wind outside. It felt like the room itself was holding its breath. Adam sat on the edge of a medical cot, his legs dangling, shoulders hunched, breath shallow. A thick ringing buzzed in his ears. *Where did this ringing come from? It's gnawing at my head.* A clean towel pressed to his forehead, too warm, too gentle, like it didn't belong in a world so broken. Even that towel hurt him. *I was hoping it would make the pain go away.* The nurse tending him moved carefully, but each dab against the gash above his brow made him flinch, as if the pain were rooted deeper than skin.

He couldn't shake the images, each one stamped into his mind like carvings in stone. The gravestones hadn't been vague symbols or illusions. They were real. Not from his imagination. A bit Cold. Blood seeping out. Images flashing like a polaroid camera, snapping photos. Names he knew by heart, now chiseled into silence. Not just any graves, their graves. *Could it be?* No… it couldn't be. But it was there, etched in crimson.

Rose Blackburn.
Eric Rowe.
Katherine Greenfield.

And his own. The last one… the most disturbing. He saw it. His name, imprinted into stone, cold and bloodshot red. A vision. A warning. A lie? His eyes flickered like he was changing the channel in his own head. His throat tightened. *Is that our future? Is that what's waiting for us?* His hands trembled on his lap. *Or are we already too late? Did they have us fall into a death trap?* Fighting his own thoughts. *No. No. Marie and Ronan wouldn't lead us into battle just for our deaths. Some say Ronan might otherwise.*

Across the room, Rose sat on another medical cot, speaking softly to a nurse. Her shoulders were tight, her voice low, like a memory Adam couldn't quite reach. Eric stood beside her. Their eyes met for a moment, just long enough for Adam to feel the wall still standing between them. Then Eric looked away. He knew that look. Not guilt. Not even anger. Just… avoidance. Like Eric had gotten what he needed, and Adam was just a reminder of what he didn't. The nurse stepped aside, her presence vanishing like a shadow in retreat. Silence settled in, thick and unnatural, as if the world had been dipped underwater, sound muffled and warped. Even the breath in Adam's chest felt distant, like it didn't belong to him.

And then—

Footsteps. Light ones. There it goes again, barely audible, the ringing in his ears… his vision weaving in and out. A figure moved toward him, blurred at the edges, like a memory refusing to come into focus. Adam didn't react at first. He just sat there, eyes distant, the sound of thousand bees buzzing in his ear. Watching the world folding in on itself. Then her voice broke through, clear and sudden, like a stone shattering glass.

"Adam?"

He blinked. A soft ringing pulsed in his ears, steady, like a siren buried underwater. Someone was speaking, but the words came warped and slow, a low *womp womp womp* that drifted in and out. His head throbbed. *What are they saying?* he wondered, caught in the static of his own mind. The sound swelled, returning to full volume in waves, until her voice finally cut through the fog.

"You haven't said anything." Katherine's voice was clearer now, sharp with concern.

He didn't answer. Although her voice was pure, like it had traveled through fog to reach him, but he couldn't move. He just stayed there, like a memory surfacing too slowly. When her hand brushed his arm, he flinched, instinctively, like muscle memory. His body pulled back, rigid, as if expecting another blow, another jolt of pain he couldn't see coming. The raid he remembered. The contact wasn't violent, but his nerves didn't know the difference between his sister or the enemy. Everything in him braced like the worst was still coming. "Adam, are you okay?" She stepped into his line of sight, forcing him to look at her.

…Silence.

"You, okay?" she asked again.

Adam exhaled, low and shaky. "Yeah," he muttered. The buzzing had stopped, the pain subsided, but his voice didn't sound like his own.

"He's been waiting, Adam," Katherine said, watching him carefully.

Adam blinked slowly, eyes still unfocused. "Who?"

"Eric." Her voice softened. "You know he's waiting for you to say something."

Adam didn't look at her. His gaze hung on the floor, where blood still clung to his boots. *Katherine doesn't even know. She didn't see the way he swung at me. The way he shut down. Like I wasn't even there. But sure. I'm the villain now. That's rich.*

She stepped closer. "You're really going to let it sit like this? Go fix it."

Adam's throat tightened. *Must I always be the one to mend the hearts of men?* The thought scraped across his mind like rusted iron, bitter, unspoken. "What?" he muttered. "It's not like we haven't talked before."

Katherine exhaled, slow and tired.

"This is different."

Adam sat in silence, the echoes of Katherine's words still hanging in the air. *I guess she's right.* He just stared at his trembling hands, blood-streaked and still. Even now, they couldn't stop shaking. Not even the wind within him could shake it. His gaze drifted to the window, to the shifting shadows outside. Something felt… off. Like the world itself had paused. Something twisted inside him. A pressure. A weight. Like a tether snapping loose, or something waking up. His eyes wandered beyond the fogged glass of a world he never knew. Something is coming.

The wind howled just beyond the northern tower stone fractured, in ruins, walls scorched, as if the room itself had been ripped open by unseen hands. Shafts of light pierced through the cracks, illuminating the wreckage like spotlight beams through a burning cathedral. Smoke hung in the air, curling like restless spirits above shattered pillars and debris. Every breath felt heavy, tainted with ash and ruin. Emperor Zion stood motionless at the center of the devastation, his long coat pooling around him like a shadow. Before him, the pedestal that once held *The M'ra Sphere* now sat empty.

It was cold. Silent. Felt like betrayal. The air around it pulsed with absence, as if the sphere's removal had torn a hole in the fabric of the room and in Zion's control. His breath was steady, but his eyes blazed and reptilian. His jaw clenched. His breath slowed. Then it happened. A spike of rage lanced through him, sharp and immediate, like a blade beneath the skin. He didn't move. Didn't blink. He couldn't. If he took one step, he'd burn the entire lair down. The sound of footsteps echoed behind him, measured, quite hesitant. He didn't turn when The General entered. He didn't need to. "Your Majesty…"

With no warning, Zion's hand swept behind his back. A dagger gleamed, in a swift motion, a slashed across The General's throat in one fluid execution. The man staggered, gurgled, and dropped to the floor, like a thud, in a pool of blood. Zion didn't flinch. He stepped over the body, eyes fixed on the empty pedestal. His breathing turned heavy, heaving.

He didn't need to speak. The truth bled into the silence. They had taken it. They had dared to take The M'ra Sphere. He roared, his voice rising like a beast unfurling in the dark. The scream shook the chamber, rattling the broken walls and echoing across the lair like a declaration from the depths of hell. The pedestal still pulsed faintly, an echo of the power that once rested there. Dust trembled in the silence, curling in the air like breath held too long. Even outside the chamber, footsteps retreated, afraid to enter. The footsteps knew this means war.

Even on New Earth's soil, Marie didn't hear the scream, but she felt it. Like a ripple in her chest, it was sharp and uninvited. Some instincts were deeper than magic told her: Zion knew. The chamber knew, it buzzed with energy even before the casing opened. Ronan stood beside Marie, his skin pale beneath the flickering vault light like he'd seen a ghost. *The M'ra Sphere* pulsed in his hands, brighter than ever, its pure white glow swirling inside like fog trapped in glass, silent and unnerving in its calm. It whispered mutters no one could hear. Marie's fingers hovered over the latch, trembling slightly. Her breath caught, was it the sphere, or her own fear making her hesitate? Then she unsealed it, and the top hissed open with a soft click that echoed louder than it should have. Ronan placed the sphere inside, and the moment it touched the cradle, the air shifted. Just like that. It was charged and waiting.

An enormous shockwave of white energy surged outward from the sphere, rippling through the marble like a breath of divine force. The walls quaked, but Ronan and Marie didn't move. They stayed there as the white energy flows through them. Symbols etched into the floor flared in brief succession, glowing white before fading into silence. Light licked across the chamber in branching currents, climbing the pillars and exploding through the vault ceiling in a towering beam that lit up the sky. The blast didn't stop at the vault.

The pulse shot across New Earth like a lightning storm ripping through centuries of shadow. The sky viciously cracked open— one half stained a deep, aching sunset blue, the other streaked in red-pink like an infected wound. Forests trembled as black goo and tendrils curled and burned away, shriveling to ash beneath the cleansing surge. Crops lifted their wilted heads in slow, cautious bloom. Birds burst from the trees, wings slicing the air, while distant howls echoed from hidden dens as creatures emerged from long-held silence. Nothing was the same, it couldn't be. Sometimes things never happen the same way twice. Even the land was not whole. It only had awakened.

Yet far beyond the forests and fields, past the ridges still choked in smoke, something stirred. A sliver of land once sealed by ancient spells began to fracture, stone parting, light seeping through like veins rediscovered beneath old skin. Mountains shifted. Earth yawned open. And for the first time in orcas, the Nexus, New Earth's capital, born of a new world taking shaped, breathed again. It began with the Celeborn Castle, long dormant, now reclaimed by its true heir. High upon the cliffs, its towers stood defiant above the sea, casting shadows over the land it once ruled. The Old Dominion, an ancient coliseum forged for battle, flickered to life deep within.

Hidden chambers stirred. Forgotten corners awakened. Something ancient had been unlocked. Only a glimpse. But enough to suggest that the balance had not just been restored… it had moved. The corruption withdrew, but the scars remained, like a torn heart. The trees stood brittle and hollow, their bark stripped like flesh from bone after the black goo retreated. Rivers still ran dry, winding through the land like veins full of ash. New Earth's core balance had not been restored. Only postponed. Marie steadied herself, blinking against the light as it faded. *The M'ra Sphere* now rested in stillness. Quiet. Dormant. But its glow hadn't dimmed. It was waiting. "He'll be back," she said, breath still catching in her chest. "We have to warn the others."

Ronan didn't look at her.

"No! Not now."

Marie turned toward him, her voice sharp. The sudden bark in his tone made her flinch, it wasn't fear. It was something else. Something colder rising in him. "No? In case you've forgotten, the war has already started. He and his army…"

"It will be too risky for them to know now," he said in a quick breath.

"What's risky is not telling them," she snapped. "We need to prepare before we get ambushed again."

"Not like this," Ronan said.

"This way I know we can protect them."

Marie's eyes narrowed. His posture. His tone. There was a coldness in it that hadn't been there before. "Ever since the raid, your judgment has been... off."

"What matters," he said, "is that we keep The M'ra Sphere safe. Out of Zion's hands." Marie's gaze dropped to the case. "It sounds like it needs to be out of your hands," she said. The light inside pulsed, slow, rhythmic, almost like it breathed. It flickered across Ronan's face, casting sharp, unnatural shadows. And in that moment, the truth settled in her chest like a stone. It wasn't just protecting him. It was feeding on him. Consuming him from the inside out, creeping through his veins like a parasite inching toward escape.

Her voice fell to a whisper. "When I become Queen, I'll see to it that you never lay a hand on the M'ra Sphere again."

"Ah. There she is. Queen Marie, always thinking we're part of a disease. Giving orders like we're still in love. For the record, I'm not sick." Ronan's voice stayed level, but the edge was unmistakable. He just stared at her, not angry, not defiant. Just... composed. They argued like a bitter couple. Like someone holding onto something already lost. There was more between them than power and duty. There had been once.

And maybe, in that silence, it showed. She turned and walked away, faster than she intended. She didn't look back. Her mind swirled. *Time moved differently here. Seasons could pass in a matter of moons, children grew in blinks, and love unraveled faster than it formed.*

The vault doors sealed behind her with a low, final thud. Silence returned, thick as stone. Outside, dusk had settled over the palace grounds. The air cooled. Somewhere beyond the northern wing, a wind stirred through the blue gardens, soft, but steady. Petals danced like whispers across the stone paths. Ronan stood alone beneath the shifting light, his gaze distant. The weight of *The M'ra Sphere* still echoed in his chest, but his face gave nothing away.

Later that night, Katherine stepped into the courtyard, her boots brushing softly over the worn stone path. The air was cooler here, earth-kissed and still, like the breath of something ancient holding its silence. Ivy curled along the outer walls, their leaves trembling faintly as she passed, reacting to her presence without fear. She walked in near silence, fingertips grazing the cobblestone's ridged surface, its grooves slick with night dew. Each step echoed like a whisper beneath her soles. Moonlight spilled across the garden, casting long shadows between the hedges and fractured statues. The stones beneath her feet shimmered faintly, their cracks laced with moss and flickers of bioluminescent green, as if the land itself was alive, watching, memorizing. Somewhere deeper in the garden, wind moved through the trees like breath through a sleeping giant. The air pulsed softly, as if the ground were exhaling. She didn't speak. There was nothing to say. The silence said it for her: a silence thick with the ghosts of battles past, of choices not yet made. And still, the Earth remained, tangible, patient, unmoved. A quiet witness to the war on the horizon.

Around the corner, a strange green glow lit the night, soft at first, then brighter, pulsing like a heartbeat beneath the soil. The light spilled across the garden floor in uneven waves, casting the statues in ghostly silhouette. It radiated from a sunken pool near the center, its surface rippling without wind, as if stirred by unseen hands. The air here was thicker, tinged with something metallic and old, like rain on stone or blood on iron. Katherine slowed, her breath catching as the garden shifted from quiet to sacred.

She stopped short. Something glowed ahead, dim, beckoning. A pool, sunken deep into the ground, flickered with trapped light, a haunting circle of translucent water. Ghostly radiance shimmered across its surface, and pale faces shifted beneath, flickering like echoes caught in time. She stepped forward. Sat slowly at the edge. Her hands rested on her knees, shoulders slumped, as if the weight of everything pressed down at once. She stared into the pool.

"Only if you knew what I'm going through," she said quietly.

The surface of the pool rippled, as if it had heard her. The light within shifted, subtle, slow, like breath beneath glass. For a moment, the water seemed to listen, holding her words in its depths. Then it stilled again, silent as the dead. Behind her, a figure emerged from the shadows of the archway. His footsteps were nearly silent, swallowed by the hush of the garden. He moved with purpose, but not urgency, like someone stepping into memory rather than confrontation. She didn't turn right away, but something in her chest tightened, recognition without sight.

"I do," Ronan said.

Katherine turned, startled by the sudden presence. He walked toward her with measured steps, his face unreadable in the wash of moonlight, shadow and silver softening every edge. For a moment, neither spoke, only the rustle of leaves filled the space between them. Then he sat beside her in silence, like he'd been there before, and knew exactly what not to say.

"How did you know I was here?" she asked.

"I may not read minds, but I can read a heavy silence," Ronan smirked.

She gave a tired laugh, dry, brief. It wasn't joy, not really, but something more like release. A crack in the armor. Her gaze dropped to the pool again, chasing the ripple before it faded. "Why are they here?" she asked, nodding to the souls.

"They're the fallen warriors and guardians," he said. "Men and women who gave everything to protect New Earth."

Katherine looked back into the pool. The faces shifted again, their outlines warping in the rippling surface like restless spirits trapped between worlds. Some wore expressions of peace, as if they'd found rest in the depths. Others contorted in silent screams, mouths stretched wide in frozen terror. One blinked. Another twitched. The water shimmered around them, a canvas of memory and mourning. She didn't flinch. She'd seen worse. "Why give up your whole life for a world that might never appreciate you?" she asked.

Ronan's voice was low. "Because it mattered. And they knew it. The world is built on fear, but they chose purpose. They stood when others ran." Silence passed between them. It wasn't empty, it carried the weight of everything left unsaid. The kind of silence that settles in when grief and understanding meet halfway. And then, quietly, he broke it. "I know why you're here," he said.

Katherine didn't speak. The silence stretched. Her gaze stayed fixed on the water. Shadows from the pool flickered across her features, catching on the sharp lines of her jaw. She sat perfectly still, as if breaking that stillness might let something else rise to the surface. Then, quietly, she said, "You don't know what it's like… to be that close to someone. To feel them slip away. To live with the regret. The not knowing." Her voice caught, barely audible. "If they died… would they even remember me?"

Ronan didn't answer right away. The air between them felt heavy, charged with memories neither had spoken aloud. "I do know the feeling," he said at last, his voice low. "I lost my father to Zion." He let that linger, then added, "It's not easy, losing people. Carrying the weight of the ones you love. And now, being asked to fight again… to unlock something you never asked for."

She clenched her hands.

"I don't think I can do it."

"You were chosen for a reason," he said. "You're stronger than you think. You've already made it this far. Don't lose hope." He glanced at her, gentler now. "Sometimes we all just need a little push."

Katherine took a deep breath, steady but slow. The pool shimmered beside her, casting ripples of green light across her face like a ghost's hand reaching from below. It brushed her cheek, soft and cold, as if testing her determination. She didn't move, just sat there, letting it touch her, letting it pass. Then something itched faintly at the side of her neck. Katherine brushed her fingers there, just below her jaw, above the collarbone. Her skin felt warmer, pulsing gently beneath her touch. She turned toward the pool's reflection, and saw it… A mark.

Faint, but unmistakable. It curved like stone fractured under pressure, etched in the shape of roots twisting through soil. It didn't glow, it throbbed, quietly, like a heartbeat buried deep underground. Not a wound. Not a scar. It felt… inherent, as if it had been there all along, waiting for the moment she was ready to see it.

"Just don't forget to breathe," he said. Then, with a quiet nod, like he'd seen something and chosen to let it be, he rose and left her with the garden and the ghosts of the past.

Katherine allowed herself a faint smile, small and fleeting. For the first time in what felt like ages, it didn't feel forced or borrowed from someone stronger. It settled gently on her lips, uncertain but real. Not joy, just a quiet exhale, like a bruise finally starting to fade. Behind her, the garden remained still. The pool shimmered and the night waited.

Chapter XXI:
Vengeance Stirs

Firelight flickered against stone. Shadows danced along the high-vaulted ceiling of the dining hall, where the four Legends sat in near silence. The long oak table stretched between them, untouched platters of food laid out like offerings to ghosts. A storm pressed against the windows, distant thunder rumbling low like a warning. The flames cast an unsteady glow across their faces, tired, hollowed, changed. Utensils remained untouched beside half-filled goblets, the scent of roasted game and herbs hanging in the stillness like a memory too heavy to savor. Every tick of silence widened the chasm between them, an invisible grief threading through the air. Outside, wind howled through the cracks in the stone walls, as if the world itself was mourning something not yet lost.

Adam sat at the head of the table, his eyes fixed on the empty space before him. A half-eaten piece of bread rested near his fingers. To his right, Katherine's back heated near the flames, her arms folded tight across her chest. To her right across from Adam, at the other end, Rose sat stiffly, posture upright but eyes unfocused, the fire's glow painting the sharp lines of her face in molten orange. Eric sat across from Katherine, hands clasped, one thumb gently rubbing across the other in restless rhythm.

No one spoke. What could they even say? Fractured minds. Fractured places. It felt less like a gathering and more like a shared captivity, like they were trapped inside a nightmare no one could wake from. The silence wasn't peace. It was a prison. Then the clatter of a fork against a plate broke the tension like a slap across still water. For a split second, Adam wasn't sitting at the table at all, he was somewhere else, hovering outside his own body, watching the scene from a cold, unreachable distance. The sound yanked him back like a ripcord.

Adam blinked, startled by the sound, and dragged himself out of whatever spiral had taken hold. His eyes refocused on the table in front of him, though the room still felt distant, like he was watching it from behind glass. He hadn't even realized he'd been holding his breath. "Sorry," he muttered. No one responded. The silence returned.

Rose stared ahead, unmoving. Her plate sat untouched, the food was made up of dried meat and uncooked vegetables, had gone cold. Across the table, Eric shifted slightly. Adam noticed his hand disappear beneath the table, subtle, but careful. Rose didn't look at him. But her jaw clenched, just enough to betray something unspoken. Finally, Katherine exhaled. "We should talk about what happened."

Adam didn't lift his eyes.

"What's there to talk about?"

"Everything," she said.

"You nearly almost had psychotic breakdown," Rose added, voice low but sharp. "Don't act like it was nothing."

Adam's eyes flicked toward her. "And you didn't?" He looked at each of them. "None of us made it out clean."

Katherine leaned forward slightly, studying him. "What happened to you in that hallway, Adam? You changed."

He didn't answer right away. The weight of the vision still clung to his chest like a stone; those gravestones carved with names he wasn't ready to lose. Katherine's had been one of them. And now she sat across from him, alive and breathing, but his mind kept looping Asterius's words: *Just a figment of your imagination.*

"I don't know," he finally said. "It felt like… like something saw me."

Eric leaned forward.

"What do you mean?"

Adam shook his head. "I couldn't see its face. Just shadows. But I felt like it knew me. It knew what I'd done… what I'm afraid of. It whispered like it had the answers, but none of it felt real." The others watched him. A beat of quiet passed. The fire cracked.

"I didn't mean to," Adam said.

"But I did..."

Rose narrowed her eyes.

"What are you talking about?"

Adam's voice was low. "I saw his face again… the man I killed." He kept his eyes on the firelight, the flames casting shifting patterns across the long stretch of dark oak between them. No one spoke for a moment. The fire cracked again, casting warped shadows across the table, like judgment. Then, quietly, as if the thought had just escaped her lips, Katherine said, "It's okay."

Adam blinked slowly, but before he could respond, Rose's voice cut through the quiet. "What do you mean it's okay?" Her tone was sharp and brittle. She stared at Adam, her expression unreadable but laced with something taut beneath the surface.

"You killed a man. That's never okay."

The fire crackling as the silence returned, with swollen things unsaid. Eric shifted in his seat. "It's not like that," he said softly, trying to ease her fire.

Adam didn't look up. He couldn't. If Rose truly knew the story... If she knew that Eric had been part of it. She knew the blood was on his hands, that it had spilled between us. It would tear them apart. Across the table, Eric's jaw tightened. His eyes locked with Adam's. Tension hung between them, unspoken but loud. Adam dropped his gaze again, then over to Rose. She was quiet now, looked toward the fire. It reflected in her eyes, but she wasn't really looking at it. Something had pulled her inward. Adam watched her jaw tighten. "It was an accident."

Rose cut her eyes. "What?"

"The man I killed" Adam said calmly.

Rose turned away. The room held its breath. And then it came, not a sound, but something in her face. Her shoulders tensed. Her eyes brimmed, but the tears refused to fall. A scream he couldn't hear. A memory he couldn't see, but could almost feel. Zion's voice. The temptation. A cliff. The drop. The wind.

Rose shut her eyes. The silence around her cracked like thin glass, ready to shatter. She drew in a breath, then held it, as if even the act of exhaling might unravel her. Adam watched as she shifted slightly, lips parting. But whatever she meant to say died in her throat. The fire popped. No one moved. Katherine noticed and turned to her. "You don't have to carry it alone, Rose."

Rose's voice trembled. "He threw me off a cliff. I should've died." The room fell still. Too quiet. The fire cracked, loud, sharp, like a spine breaking. Adam flinched. The silence around them made the sound feel unbearable. Eric's voice cut through it. "But you didn't."

"No," she said. Her eyes flared. "And now I have to pretend I'm fine. Because we have a job to do."

Adam didn't move. Didn't breathe. He knew that feeling too well. The weight of pretending. The ache of holding it all in just to keep going. She was breaking in front of them, and still holding the line. Just like he had. Just like they all were. *How could he stay angry at her for saying the truth? When she was barely holding herself together, just like he was.*

None of them said a word.

The fire kept cracking.

But there was nothing left to burn.

***

In other lands, the sky hung heavy with smoke and fire, and the rivers no longer remembered their names. They flowed like lava. The trees stood hollow, bark peeled back like flayed skin. Blood dripped from Zion's fingers, painting the ground in wet, soundless screams. He didn't wipe it off. It fell in steady drops, soft against the stone below. His hands dangled at his sides, crimson painting the silence.

He watched his Horsemen feed; lips sealed around his wrist like hounds at a vein. Each drop sizzled where it landed, feeding the lair with something ancient. His eyes held no remorse, only the cold gleam of conquest, as if every life lost had only sharpened his resolve. The wind dared not speak his name. The chamber was quiet, too quiet. A low hum echoes from the throne, as if the stones themselves are holding their breath. Zion sits in darkness, both arms outstretched, his Horsemen feed from his wrists like ravenous beasts, fangs tearing gently into the flesh of a god.

"Yes," he whispered. "You are my children. Feed. Take what you need."

Vienna looked up, her mouth smeared red. "Yes, master." She sank her teeth in deeper, hungrier this time. The flickering torchlight danced across Zion's face as the pain began to ease. His jaw tensed, but his eyes rolled back, not from agony, but something closer to pleasure. A twisted relief washed over him.

Then-

Zion flinched, just barely. The pain was dull at first, almost ceremonial. But then something changed. The sharpness pierced through. The drain was too much. He yanked his arms back and rose from the throne. He stared down at his left arm. Two of the wounds were sealed, but the others. Still open. Still bleeding. Normally, they would've closed within seconds. Now… they pulsed. Red. Exposed. Vulnerable. He touches one, and more blood leaks through his fingers. Fear crept in, just for a moment. *Not now. Not without the Sphere.*

"Is everything okay, master?" Asterius asked, voice calm, despite the blood sliding down his neck like spilled wine.

Zion doesn't answer. He stares at the blood pooling in his palm, transfixed by the way it glistens in the firelight. His chest rises, falls, slow at first, then sharper, each breath scraping the back of his throat. Something's wrong. He can feel it, not just in his skin, but in the silence pressing against the walls like the room itself is waiting for him to break.

"Master?" Asterius insisted.

Zion steadies himself. His voice, hoarse but sharp "Haiti!" A chill swept through the throne room. The torches flickered low, shadows twisting unnaturally as the air bent with something unseen. It was as if the stone itself whispered, low, unintelligible murmurs curling through the cracks in the walls, too faint to name but impossible to ignore. Every flame wavered like it feared what was coming. Even the silence seemed to press inward, heavy and thick, as if the room had caught on to what Zion would not say out loud: he was no longer whole.

Haiti drifted through the far wall like smoke, limbs unraveling as his form floated forward. Not a man. Not anymore. Just a whisper of something that had once lived and now wore shape like a mask, thin, stretched, almost human. His presence pulled the warmth from the room, bending the air around him like gravity itself recoiled. Even the shadows hesitated, as if unsure whether to follow or flee. He hovered in front of the Horsemen. Zion didn't speak. He already knew. Haiti's form split—four orbs peeling from his center, black as void, humming with low, unnatural sound. The orbs hovered. Hung. Then slammed into the chests of each Horseman. One. Two. Three. Four.

They convulsed, bodies seizing as if the air itself was trying to rip them apart. Their spines arched unnaturally, bones cracking beneath the strain, jaws stretching in silent agony before the scream finally tore free. It wasn't human, it was something deeper, guttural, like the sound of souls being reshaped. The chamber pulsed with their cries, echoing off the walls like a funeral dirge dragged from the throat of the dead. Then stilled.

Their eyes burst open—no longer eyes. Just light. Cold. Blinding. Not fire, not magic, just the hollow glow of something that wasn't meant to return. There was no soul behind it. No thought. Only command. The Horsemen rose together, shadows steaming from their skin like smoke from ash, as if their bodies were still deciding whether to accept the life forced back into them. Zion steadied his breath. Not from pain, but satisfaction. The Horsemen stood before him now, reborn, their forms brimming with power he had only tasted in dreams. Shadows swirled behind their eyes, just waiting. Watching. They didn't speak. They didn't need to. In their silence, he saw allegiance, and, in that silence, he smiled.

***

The fire crackled low, casting faint light on the stone walls as Adam stared into the flames.

397

His thoughts were loud. The kind of loud that lived behind the eyes. He didn't speak. Adam sat back, but not really seeing it. His mind had been racing ever since the vision, ever since the truth clawed its way into his chest like frost under skin. He hadn't said anything, not really. Not about the Sphere. Not about the thing that touched him. Not about what he *felt* when he stood at the edge of death and saw… names. None of them spoke. *Is there really anything left to talk about? All of our minds are probably racing like a hamster on wheels, constantly busy and reaching for something… but not necessarily achieving any meaningful progress.*

He looked around the room. Eric's hands were still, calm, for once. Katherine's gaze had softened again. And Rose… even broken, even after everything, she carried a kind of fire he didn't know how to name. Adam rubbed the back of his neck. Something tingled there, not pain, not warmth. Just… something. Like a whisper under the skin. He hesitated. "Have any of you noticed something… strange?"

Katherine tilted her head. "Like what?"

He turned toward her, gesturing. "That."

She blinked. Rose and Eric followed his gaze. There, just above Katherine's collarbone, a faint symbol glowed, soft but visible. Like stone fractured under pressure, etched in the shape of roots curling deep into soil. It pulsed once, then faded to a faint shimmer. Rose instinctively brushed back her hair. A similar mark had appeared just below her jawline, flame trapped behind glass, flickering quietly.

It wasn't just glowing marks. It was proof, something happening to them. Something he wasn't part of. He tried not to let it show, but it settled in his chest like a quiet question:

Why them… and not me?

Eric's mark had begun to show too, a swirl of water mid-motion, like the tide frozen in time beneath his skin. It shimmered faintly, pulsing with a quiet rhythm all its own. For a moment, it didn't look like a mark at all, but a ripple waiting to move, to flood, to rise. Adam watched it, silent, the thought creeping in again: *Why them… and not me?* He touched the side of his own neck. Nothing. He forced a smirk.

"Guess I'm the odd one out."

Rose looked at him, her gaze lingering.

"Maybe not yet."

The words should've comforted him. But they didn't. Not entirely. They fell into quiet again.

The fire crackled. Shadows swayed. The storm beyond the windows seemed to retreat for just a moment, giving them this stillness. Wounded. But not broken. Together. And then, faint at first, a sound. Raised voices. Muffled. Coming from the hallway. Rose lifted her head, her brows furrowed, and looked at Adam. He glanced toward the noise, listening. His eyes met Katherine's. She tilted her head to Eric, who was picking it up too. Eric looked to Rose, then back at Katherine.

Eric's brow arched. "Is that…?"

Katherine leaned forward slightly.

"Can they get a room?"

Rose snorted, then caught herself. "Tell me about it. They sound like an old bickering couple."

For the first time in what felt like days, laughter broke the tension. Soft, surprised, but real. The sound of their laughter surprised Adam. It had been so long since he'd heard it. Since he'd felt it. Just for a breath, it felt like home again, like before everything broke. Their eyes met around the fire, and something unspoken passed between them. This, this moment, one of a kind. Sacred.

Then came the voices. Low at first. Muffled through stone. But his senses were sharper now, like the world had leaned closer. Something was happening. And whatever it was… it was coming for them.

The corridor walls caught every echo. Marble, cold, veined with age, and sharp enough to wound. The torchlights hanging along the walls flickered with every shift of wind, shuddering like they, too, were afraid of what was coming. Every footstep, every breath seemed to linger too long, like the stone itself was listening. Shadows bled from the torchlight, stretching across the floor like silent witnesses to the tension coiling in the air "I'm not asking for your permission," Marie snapped, her voice sharp with strain.

Ronan stood across from her, arms crossed, jaw tight. "That's not what this is about."

"Oh no?" she shot back. "Then tell me, what is this about? Because from where I'm standing, it sounds like you're more afraid of failure than of doing nothing."

The silence between them pressed like stone. Unyielding. The kind of quiet that didn't wait to be broken, it demanded it. Every second stretched thin, pulled tight with all the things neither of them were willing to say. And still, the air crackled with everything they meant. "I'm doing this," she continued, softer now, but no less fierce. "With or without your help."

Marie turned, the sapphire glow at her wrist flickering as she started down the hall. Her footsteps echoed, steady, deliberate, echoing like a drumbeat in stone.

Ronan didn't follow. Not yet. He watched her go, the weight of too many choices pressing against his ribs. She was walking toward a crowd that might not listen, against an army that might not wait. And still, she walked.

"You're going to get yourself killed," he murmured under his breath. She reached for the doors, both hands steady on the handles. Then, she stopped. Her shoulders tensed. Slowly, she turned her head back, just enough to see him over her shoulder. Her voice was quiet. Deadly calm. "Be careful with your words, Ronan. Fate has a strange way of circling back." And then she pushed open the doors, stepping into whatever storm waited for her on the other side.

The doors groaned open behind her as Marie stepped out. Overhead, the sky remained split, one half a bruised twilight, the other veined with bleeding red, as if the heavens themselves had cracked under the strain. Balance had not been restored. Marie stood still beneath it, heart pounding. The sky hadn't healed. New Earth's balance hadn't returned. Maybe it never would. But the people were watching and if the world was going to break again, she had to be the one standing in its center when it did.

Torchlights licked the cream-colored outside walls of Ronan's castle, casting the courtyard in dim orange hues. The shadow beneath her feet glowed faintly under the firelight, but beyond the steps, a crowd waited, silent, tense, hundreds of Shikarians and New Earthians. Skeptical. Some held torches. Others held onto fear. Shrouded in cloaks, wrapped in whatever remnants of warmth they had left. Their eyes watched her like she was a ghost of the past, not a leader of the present. She wasn't, but she had to be there.

Her pulse thudded. Not from fear. From the weight of everything she carried. She stepped forward, standing tall on the old stone podium Ronan's guards had erected at her request. Wind brushed past her shoulders, pulling strands of her blonde hair loose. She took one breath. Then another. It almost felt foreign... like a taste of her mom's cooking before being crowned royalty.

Almost forgettable. "My fellow New Earthians… my Shikarians…I know you didn't ask for this war. I didn't either. I know you've lost more than anyone should ever be asked to bear. But I stand here, not as royalty. Not as Ronan's ally. I stand here as one of you."

Silence. The silence was cold and seeping in like a parasite. Marie's chest tightened. Still, nothing. She scanned the crowd, mothers clutching children, scarred hands gripping worn tools, eyes dark with disbelief. Then, she raised her wrist, letting the sapphire light coil in her palm, shimmer through the night. And in the old tongue, the language she was never meant to speak, but had learned in quiet defiance. She lowered her wrist, spoke in Shikarian for the first time in a long time and called out:

"T'val shei norra. Vek shan'tai me."
I do not stand above you. I fight beside you.

A ripple moved through the crowd. Not loud, but there. One man leaned toward another, voice low but sharp: "If you trust her… she's one of them."

"Sha'tai ven'kor et sulem. T'alava korinth et selven, t'alava rion, et t'alava ves."

I stood beside them and fought. I stood with my mother and father, the King and Queen of New Earth, until their final moments.

"Zion et valkor en'orca, et vel du'sai."

Zion has been our enemy for orcas, and still, he hunts us.

"Tai'ven kai shal'vos. Tai'ven dor'kai rion. Tai'ven dor'kai ves."

Today, I fight for you. I fight for your children. I fight for your future.

Still no reaction. The torches crackled. The flames danced. But the people did not. The silence was dead. Marie's gaze scanned the crowd. They stared back, unmoved. Murmurs passed between them like cold wind over cracked earth.

"Tai'kar e'ven tor'en?" she said louder.

Have I not proved where my allegiance lies?

No reaction. Not even a murmur of belief. Marie felt the silence clawing back at her, unreadable. Had she misjudged them? Had her words meant nothing? The weight of their stares pressed in like fog. She steadied her breath. If Shikarian couldn't reach them… maybe truth could. Marie's jaw clenched. *Let's try this,* she thought. "My name is Marie. Daughter of King Theodore and Queen Elena… Our reigning King and Queen perished defending what held deep to their heart. What was meant to keep everything in balance and in order was also taken that night. I know you didn't ask for this war. I didn't either," she said, voice steady but quieter now. Her eyes swept across the crowd again.

"I didn't ask to lose my parents… as they bled for a future they never got to see. I didn't ask to be part of a prophecy I never fully understood." A few faces turned toward her now. "But I stand here, not as an heir. Not as a leader in some castle tower. I stand here for you. As King Theodore and Queen Elena would."

The wind stirred again. It swept across the courtyard like a warning, curling around Marie's boots and tugging at the loose strands of her blonde hair. The torches lining the castle walls hissed and flickered, casting dancing shadows across the stone. For a moment, it felt like the world itself was holding its breath.

"Tonight, we stand together. United. As one nation. It will be the end of Zion's reign," Marie stated.

"Liar!" The cry pierced the air, sharp and immediate.

"You left us to die!" Another voice, rough and broken, rose from the far left, closer this time. The anger was real. So was the grief.

"Where are these so-called heroes you speak of?!" The scream drilled the air, closer than the last.

Marie stiffened. The weight of their voices hit harder than she expected. *Why are they screaming at me like this? Do they really feel I let them down?* Even without the crown, she had carried the burden. She tried. Her parents had, too. But somehow, the people still believed they'd been betrayed. Even if it had happened orcas ago.

Back in the dining hall… The fireplace flickered low, casting shadows that danced across the stone floor. Adam stiffened. At first, he thought it was just the wind howling through the cracks in the walls, but no. There it was again. Raised voices. Distant. Muffled. Closer than they should be. He straightened. "Do you hear that?" he asked, his voice barely above a whisper.

Rose lifted her head, her expression tightening. Eric turned toward the far corridor, listening. Katherine's brows furrowed. "That sounded like shouting."

Then—

"Traitor!" The word cut through the air, faint but unmistakable. Another followed. "Monster!" And another "There is no prophecy!"

Adam's heart kicked. He rose slowly, his hand brushing the edge of the table for balance. Each word echoed like thunder cracking across the plains. He moved toward the window. Peeked out to hundreds of civilians outside. And Marie was alone. *What is going on? What happened to Ronan?* The others close behind. Adam rises. "They're mocking her," he muttered. "Not on my watch. We should gear up." No words were spoken. There didn't need to be. They left the dining hall with heavy silence between them and returned moments later, suited in what the world had come to fear: their elemental garb.

Back in the courtyard, Marie stood tall. Took the burn of their judgment like flame. And still she spoke: "The prophecy is real. I did not come here full of shame. The Legends have returned. And I will not let Zion have this world. Let him see what we've become. We will not stand down! We are not broken! We are not alone! And we are not afraid! I promise you my fellow citizens." She paused. Let it breathe. A ripple moved through the crowd, not roaring, not yet, but real. A few heads lifted. Someone lowered their torch. One woman nodded through tears.

The silence didn't vanish, but it shifted. Like maybe, just maybe, they believed her. "We lost ourselves. That doesn't mean we forget what we're here to do. My parents died for this world. I will not let it fall while I still draw breath. We will fight to the death, by any means necessary. This is our home. And if Zion wants a war…" She turned her gaze toward the horizon. "Then we'll give him hell." She drew in a breath, steady now. Whatever fear remained, it would not rule her. Not tonight.

Then, and only then, the doors creaked open. Light spilled from behind them, catching the faint swirl of dust in the air. A hush rippled across the crowd as four figures stepped out of the castle. At the center, Adam walked forward. The others followed, Rose, Katherine, Eric, flanking him in quiet formation. Their elemental garb shimmered in the torchlight, a haunting contrast to the fear thick in the air, but it was their elemental marks that silenced the crowd. Each one burned faintly beneath their skin, living sigils of fire, earth, and water, pulsing with power no mortal could possess. In the torchlight, they looked like legends. *I didn't.*

Adam's heart thudded louder with every step. Gasps escaped from every side. Not words. Not cheers. Just breath, held, then exhaled. He didn't know why he felt compelled to move toward the crowd, toward their expectant stares. *What are they all looking at?* he thought. *Do I look like a ghost to them… or a savior?* But he didn't feel like either. Just a boy in borrowed armor, stepping onto a stage he never asked for, blinded by the weight of their belief, like camera lights flashing straight into his soul.

He walked at the center, unmarked. But not unseen. Marie turned, her gaze locking with Adam's. She gave the slightest nod. And something in him responded. He wasn't sure when his feet started moving. The crowd didn't move all at once, but slowly, instinctively, they took a step back. Not in fear. In reverence. In awe. His pulse pounded, but his body moved like it already knew the steps. *What am I doing? What if I fail them? What if I'm not enough?*

But still, he walked. Then she appeared. A woman pushed forward from the crowd, her face drawn and desperate. Her hand shot out, clutching Adam's arm with a strength that startled him. "Can you save us?" she asked. Her voice cracked, barely a whisper, yet it cut through everything. He froze. Words didn't come. Not right away. He looked into her eyes and saw everything, grief, hope, fear, all knotted into a single plea.

Adam swallowed, even though it felt like dry rot. "…We'll try," he said quietly.

The woman tugged his arm again, more desperate now. "Please," she whispered.

He saw it then, really saw it. The grief in her eyes. The panic. The helpless hope. His breath caught. His eyes widened, not in fear, but in understanding. He nodded. "Okay… we will," he said again, this time firmer. Not for her. For himself. But inside, something shifted. The weight settled in, and deep down, he knew this was only the calm before the storm.

Chapter XXII:
We Were Never Ready

The wind soared, slow at first, then rising like a breath held too long. It swept through the courtyard, tugging at cloaks and torched flames, curling around the Legends like an omen. The scent of ash and iron hung in the air, thick with the silence of what hadn't yet arrived. Something was coming. Adam knew it. The wind knew it. He stood exactly where the woman left him, where her hand had gripped his arm, trembling and desperate. *Please.* The word hadn't meant much at first. But now, it echoed, soft, steady, lodging itself deeper than he expected. He hadn't realized how much it affected him until after he said the words back. Not for her. For himself. *How could this be? Is this really me? Does she actually see me as a hero? A savior?* It didn't make sense. Not with all the guilt he was still carrying. *Does it take one to know one?* he thought. And for the first time, he wasn't sure of the answer.

The sky was sick with color, twilight fading into bleeding red, the air thick with smoke that drifted like ash-born fog. The scent of it clung to everything, even the back of his throat. Somewhere, far beyond the castle, something burned. He didn't know what. Maybe it didn't matter. He could feel it, the weight of what was coming. Of what had already been lost. His jaw tightened, the woman's voice still echoing in his head. *Please.* Not just a word. A burden. One that had been passed to him without warning. He didn't know her name. Didn't know who she'd lost in the last raid—husband, child, family… but her grief lived in his chest like it belonged there.

The others stood behind him. Katherine. Rose. Eric. Quiet. Watching. Even Marie didn't speak. Not yet. There's such a stillness in the air… even now. The ground rumbled, low at first, like a distant growl beneath the soil. Adam felt it in his boots, a slow vibration rising through the soles and into his bones. Around him, the air seemed to hold its breath, the silence pressing tighter with every second. Something was coming and the earth knew it before they did. Marie's voice cut through the stillness. Barely a whisper.

"He is here."

A hissing sound coiled through the air, low and unnatural. It didn't come from the crowd. It didn't come from the sky. It came from everywhere. The air shifted. Cold. Dense. The kind of silence that pressed against the eardrums, flattening everything else into a hum. The torches along the courtyard walls flickered, some extinguishing entirely, as if the flame itself had been warned. Civilians tensed. A child whimpered. Somewhere in the crowd, a metal weapon clattered to the ground, forgotten by the soldier who no longer trusted their grip.

The wind dropped. Not a breeze. Not a whisper. Just stillness. An unnatural pause in the lungs of the world. Adam turned slowly, his eyes scanning the treetops beyond the courtyard, then the rooftops above the castle. But there was nothing. Only smoke creeping along the horizon, and that sound, that hiss, curling tighter around them like a serpent preparing to strike.

And then—

A deep vibration, low at first, began to pulse beneath their feet. The stones beneath Adam's boots groaned. Civilians staggered. Some gasped. Others dropped to their knees in prayer. Marie's jaw tightened. "He's toying with us," she murmured under her breath. But the fear was already here, climbing up every spine, clawing through every chest. And the voice hadn't even spoken yet. It slithered through the marrow of Adam's bones. Through every stone in the courtyard. Through every soul holding their breath.

You think you're the chosen ones? Each time destiny brings us all back together, I wonder… who will fall first?

The voice wasn't angry. It was calm. Controlled. Cruel.

I am grateful… For a new world that knows not of what's to come. I will tear this world to its core. Strip it of suffering, of guilt. And from the ashes, birth a new nation from the M'ra Sphere.

The ground trembled beneath Adam's boots. A rumble echoed in the distance. Thunder cracked. And still… the voice smiled.

My men will rip you apart and leave nothing that holds even the slightest significance to your name. That's what I call a merciful universe. Unfortunately… you won't be around to see it.

Screeches cut through the air, high and sharp, like steam escaping a dying machine. Not human. From the pitch-black sky above, shadows moved like liquid glass, glinting with faint shimmer of distant firelight. Then they dropped like hail, hard and fast. They weren't just beasts. They were Prylyn Stalkers, the twisted spawn of something ancient and merciless, bred from shadow and venom, something that carried his scent. And they had come to feed. Wings outstretched, fangs gleaming, their skin slick with black ooze that caught the light like oil.

The courtyard erupted. Screams tore through the crowd. Torches fell. Claws tore through flesh. Blood. Bodies hitting the stone like broken drums. In seconds, dozens were gone. Adam turned, watching a bloodbath unfold. The courtyard was a slaughterhouse. Civilians dropped like ragdolls. Ugly bursts as the Prylyn Stalkers descended, more of them, faster now. "No. No. This isn't supposed to be happening." He could barely hear himself. A woman tripped behind him, eyes wide, mouth frozen mid-scream.

Adam moved without thinking. He planted himself between her and the thing lunging forward, limbs too long, wings slick with black rot. He threw his hand out, wind cracking like a whip, blasting the Stalker backward into the wall with a sickening crunch. To his right, Katherine spotted movement. A child, barely more than a toddler, crawled through the chaos, sobbing. She darted forward, scooped the girl into her arms, and ran for the castle steps. "Hold on," she breathed. She shoved the door open, dropped to her knees, and set the girl inside.

"Go. Run. Don't stop."

Rose stood with her arms raised, flames spilling from her hands like a living beast, casting hellfire across the courtyard. Fire clung to the Stalkers' black ooze, consuming them from within until they fell, collapsing one by one like dying trees. For a moment the courtyard was silent. The others stood next to Rose as her fire died out. They took formation without needing to speak as the civilians lined up behind them, a line, united as Legends of New Earth. Seconds later, Marie joined with them. And as more creatures dropped from the sky, as black smoke curled across the horizon, Adam's breath caught in his throat. This wasn't a war they had prepared for. But they were here now. And they would not run.

There was a silence thick as fog. Adam and Rose exchanged a look. He gave a subtle nod. No words. Just understanding. Together, they lifted off. Rose burned bright throughout, fiery red, a streak of flame against the storm. Wind coiled around Adam, lifting him gently but with force, like the sky had claimed him. From the ground, they ascended toward the castle's heights, rising like twin omens into the storm-dark sky.

The ocean rustled as waves crashed violently against the shore. Smoke like fog rolled in thick coils across the sand, swallowing the pitch-black sky. Thunder cracked, sharp and cruel, as a dark silhouette emerged from the veil of fog. Adam's breath held. Zion. And for a single heartbeat, Adam forgot how to breathe. *He's not the same from the raid. He's here and he's deadly,* Adam thought.

Zion walked through the smoke like a deity through ruin. No horse. No beast beneath him. Just boots crushing the earth with slow, certain steps. His black cloak dragged behind him, heavy as death, soaking in the storm's fury. His eyes, burning with that otherworldly, serpentine, silver light, cut through the fog like blades. He didn't look left or right. He didn't need to. The world seemed to part for him. Behind him, four figures flanked his sides—The Horsemen. Asterius. Vienna. Barricade. Jarvis. Their armor grotesque and ceremonial, like they'd been forged in the underworld. And behind the army.

Hundreds, maybe thousands, marched in from the dark, a monstrous tide of corrupted flesh and armored bodies. Some were once men, now twisted, reformed into something unrecognizable beneath jagged plating and soulless eyes. Others crawled and slithered in unnatural shapes, limbs bent wrong, mouths too wide. Two massive siege catapults rolled behind them like giants reborn, groaning with every turn of their wheels. The horizon rippled with shadow and movement, as if war itself had grown teeth.

Adam swallowed hard. From his vantage, he saw it all, civilians huddled like broken pieces of a world that had just begun to shatter. Dozens of them remained. Faces pale, breaths shaky, still stunned from the chaos. Marie stood frozen in the aftermath. Eric was checking the perimeter. Katherine hoisted like a fuse waiting to blow. Zion stopped. The storm churned behind him, casting his figure in jagged flashes of lightning. Slowly, he lifted his chin, his face pale as bone, framed by damp strands of midnight hair clinging to his skin. His silver serpentine eye, cut through and his gaze found Adam's like a curse spoken in silence. There.

No fury. No rage. Just a cold, disturbing calm, as if the world itself dared not breathe without his permission. The contact was a blade through bone. Adam didn't breathe. He couldn't. Those slithering eyes froze him, like venom sliding beneath the skin. His muscles locked. Something about that gaze made his soul recoil, as if Zion wasn't just seeing him… he was inside him. He knew he was the one. *Back at Zion's lair… I thought it was just a nightmare,* Adam realized. *Those claws… reaching for me in the dark. Do they belong to Zion… or to the One Who Cannot Be Named?*

Zion flickered his eyes away from the fable boy, he never believed it. He didn't want to. He opened his mouth. With a lingering roar. All rage. "Ronan!"

And the world began to fall apart. Ronan was nowhere to be found. *Did Ronan just abandon us?* Adam thought. Panic prickled beneath his skin. The ground hadn't even started shaking, but something inside him already had. The civilians looked around, voices rising, a tremble running through the crowd like a prelude to collapse. *He wouldn't leave us… would he?* Adam searched the field again, desperate for a sign, any sign, that someone was still in control.

Eric and Katherine took their positions. Their eyes met, brief, but unyielding. No words passed between them, but something did: a silent vow, forged in fire and fear. Whatever came next, they would face it together. The storm howled above, but neither of them flinched. Marie stood in front of them, closer to Katherine's side, but forward enough to lead. Her presence was the thread between them, the signal that the moment had come. All that remained… was Ronan.

"RONAN!" Zion roared again, louder, sharper. His voice boomed across the storm, thunder folding beneath every syllable. "This land won't remember your mercy! It will remember your silence! Come out, King before I crown myself in your ashes!"

The castle doors groaned open, and Ronan stepped into the storm. Boots striking stone. Eyes locked on the battlefield ahead. He didn't speak. He didn't need to. The crowd parted as if the wind itself carried him forward. From his perch above the battlefield, Adam watched him, watched Ronan move with that same unshakable presence he'd seen during training. But this was different. And when Ronan's eyes found Marie, Adam could feel it, something unspoken passed between them. A tether. A final breath before the storm broke loose. "This is the end, Zion!" Ronan shouted. "It's over. Unless you'd rather watch your army fall first."

"I thought you might say that," Zion replied.

"If we fall, we fall as one." Ronan's voice cut through the chaos. "The ground will drink your blood, Zion… and Death will know your name."

The wind shifted, sharp and sudden, like the world itself was holding its breath. Something changed. One by one, the civilians began stepping forward, their fear still clinging to them like shadow, but no longer in control. Some held rusted weapons. Others held nothing but clenched fists and fire in their eyes. But not a single one turned away. Adam saw it happen and felt it. Ronan's words weren't just a rallying cry… they struck something deeper, something primal. *They believe him*, Adam thought. *They're really going to fight.* His pulse thudded. Whatever came next, it had already begun. They weren't just standing their ground. They were choosing it.

Zion didn't hesitate. He turned to his army, eyes gleaming beneath the storm-fog sky, then back to Ronan. The wind lashed around him, carrying the scent of smoke and blood. Then his voice rose, not just with command, but with brutal certainty. "Charge!" The word cracked like thunder, ripping across the battlefield with deadly intent. His soldiers loaded dark, jagged obsidian stones into massive catapults. With a brutal groan, the first payload launched, whistling through the air like death made solid. No flame. No light. Just impact. The sky above in pitch-black, casting a ghostly haze over the courtyard as the projectile struck the castle wall with a bone-rattling roar.

"Attack!" Ronan bellowed.

The front line surged forward, boots pounding, power igniting, hearts ablaze. Marie ran beside him, eyes fierce, hair snapping in the storm wind. Katherine charged ahead like a quake unleashed, stone cracked beneath her every step, the air thrumming with the raw fury building inside her, while water swirled at Eric's side, coiling and slicing with every step. The civilians followed, some armored, most not, but all unyielding, as they swept across the battlefield like a tidal wave of defiance. And ahead, Zion's army, grotesque, snarling, endless, met them in a furious clash that shattered the silence and split the night wide open.

The cliff buckled beneath them as the obsidian stones slammed into the high towers. One after another, the ancient spires collapsed in a rain of shattered stone and screaming wind. Debris plunged down like judgment, pulverizing everything in its path. "Take cover!" Rose's voice cracked like fire through smoke.

Adam turned, blinking against the dust and wind. Rose's silhouette blazed against the sky, hands lit, stance braced, eyes locked on something above them. She saw it. He couldn't yet. But the panic in her voice was enough. His chest tightened. *Whatever it was… it wasn't going to miss.* His mind screamed, *Move! Do something!* But all he could do was stare as the world cracked open beneath him. This wasn't battle. This was execution. But something clicked.

Not instinct, his will. Adam lunged through the smoke, grabbed Rose by the waist, and pulled her down just as a boulder the size of a wagon slammed into the stone behind her, exploding into shards. They tumbled hard, crashing behind a jagged slab of fallen masonry.

Down below, the battlefield erupted. The clash hit like a quake, limbs, bodies, fury colliding all at once. Katherine barreled into the fray, rock gauntlets fused to her arms, each strike sending a Prylyn creature flying back in shattered bone and black ooze. Beside her, Eric's arms reflected, encased in churning water, gauntlets forming and reshaping with every punch. He moved like a tide made flesh, sliding through, crashing through enemies with brute force and fluid grace. The ground was chaos. Screams. Steel. Stone. The scent of residue and blood stained skin. And the sky, still broken. Still mourning the night.

Then came the creatures. Prylyn Stalkers, dozens, then hundreds, unleashed from Zion's horde like a plague with wings. They shrieked like banshees, the sound ripping through the sky in waves of pure terror. Wings sliced the air. Claws glinted wet in the fractured battlefield. Jaws stretched too wide. The sky filled with them, wings, shadow, and decay, an apocalyptic swarm blotting out the stars.

Below, chaos ensued. Civilians screamed. Fighters froze mid-step, staring up as the creatures dove. Others stood paralyzed, just paralyzed. Some ran, but it was too late. There was no mercy. The first wave tore through the crowd like wildfire. Claws tore through flesh. Wings slammed bodies to the ground and the castle walls. Screams became gurgles. Limbs snapped in half. Blood sprayed the stained stone floor. The attack was a pure blade cutting through the fog.

A man threw himself over a woman, arms outstretched in a desperate shield. But the Stalker was faster, talons unfolded, cleaving through flesh before breath could even catch. A scream tore loose, then silence. When the dust cleared, there was nothing left but blood on the ground and the echo of a moment too slow. One woman screamed and swung her blade wide, striking air and shadow. Another lunged forward with a torch, flames dancing in her grip as she struck a creature square in the chest. For a moment, it shrieked, and then more came. Dozens. Claws, wings, teeth. The women were swallowed in seconds, their cries drowned beneath the onslaught.

The Stalkers tore a path through the battlefield, wings slicing low as they descended like a nightmare unchained. Screams split the air as bodies were lifted, flailing, into the sky, only to be ripped apart mid-flight in showers of blood and skin. They carved through the lines with grotesque precision, leaving limbs and entrails strewn across the field. Terror moved like a current, wild and contagious.

From above, Adam crouched, walked from the jagged slab and saw it—bodies flung like ragdolls, the ground-soaked red. All the civilians deaths who tried to reclaim New Earth. The carnage. Now gone. But from the fractured ledge of the upper tower, where wind screamed through broken stone and smoke veiled the horizon. His breath slowed as the scene below twisted into a nightmare he couldn't wake up from. He gripped the stone ledge, knuckles bloodless. But his legs wouldn't budge. Moments before, he witnessed a man throw himself over a woman, shielding her just before the Stalkers descended. And in that moment, Adam felt it, that creeping, crushing certainty that they were already too late. A current surged through him, sharp, clean, and electric. It didn't make him brave. It made him ready. *We have to do this,* he thought. Adam turned to Rose, heart hammering as the shriek of Stalkers pierced the air above them. Smoke curled through the fractured stone, and the sky stirred with wings. Rose dazed, but when she looked up, her eyes met his. She was still in it and so was he.

Black wings. Twisted shapes. Hundreds flooded from the fog like nightmares loosed from another world. Their forms shifted as they came into view, limbs bending wrong, mouths stretching too wide, eyes glowing with unnatural hunger. The sky writhed with them, a living storm of shadow and shrieks. Every flap of their wings sent dust swirling trembling, as if the air itself recoiled.

Adam's chest tightened again, like a warning he couldn't swallow. His heart was still pounding, as he offered his hand to Rose, out of finality. *This is it,* he thought. *There's no turning back.* He turned to the sky, where the shadows twisted and shrieked, drawing closer by the second, then back to Rose. "Ladies first," he said, voice low, calm… ready.

Rose didn't hesitate. She took his hand, eyes fierce, and pulled herself to her feet with a steady breath. Her gaze cut through the fog, narrowed on the swarm that darkened the sky. Then, without a word, she ran straight toward the ledge and launched herself into the abyss. Midair, her body ignited. Flame roared to life across her shoulders, her back, her arms, a living blaze. Fire danced along her spine as her limbs snapped into control, her body leveling as wings of heat flared outward. She blazed upward like a comet let loose, spinning once before hurling herself toward the swarm. Her hands lit, and then—*fireballs.*

Bright, burning comets exploded from her palms, striking the first cluster of Prylyn with relentless precision. The creatures shrieked and burst apart in the sky, black fluid trailing behind them like smoke. Bone fragments spun through the air. Wings were torn clean from sockets. They didn't fall; they disintegrated.

Adam dove after her, dropping fast into the fog, letting gravity take him before catching the air with a violent shift of his arms forward. Wind bent to him, curled beneath his limbs like unseen wings. Just before he struck the earth, he banked, hard, rising like a slingshot through the clouds. His momentum ripped through a line of Stalkers, bodies shattering on impact as he tore past them like a blade of air. The sky trembled around him. Adam floated mid-air, scanned the horizon, spotted a wave of creatures, pulled the wind deep into his lungs, through his ribs, down to his hands.

Then, with one motion, a forceful clap, he released it. A thunderous gust erupted from his hands, the air splitting like lightning, the blast tearing through another wave of creatures like paper. They scattered. They screamed. They vanished. He looked up at Rose, flaming, fearless, untouchable, and felt the truth settle in his chest. *This is what they were made for. Whether they wanted it or not.* They didn't just fly. They danced through the battle, two forces of nature unleashed.

And below, the battle had only just begun. Ronan carved his way through the chaos, a storm of steel and fury. His two-handed sword swept wide, slicing through Prylyn with practiced force, dark bodies cleaved in half, black ooze spraying across the battlefield. His armor was streaked with fluid, his face set like stone, eyes locked on the next target before the last had even fallen. He moved with precision, rage, and purpose.

Beside him, Marie stood tall, her sapphire dress whipped by the wind, her staff glowing with a sapphire light. Back-to-back, they fought, an unlikely duo, but unstoppable in rhythm. She struck down one creature with a burst of arcane energy, the blast sending it reeling into a pile of twitching limbs. Another rose in its place. She didn't flinch. Then came the shriek. A Prylyn creature burst through the fog on all fours, faster than the others, spiderlike in movement, its spine bent at unnatural angles, jaw unhinged as it bounded toward Marie. It leapt, midair bones cracking, flesh shifting, its right arm twisting into a jagged rod of black bone, sharp as a spear. Ronan turned too late.

The creature slammed into the ground where Marie had just stood, the rod-arm plunging into the earth with brutal force. But Marie was already gone, flipped backward into a somersault, twisting midair like she'd done this a hundred times. She landed behind it, low and precise, her sapphire dress streaked with ash. The air shimmered around her fingers, like a whisper in the bloodstream. This wasn't survival. This was purpose. This was who she'd always been. Before it could rise, she moved. With one fluid motion, she swept her staff around its throat, locked it in place, and twisted hard. The creature let out a final, garbled hiss before its neck snapped sideways with a sickening crack, black ooze spraying as it collapsed in a twitching heap.

From below, Zion's Prylyn hybrids swarmed the scorched ground, twisted creatures that once bore human faces, now fused with dark matter and bound to his will. Their bodies twitched with unnatural spasms, spines curving in jagged angles as they scrambled into position. With jerking precision, they loaded the catapults, their clawed hands tightened over obsidian stones that pulsed faintly with volatile heat. The scent of sulfur and rot thickened in the air as the launch mechanisms groaned, preparing to send death into the sky. Above them, Adam flew in a wide arc, scanning the battlefield from high above. He spotted Zion below, arms crossed, unmoving, as the hybrids locked into formation. *He's not aiming for the ground,* Adam realized. *He's aiming for us.* He twisted midair, cleaving through the last Prylyn creature that came too close, slicing it in half with a burst of wind. It screeched, split apart, and tumbled from the sky in a spray of black ooze. "He's marking us," Adam muttered, his voice tight. A guttural screech tore through the air.

The first obsidian stone exploded mid-flight, sending burning shards in every direction. The shockwave cracked the sky like thunder. One fragment sliced past Adam's leg, close enough to sear the edge of his uniform. He snapped into motion, rising hard into the sky. Rose dropped low and spun through the chaos, flame licking throughout her body, as she cut a spiral through the shrapnel. "Brace yourself!" she shouted, already dodging the next wave. Obsidian projectiles ripped past them, splitting the clouds, threatening to drag the heavens down with them.

On the war-torn ground, chaos screamed. Marie staggered as a Prylyn creature slammed into her, driving her backward across the blood-soaked earth. Its claws scraped against her staff, trying to force her down, their bodies locked in brutal tension. Her boots skidded, knees bending low as she gritted her teeth and surged upward. With a twist of her arms, she knocked the creature's grip aside, then swept the staff across its head with a sharp, brutal crack. It dropped to the ground with a rasping hiss.

With a flick of her wrist, the staff vanished in a swirl of blue light, called back only when needed. Marie exhaled once, then raised both hands. Blue hexes surged through her palms, charged shapes flickering. And with one motion, a forceful clap, then a slam into the earth. A wave of glowing energy rippled outward. Prylyn creatures convulsed on impact, their twisted bodies seizing before collapsing in heaps of blackened ooze.

Zion stood overlooking the battlefield, twisted with rage as he tracked the Legends. He didn't flinch. His silver serpentine eye were darkened, but not empty. Beneath his jaw, just past the collarbone, something moved. A glimmer of scale peeked through, thin, oily, almost reptilian, as if his skin was a mask barely clinging to something else. Marie turned back toward the palace. Something pulled at her, deep and familiar. Not a sound, not a voice, but a presence, like pressure behind her eyes, like a memory half-remembered. Almost like her mom called out:

The M'ra Sphere.

It wasn't just calling. It was disturbed, touched by something it did not choose. And

Marie felt it ripple through her bones like thunder waiting to break. Whatever had found it… didn't belong. *She didn't know how she knew. She just knew: The M'ra Sphere was calling.* It was time. She conjured her staff, raised it. With a sharp cry, she slammed it into the ground, blue lightning sparking through the soil. The shockwave fried the surrounding creatures as Marie launched into the air, soaring toward the palace doors like a streak of blue fire.

Katherine clenched her fists, jaw tight as dirt caked her skin. The gauntlets on her arms pulsed once, then detonated. Rock shards burst outward in a deadly fan, slicing through the swarm of Prylyn in brutal, unrelenting strikes. Screams erupted across the battlefield, limbs torn as the earth itself became her weapon. She stepped forward, unshaken, planting her boots into the blood-soaked ground as if daring the next wave to come. Then, she roared and slammed both fists into the dirt. The sound echoed like thunder cracking through stone, loud enough to make the air recoil. Power surged from her core down through her arms, channeled into the trembling soil. Dust exploded around her as the earth groaned under the force, no longer a battleground but a weapon she controlled. Cracks spiderwebbed outward, glowing faintly as they raced across the field like hungry veins. The earth split with a violent tremor, entire chunks of land shearing open into jagged voids.

Prylyn creatures screamed, their claws scraping uselessly against stone as they plummeted into darkness. One by one, they vanished into the abyss, no light, no sound, just the final silence of things buried alive. Cracks split the battlefield, steam rising from below. The dead were still rising. The living barely stood. And in the silence that followed, one truth remained:

They were never ready.

Chapter XXIII:
Bloodbath

The halls of the palace were colder here, carved from ancient stone and lined with dying torches that barely held their glow. Marie's boots echoed with each step, steady and deliberate, until something made her pause. The air. It had changed, a bit thicker now, not just with magic, but with weight. Something unseen pressed in around her, heavy and vigilant, as if the walks themselves were listening. A chill moved up her spine. In that moment she knew she wasn't alone.

Ahead, two Prylyn creatures scuttled into view, their elongated limbs twitching with every step. Their claws scraped against the stone floor in erratic bursts, leaving trails as they scrambled forward like insects caught in a trance. They weren't holding The M'ra Sphere, but they were headed straight for it. Their movements were jerky, obsessive, like they were being pulled. Marie's eyes narrowed. *Not this time.*

She stepped into the open, calm and careful. The creatures froze, claws twitching in the dim light. "Hey boys," she snickered, the sound low and amused. They shrieked, heads twisting toward her like insects drawn to heat. Their jaws snapped open, too wide, too fast, hinges unhinging with wet clicks. Claws scraped against stone as their bodies jerked into motion, limbs folding and unfolding like broken machinery.

They didn't hesitate toward her, but with a sharp twist of her wrists, Marie snapped her staff in two. Light flared along both rods, her escrima sticks, charged and ready. The corridor crackled with energy as more creatures emerged, climbing across walls, crawling from the shadows. Marie gave a grim smile. "Fair enough." They lunged, and the fight began. She moved like wind through water. One blocked, she ducked. Another swiped, she flipped backward off the wall, twisted midair, and drove a rod straight through its chest. It screamed, shuddered, collapsed. The second one leaped from the ceiling. Marie slid beneath it, caught it mid-fall, and rammed her second rod into its throat.

Black ooze sprayed across the walls. More crawled forward, three, four, maybe more. Marie exhaled once, centered herself, then slammed both rods together. A shockwave of blue light exploded outward, arcing down the corridor like a pulse of divine energy. The remaining creatures convulsed and dropped, smoke rising from their scorched bodies. Marie stood alone, her chest rising and falling, each breath steadying the sapphire energy still burning in her veins. Slowly, she turned toward the far end of the hall, drawn by something she didn't fully understand but couldn't ignore. And there it was. Suspended above a cradle of stone, hovered in silence, swirling with pale light that pulsed like a heartbeat. It wasn't just waiting. It was watching.

The M'ra Sphere.

Its glow was dim, soft white light turning slowly within the glass, like a storm caught in stillness. There was no hiss, no hum, no beckoning voice in her mind. It didn't halt her. It didn't tempt her. It simply waited, quiet, contained, as if recognizing the one who had bound it. Whatever power still stirred inside, it no longer needed to announce itself. It was already hers. She stepped forward. Not to take it. Not to wield it. To protect it. She placed a hand gently against its side, just enough to steady it in its cradle. Then she whispered a phrase in the old tongue, words passed down through ancient texts she barely remembered reading.

Light swirled from her palm, wrapping the Sphere in a delicate cage of blue sigils, symbols rotating like a celestial lock. The markings shimmered, each one ancient, flickering with power older than language. They turned in measured rhythm, orbiting the glass like constellations bound by intention. It wasn't just a seal. It was a vow. "Rest now," she whispered. "We'll protect you until it's over." The glow inside The M'ra Sphere dimmed, calm, but not tamed. Marie exhaled and backed away slowly. Then… A shiver. A chill down her spine. Not from the Sphere, but from something else. Far beyond the vault walls, beyond the palace, something was wrong. "Ronan," she whispered. She didn't know how she knew. She just did.

Through the shattered battlefield, Ronan carved through the chaos with newfound fury, having ripped the gauntlet shields from the arms of a fallen civilian, another soul lost in the dirt. He didn't have time to mourn, only to fight. Each strike landed with brutal precision, cleaving through Prylyn abominations in sickening bursts of black ooze. His breath came heavy, armor streaked with gore, but he didn't stop, not while any of them still stood. Not while anyone still could fall.

A roar echoed from the shoreline, Eric charged forward, water gauntlets blazing along his arms, the liquid spiraling and coiling like serpents preparing to strike. He moved like a storm given form, target to target, releasing precise blasts that burst through the chest of each creature. Each one crumpled in his wake, bones snapping, black ooze hissing as it hit the scorched earth. The battlefield rippled with the aftershock of his path, a straight line of destruction cut through shadow and blood. They came from all sides, a frenzied pack of Prylyn beasts, screeching as they lunged with twisted claws and snapping jaws.

They swarmed him, pouncing, slashing, and thrashing, their ooze-like hands, dragging him backward across the blood-slicked battlefield. Eric twisted, kicked, fought like hell, but there were too many, and their limbs coiled around him like chains. In one violent motion, they hurled him into the ocean, his body sailed through the air, limbs drooping, blood trailing like ribbons behind him. The ocean filled the frame, endless, dark, and even expecting. And then without a sound, impact. He pierced the surface like a blade through silk, vanishing beneath in one fluid motion. The water swallowed him whole. For a heartbeat, he didn't move, suspended in the depths, arms drifting, eyes closed, like a man suffocated from drowning. He was just still. The ocean stirred, trembling from some force deep beneath its surface, like the sea itself had drawn breath.

Then—

It erupted. A geyser of water exploded skyward, towering over the battlefield like a summoned storm. From within it, he emerged, Eric, small at the heart of the towering waves. Cloaked in spiraling tides of water, his body blended in a living tide. He hovered in the air like a god unchained, Poseidon, forming around him. His eyes glowing faint blue, the ocean shaping itself around him like armor. For a second he was unstoppable. Every Prylyn on the field stopped. Snarled. Watched. But he didn't speak. He didn't need to. The water spoke for him. It coiled around his limbs like armor, rising and falling with every breath, as if the ocean itself awaited his command. And then—

He dove. A blur of motion and fury, he crashed into the battlefield like a tidal spear. Water erupted outward in a blast so violent it split the earth, sweeping Prylyn creatures off their feet, tearing through their ranks with merciless force. Bones shattered. Screams drowned. Black ooze scattered across the field like ink in a rising tide. When the wave settled, silence followed. Only one figure stood at the center of the wreckage. Soaked. Steady. Eric.

Zion stood at the edge of the battlefield, watching as the sea swallowed his creatures whole. Not with awe. With contempt. His lips curled, not in pain, but in cold revulsion. *The M'ra Sphere* had gone silent. It no longer called to him. That silence was betrayal layered over lifetimes, Orcas upon Orcas of dominance undone in a single breath. His army, his grand design, lay scattered in ruin. Shattered bones. Empty eyes. Smoke rising where loyalty once stood. His hands clenched at his sides, nails digging into flesh. His jaw tightened. A ripple of power coiled beneath his skin, barely contained. He didn't shout. He didn't scream. He simply said, low and venomous,

"Take them."

Behind him, the Horsemen stirred, four shadows cloaked in silence, their eyes aglow with unnatural light. They had waited long enough. Now, like wolves released at last from the leash, they stepped forward. The air warped around them. The hunt had begun.

From above, Adam felt the shift. The wind tightened. The sky had darkened, fractured with streaks of silent lightning. He looked up, breath shallow. *Was New Earth finally coming back together… or falling apart all over again?* Energy warped beneath his feet, as if something unnatural had just been loosed. He looked down. He didn't see Zion's lips move, but he felt the command in his bones. *They were coming.* Rose at his back, watching his six, fire flaring through her body and her hands. They hovered mid-air, surrounded on all sides. Back to back, wind and flame crackling from their limbs. The sky burned with movement.

"Ready?" he muttered.

"Always," she breathed.

Then came the scream like a banshee. A creature of the night launched toward them, wings stretched wide, claws out. It slammed into Rose, knocking her sideways through the air, with a blast of fury. Adam's breath caught, but he had no time to react. Another creature lunged from the smoke, talons first. But he never saw the second one. It hit him like a meteor. Air fled his lungs. The sky bent sideways. His body spun, plummeting fast, down, down, down faster than thought. He hit the ground with a thunderous thud. Every part of his bones shattered. His head throbbed, blood warm against his temple, vision swimming in fractured light. *What the hell hit me?* he thought, dragging himself to his knees. Every bone screamed, his breath shallow as ash. Then, through the smoke, came Asterius, tall, brutal, smiling like the bastard had waited lifetimes for this. *Not this joker again,* Adam thought, forcing himself upright. *Bring it, you smug piece of shit.*

"Hey, buddy," he purred, fingers curling around his fist. "Miss me?" Without warning, Asterius's fist rocketed upward, an uppercut that lifted Adam clean off his feet. His jaw snapped back with a sickening crack as the world turned sideways. The sky twisted as he flew, wind howling past his ears, his body weightless for a fraction too long. Then—boom—Asterius was there again, faster than thought, he zipped to Adam, appearing mid-air like a phantom. His fist came down like a clobber. The impact was cataclysmic. Adam slammed into the ground with bone-breaking force, stone shattering beneath him in a brutal explosion of dust and blood. Something in his ribs gave way. His breath fled his lungs in a sharp gasp, and for a moment, just a moment, the world flickered to black.

Adam groaned, fingers scraping across broken stone as he struggled to rise. Every inch of him ached. His ears rang from the impact, head spinning like the wind itself had turned on him. *What does this guy want from me?* he thought, grimacing. *Feels like he's trying to break me in half just for fun. At least ask me out on a date first.*

Then, something caught Adam's attention. Not flame. Not wind. A shimmer twisted across the field, like metal trying to vanish. He saw Eric, tense, gauntlets raised. And then, just distortion. There was no warning. Only a shimmer, brief, like a mirage breaking through smoke and then silence. Eric turned, gauntlets raised, heart pounding like drums in a war tent. The battlefield had darkened, storm clouds swallowing what little light remained from the moonlight. She was here. He couldn't see her... but he could feel her.

Then—

Crack. A rib snapped under the blow.

Crack. His jaw jerked sideways.

He stumbled back, coughing, water already forming at his fists. Another strike came, too fast to brace for. He dropped low, instinct taking over, dodging the next blow. A burst of water shot from his palm, spraying blindly and for a moment, he saw her. Vienna. Invisible. Outlined in the mist like a phantom. Twin swords mid-swing, her body half-formed in shimmer and rage. The water clung to her, outlining a skeletal shape of death. Eric didn't wait.

He fired again, pulse after pulse of water, not to wound, but to reveal. She hissed as the blast collided, forcing her to materialize fully for a heartbeat. Long enough. They clashed. Steel met pressure. Ghostlike blades shimmered against water-forged gauntlets, their edges flickering in and out of sight as if resisting full form. Sparks flew. She twisted, struck low, he blocked, swept, blasted. The battlefield echoed with crashes and screams of elements striking steel.

Eric gritted his teeth. "Come on, then," he muttered. "Let's dance."

Across the battlefield, Rose didn't move at first. The weight of the creature's charred carcass pressed against her, harsh smoke curling in her nostrils. Then, heat surged. A pulse from deep within her chest, burning through the suffocating dark. She ignited. A blast of fire erupted beneath the corpse, incinerating it from the inside out as Rose shot upward like a missile—hair ablaze, eyes fiery red, body flamed throughout. A girl on fire. *You want a fight? I'll give you the damn sun.* She didn't hesitate. She locked on to Barricade mid-roar and blasted straight into him, fire trailing behind her like a comet, both of them hurtling across the battlefield toward the nearest wall.

She slammed him into the wall with a force that split stone, cracks webbing out like veins beneath thunder. She didn't wait. She launched back, a human inferno, fire erupting from her fists. She struck, once, twice, a third time, flames searing skin, bone crunching beneath each blow. Barricade's head snapped to the side, blood spraying, but he blew steam through his nose, teeth red, eyes wild. The flames did not affect him as much. He snatched her wrist like a vice and slammed a fist into her ribs. The sound was obscene, wet, shattering. Rose gasped, flames faltering as she hit the ground in a heap of dirt and agony. The blow had landed like a sledgehammer, cracking through her defenses, stealing the breath from her lungs. For a moment, all she could do was lie there, the taste of iron thick on her tongue, the world spinning around her. "You work too hard, sweetie," Barricade murmured, wiping the blood from his cheek with the back of his hand. The smear left a streak like war paint. "Let me help you rest."

Rose growled, flames sputtering across her skin, but it was too late. His massive hand clamped around her throat, fingers tightening with brute, gleeful force. Her fire flickered once, then vanished. "Now it's my turn," he hissed. With a roar that shook the air, he lifted her like she weighed nothing and hurled her into the sky. She barely had time to gasp before he leapt after her, closing the distance with beastlike speed. Mid-air, his fists came down like twin hammers from the gods. Thunder struck.

Both fists collided against her with sickening impact, a thunderous blow that sent her hurtling toward the earth like a broken star. She crashed into the ground like a meteor, the impact snapping stone and throwing dust into the air. The earth caved beneath her, a shallow crater forming where she landed. For a moment, nothing moved. The silence was almost cruel. Too cruel.

Not far off, Jarvis lunged again, a snarling mass of twisted limbs and shadow-stretched muscle. Black goo frothed from his mouth, teeth like daggers, hissing as it hit the ground like acid, trailing behind him in venomous ropes. His movements were jerky, unnatural, like something dragged back from the dead and stitched with fury. Katherine didn't flinch. She stepped into his charge, rock gauntlets slamming into his ribcage with a force that echoed like a cannon blast. He reeled, but not for long. They collided again, a savage flurry of fists and grit. Katherine gritted her teeth, driving forward with every ounce of strength, matching the beast blow for blow.

Jarvis struck like a creature unchained, black ooze dripping on the battlefield, flinging sludge with every swipe, screeching through his dagger-like teeth. She drew dirt from the battlefield, threw up a stone wall from the ground with one hand, just in time, the sludges splattering against it in thick, hissing ropes. The ground

cracked beneath her stance, but she didn't budge.
Then, he spit. A black orb of corrupted energy
spiraled through the air. It struck her square in the
chest. The blast knocked the wind from her lungs.
She was airborne before she realized it, slammed
into the stone wall with a brutal crunch that split
the air. Cracks webbed outward like lightning.
Dust rained down in clouds. She didn't move. She
couldn't. She was pinned.

Adam groaned, pushing up from the
cracked earth. Pain bloomed across his back, a
red-hot brand seared into every rib. His arms
shook beneath him. Blood clung to his lips, warm
and metallic, his vision a blur of motion and
nightfall. *Everything hurts.* The wind carried the
taste of clouds. Somewhere beyond the haze,
footsteps echoed, slow, deliberate. Asterius
emerged from the smoke, grinning, bloodied, the
samurai blade in his grip gleaming like it had
already tasted victory. His eyes were feral. "Your
lungs are failing, Adam. Maybe I'll crush your
throat next. I want to savor every breath you lose.
See how long the wind carries you then." he
sneered, voice dipped in venom.

Adam wiped the blood from his mouth.
He spat to the side, vision tunneling through the

pain. *He's not stopping. Then I won't either. Let's give him a show.* "Wanna bet," he rasped. Then, Asterius leapt. A blur of motion. Blade raised. Wind screaming. Instinct took over. Adam threw out his hand, *please, please… let this work*, and the wind answered. A nearby sword tore from the earth, spiraling through the air like it had a soul of its own.

In a blink of an eye. Clang, the two blades met in a blinding clash. Steel scraped steel, sparks igniting the space between them. They clashed again. And again. Moving like phantoms in a whirlwind. Adam pivoted. Just one breath, and then he struck. One clean slice. Adam's eyes low. Asterius screamed. His hand, fresh off the bone, hit the dirt before the sound even registered. He dropped to his knees, clutching the gory stump, face twisted in agony. Blood gushed between his fingers and arms. His breath came in short, wet gasps. Adam stared down at him, sword still humming with energy in his grip. *What did I just—* He let it fall. Let it all fall. The sword. The fear. The doubt.

He asked for it.

He would've killed me.

I didn't choose this element. The element chose me.

Now it's my turn.

He ascended.

Wind whipped around him as he lifted off the ground, slow and steady. Lightning roared. The battlefield spun beneath his feet, debris spiraling in his wake like the world itself recognized the shift. Higher he climbed, until he hovered midair, arms outstretched, eyes pure white with power. And then, everything began to thrash. Winds gathered like vengeance, spiraling around him, shrieking louder with each passing heartbeat. A storm was brewing. It answered him now, not gently, but with wind speed like a god.

In front of him, the gale twisted into a cyclone, howling his fury. Asterius trapped within the shrieking air. Leaves, dust, shards of bone lifted into the air, spinning faster, wider, until they formed a dome. He was shaping it. Controlling it. A storm born of will. Adam's will. Asterius staggered, trapped. Shivering. The wind drowned out everything. The gale beat down like a god's hand, keeping him to his knees. There was no escape. Not anymore.

Adam hovered in the eye of the storm, bloodied but unshaken. Eyes pure white. Wind shrieked around him, yet none dared touch him.

The chaos bowed to his presence, parting like a veil as he descended. He didn't fall, he commanded the air beneath him, drifting down like judgment given form. As he landed, he raised a single hand, fingers outstretched.

"Breathe this."

The wind condensed, tight, whirling, merciless. Oxygen tore violently from Asterius's lungs in visible currents, flowing from his chest and lungs, like taking iron from blood, drawn straight into the spread fingers of Adam's outstretched hand. It gathered there, swirling into a small, foggy sphere of breath, suspended in the air like a captured soul. Asterius clawed at his throat, mouth wide open, unhinged, in silent horror, veins bulging, eyes wide and wild. His body convulsed violently, spine arching.

Adam stared down at him; at the thing he had just unmade. In his palm, the orb of stolen breath hovered, white, foggy, and trembling like a newborn star. He clenched his fist in anger, like gripping reins on a horse. It vanished. Gone just like the wind. Asterius stilled. Mouth wide like an unseen horror. Pupils dilated. Frozen. Lifeless. There was no air left. He crumbled to the ground like a fallen star.

What came over me? That wasn't me… or was it? Was that the power inside me all along? I could see everything, so vividly, but I couldn't stop. I wouldn't let him take me down. If I did… then all of this was for nothing.

Silence fell, heavy, unnatural. Adam stood at the center of it all, chest heaving. His hand was still clenched, knuckles white. The warmth of stolen breath was gone, scattered to nothing. He looked down. Asterius lay twisted in the dirt, eyes frozen wide. Mouth parted like he'd tried to scream, but hadn't made it in time. It didn't look like death. It looked like erasure. Adam's heart thundered. He opened his hand slowly, half-expecting something to still be there. The cold lingered for a bit. The taste of power clung to his tongue, metallic, bitter, and wrong. That wasn't instinct. That was something else. The idea still clung to him, *Am I becoming him?*

He didn't finish the thought. He couldn't. Because in the next heartbeat, the storm moved again, this time, in the dirt, where Katherine rose through earth and fury. She ripped the last of the black goo from her arms with her gauntleted fists, flinging it to the dirt. Another glob shot toward her like a shrieking specter, but she ducked, barely. It splattered behind her with a hiss.

She surged forward to Jarvis, fist to ribs, elbow to throat, again and again, landing blow after blow into his torso, each strike laced with raw fury. A low, guttural growl rumbled from Jarvis's throat, feral, unholy. His fingers twitched once… then split open, birthing claws like jagged bone forged in the pit of some forgotten hell. The ground pulsed beneath him, as if the earth itself felt his hunger. His eyes locked onto Katherine, no words, no mercy, just the quiet promise of death. Then she paused, sensing the shift. She blinked at the claws. "You gotta be kidding me."

He lunged. Katherine thrust her palms to the earth, yanking a wall of rock upward. She hurled it forward like a battering ram, but Jarvis tore through it, unscathed. Two sharp slashes ripped across her face and forearm, blood blooming instantly. Then his clawed hand backhanded her hard, sending her flying across the battlefield. She skidded across the torn soil, coughing, crawling backward as debris whirled around her. With a grunt, she hurled the shards, formed out of her hands, at Jarvis. He rushed through them, smashing each piece aside, unstoppable. Then, she vanished, sinking into the earth like it was part of her, and she part of it. The earth had swallowed her whole.

Jarvis staggered. Confused. Then a tremor surged, as the dirt beneath him shifted, not crumbling, but parting. A hole tore open in the battlefield like a mouth yawning wide. Katherine surged up through it, riding a jagged slab of stone that lifted her above him like a rising god, enthroned midair. Debris spiraled around her in a cyclone of vengeance, her eyes burning white, locked on him with finality. With a twist of her fingers, the dirt beneath Jarvis erupted, snaring his legs like vines of stone. Katherine raised her hands. Two enormous slabs of stone erupted from the ground, trembling on either side of Jarvis. For a beat, they hovered, she waited, ominous. Then, they slammed inward like a god's fist. The impact cracked like thunder, echoing across the battlefield. When the dust cleared, Jarvis was no more.

Not far off, another storm was building. Eric moved. Water surged to Eric's fists, solidifying into gauntlets with a sharp splash. In one fluid motion, he struck out, disarming Vienna. Her twin samurai swords went spinning through the air, clattering across the dirt.

He didn't pause. With a fierce thrust of both hands, he summoned a full-force blast of water. The torrent struck Vienna in the mouth, mid-scream, lifting her off her feet, her jaw cracked open with a sickening snap as the wave carried her backward like a ragdoll caught in a current, then slammed her into the stone wall, neck snapped on impact. Her body crumpled to the ground, jaw hanging loose, the noose of her own broken neck. That is where fire met brute force. Everything was fire.

Or maybe that was just the pain. Rose didn't know how long she'd been down. Time felt fractured, measured in pain, in the pounding echo of her heartbeat buried beneath stone. Everything throbbed. Her ribs screamed. Her lungs ached like they'd been branded from the inside. Where was she? What happened? Then came the heat. A flicker. A breath. It stirred in her chest, low and defiant. Pain blurred with memory, Barricade's grotesque grin, the feeling of weightlessness, the sound of cracking bone. Rage surged through her veins like kerosene meeting flame. *Not today*, she thought. Her fingers twitched against the shattered ground. Fire gently coiled at her palms, then faded. Her hands, they were rough. Tired, but unforgiving. Barricade yanked her upward, hoisted like a doll in a brute's grip, baring her body to the sky, like he meant to snap her spine in half. Her limbs dangled, she was unconscious, helpless, every nerve screaming in protest, but she couldn't do anything. She couldn't move. His grip tightened, fingers digging in like iron shackles as her back arched unnaturally. For a breathless second, the world tilted, her face to the sky, the battlefield spinning below, slightly unconscious, caught in the hands of a monster who wanted to break her. "Show me a real fight," he snarled, voice grotesque and guttural. She writhed in his grip, every nerve screaming. Pain lanced through her ribs, her spine, her skull, but it was the helplessness that burned worse. He pulled her limbs down from both ends, extending her. Stretching her arch like a rubber brand. *No. Not like this. Get up.* Her thoughts clawed against the darkness, against the weight crushing her from the inside. *You didn't come this far to die in his hands. Get up!* Her vision blurred. Her breath stuttered. *Move!*

Then—heat. Fire—her body flamed on!

It emerged from within, wild and defiant. Her teeth clenched. She pulled; her fingers curled around his grip. The spark caught. She ignited.

Fire exploded across her skin, crawling to the edge of her hair like a phoenix reborn, engulfing them both in a sudden inferno. Barricade roared, hands searing from the blaze, and dropped her. She hit the ground in flames and thudded, held there for a second, fully flamed on, she lifted her head to him in fury, flames roaring to life around her. Eyes sparked in fire. Face to face, defiance to defiance, heat crackling between them. For a breathless beat, neither moved. She remembered her parents, the silence of her old bedroom. The hum of the ceiling fan. The ache in her chest. The weight of everything unsaid. The nights she stared at the ceiling, whispering to herself, I have to do this. From almost dying in the hands of Zion. And now, here, on a scorched battlefield, smoke curling around her like old ghosts, she finally could. Not for vengeance. Not for power. But because someone had to end this. And it damn well wasn't going to be anyone else.

She roared like a warrior, loud like a thunder in the clouds, fire in the furnace, with her mouth wide open, feral eyes, nothing, but fire surrounded her essence, only a raw, death by daylight battle cry that tore through the darkness like lightning. It was over. Flames ignited around

her in a sudden burst, casting her in a blinding
halo of fire. She moved. She flew. Zipped. A fast-
whipping blur of heat and fury, toward Barricade,
a streak of blazing vengeance spiraling around
him. With every pass, every turn, she spun tighter,
higher, building a tornado of fire that scorched the
ground and lit the night ablaze.

Higher and higher, the fire climbed with
her, feeding on her rage, her rage that Zion felt
and diminished, until the night itself seemed ready
to combust. Barricade roared like a stallion,
swinging wildly into the inferno, his punches
through the fire, fast at first, but then slowed,
limbs blistering. The fire clung to him, peeling
flesh from his muscle. His hair burning at a crisp.
Skin blackened. One arm caught alight entirely,
bone flashing beneath the bubbling ruin. "No!" he
howled, the voice cracking as fire peeled away
from his muscles and his face. His eyes clouded
white, bubbling beneath the blaze like glass
melting in a forge, then bursting under the heat.
The scream that tore from him didn't sound
human; it was the sound of something unmade.

Rose didn't stop. She couldn't. This was the first time she felt free. Free from fear. Free from Zion. She was boundless. She roar again, louder and louder, poured everything into the tornado of fire. At the tip of it, a final flare burst outward from her core, collapsing the tornado inward. And when the fire cleared… when it was said and done, there was nothing left but ash.

Chapter XXIV:
At the Edge of War

The fire was gone, but its echo still burned in the air. Crisp even. Adam hovered above, the wind still humming beneath his boots. He didn't see the flames, he felt them. A pulse. A scream. A wildfire of rage that wasn't his, but could've been. Almost was. If he had let himself go that far. But her fury had ignited, and nothing prepared him for what followed. The fire hadn't just consumed Barricade. It had nearly consumed her. Adam descended slowly beside her. Rose stood amidst the smoke, scorched and trembling, fire still flickering faintly across her arms. She wouldn't look at him. Her jaw was locked, eyes fixed on the smoke. What if she had taken it further than this?

"You good?"

She nodded once. No words. That was enough. Adam looked at her a second longer. *She's changing too,* he thought. *Maybe we all are.* He glanced away, breath still ragged. His hand, once clenched around a stolen life, now hung open and shaking at his side. *We're all monsters now, huh?* He didn't say it out loud. He couldn't. Not after what he did. Not after what she just did. *Was that… was that her breaking point?* Part of him wanted to ask. *How did you do that?* But something in her silence told him: *Don't.* Whatever she'd unleashed, whatever he had, it came from somewhere deep. Dark hiding in their soul. He let the moment sit between them like cooling ash. He turned his head. Adam looks across the battlefield. Zion stood shirtless, sweat-soaked, ash-streaked, blood smeared across his chest. A soldier masquerading as a god. Ronan stands across from him, sword at the ready. Adam's breath caught. *This is bad. This isn't our fight… Not yet.*

Behind them, boots pounded through the broken terrain, Katherine and Eric, bruised and bloodied, crossing the chaos to reach them. The last ones standing. "They're over there," Rose said quietly beside him. Adam nodded. He didn't move. Katherine reached them first. "Where's Ronan?" To his right: Zion and Ronan, already engaged in vicious, blade-sparking combat. Steel clanged like thunder. Sparks flew. Adam looked toward the blur of flashing steel in the distance. "Fighting Zion."

Eric's jaw tightened. "We're just going to let him do that alone?"

"We need to move," Adam said, but the words barely left his lips before his thoughts caught up. Adam's jaw clenched. *But I didn't move. Not yet. My body wanted to. My heart didn't. Does it make me a bad person if I tell them we need to run? That we might survive if we leave him behind? He wouldn't have left us. I know that. And maybe that's why we can't leave him either.* They circled each other like beasts in a cage, filthy, blood-soaked, teeth bared. Steel clashed with steel. The sound rang out across the battlefield like a tolling bell. Sparks scattered.

Ronan ducked under a sweeping strike and slashed across Zion's ribs. Zion stumbled, growled, swung. Their blades collided again with a sound like bone snapping. Each step dragged blood and dust behind them, their bodies moving like titans, flesh and rage, prophecy and vengeance colliding in steel. "You were mine," Zion said, voice cracked and low, "the day your father fell. And now... I'll finish what he started."

Ronan didn't flinch.

"You'll die alone, same as him."

Zion roared and lunged. The sound was animal, raw fury erupting from a throat no longer entirely human. He launched forward with terrifying speed, blades flashing, eyes lit with something beyond rage, something ancient, unhinged, and all-consuming. Steel clashed with steel. Ronan blocked, parried, stepped in. A fist connected, Zion's jaw cracked sideways. Blood stained the battlefield. Zion spat the blood from his mouth and laughed, a sharp, broken sound that cut through the chaos. Every strike bled history, each clash echoing with wars long buried and betrayals never forgotten. Every step dragged the weight of the past behind it, cracking the earth beneath their feet like time itself was fracturing.

Then—

Zion staggered, just enough to sell the lie. Ronan hesitated. Just for a second. He thought Zion was slipping, wounded, winded, breaking. Maybe this was it. Maybe they could end it. But Zion wasn't finished. He was baiting him. In a blur of motion, Zion surged upward, teeth bared, blade flashing. The steel cut into Ronan's side, like puncturing a heart, pressure too thick to burst, with a sickening crunch, buried deep beneath bone. The breath left Ronan's lungs in a single, brutal gasp—a sharp exhale that sounded almost like surprise. Time fractured around them. His body stiffened, eyes wide, the pain blooming too fast to process. His fingers opened without meaning to, and the sword slipped from his grip, clattering against the stone with a sound that felt far too final. He just froze. Every racing thought of his father, Varek Valemont, stamped in his head. A blacksmith who dreamed beyond the forge. Worked with salvaged elemental tech and ancient conduits that could've advanced New Earth without corrupting it. His father's legacy flashed before his eyes. Zion had to eliminate him: to kill both a threat and a dream. Now it was all his. And this time, there was no one who could save Ronan.

Zion's blade twisted in, slow and deliberate. Ronan's body jerked, not once, twice. A convulsion of sorts. A strangled sound escaped his throat as steel scraped bone. Then Zion pushed in deeper, until there was nothing left between them but the blade and the blood. "You didn't let the M'ra Sphere consume you... did you?" He leaned in closer, his breath cold as stone, curling against Ronan's cheek like a final insult. His lips hovered near his ear, mocking, intimate. "I hope they remember you." A pause. "Say hi to your father for me," and twisted the blade once more. Ronan winced like a lost puppy, his body twitching one last time as the pain surged through him. He couldn't speak, only blood pooled around his mouth in a sputter. The scariest part of it all, from the shattered castle doors, Adam saw Marie burst onto the field, eyes wide, breath frozen. She arrived just as Zion drove the blade into Ronan's chest. Time didn't slow. It stopped. The battlefield fell into silence, as if New Earth forgot how to breathe. Adam saw it too. The blade. The blood. The way Ronan's body jolted, then stilled. His breath caught in his throat, too tight to release. *No…* Across the field, he stood frozen with Rose, Eric, and Katherine. All four had regrouped, bloodied and breathless.

The sword ripped out in one vicious jerk. Ronan squealed, taking his final breath, his eyes froze as his mind recorded the last image of New Earth, and it was no one other than: Zion. Not Marie. Not the Legends. Just Zion. His body crumpled, folding to the ground. A thud echoed across the battlefield. Marie's scream cracked the sky, a raw, grief-stricken cry, like a thunderclap in a cathedral of war. It wasn't a cry. It was a rupture.

The sound echoed through the battlefield, cutting through the debris like a blade of glass. Thunder cracked above them, loud enough to shake the bones beneath the battlefield. Lightning tore across the sky in a blinding arc, freezing the chaos in stark white. For a breathless instant, Zion stood at the center of it all, next to Ronan's body, cast in silhouette, jagged, monstrous, divine. He looked less like a man, and more like a storm given flesh. Lightning forked above them, twisting, clawing, carving through the clouds like a vengeful god had drawn his blade across the sky. The light split the heavens open, casting the battlefield in flashes of white fire and shadow as the dust calls.

Thunder followed, not once, but in brutal waves, each crack louder than the last, as if the sky itself was breaking apart. The final boom hit so hard it rattled Adam's bones, vibrating through his chest like a warning he didn't yet understand. He turned. And that's when he saw it. A bolt of lightning, massive, blinding, came down like judgment, ripping through the sky and slamming into the highest spire of Ronan's castle. The impact wasn't a strike; it was an execution. Stone shattered on contact, the tower split open like bone beneath a blade. The earth heaved with the force of it, windows bursting outward in a scream of white-hot glass as the wind howled through the ruins like something mourning the dead. Then came the glow.

The conduits, buried beneath the castle since the time of the Ancients, lit up like veins under skin, pulsing with unnatural light. Lines of energy, long dormant, now surged to life with a violent, erratic rhythm, as if the world's buried lifeblood had been shocked awake. These weren't decorative etchings or forgotten relics, they were a living network, built to carry elemental current across the land. Old-world channels, sacred and dangerous, designed not to empower the flesh, but to contain the chaos. But nothing was containing it now. The storm had activated them. And Zion… Zion was waiting.

Eric stepped forward, mouth slightly open. "What is that?" No one answered. Not even Marie, who knelt beside Ronan's lifeless body, lips trembling, eyes wide. The wind howled louder now, and Adam could feel something vibrating through the soil, like the heartbeat of something buried beneath them. The sensation crawled up his legs and into his spine, cold and pulsing, as if the ground itself was trying to warn him. He

gasped. *The conduits… They're waking,* he thought.
The same ones from the Chronicles.

Whatever was coming… it wasn't natural. It wasn't right. Suddenly, cracks split open across the battlefield, tearing through stone and soil with sickening force. From the wounds in the earth, black goo erupted, stretching upward in long, sinewed strands that writhed like muscle torn from bone. Prylyn creatures. Dozens. Crawled out of the ground, faceless and twitching, as if pulled from the marrow of nightmares. They formed a line with eerie precision, their bodies still, their heads tilted just slightly, as if listening for a voice that hadn't yet spoken. Another lightning bolt ripped from the sky. This time, it struck him. Zion.

The lightning hit his chest like divine fury, but he didn't fall. His body convulsed violently, then froze mid-arch, as if something unseen had taken hold. His arms lifted, bones cracking beneath the skin, and his head jerked back in silent ecstasy, or agony. The conduits responded like they had been waiting, their energy surging upward in tandem, threading into his body in tendrils of light, as if New Earth itself had mistaken him for a god… and offered him the keys to the underworld. For a moment, the air shimmered around him, as if reality were trying to reject him, but couldn't. The ground blurred, and the sky rippled like heat on glass.

Then, stillness.

Rose gasped. Katherine backed away, shaking her head. "What is happening…?" Adam didn't answer. He couldn't. He instinctively threw his arms out, blocking Rose with one arm and steadying Katherine and Eric with the other. His body moved before his mind could catch up, muscle and fear acting as one. The heat from the lightning still pulsed in the air, making his skin prickle, but he didn't back down. "Don't move," he whispered, eyes locked on the storm ahead, not as a command, but a warning. The wind surged, harder, louder, like the earth itself was bracing for what came next. And then, from the center of the storm, something monstrous stood, tall, twisted, barely recognizable as anything that had ever been human. Lightning still licked across its body in slow, flickering veins, casting its silhouette in flashes of bone and shadow. It didn't speak. It didn't breathe. It simply existed. Waiting.

Adam's voice left him in a whisper:

"What the fuck did we just unleash?"

473

Chapter XXV:

Let It Burn

The world had fallen silent, too silent. Adam stood still, boots rooted in cracked earth, air humming around him like a breath caught in the lungs of a dying god. His heart was pounding so hard it felt like it echoed through the sky itself. That blue haze before dawn. He'd seen it before, as a child arriving to school, the fresh scent of moss in the air, the cold breeze curling in his hair, but not entirely like this. Time fractured, not in seconds or minutes, but in the space between heartbeats, where this time, everything burned and reeked of old blood. He didn't know what this thing was, not really. But he knew what it wasn't. It wasn't Zion anymore. Zion's silhouette began to shift, slowly, grotesquely, as if the shape of him was being rewritten against his will.

His limbs stretched in unnatural jerks, bones snapping with sickening cracks as his body began to swell, taller, broader, heavier. Skin split open in jagged lines, leaking light instead of blood, as though something ancient was crawling out from inside him. His veins pulsed with a furious glow, mapping something unholy across his body. Whatever humanity he once held burned away with every breath, scorched out by something older, something wrong. This wasn't a spell. This wasn't magic. This was mutation. This was the world trying, and failing, to reject him. A forced evolution. A rebirth no one asked for, and no world was ready to witness.

His bones weren't just growing; they were being rewritten, sculpted by something that didn't care if the flesh could keep up. His frame expanded with every pulse of energy, limbs thickening, spine elongating, shaped not by nature, but by violence. He wasn't becoming more. He was becoming something entirely out of this world. From the crater of lightning and ash, the creature awakened, slowly, monstrously, as if the earth itself was being peeled back to let it through. Smoke clung to its form like a veil of scorched fabric, unveiling a figure towering over them like a fortress given flesh. Limbs thick as tree trunks, claws like spears, its presence alone bent the battlefield around it.

Towering like a three-story nightmare, dragged from the underworld, it didn't just rise, it dominated, a living colossus born of storm and fury. Its shoulders scraped the blue haze, and its hands looked big enough to crush a man like fruit. His limbs shifted with flickers of unnatural light, each movement cracking reality around him. His skin was slick with a greenish-black sheen, scaled in patches like something caught between flesh and serpent. His face… if it could still be called that, was stretched and wrong, cheekbones too sharp, the nose flattened, and his mouth torn wider than it should be. And his eyes… those reptilian eyes, gleamed like obsidian glass, yellow at the core, pupils slitted thin, milky at the edges, reflecting nothing but the blue haze and the slaughter to come.

The battlefield groaned in silence. And out of the silence, a rumble built in his throat until it erupted, a guttural, inhuman roar that shook the ground beneath their feet. Adam didn't move. He couldn't. The breath trapped in his chest wasn't fear, it was something thicker. Like a golf ball lodged in his throat, sharp at the edges, impossible to swallow. He didn't know how they were supposed to fight this thing. But still… *I wasn't ready. But I'm standing here anyway.*

The Prylyn creatures answered the call. From every corner of the battlefield, they emerged, twitching, gliding, galloping, screaming, as if the ground itself had given birth to nightmare. Their bodies jerked with unnatural rhythm, eyes glowing, claws tearing through what remained of the earth. And the Legends—bloodied, breathless, burning—took their stances in silence, side by side. They didn't speak. They didn't have to. The storm had come, and they were New Earth's last defense.

Adam stood at the front, eyes locked, breath steady. Rose stepped beside him without a word, her presence as fierce as the fire building at her fingertips. Eric and Katherine flanked them, the four of them forming a line, not scattered, not running, but ready. For the first time, they stood as one. No commands. No words. Just motion.

Katherine slammed her fists into the ground, jagged stone exploding upward, hardening into gauntlets that locked around her arms like armor forged from the earth itself. Eric's hands shimmered as water coiled around his wrists, shaping into twin blades that pulsed like living current. Rose's flames reignited, licking around her body and spiraling through her fingers in defiant rhythm. Adam exhaled, and the air around him tightened, spiraling into a cyclone of force, the wind answering his call like it had always belonged to him.

The creature didn't move. It didn't have to. The Prylyn horde surged first, screeching, twitching, a wave of shadows and limbs tearing across the battlefield with inhuman speed. And the Legends, united now, breathless but unbroken, met them in motion. Adam and Rose flew skyward like twin comets, while the ground quaked beneath Katherine and the water gods motion Eric to the sea, as they charged forward into the storm. Rose hurled fireballs down from above, lighting the horde aflame. Eric slipped between enemies like a ripple of water, blades slicing through tendons and bone. Katherine launched a barrage of earth-bound spikes, the ground cracking beneath her as her shards ripped into the enemy ranks.

But nothing slowed the creature. It raised a single arm, and brought it down like thunder. The ground erupted in a blast of debris, the shockwave knocking Adam and Rose off balance in mid-air. Below, Katherine grabbed Eric and braced, she pulled stone from earth, rising like a shield to protect them as the impact crashed across the field. From above, Adam caught the chaos: the earth rippling, bodies flung, flame trailing through smoke. He summoned the wind beneath him, circling a dead tree into the air, hurling it toward the creature like a missile. The creature turned. It swatted the tree from the air like a twig. Adam didn't hesitate; he dove.

He shot forward with a blast of wind, spiraling like a tornado toward the monster. But the creature met him mid-flight, a snarl twisting its half-shifted face. It lunged, swinging a massive fist. Adam tried to dodge, but—

CRACK.

The blow sent him soaring backward, flipping end over end through the air like a ragdoll in a hurricane. He crashed into the earth with a thunderous crack, tearing through dirt, stone, and shattered bone as his body carved a jagged path across the battlefield. Blood sprayed with each impact, smearing the ground behind him like a trail of red ruin. When he finally slammed to a stop, the silence around him felt louder than the impact. *Get up*, he thought. Though every breath scraped like fire in his ribs. *You're not done. Not yet.* He barely had time to rise before the roar hit again. Katherine was already counterattacking, spires of rock slamming toward the creature like spears. One impaled its foot. It roared and shattered the spike by snapping the loose end and hurling it like a blade. She jumped, but it came too fast, slamming her in the side, flinging her across the field.

Above, Rose dove through the air, fire roaring throughout her body, from her hands, fire concentrated in a stream that lit the sky in orange and gold. The flames slammed into the creature's chest, but it didn't flinch. It turned with terrifying speed, caught her mid-flight, and clenched its clawed fist around her like she was nothing. She screamed, thrashing, her flames flaring wildly, until, with monstrous force, it hurled her into the concrete. The impact cracked the ground beneath her. Her fire sputtered. She rolled once, and then silence. Eric appeared behind it, water rushing beneath his feet as he dropped low into a slide. Blades of water extended from his hands, sharp, quick, and deadly. He sliced across the creature's legs in one smooth motion, one, two, three cuts in rapid succession. Blood spilled, thick and steaming, but it wasn't red, it was like something from a tar pit. The creature roared, whirled around, and brought its claws down like a guillotine.

Eric raised both arms, water whipping up into twin blades just in time to block, but the sheer force behind the strike drove him to his knees. The ground cracked beneath him as he strained to hold it back, arms shaking, water overflowing out of him from under pressure. With a final bellow, the creature crushed his fist downward, and Eric vanished, bursting into water with a violent splash. Quickly, water spiraled up the creature's body like a living stream, wrapping around its throat. It wrapped around, coiling tight, until Eric began to reform behind its neck, choking it with his full weight. The creature flailed. Then grabbed him. Eric's form snapped back into solid flesh, trapped in its grasp. The creature lifted him high, face-to-face with its burning, steaming breath. They locked eyes for a moment. In that moment, the rage, the anger, the frustration Zion felt holding the prophecy in its grip. It knew New Earth was all his and it had the power to end it all. It exhaled, the reptilian eyes hung low, a blast of hot scalding vapor like a furnace venting. Eric thrashed against its hold, desperate, but there were no more chances. This was it. Death by degree. The creature hurled Eric across the battlefield. He crashed through debris and stone, skidding to a halt in the dirt, just feet away from Rose's motionless body. Neither of them moved.

Above it all, Adam jetted upward, wind spiraling in tight coils around his arms and legs like a storm taking flight. His eyes burned, not just with elemental power, but with a gathering force like a summoned storm. They were down: Rose, Eric, Katherine. Even Marie. She couldn't, not anymore, not after Ronan. It was just him now. And whatever this thing was, it didn't get to win. *You don't get to win today.* He flew forward, slicing through the air like a spear of vengeance, wind screaming in his wake. A storm spiraled behind him, white eyes burning as he hurtled toward the creature with everything he had left. But it didn't flinch. It turned.

And with one massive backhand, it swatted Adam out of the sky like nothing. His body twisted through the air, slammed into stone, and bounced off earth like broken cargo. He landed beside Katherine. They lay where they fell, battered, broken, and forgotten by the sky.

What once stood as New Earth, a place of resilience was now disbarred, broken, draped in the smoke of defeat. The castle was torn open, its towers fractured, its gates shattered. Scattered across the land were bodies, soldiers, civilians, the fallen. Four Legends lay in ruin like broken relics, and in the shadows behind it all, half-hidden in ash and silence was Marie, who wept beside the dead.

Chapter XXVI:
It's Time

The forest shimmered like a half-remembered thought. Light filtered through the trees in soft dapples, catching on silver mist that hovered above the ground like breath held too long. Everything was quiet… too quiet. No birds. No wind. Just the hush of something unspoken. Adam stood alone between the trees, between the leaves, between the hush, boots crunching softly over moss and fallen leaves. The air was thick, but not heavy. Gentle. Almost dreamlike. He didn't remember walking here. He didn't remember anything at all. He looked down, opened his hand slowly, and turned it over. Not sure what to expect. Then he saw it.

A unicorn, pale as moonlight, stood in a clearing ahead. Its coat glowed faintly under the filtered sunlight, almost translucent. It chewed slowly on leaves from a low-hanging branch, calm, unbothered, like it had always belonged here.

Light flickered across its body like a moving prayer. Adam stared. Not in fear. Not in awe. But in something between. He wasn't sure of what to make of it. The unicorn turned its head, meeting his eyes. They were dark. Deep. Older than the forest itself. He stepped forward, breath grasped. Another step. Another. He reached out to touch the unicorn. "Adam…" A voice, distant, broken, familiar. "Adam, wake up."

He paused. Turned slightly, like he could see through the trees to the voice calling him from somewhere he didn't want to go. But something pulled him back. He looked at the unicorn again And this time, the tip of its horn was dripping in blood. Adam stood there frightened. Eyes wide. Blood struck. The light fractured. Then a deep, roaring groan. The forest shattered, crumbling into pieces. The sound of Katherine's voice cut through like thunder—

And the dream tore apart at the seams.

"Adam, come on... wake up."

A voice broke through the darkness— urgent, desperate. His name came again, fractured by sobs. "Adam, please." His eyes opened to a world smeared in blood and ash. The sky hung low, choked with smoke, casting everything in a blue haze right before dawn approached. Fires still burned in the distance, slow and spiteful, while the wind dragged soot across the corpses like a shroud. Nothing moved, except the pain crawling back into his body, reminding him he was still alive. Katherine hovered over him, her face streaked with dirt, blood, and tears, her voice cracking as she pleaded. He blinked through the haze, her face blurring in and out of focus like a fading memory. Every breath was shallow, sharp, the air thick with smoke, copper, and something burning. His vision swam, fractured by pain and panic, the world tilting beneath him like it couldn't bear to stay upright. "Are you okay?" he whispered. She didn't answer that. She was too focused on helping him. Her hands were already under his arms, dragging him up. "Come on. Get up. We don't have time."

Adam groaned, the sound raw and broken as pain tore through every inch of him like fire licking bone. Blood poured from a deep gash at his temple, hot and blinding, but he didn't fight her grip. He let Katherine pull him through the rubble, each jagged edge scraping against bruised skin. She set him upright and sat next to him. Around them, the battlefield was unrecognizable, a graveyard of steel and ash, choked with smoke and silence.

The creature, Zion? No, not anymore, rampaged in the far distance, moving in the ocean, shadow and fury incarnate, tearing through anything that moved. Lightning crashed one last time, splitting the sky as it struck the castle behind them. The dome shattered with a sound like the sky itself cracking open. Shards of stone and steel erupted outward, raining down in all directions like the teeth of a broken god. Flames beat through the fractures as the tower caved in, swallowed by its own collapse. What once loomed as a fortress now crumbled into ruin, devoured by the wrath it tried to contain. A wave of fire and stone erupted from the blast, the tower collapsing in a storm of molten ruin. The place that had once stood as a symbol of power now burned like a funeral pyre.

Adam turned in every direction, heart pounding, eyes wide with disbelief. Everything that had once stood, walls, towers, people, was either burning, broken, or gone. The air itself felt hollow, like New Earth had taken a breath and never let it go. This wasn't just a battlefield, it was the end of something, and he could feel it breaking inside him too. Marie crouched in the shadows, her arms wrapped tightly around Ronan's limp body, as if holding him could somehow undo the inevitable. Her face was ash-covered, eyes empty, like the grief had hollowed her out from the inside. Nearby, Eric clung to Rose, both of them bruised and bloodied, shaking as they leaned into each other for warmth that the world no longer offered. This wasn't war anymore, it was aftermath, the raw, quiet fight to simply endure. *We can't stop him.* He thought.

Then he saw it, a few feet ahead, half-buried in the debris. A jagged metal rod, glinting faintly in the ash-thick light. Long enough. Sharp enough. It didn't move. It didn't call to him. But somehow, he knew it was meant for this. Adam turned slowly to Katherine, his gaze heavy, not with fear, but with quiet resolve. His voice cracked. "There's no way we can stop him…" *Could this be? Am I the one to make this decision?* Adam thought. He looked to Katherine again, seeing little Katherine dancing around the kitchen table. Happy as can be, then he looked away. *Am I the one to save her? She has a whole life ahead of her. They all do.* "But I can," he said. *I am not sure if I am thinking clearly… I did lose a lot of blood, but everything from this moment, stepping foot in New Earth, led me here. Maybe this is my second chance.*

The guilt.

The man I killed.

I have to do this.

I have to do this to save my family.

Katherine sitting next to him, grabbing his arm. Her voice cracked. "No. You said we would make it out of here together." *Maybe this is what I was made for. A life for a life, right? There's no easy way out of this.* He thought. His heart broke, shattered into millions of pieces, like wind fled from his lungs. Tears fell valiantly from his eyes. But his eyes were clear now. The wind stirred at his body, spiraling. It circled his ankles, his legs, his waist, lifting him. He met her gaze. "I was able to get a second chance at life…" His voice cracked. A tear slipped down his cheek as he looked at her, really looked at her, like he was seeing her for the last time. "A life for a life, right?" And before she could protest, he reached for the rod.

"No, no, no." Tears fall from Katherine's cheeks. "You promised."

"I love you, sis," his voice whispered.

Before Katherine could reach for him, Adam was already rising off the ground, then surged forward like a lightning bolt torn from the earth, a streak of power ripping through the air toward fate, wind bursting around him in a violent spiral. He shot toward the creature like a divine arrow, every fiber of his being honed on one purpose. It wasn't flight. It was a final act of will.

"No!" Katherine screamed, falling over in the attempt to grab him. Adam gains momentum, flying across the plain, warped at god fearing speed. He gripped the metal rod tighter. It bit into his palm. Blood streamed down his wrist. Just beneath the curve of his jaw, above the collarbone, something. A mark, faint but distinct, curled like air caught in motion. It rippled slightly, as if it had been waiting beneath the surface of his skin all along. The mark. The mark he has been waiting for. Not stamped. Suddenly appeared. He earned his stripes as a Legend.

Adam flew faster, wind spiraling tighter around him with each passing second. The world below blurred, a rush of cool wind from the sea, a battlefield fading beneath a singular purpose. His limbs ached, blood trailing behind him, but he didn't stop. He couldn't. He wasn't flying anymore, he was ascending, drawn by something greater than rage or fear. *It's too late to turn back now.*

I am not even sure if this makes sense. I know the guilt will rid of me free and this is something I have to do.

Back at the battlefield, Eric and Rose rushed through the smoke-streaked air, scrambling across debris as the chaos closed in. They reached Katherine just as her scream tore through the battlefield, raw and full of helpless fury. Eric threw himself in front of her, arms outstretched, while Rose leaned firm at her side. Together, they shielded her, not just from the storm, but from the shattering truth none of them were ready to face. The creature turned, slow and deliberate, as if it had sensed more than seen him. Its yellow reptilian eyes, pupils thinned, locking eyes with Adam mid-flight. For a breathless instant, the world seemed to hold still, just the two of them, suspended in a moment carved from wrath and fate. Then it moved, and everything in Adam screamed to keep going. *Is there an afterlife for these things?* He thought.

The creature roared, a sound that split the air like a blade, primal and thunderous, shaking the ground and sky alike. The cry echoed with ancient fury, the kind meant to break spirits before bodies. And Adam answered, not with words, but with motion, with will, with wind rising around him like a second skin. He flew faster, fiercer, as if defiance alone could tear through the impossible. With every ounce of strength left in him, Adam gripped the jagged rod, with wind shrieking around him like a battle cry from the heavens. He didn't throw it. He held it firm, his hand clenched tight, and drove it straight into the creature's heart, piercing through scale, sinew, and darkness itself. But at the very exact moment, the creature's claw burst through his chest, ripping through ribs, tearing into his heart like fate had struck back. For a second, time bent once again, not in seconds, but in the space between heartbeats, a blinding light exploded across the battlefield, drowning the war in silence. Sound vanished behind the ocean shore. The world sat fractured. And in the stillness that followed, he was truly gone.

***

When the light faded, a calm breeze floated in the blue haze, they found him near the southern ridge, where the land dipped toward the sea, his body sprawled beside the creature's remains. Somehow, he'd landed near it again. Or maybe the world had pulled it back to him.

The air felt different. The battlefield lay in ruins. Smoke spiraled above crumbled stone. Fires cracked against broken trees. The dome was gone. The sky, a soft blue. Too soft for this much death. Adam lay still. His body lay broken, unmoving, limbs twisted at unnatural angles. A deep gash cleaved through his chest, blood soaking the earth beneath him in dark, spreading silence. The jagged rod jutted from the creature's heart where he'd left it, buried to the hilt, unmoved. And beside the fallen beast, Adam remained still… like the final breath of a storm. Katherine was the first to reach him. She stumbled through the wreckage, knees buckling as she dropped beside his body. Her hands trembled as they hovered over his chest, not ready to touch what she couldn't bear to confirm. "Adam…" she whispered, voice cracking like glass. The blood told her everything, but still, she searched his face, begging for even the faintest breath. "No. No. No. No, come on…" She cradled his head, shaking.

Her fingers threaded through blood-matted hair as she pulled him close, rocking him like a child who might still wake. His chest did not rise. His eyes were open, wide, unblinking, staring past her, past the sky, past the world like a broken clock. And in that hollow gaze, she saw the finality she wasn't ready to accept. Eric and Rose arrived seconds later battered and bruised. Rose dropped to her knees beside them, her breath catching the moment she saw his eyes, wide open, glassy, and just still. It didn't look like sleep. It looked like the world had forgotten to close him. She pulled Katherine into her arms, trembling, then leaned in, brushing a hand over Adam's brow. "I'm so sorry," she whispered, her voice breaking as she gently closed his eyes. Eric's face crumpled. He turned away.

Marie stepped forward last. She knelt beside them all, quiet. Her eyes were crimson red, but no tears fell. Just silence, carved in grief. *This wasn't supposed to happen, not like this.* She thought. She hovered a trembling hand above Adam's chest, her fingers barely an inch from his blood-stained uniform. There was no heartbeat. Katherine turned, her voice broken. "What are you doing?"

"We lost two legends today," Marie said, voice steady but quieter. She closed her eyes, whispered in *Shikarian ancient language.* Something deep. Something dark. Darker magic than time itself. Something forbidden. Nothing like we've heard before. A parallel, perhaps? Her hand began to glow, sapphire blue, faint and flickering, like a dying star. She moved it over his face… then lower, over his heart. The light pulsed once. Then nothing. Marie's hand dropped. The glow died. And Adam… well Adam, he didn't move. He was dead. Behind her, no one spoke. Not even the wind. This is the first time the world stood still.

Chapter XXVII:

All That Remains

Time ran faster here, but slow for the
Legends; days that followed blurred into smoke
and silence, each hour indistinguishable from the
next. Grief settled over New Earth like a second
sky, vast and suffocating. The fires had died, but
nothing felt healed. Not the land. Not the people.
And certainly not the four hearts left behind to
carry the weight of what they'd lost. Katherine sat
alone on the cracked stone steps of Castle of
Celeborn in an open arch way, the wind moved
through the windows openings like a ghost,
brushing over her as she tucked her knees to her
chest. The royal castle of Celeborn, once home to
Marie's family, had finally been reclaimed. Zion's
fortress had fallen, but her family's legacy had not.
After Zion's reign twisted much of New Earth,
this place remained sealed and untouched. Now,
with Marie the last surviving heir, it stood again,
restored by her own hand, her bloodline's legacy

preserved within its stone. Grief no longer came in waves. It was the tide itself. She didn't know why he did it. She always thought he was the tough one, but this. Sacrificing himself, did not make any sense. Why did he do it? She was left with a ghost of his past. No answers, just a raw ache in her heart that she couldn't fix. He left her and that burned a hole in her heart. Katherine's fingers slowly brushed the locket at her throat, still warm against her skin. She hadn't opened it in years. Not since their childhood. With a quiet breath, she undid the clasp. Inside was the photograph Adam had taken of them the summer before everything changed. He'd folded it to fit, as if he always knew she'd need it one day. "This isn't how it was supposed to end," she whispered, clutching her arms tighter. "You were supposed to survive. You always survived."

Far across the crumbling keep, where stone met stillness and mourning hung heavier than breath, the infirmary held its own silence. The room was quiet, dimly lit, wrapped in the kind of hush that followed catastrophe. Two beds stood in the center, opposite of each other. Adam lay on top of one, wrapped in a pale sheet up to his chest, his skin pale as frost. The second bed stood opposite of Adam, equally still, with Ronan, draped in ceremonial cloth, the silver crest of the Celeborn placed gently at his side. The wind outside pressed softly against the windows, as if afraid to intrude. Somewhere in the distance, bells tolled low, mourning tones that echoed through the bones of the city. The Council had finalized the funeral rites. The people of New Earth would gather at first light to honor their fallen. Two warriors. Two legacies. And a silence too heavy to name. Rose stood by his side, one hand gripping the edge of the bed, the other covering her mouth. Her shoulders shook. Eric stood beside her, silent, hands clasped behind his back. A nurse adjusted a nearby monitor before stepping away. "We have the funeral arrangements ready for tomorrow," the nurse said gently.

Eric nodded. "Okay. Thank you."

The nurse exited quietly, leaving just the two of them with what remained. Rose leaned down, brushing a piece of dust from Adam's forehead. His face was so still. Too still. Like a statue carved in memory, not a person they had just laughed with days ago. Or it seemed like days ago when they were on Earth. She didn't know why she did it. Maybe it was pointless. Maybe it meant nothing. But still… she had to touch him. Just once more. "I'll let Katherine know," she murmured, her voice catching. She turned quickly and left the room, tears sliding freely down her cheeks. Eric remained. He stepped closer, the floor groaning beneath his boots, until he stood at the edge of the bed. For a long time, he just stared. Stared at the bruises, the wound, the way Adam's chest no longer rose. Adam was breathless. Words gathered at the back of Eric's throat, but none made it past the grief tightening in his jaw. The way he kept his mouth quiet. He couldn't speak. The grief from their last argument. If he could take it back, he would, but it was too late. He knew he lost his best friend. Then: "Why'd you do it?" he whispered. "It should've been me." His voice cracked, the words barely surviving the weight in his throat. Slowly, he reached out and placed a hand on Adam's cold shoulder. It was definitive. The skin beneath his palm was cold, unnaturally so, as if all warmth had been drained from the world with him. Still. Unmoving. The kind of stillness that didn't come with sleep. "Goodbye, my friend."

He stepped back, gaze lingering on the still figure beneath the pale sheet. For a moment, he didn't move, like some part of him still hoped Adam might breathe again. Like a memory imprinted in bone. But hope was cruel here and sometimes things are what they seem. He shut the door behind him and turned away, sealing the room in silence once more, like it was swallowing a secret it would never give back.

While the others mourned in silence, Marie turned to something older than grief. The study was pitch black, thick with silence and shadow, until the candles lit themselves one by one, snapping into life in a ring around the room like a summoned seance. Their glow flickered softly, casting Marie in the center like a ghost caught in amber. She sat cross-legged, grounded in ritual, her lips moving in rhythm with an ancient *Shikarian chant*, her voice low and melodic.

As the incantation deepened, her body began to rise, slowly, weightlessly, levitating above the ring of firelight. A weathered spellbook hovered before her, its cracked leather binding seething with power older than the palace itself. The air around it vibrated like it remembered war. Within its tattered pages was a forbidden craft, magic meant for no one, yet now spoken aloud. Marie's eyes snapped open, pure white, incandescent. She reached beyond the walls, beyond time. And the world answered.

Voices, thousands of them, rushed at her from every corner of New Earth. She fell into them like a plunge through space, through sky, through scream and prayer. Every voice. Every language. Every cry for salvation echoed within her mind like thunder. She searched and searched, through the swell of desperation and grief, for one voice, one cry, one scream, her sister, Maya Celeborn. But it wasn't there. It was nowhere to be found. "Where are you, Maya?" she whispered, softer than breath, but heavier than grief. *How could this be?* She thought. Three knocks echoed against the chamber door. The sound dropped out. A void, deafening in its absence. Marie violently fell to the ground as the seance tore apart at its seams. No whisper. No cry. No scream. No thought. Just the ache of something missing. The silence that followed her whisper didn't answer. Only the three knocks that echoed against the chamber door. "They're ready for you," said a voice from beyond. Marie stood slowly, brushing the dust from her gown. The time for mourning was over.

The halls were different here, they stretched before Marie, long and cold, still scarred from the siege, not too far of a distant memory. This place where she stood, The Nexus, nestled in downtown of New Earth was locked and sealed under Zion's reign for many orcas, since after his reign The Nexus remained full, occupied by civilians, councilman and woman, and soldiers. It was New Earth's cornucopia. New Earthians and Shikarian tribes took it as a symbol of abundance. A new hope. Marie held her head high and walked with purpose, each step echoing against the hollow stone, her sapphire cloak trailing behind like a river of resolve. She turned the corner, the right corridor, always the right, and reached the doors. Tall. Heavy. Marked by the seal of the Nexus. Two guards opened the great doors without a word. Inside, the council chamber was dim, lit only by the crescent arc of golden braziers lining the walls. Stone columns loomed like watchers in the dark. Seated at the half-moon table were familiar faces, some loyal, some wary.

Councilwoman Elara rose as Marie entered. "Queen Marie," she said. "Thank you for joining us. Sergeant Eris, please step forward," she continued. A figure stepped forward from the far end of the room. "He has a proposal… regarding the new order." Marie didn't flinch. But something in her bones knew, this wasn't the end of the war. It was only the beginning.

Chapter XXVIII:
Now You Understand Why

Time had gone still. Not in the way silence falls after death, but in the way the world holds its breath when something sacred is about to return. Outside, the sky bled morning light into the ruins of New Earth, casting gold across shattered stone and smoldering ash. Inside the infirmary, all was still, no wind, no nurses, no sound. Just two souls lay outstretched on the beds, but something was shifting. Something inevitable. And deep beneath it all… Adam lay still beneath the white sheet, his skin pale as the full moon, dead beneath it all. The infirmary held its breath, thick with the kind of silence that follows the final note of a song no one wanted to end. Shadows draped across the floor like stretched-out ghosts, unmoving. Then, barely there, underneath it all… a twitch beneath his ribs. A breath.

Color returned to his cheeks, faint at first, then blooming like dawn bleeding into frost. The ghostly pallor melted into the warm olive hue of life, as if his skin remembered the sun. His eyelids fluttered, trembled, then twitched with the erratic dance of something clawing its way back. Beneath his lids, his eyes darted side to side violently, wild, and frantic. Movements sharp and erratic, like lightning flashing through a storm no one else could see. Only he. Whatever he was seeing, it wasn't peace, it was chaos, tearing through him like wildfire on dry bone. His breath hitched, shallow and uneven, as if the dream refused to let him go. And then—

The visions came:
Brutal and prophetic,

—New Earth in flames
—Villages collapsing into ash
— Screams from civilians
— Fire choking them
— Children and civilians dead
—A void in the chaos
—Watching. Cloaked in darkness.

Then—

A flood of blinding light washed over it all. And the world went silent. Adam's eyes shot open. He gasped, eyes and mouth wide open like he'd seen a ghost. His head jumped up. His vision locked on the ceiling above him; he just stayed there, frozen, like his soul wasn't fully there. He'd seen the end. The end of New Earth.

And it had only just begun. You thought the war had ended. But the dead had only just begun to speak. You saw what you wanted. You believed the illusion. But he died… and still, something in you waited.

Now you understand why.

END OF BOOK ONE

9 798218 653651